The Old Limey

THE OLD LIMEY

A NOVEL

H. W. CROCKER III

Since 1947
**REGNERY
PUBLISHING, INC.**
An Eagle Publishing Company • Washington, DC

Library of Congress Cataloging-in-Publication Data

Crocker, H. W.
The old limey : a novel / H. W. Crocker III.
p.   cm.
ISBN 0-89526-232-0
1. British—California—Fiction. 2. Missing persons—Fiction. 3. California—Fiction. 4. Retirees—Fiction. 5. Generals—Fiction. I. Title.

PS3553. R5347 O4 2000
813'.6—dc21   00-051763

Published in the United States by
Regnery Publishing, Inc.
An Eagle Publishing Company
One Massachusetts Avenue, NW
Washington, DC 20001

Visit us at www.regnery.com

Distributed to the trade by
National Book Network
4720-A Boston Way
Lanham, MD 20706

BOOK DESIGN BY MARJA WALKER

Printed on acid-free paper
Manufactured in the United States of America

10 9 8 7 6 5 4 3 2 1

Books are available in quantity for promotional or premium use. Write to Director of Special Sales, Regnery Publishing, Inc., One Massachusetts Avenue, NW, Washington, DC 20001, for information on discounts and terms or call (202) 216-0600.

For Sally,
the only reader to give Jeeves and
Bertie Wooster Southern drawls

'For he is the minister of God to thee for good. But if thou do that which is evil, be afraid; for he beareth not the sword in vain...'

—ROMANS 13:4

'Be afraid; be very afraid.'

—LATE TWENTIETH-CENTURY AMERICAN LINGO

CHAPTER ONE

NIGEL HADN'T REALISED BEFORE how cinematic it was to crash a car. There was that moment of swerving and squealing brakes. The jolt of the impact and the sudden flipping upside down; a scraping of metal and a shattering of glass. And then voices in the darkness telling him to lie still and not move. Just like the cinema. It was almost gratifying to wipe his cuff-linked sleeve across his forehead and find it covered in blood.

Perhaps he'd been unconscious, perhaps not, but it seemed as though he saw the rotating red and blue lights of the police car flashing through his cracked windscreen almost immediately. Damned efficient, these Americans.

He envisaged himself in the Dawn Patrol, trapped in his inverted biplane, crash-landed on the fields of France. He fiddled with the seat belt, and finally snapped it free so that his body slumped down on his neck and squeezed him against the roof of the car.

A torch sprayed him in a beam of light.

'Don't move.' It was a woman's voice, kind and scared. The torch switched off. He saw the door on the passenger's side was a quarter of the way open and crushed into an irregular parallelogram. There was no glass left in the window. It was twinkling beyond in the moonlight, like frost on the cobbles at Sandhurst all those years ago.

He rested calmly in his awkward position. He heard tyres rolling slowly nearby, munching gravel, and scratchy, mechanical voices trading information over radios—reminding him of nothing so much as the urban equivalent of the squawking jungle birds in Katanga.

The passenger door was shoved open, scraping noisily along the tarmac. And somehow, in his muddled state he frankly didn't notice how, he was dragged from the car, strapped on a stretcher, and slid neatly into an ambulance.

It was odd, but the first thing he noticed was its cleanliness. He'd seen plenty of ambulances in less than perfect circumstances, but even given the advantages of peace, the Americans were a remarkably clean people, he thought.

And professional, too. One had grown used to the idea that the Americans were rather hysterical, given to mass panics and strange fears that they might never find the secret of eternal life. But the male nurse in the ambulance seemed quite friendly and calm as he put him through the usual preliminaries—taking his blood pressure, shooting something into his veins, and wrapping a cloth brace around his neck.

When they snapped Nigel out of the ambulance and into the hospital, he was told he was going into some section reserved for non-emergency accident cases. He was not, evidently, in so very bad a shape as one might expect of a man who had recently celebrated his sixtieth birthday and survived a car wreck.

And it was a good thing he wasn't in bad shape, because once the nurses had laced him onto a flat, uncomfortable slab, and incarcerated him in a rather more severe neck brace than the one he'd had in the ambulance, he was left completely alone. He could hear the voices of nurses not far away, but they never came round to see him.

After about two hours, a young doctor with owlish glasses, a white smock, and tennis shoes wrapped in plastic carrier bags shuffled in to lecture him on the evils of drink, mysteriously noted something in the file at the foot of his slab, and wandered off again.

Good Lord, thought Nigel—entertaining the pleasant idea that he'd been thrown from a horse rather than written off his car (a rent-a-car at that)—have I ridden with Prince Rupert's right wing at Naseby only to fall wounded and a prisoner to the dreaded Roundheads? It certainly seemed that way, for his next visitor was a uniformed member of Cromwell's New Model Army, a large, suntanned young man with blond hair shaved close to his head—a fine figure of the California Highway Patrol Regiment.

It seemed to Nigel that sometime in his career he had received training on how to handle interrogations when captured by the enemy. But never before had he been captured, and he couldn't remember the drill. Something to do, certainly, with name, rank, and serial number. After that, it was all rather vague.

He was shocked when he saw the Cromwellian Californian flipping through his wallet. How on earth did he get that?

'An Englishman, huh?' he said, looking vaguely and dangerously German, Nigel thought, with his chiselled Gothic face. His air was cocky and amused, as it might well be when one's opponent is chained to a mad scientist's operating table.

'Yes,' Nigel croaked. His throat was dry. He shifted uncomfortably under his bonds.

The officer nodded and puckered his lips a little before widening them into an arrogant grin.

'Kinda old for this sort of thing, aren'tch ya?' It was a question to which there was no answer; and Nigel gave none. The officer seemed disappointed.

'Technically,' he went on, shifting his weight in a manner that seemed to imply his sidearm was remarkably heavy, like a handheld Gatling gun, 'you're under arrest for driving under the influence.' He ambled with the rolling gait of a western gunfighter to the foot of the bed and came back with a clipboard in his hand. He shook his head. 'Man, your brain was fried.'

Nigel's mouth grimaced under his grey moustache. Insolent little puppy, he thought. Damned self-righteous, bronzed Puritan.

The officer stuck his tongue in his cheek. 'But then again, you guys do drive on the wrong side of the road, don'tch ya?'

Nigel's grimace twisted itself into a forced, false rictus. Damned little whelp...

'Well, anyway,' the officer said, turning businesslike, 'you're technically under arrest, as I said, but you'll be free to go once they check you out of here. It'll be up to the D.A. whether to issue a warrant for your arrest. You live in England, right?'

Yes, an England whose crown we'll defend to the last man against you and all of your republican kin, you vile dogs, Nigel said to himself before he realised his imagination had got the better of him. To the officer he only nodded as best he could given the constraints of the neck brace.

'Well, as long as you're out of the States within a week or so, I don't think the D.A. will think it's worth the taxpayers' money to bring you back for trial. After all, nobody was hurt but you. And you're damn lucky about that. You drunk drivers usually always live. It's the people you hit that get killed.'

Oh, yes, yes, thank you very much, Carrie Nation. If only you knew why I was here. Doing a policeman's work myself and doing it a damned sight more considerately than you, you Levelling, surfing, Teutonic moron.

'I'll still have to file a report, of course,' the officer said, pulling out his notebook.

Yes, very big on reports, your kind, aren't they?

'Are you in the States for business or pleasure?'

'Pleasure seems a bit ironic now, but that's fair enough.'

'You're on vacation?'

Nigel grunted. No need to lie unnecessarily.

'Where exactly were you going—before you went off the road, that is?'

'To my hotel.'

'And which one is that?'

'Oh, you know, the big one with the French name.'

'Too drunk to know where he was going,' the officer said slowly, scribbling in his notebook. 'Where'd you been drinking?'

'I believe you Californians call it a saloon.'

'A saloon,' the officer repeated, smirking. 'And you don't remember the name, do you...?'

'The "Billy the Kid" or something...'

'... or who you were with?'

'With? I wasn't with anyone. I don't know anyone here.'

The officer nodded. 'Suspect completely disoriented,' he said as he wrote. 'I think the skid marks tell the rest of the story.' He put his notebook in his pocket. 'You know, you totalled that rental. You even blew out all four tyres and bent the wheel stems. I hope you have insurance on it.'

'I have.' Nigel was enough of an old soldier to know the risks he was running on this mission, though he hadn't considered drink driving to be one of them.

'Good. That could have ruined your trip, otherwise.' He grinned again. 'You know, my grandfather's been to England. He was there to bail you out during the war.'

'Was he really?' Nigel said in mock politeness, flat on his back and unable to move.

'Yeah. He thought it was cold. 'Cept the beer—that was warm.'

Nigel nodded thoughtfully. 'Give him my apologies. But tell him it's been that way for quite some time.'

Cromwell's grinning constable took another look in Nigel's wallet, then flipped it closed. 'I'll leave this with the nurses. You can pick it up when you leave.' He waved it at Nigel. 'You'd better watch it, old man. Accidents can be gnarly.'

'Yes, can't they just,' Nigel said, his fake grin following the officer out of the room.

Well, he'd survived the interrogation, but now came the true torture that all captured soldiers risked. Torture was what they gave you after you refused to talk. He braced himself for it. In fact, strapped down as he was, he was already braced for it.

His first fright came when a nurse stopped by his bed to ask him about payment—always an awkward question when one finds oneself unexpectedly in a foreign hospital, especially when the authorities have confiscated one's wallet. But he was relieved that his being a foreigner didn't seem to cause her any anguish. Like a true die-hard, anti–Reform Bill Tory back in 1832, Nigel had always distrusted the

National Health Service at home. He'd been all of eight when Nye Bevan introduced the idea. He hadn't thought much of it then and he didn't think much of it now. But he also maintained his countrymen's common fear that an American hospital would either turn him away to die in an alley or take him by his countryman brogues and shake him down for everything he was worth.

Taking matters quickly into his own hands he got the nurse to wheel his bed to where the phone was mounted on the opposite wall. He dialled his bank in London, Messrs Coutts, announced himself, and handed her the receiver. (The nurse, he thought, was rather plain and decidedly craggy with age and he'd rather not have her face rubbing cheeks with his.) The clerk on the other end assured her that Nigel's account was in very good order. She rang off, and Nigel gave the nurse his address so he could be billed and granted her permission to copy down his bank card number as security. It was quite simple, if more mercenary than one would like from a medical establishment, which, one likes to assume, no doubt falsely, is a rather idealistic place, with Angels of Mercy floating silently through the wards like Nightingales. And of course, Nigel thought to himself, given that they already had his wallet in their custody, they could be gracious rather easily.

The next torture to be borne was more severe. This torture wasn't clever, like Chinese water torture. It was more neglectful, more modern, more bureaucratic; in fact, it was very much like the National Health Service. He was left strapped on his mad scientist's operating table, ignored, abandoned, and alone.

He lay on his rack for a good twelve hours in a position that rapidly became far more painful than the quick and irrevocable accident that had sent him there. Whenever he tried to move, the apparatus blocked him. It was like trying to roll over in bed, only to have Helga of the SS pin his shoulders back, saying, 'You vill sleep on your back and you vill like it.'

It would be wrong to say that he was being kept under observation, for he was barely observed at all. And then it was only to wheel him in to be X-rayed—which they did twice, because the first batch didn't come out properly—and to stitch up a cut near his eye.

Nigel hadn't been seriously injured before he entered the hospital, but by the time he left—when a doctor happened upon him and said, 'Hmm, they haven't let you out yet. That's funny.'—his spine felt as though it were about to snap.

When he was finally discharged and in receipt of his confiscated valuables, he stepped into the remarkably hot October sun—a portrait of elegant, unclimatic dishevelment: blood-spattered cavalry twill, a Frankenstein-monster scar on his forehead, and a swollen black eye that he tried to hide by giving his Panama a rakish tilt.

He knew he was not a pretty picture. And at his age he knew it would be a bit hard to claim it was all a result of a stirring round of fisticuffs—his glory days as a pugilist for Eton were long behind him.

But it was a very pretty picture that had plunged him into this mess. A very pretty picture indeed. It was a leg, actually. Or rather, two pairs of legs, belonging to two young women who were the very embodiment of a 'Come to California' tourist advertisement.

He remembered walking down a sunbaked street lined with flashy shops, coming to an outdoor café, where his eye was caught by the long, suntanned leg of a beautiful blonde whose face had what he assumed was called 'an innocent, all-American look.'

Plan A, thought Nigel. Whenever, in his long and distinguished military career, he had had to do a recce up country, in darkest

Katanga or the border country round Crossmaglen, he'd invariably enlist native support to help him catch his prey. There was Ngube Mboto, who'd led him to the Katanga rebels, whom he secretly—and rather dangerously for his career as a wet-behind-the-ears lieutenant and military observer—advised in their secessionist war against the Congo's communist government; and Paddy O'Rourke, who drank with the Provos. These two lovelies might well serve the same purpose. Except the objective now was not settling the borders of the Congo or keeping a close eye on the IRA, but recovering his own goddaughter. She was twentysomething; these girls were twentysomething. Perfect. Plan A.

As he passed the blonde, he touched his Panama in greeting. He then walked straight into a chair that was shoved in his way by a woman getting up at the next table.

Nigel remembered feeling momentarily quite proud that though he was stumbling in a strange, hopping, froglike sort of way, his hands skipping along the ground, propelling him forward if not upright, he hadn't yet fallen flat on his face.

He did, however, propel himself full force into an unoccupied table, bringing it crashing to the ground, its umbrella, a chair, cutlery, salt and pepper shakers, packets of sugar, and other odds and ends falling on top of him. A purple ceramic vase with a single colourful flower plopped on his lap. He quickly brushed it aside so that it shattered on the pavement into convenient shards for cutting his hands. And to his shame he saw that the vase's water had spilled out into a Rorschach ink blot on the crotch of his trousers, which quickly emitted a sheepish smell to match the sheepish look on his face.

He heard a woman say, 'Oh my God' (it was the woman who had knocked him over), and he groaned a bit. He was much too old to be playing rugby with furniture on the pavement, his erstwhile fame as scrum half for Eton but a distant memory. Surely a few bones were broken. Perhaps he was paralysed.

He shut his eyes for a moment, making a quick mental catalogue of his pain before he decided to move. When he opened his eyes, he was surrounded by the sound of shoe leather scraping on the pavement and the umbrella being wrenched aside. The blonde siren knelt beside him and put her hand on his Panama. 'Don't move,' she said to him. 'Are you all right? Do you want me to call an ambulance?'

'No, no,' he said, half bravely, half in fear of causing even more of a scene. 'I'm quite all right. Really, it's my own damn fault for not looking where I was going.'

'Are you sure?'

'Quite sure.'

'You're sure nothing's broken?'

'Yes.'

The blonde nodded to a very pretty brunette, and they each took an arm and helped him up. He came to a wavering upright position. They let his arms go slowly and stood by him, as though he were a babe who might tumble over. Plan A was working perfectly. Silly old limey duffer, completely out of his depth, needs help. He could practically read the advert in the local paper.

'Ah, there,' he said, feeling more unsteady than he wanted to let on. He spread his legs a bit to improve his balance.

The woman who'd broadsided him rushed towards him with profuse apologies. No wonder she'd capsized him. It was like a hippo ramming a punt—the latter might be elegant (like Nigel) but the laws of physics determined he was no match for Hermione the hippo's well-fed bulk.

'Yes, I'm fine. Please, I'm perfectly fine. I do it all the time. No peripheral vision at all. Always knocking things over. Really. Perfectly, perfectly fine.'

Roar as solicitously as she could, Nigel had no interest in pursuing a conversation with this emigrant from Lake Victoria, and bravely, if gently, brushed her aside, the way a daring crocodile might, and moved boldly to his original objective—the blonde, who had retreated to her table with her friend.

An officer ought always to take the initiative, he thought. What was it Frederick the Great had said? 'An officer awaiting an attack shall be cashiered.' This was especially true when on special operations. It was, after all, imperative to secure the loyalty of the locals.

'May I join you?' he asked, bowing slightly at the waist, interrupting the blonde and brunette, who had already fallen back into their pre-Nigel-falling-on-the-ground conversation.

The blonde nodded, her lazy, bedroom blue eyes lighting with apparent deep concern for Nigel's well-being. 'Oh, yes.'

'I'm sorry about all this. But I think I need a bit of a rest.' He slowly lowered himself into a chair. He was pleased his bones didn't creak as he did so.

A young waiter with shiny black hair hurried to their table, his worried eyes watching a couple of Mexican busboys cleaning up the wreckage from Nigel's fall.

'Are you all right, sir? Shall I call a doctor?'

'No, no, I'm perfectly fine,' said Nigel, who couldn't help but consider the waiter a damned nuisance. He had a sun-drenched table with two beautiful young women. What the devil did he need with a pretty-boy waiter with slicked-back hair?

'Can I get you anything? A glass of water?'

'You can bring me a beer.' The waiter recited the dozen beers of the house. 'A Bass will do me fine.' Nigel looked at his companions, but they were happy enough sipping their fizzy cola drinks, as Americans were wont to do.

Nigel felt fairly knowledgeable about Americans from his days cooperating with them ousting the Iraqis from Kuwait. Many were the hours he'd sat in the Pentagon with Schwarzkopf and Powell breaking pencil nubs and working out the finer points of the Mother of All Battles. He had to admit to being a *little* hurt when Stormin' Norman gave all the credit for the Gulf War to the tactics of Alexander the Great and not so much as a mention to Nigel the Pretty Good Really. But the last laugh was his now, wasn't it? While Schwarzkopf and Powell were reduced to attending old soldiers' reunions or dull, formal dinners with desiccated, boring foreign policy mandarins, here was Nigel enjoying the café life with two radiant, sun-kissed creatures.

'You must be from England,' said the brunette.

'Yes, yes I am.'

Apart from acknowledging her amazing powers of deduction, he also carefully noted her features: warm brown eyes, though brown eyes always reminded him of animals rather than people—still, hers seemed affectionate, beautiful doe eyes; a bright, welcoming smile; a walnut tan...

'I'm April,' she said, 'and this is Penelope.'

'I'm pleased to meet you both. My name is Nigel, Nigel Haversham.'

'Are you all right? That was quite a fall you had.'

'Oh, yes. I suppose I was rather blinded by the sun. In England, we usually have rain in October—and every other month of the year.'

'Would you like something to eat?' asked Penelope. 'We haven't ordered yet.'

'Oh, haven't you?' he said, accepting the menu from her hand. He looked at it briefly and put it aside. Looking at Penelope was more interesting: tall, blonde, and beautiful, with pouting lips, and eyelids that rested half unfurled, reminding one of the joys of the long Norwegian winters. 'It gets rather warm here in L.A., doesn't it?' he asked, easing his shirt collar.

'Yes,' she said, smiling politely.

Nigel shook with a violent cough.

'Are you sure you're all right?' she asked him.

'Yes, I think it's just the smog.' He coughed again in wrenching spasms. *Good Lord, did I dislodge my intestines?*

'Here, have some water,' April said, handing him her glass.

Drinking someone else's water in a sexually promiscuous and Aids-infested area like Los Angeles was undoubtedly dangerous, but Nigel had a long streak of fatalism in his character; and anyway, better to swig someone's water and die of Aids than to sit here and embarrass everyone with one's uncontrollable coughing.

'Isn't it awful?' asked Penelope.

Actually, Nigel thought it tasted quite pleasant—cold, clean, and quite free from every disease from the Tropics, without even a hint of tsetse. His eyes were question marks.

'The smog,' she explained.

'Oh, it's not so bad. We invented it, you know.' *He didn't want to appear an ugly Englishman.*

'Do you live in England?' asked April.

'Yes, smoggy old London. It's quite as bad as here. Diesel fumes, mad motorcyclists, a jogger's nightmare. Perhaps that's why we don't have any; joggers, that is. Not like you Americans.'

'Oh, we don't jog. We do Tae-bo,' said Penelope.

'Tae-bo?'

'Yeah, you know, like aerobics and kickboxing.'

'Ah, savate,' he said, thinking of the secret foot-fighting technique practised in the dangerous alleyways of Marseilles, something he'd picked up during one of his more adventurous school hols.

'Gesundheit,' said April.

Penelope glanced heavenward, 'I don't like jogging in this air.'

Nigel was just on the point of imagining Penelope in one of those form-flattering outfits he knew were *de rigueur* for any self-respecting exercising Angeleno, when his view was suddenly blocked by the waiter bending over the table. He gave a growling sigh as the toy boy produced a glass, filled it halfway, and placed the sweating bottle beside it.

'Thank you,' Nigel said sourly.

'Are you ladies ready to order?' the waiter asked, flipping out his notebook.

'I'll have the turkey on whole wheat, lettuce and tomato, with mustard, but no mayonnaise, please,' said Penelope. The waiter scribbled.

'I'll have the taco salad. And can I have rice instead of beans? And hold the meat. And could I have some extra guacamole and tomatoes?' asked April. 'Oh, and can you hold the peppers?'

'Do you want something, Nigel?' asked Penelope.

He almost laughed. Here I am in a foreign land and all I have to do is sprawl on the pavement to get invited to luncheon with two beautiful young women. This was really too good to be true. 'Ah, yes, yes... hmm... roast beef?'

'Sandwich, sir?'

'Yes, yes, sandwich.'

'And what kind of bread?'

'Uh...' His mind raced. 'Sourdough!' It seemed to him he remembered reading somewhere that sourdough bread was the delicacy of the California gold miners, even if the Forty-Nine was some time ago. And roast beef? Surely that's what the California cowboys ate, along with their buffalo chips and endless beans.

'Mayonnaise?'

'Yes.'

'Lettuce or sprouts?'

Sprouts were green vegetables one has with the turkey at Christmas. But in a sandwich?

'Lettuce.'

'Tomayto?'

'Tomahto.'

'Thank you.' The waiter gathered their menus and disappeared.

'Like, I love the way you say,' April mimicked him as though he were Colonel Blimp, 'tomahto.'

'All a matter of upbringing, I suppose,' he responded. Good Lord, he thought, don't raise my hopes just to make me a figure of fun.

'So are you here on vacation?' asked Penelope, whom he much preferred.

'Yes, a holiday,' Nigel lied. 'I came here for the sun.'

'Then you should be like, you know, wearing shorts and a tennis shirt. Aren't you hot with that tie on? Take it off.'

'Yes, well, you see I need my cavalry twill—it cushions my falls. And my tie, well...' He smiled and loosened the knot.

'Where do you work?' asked April.

'Oh, Katanga, Cyprus, Aden, the Falklands,' he smiled mischievously. 'Or I used to anyway. I'm a retired officer of Her Majesty's Army.'

'Oh,' they said, with obvious boredom and disappointment.

Nigel assumed that with his debonair good looks and their California ignorance, they had probably taken him for a gentlemanly fashion photographer, a sort of Lord Lichfield. But to a more discerning eye, an English eye, Nigel knew his looks would have given him away—neat, grey, military moustache; surging white-water eyebrows over intense blue eyes; the handsome, ruddy, weather-beaten face that retained, if he said so himself, a certain Fairbanksian charm.

He thought it only good manners to shift the conversation back to his hosts, especially since he needed to gauge their worth for Plan A. 'Do you girls have jobs in L.A.?'

April laughed as though there were something funny about the way he said L.A.

'Not real jobs,' said Penelope. 'We're Xers. You know, like Generation X. The baby boomers have all the real jobs. All we have are part-time, go-nowhere, do-nothing jobs.'

'Yes, very difficult, I suppose,' he said, adopting a look of pained concern for their difficulties, while he wondered what they were talking about and what they would have made of the depressions and wars previous generations had faced, and also how they had failed to make the cool million that apparently every other twentysomething American was making via computerised commerce of some sort. 'Do you aim to be movie stars?'

'That'd be fun, but it's really hard,' said April, with a gleaming smile that seemed as bright as any Hollywood star's. 'Actually, I'd like to get married,' she said sincerely.

Nigel was touched. He didn't for a moment think she had him in mind—no, of course not. But it was touching, wasn't it, in this time of women's lib, massive divorce, and enormous pressure on young girls to lift weights, dye their hair green and purple, and put pins through their noses (and other places), to find an unspoiled young thing whose choice was for the kinder and gentler ideal of matrimony—even if they apparently, and disconcertingly, practised savate on the side?

He warmed to her. His every fibre cried out in wonder at her. *Ecce femina!* he wanted to shout to the women of the Western world, conjuring up his classics from the old school—*Floreat Etona!* Behold the woman, behold her dignity and charm, behold this untarnished—though she is delightfully tan—paragon of the unbought grace of life!

If only his goddaughter could see this girl's example and appreciate what it means—the proper path, the right course, the future of England—even if, in this case admittedly, the golden exemplar happens to be a Californian.

April touched his forearm, startling him from his reverie and melting him even further. 'But right now we'll do anything for money.'

'Well, almost anything,' said Penelope, laughing in a rather coarse, horsey way that distracted from her natural endowments and brought Nigel's dreams crashing down like crockery hurled off a mantelpiece by a California earthquake.

'Believe me,' said April, stroking his sleeve, 'we Xers need money.'

Nigel forced a smile, feeling very self-conscious. Surely he wasn't being propositioned. This was just the way our American cousins showed their frank, unrepressed, friendly equality... wasn't it?

Well, if it was, he couldn't help thinking that their frank, unrepressed, friendly equality was rather like walking around naked. It might be very comfortable for you, but it's damned distressing to your neighbours.

'How do you support yourselves now?' he asked. He'd never raised a daughter himself, or been married for that matter—though of course he did have his goddaughter, the reason he was here. But he was already becoming rather concerned for the welfare of his two beautiful companions.

'Oh,' said April, 'our parents pay for us. Pen and I live together in Westwood.'

'Well, have you been to school? Do you have any qualifications?'

'We want to get into public relations, but, like, nobody's hiring,' said Penelope. 'We're thinking about setting up our own public relations firm, but you can't do that without money.'

But surely, thought Nigel, that's what striving young men are for, to take care of beautiful young girls like these, set them up in flower shops, or public relations boutiques if that's what makes them happy. 'Public relations... who would your clients be?'

'Athletes.' Penelope's beauty had kept Nigel from noticing her voice, but now he decided it was rather odd—thick, as if her tongue were swallowed by the swelling of her bee-stung lips, and whining.

'Athletes,' he repeated after her, thoughtfully. 'Do you know any?'

'Like, we were cheerleaders,' she said condescendingly, as though it had been on the front page of *The Times* for weeks.

'Quite. And what would you do for them?'

April giggled and flashed her shiny teeth, but Penelope held forth as though she were Lord Keynes confronted with a particularly ignorant, ugly, heterosexual boy. 'We'd be their image consultants. A lot of them aren't very smart, you know. They need an image consultant so we can market them for promotions and commercials. We'd match athlete,' she stuck up one finger, 'and product,' she stuck up another finger and brought the two together. It wasn't a very flattering gesture, especially as Nigel thought it meant something rather offensive in California. It also exposed Penelope's rather large hands.

Obvious Viking blood, could run to Rhine-Maiden-fat in the future, Nigel thought.

But he said: 'Very clever. No wonder you outdo us economically. Born entrepreneurs, I'd say.' He looked at the girls beneath his surging waves of eyebrows. There was a veiled intensity in his look. Undoubtedly, it made them slightly uncomfortable. But he imagined they rather liked that, making them feel as though they were in the presence of a personality of startling masculine magnetism, rather like Sir Richard Francis Burton, that fiercely handsome nineteenth-century soldier, explorer, linguist, secret agent, Sufi mystic, and all-round Rambo of the 'forces of conservatism', so feared by Prime Minister Tone and so revered by Brigadier Nigel Haversham.

'Oh, look,' said April, pointing across the street. 'There's one.'

'There's what?' Nigel asked, looking around somewhat angrily.

'That giant white poodle. That's what I'm talking about, Pen. Don't you want it?' A woman with an enormous hat and dark glasses was strolling by across the street, a vast white dog on the end of a leash.

On the other hand, Nigel thought, young girls are rather self-absorbed creatures, aren't they? Liable to miss subtleties, or not feel appropriate awe. Put that old scoundrel Benjamin Disraeli in front of them and they'd probably advise him on where to find a better hairstylist. Give them Sir Richard Francis Burton and they'd advise a plastic surgeon to cover up the scar on his cheek, won honourably from a Somali spear.

Nigel's stare—the sort of stare, he thought, that might become a Brontë hero, rather wuthering, in a way—bore into April's excited brown eyes. But she didn't even notice him. Already she and her blonde roommate were discoursing on the pros and cons of giant poodles.

Oh well, Nigel thought. It's not as though he didn't already know and hold as a principle of life—especially after meeting his god-daughter Alexandra's friends—that young women were really rather like miraculous talking cows who, when one's conversation didn't involve them personally, when one took the conversation onto some higher, theoretical plane, would suddenly remember that they were indeed cows, not human beings at all, and turn away, chewing their cud, gazing in contented vacuity over the long green fields—or in these girls' case, over the large white poodle prancing in front of the long row of shops on the opposite side of the street.

The waiter bent in front of him and broke his stare. He was welcome this time. If he was going to be ignored, he might as well lose himself in his food and play the part of a hungry old man in need of nourishment to build his strength, to restore his brittle bones.

And the food was delightful. The Americans could certainly set a fine table. The roast beef was as good as any in England. (Better, perhaps, he conceded to himself, what with BSE and mad cows and all.) And the sourdough bread was wonderful. His imagination made it seem quite rustic. Every bite made him think of bearded men panning for gold, calling the wind Maria. And every gold miner he dreamt of was somehow a remarkably active and agile old duffer only just in his sixties.

Nigel remained polite and occasionally dipped his oar in the stream of the girls' conversation—saying, 'No, no, April's right. Giant poodles can be charming. Prince Rupert had one, you know. He was the nephew of our King Charles. No, no, nothing to do with Diana. But Irish wolfhounds, there you have the real thing.'—which would win him a smiling glance of acknowledgement from April, but leave him otherwise beyond the pale of the conversation. It was a no-hoper.

None too soon, the waiter slipped the bill on the table. Nigel gracefully slid his left hand for the bill and his right into his coat for his wallet. April and Penelope leaned for their handbags.

'No, no, ladies. I'll take care of this,' he said gallantly. At least it gave him something to do. There were the usual protests, but they were put down. He filed his American dollars beneath the bill and paused over the dregs of a second beer.

'Do you know anyone here in L.A.?' asked Penelope.

Here was a surprise. He looked over his shoulder. The poodle had passed out of sight. 'No, not a soul.'

Her arms slammed on the table and her head jumped towards him like a jack-in-the-box.

'Good Lord!' Nigel exclaimed, thrown back in his chair, at rigid attention.

'Then let's show you the city. It'll be really fun.'

Excellent, thought Nigel, Plan A clicking into place without even a nudge from him.

He looked at April. She was quickly brightening to Penelope's fevered look.

'Wouldn't I be in the way?' he said. 'Don't you have appointments to keep?'

'Come on, Nigel,' said Penelope. 'We can take you drinking at the Guards. It's very English.'

'The Guards?' Nigel echoed.

'Do you know it?'

'My dear girl, I was *in* it—the regiment, that is.'

'It'll be really fun,' said April, grabbing his sleeve.

So he tottered to his feet, though he was feeling much better now, and followed the girls to their car (his rent-a-car was not far away), and he agreed to follow them wherever their inspiration might direct.

Driving in a strange city in a strange car on the wrong side of the street was, he thought, strange. But Los Angeles was a fairly orderly town, and the traffic moved slowly. It wasn't difficult following Penelope's white Mustang convertible in the slow, meandering lineup of metal, the girls' hair streaming behind their sunglasses like Mercury's wings whenever they could pick up speed.

The day was turning a bit overcast. The air looked as though it had been heavily laced with black pepper. He pulled up alongside of them. 'I say, girls,' he called out, 'do we know where we're going?'

April shouted to Penelope, 'He wants to know where we're going.'

He heard Penelope shout back, 'The Queen Mary. He's old. He's English. He'll like it.'

He did, rather. It wasn't the ship so much, cresting the Cunard waves with her 81,000 tons, or the nostalgic memories of a bygone era that it could have evoked from him. It was the sight of these two young women, tripping their long legs on the deck, giggling hysterically at private jokes that meant nothing to him. The Queen Mary was in dry dock, the Empire was a Commonwealth of criminality to chisel money out of the old country and snigger at the Windsor family, but at least girls were still girls. They could still make one feel rather like Maurice Chevalier. And for that he was grateful.

So the afternoon was spent pleasantly enough. And as dusk crept over Long Beach, casting long red shadows, his companions' high spirits surged even higher. It was the Guards! Yes, they had to take him to the Guards! 'Oh, you'll have to meet Tom! I'll call Mike. He'd get such a kick out of you!'

They punched their cell phones as quickly as a Chinese flipped beads on an abacus, but neither of the men could be found. Perhaps they were there already. So on to the Guards it was!

The Guards was in a ritzy part of town. It was dark, but livelier than any pub he'd been to recently, and the clientele was a good deal better looking.

They settled into a rounded booth, and the girls plumped him beneath a large portrait of Winston Churchill, looking for all the world as if he'd just lost the 1945 election. They thought this was very funny. Nigel smiled graciously beneath his grey moustache. And when their pints of Courage arrived, he led them in a toast to the great man.

'To Winston,' he growled. Their glasses clinked, and immediately Penelope and April fell into excited conversation over clothes that they'd seen either on the Queen Mary, or on the drive over, or here in the pub, or… Nigel didn't really know where. It didn't seem to matter, and he took his being ignored with wise equanimity. He was happy enough sitting with his pint, watching the beautiful people, an even-tempered gentleman beneath the determined bulldog face of the prime minister. Yet all the time the even-tempered gentleman's eyes were watching. His goddaughter was here somewhere in California. Perhaps this was the way to find her. Plan A.

The girls turned to him occasionally to ask whether he wanted another, to which he always replied, 'Yes, I believe I will,' until he found his mind bobbing up and down like a cork on a wine dark sea.

Eventually he was inspired to interpose in the girls' conversation. 'I should tell you,' he said, slightly slurring his words but within a suave, self-disciplined sense of verbal control, 'that I think you two are dressed quite handsomely, showing a long bit of leg, I grant you. But colourful. And you can do it. You're the right age, you're fit, you're quite… charming.'

Their blank looks were starting to crease into knowing smiles.

Nigel felt compelled to warn them. 'But life, you must remember,' he said, 'is rather a sort of struggle of some kind in which one must be aggressive of course but graceful as well. You must always remember that, and remember the absolute importance of character. I'm always amazed at the absolute tyranny of weakness. So many weak people. How do they survive? I mean people who lack character. Life always destroys them. Crushed and tossed away, they are. You mustn't allow it, you know. Especially if you're to dress like that.'

Having delivered his fashion credo of the hour, he swung himself back into the padding of the booth and looked at them with powerful, sceptical, gimlet eyes that were seeing as through a beer glass darkly.

They looked at him for a moment—April puzzled, Penelope smirking—and then resumed their conversation, casting concerned looks at him every now and again.

Then two young rugby players, all jock straps and rolling mauls, hurled themselves into the booth, to the joyous rapture of Penelope and April. At last, the competition had arrived.

'Phil and Steve, this is Nigel. He's an Englishman.'

The lads were very friendly and offered their hands. Nigel gave Steve a rather flinty, sidewise look that had the desired effect. He backed off. He'd been sitting on the tail of Nigel's coat.

They tried to include Nigel in their conversation, but his mind was slipping far away. It was thirty-six years ago, Katanga, the Congo. His chin dropped to his chest and he stared deeply into the amber in his glass.

The jeep bumped along the treacherous dusty road full of rocks and potholes. They were climbing a steep incline to where the United Nations troopers were dug in on the hill. The African sun was a dying ball of fire behind the purple bars of the clouds. He pulled the lapels

of his coat tight around his neck and felt for his pipe, suddenly shiv-
ering in the knowledge that night was the winter of the Tropics.

''ang on, sir!'

The jeep bucked and jolted, nearly throwing him clear, and then a
hand pulled him back by the shoulder.

'Nigel!' It was Penelope.

'What?'

'I'll call you a cab.'

'No, don't bother. Please don't.'

'You shouldn't be driving.'

'Are you leaving?'

'It's very late, Nigel.'

He noticed that April, Steve, and Phil were talking amongst themselves behind her.

'Oh, I'll be fine. I'll just sit here a while, if you don't mind. I'll have
some coffee.'

'Are you sure?'

'I'm perfectly fine.'

'Do you know how to get to your hotel?'

'Yes, I'm sure I can manage. I have a map.'

'Which hotel is it?'

'Le Grand Extravaganza. I'm sure I'll be fine.'

'Here.' She reached into her handbag and scribbled her phone
number on a scrap of paper. 'Call me if you need any help.'

HE STOOD OUTSIDE THE HOSPITAL in the late morning sun, sweating in his cavalry twill, feeling damned uncomfortable. He reached
into his pocket. Sure enough, there it was. He needed her now.

CHAPTER TWO

HE WANDERED BACK INTO the air-conditioned hospital, looking, he imagined, rather like a monster, with a black eye stitched up on the side. He roamed the antiseptic halls full of very septic patients. Perhaps he had merely been unlucky in his choice of hospitals, but Our Lady of Guadalupe Charity Memorial Hospital seemed patronised by a white, urban proletariat of fat, loud, ignorant women and wheezing, sun-dirtied, tobacco-stained men, and an equally large Mexican peasantry, who were very brown, very humble, and very quiet. When they did speak, it was inevitably in Spanish. Nigel had never seen real Mexicans before. Only celluloid ones in *The Magnificent Seven* and *Juarez.*

He eventually found a pay phone in a quiet, isolated corridor leading to an exit. Sun splashed through the corridor's wall-length windows, making Nigel thankful for the air conditioning in this unseasonably hot October. This was the best of all possible worlds—sunny days, artificially cooled.

He fiddled in his pockets for the proper change. He'd already learned that the phone system was one of America's true marvels. Everywhere one found a phone it was perfectly maintained, the connections were bright and clear, never the slightest problem. And over such a vast country as America—a truly remarkable achievement. My compliments to Alexander Graham Bell. A Scotsman, wasn't he?

'Uhhhh-huhhh. Hello?'

'Hello, Penelope?'

'Yes.'

'It's Nigel.'

'Well, hello.'

'Sorry to trouble you like this, but I've had a bit of an accident, and I was wondering if you could help me out. It seems I crashed my car. I'm calling you from hospital. I was wondering if you could give me a lift?'

'Oh my God. I've got to sit down. Are you all right?'

'Yes, I'm perfectly fine. But I was wondering whether you could come and fetch me, my dear? I'm at Our Lady of Guadalupe Charity Memorial Hospital, if you know where the devil that is. Do you have any idea?'

'No, but I'll find it in the phone book. What's the number there, Nigel? I'll call you in five minutes if I can't find it.'

Nigel read off the number on the pay phone.

'I'll be right over.'

He hung up the receiver with a grin on his face and a chuckle in his throat. Dealing with Penelope, he couldn't help but feel like an elderly rogue. It took a bit of imagination to remember that he really had been in a serious accident, that he really had nearly killed himself, and that he really did need Penelope's assistance. Not just to find his goddaughter, but to get him from A to B. He hadn't just invented this story to see her again. Worse luck for him.

He sat on a padded bench and looked out of the window-walls at the flowered gardens—green, red, and pink—around the hospital's parking lot. And he looked out at the palm trees that shielded the hospital from the street. A fine thing, palm trees. Tropically pictur-esque, they were. They reminded him of Cyprus.

Then he looked back down the corridor towards the hospital itself. What a bloody awful hell hole. It wasn't gruesome and filled with flies and terror, as in Africa. But it was, for all its efficiency and probable economic success and medical achievement, a painful, hard, and antiseptic place. Why couldn't they make hospitals rather more like hotels? Wasn't the idea to bring comfort to those in pain? Instead, all hospitals seemed very Swedish or Germanic. A bunch of very bossy people in very clean surroundings making one's life an absolute hell.

But I suppose, he reflected, it must be a hard job dealing with a constant round of suffering humanity—especially when they are as ugly and ignorant and full of foulness and runny noses as this lot. Still, he thought the priests of his acquaintance—he'd met rather a few padres in his time in the Army—had a rather better bedside man-ner than the nurses and doctors he'd met here. At least the chaplains granted that one had an inherently valuable immortal soul, which was a comforting thought when one was risking one's life. These American medics seemed rather to regard one as merely another experimental cadaver temporarily animated by some natural electri-cal current.

He thought of the Congo. It was the mission station, set on a green hill, in a verdant forest. But there were screams—grotesque, terrifying screams. He came running up, little Père Abelard holding his black skirts and hurrying furiously at his side. They saw a horrible tableau: drug-maddened Congolese whose pangas thudded sickeningly into nuns, lying prone, perhaps already dead, splashings of blood staining the criminals' sans-culotte trousers and torn and dirtied shirts. Nigel didn't stop to count them—to measure the odds if they turned his way—but seized his service pistol and fired until the pangas thudded no more.

Père Abelard never stopped running, and when he came to the fallen nuns, he reached into a satchel he kept with him and did what was required, performing the last rites. Nigel holstered his pistol and stared. The epiphany hit him hard, and never left: to Père Abelard, the nuns weren't really dead, not in the sense of finality; some part of them lived on.

Now here he was, far removed from that wretched horror. Yet for all this hospital's gleaming machinery, all its mighty learning and Teutonic efficiency, these doctors, he thought, were wrong about the electrical current, and little *Père* Abelard—who'd probably met his Maker by now—was right. Or so an old soldier had to believe.

Nigel decided his five minutes of waiting were up, so he strolled outside to let his wounds soak up the sun and to inhale the dark brown air.

There was a large, shady tree and an expansive grassy area forming a sort of island in the middle of the car park. Nigel figured this was as good a spot as any to await his rescuer. He sank beneath the tree and tilted his Panama over his eyes.

He was very tired, and after half an hour of waiting, he fell asleep and dreamt of the cold, green moors of the Highlands. *He and a band of hearty old men, all of them nudging sixty, with twelve-bores cradled in their arms, tramped through the heather, the clinging peat squishing beneath their wellies, the wind buffing their faces to a Stuart tartan red and stinging their ears.* One of them would break stride occasionally to pull a flask from his pocket and wash a little Glenfiddich down his throat.

Suddenly, Nigel spun round, shoved his shotgun into his shoulder, and aimed for the heavens. The recoil jerked him awake and he found himself confronting a healthy bosom protruding beneath a white T-shirt, a long arm gently embracing his shoulders. His head twitched, and his neck felt the sharp pain of whiplash.

'Nigel, I've been looking all over for you.' She saw his eye, and the blood on his shirt. 'Oh my God, how could I have let you drive?'

She helped him up as he struggled to his feet. 'Please, my dear, it's not your fault. I was the idiot driver. I'm afraid I just wasn't used to driving on the wrong side of the road.'

She led him to her white Mustang convertible, and he slumped in the passenger seat. Yes, he was tired. But the furnaces of his mind were gaining fuel, driving him on. He was here for a purpose, after all. Plan A was still intact.

'Did the doctors say you were all right?'

'Perfectly. But I'm technically under arrest.'

'Oh, Nigel.'

'Rather late in the day to become a lager lout, eh?'

'What?'

'A drunken hooligan. We've rather a lot of them at home. Young layabouts who'd benefit from a spot of National Service—that's the draft to you.'

'I should never have left you alone.'

'You can hardly be held responsible for the actions of a man old enough to be your grandfather. Surely I should be the responsible one.'

'You were drunk, Nigel.'

'Only momentarily, and I usually function quite well in that condition. It was the roads and your customs that did me in. I was confused. And when everyone began screaming and honking their horns, I swerved into oblivion.'

'My God. What happened to the car?'

'The police officer told me it was a complete write-off. Tyres flat and torn off, windows blown out, the grille smashed, resting on its roof. I felt as though I'd crashed a biplane and was hanging upside down. The emergency chaps were there right away. Pulled me out quite cleanly. A good operation, that.'

'Oh, Nigel. You're lucky to be alive.'

'Yes, aren't I just?' he chuckled and looked out of the window.

'Which hotel did you say you were staying at?'

'Le Grand Extravaganza. I hope I'm not taking you away from anything.'

A smile crept over her face like a blush. 'No, I was just getting up.'

Nigel's eyes roamed thoughtfully over her body. Rather like a well-exercised leopard's, he thought. It must be something to watch it stretch and sigh in the morning.

'You must feel awful,' she said.

'No, not really. But I could use a drink. Hair of the dog, as we say back home.'

She giggled. 'Well, when you're feeling better, I'm going to give you my lecture on drunk driving.'

Nigel confessed to himself that he usually wasn't one for lectures, not after classics at Eton and the special course he'd had in Swahili while at Sandhurst—'*Jambo, Bwana Thorpe, uhali gani?*' he had to address the blighter every day; he never learned the really useful phrases one needs for Africa, such as, 'How much for that chap's ears?'—but he might rather like to attend this one. He imagined her candlelit flat, a chalkboard on an easel, and she in gown and mortarboard using a pointer to illustrate the insalubrious effects of alcohol on the body of a chalk-drawn man. And Nigel, his Number One tunic unbuttoned, body sinking into an overstuffed, leather chair, listening intently with a cigar burning in one hand and a brandy cradled in another, like that famous painting of Fred Burnaby of the Blues that used to hang over his grandmother's fireplace. He thought the old girl probably had a thing for Victorian soldier-adventurers with huge moustaches.

'You're not in shock, are you?'

'No, my dear, I was just thinking.'

'The shock will come later.' She turned to him and looked him directly in the eyes—at least, he thought she did; he couldn't tell through her sunglasses. 'Nigel, if you need anyone to talk to, I'll come over.'

'That's jolly decent of you, my dear.'

'I'm serious. Call me if you need me.'

What a charming, thoughtful young girl she was. These Americans were certainly very friendly. No one in England would ever behave in this way. In England, one would be expected to bear one's torments silently and in private so as not to impose on the privacy of others. In any event, in England nobody really gave a rat's arse about anybody else's problems anyway.

Of course, he had to confess, in England it would have been thought that he, Brigadier and all, was made of sterner stuff, that

Penelope's beneficent attentions weren't entirely necessary to a man who'd been in much tighter jams than this, with bullets buzzing all around and artillery shells ploughing furrows next to one's speeding jeep ricocheting between potholes while one calmly remarked, 'Speed it up, boy. I mustn't be late for my appointment with the Colonel; I'm making up a foursome for bridge.'

England, bloody England, how demanding it was. And October, too. How wet.

Penelope pulled her Mustang into the driveway of Le Grand Extravaganza—a long, rectangular, bronze-coloured building with enormous arched windows all along its front. A parking valet in a top hat trotted to Penelope's door. Another opened Nigel's door.

'Would you like me to park your car, ma'am?'

'I think that's a splendid idea,' Nigel interjected. 'Don't you, my dear? Would you consider joining me for some tea?'

Penelope thought for a moment and then smiled and said, 'Yeah,' in that peculiar, thick, whining voice of hers.

He heard the parking valet say, 'Please leave the keys in the ignition, ma'am,' and saw him help her out of the car. He seemed extremely attentive to her. Nigel wondered whether being a beautiful woman would give one a particularly rosy or a particularly cynical or perhaps merely a particularly spoiled view of the world.

Nigel tilted his Panama over his eye and offered her his arm as she trotted round to him. She took it, thank goodness, and Nigel's chest swelled like a courting pigeon's. That should put that damned parking spiv in his place.

He wondered whether—with the rakish tilt of his Panama—he might possibly look like Field Marshal Slim in his slouch hat, all jaw and swagger with his 'forgotten' army in the sweating jungles of

Burma. He strutted through the electronic glass doors of Le Grand Extravaganza, his jaw jutting to match his chest, the beautiful, tall, blonde Penelope on his arm.

It was a fine, luxurious, expensive hotel. And very American, or perhaps Californian for all Nigel knew; America had left the Empire far too long ago for Nigel ever to have spent *that* much time on her shores. Although in his more bullish moments, he fancied he'd have given Washington a run for his money at Yorktown, outnumbered and surrounded though he would have been.

The hotel guests strolled through the reception area, the bar, and the gift shop, dressed in everything from immaculate suits, to tennis shorts, to roller skates. Much of the clientele was handsome, but much was swarthy. London was like that too, nowadays. Didn't the Arabs own Belgravia?

'Shall we go up to my room? I think I'd rather try the room service, if you don't mind. I'm not used to looking like Frankenstein's monster yet.'

They walked across the lobby to the lifts, Nigel trying to look as inconspicuous as a bloodstained old man with a shiny black eye and a beautiful blonde on his arm who's wearing tight pink jogging shorts, exposing shapely, long legs that make her almost as tall as he is, can.

He pressed a button and brought Penelope into a glittering marble-floored lift, with mirrors forming an arc from waist-level to the ceiling. He pressed the button for the fourteenth floor, and the lift chimed as it passed each one. At the fourteenth, Penelope followed Nigel's purposeful stride to his room.

'First time I've ever used one of these,' he said, showing her the card he used as a key.

His room was spacious, with a balcony like many another hotel room. Penelope was surprised, however, to find a large map of the greater Los Angeles area taped over the mirror above the writing desk, with 'PLAN A' written across its top.

'You're a serious tourist, Nigel.'

'Yes.' He snapped up the phone. 'Hello, room service... Yes, this is indeed Mr Nigel Haversham, how kind of you to notice. Now listen, I'd like a bottle of champagne. Something reasonable. You know, Moet et Chandon or something. And sandwiches... Oh, it doesn't really matter. Something Californian I think would be appropriate... Yes, and two glasses. Thank you.'

He plopped himself on the edge of the bed and tossed his Panama onto the table near the balcony.

'I thought we were having tea,' said Penelope.

'I'm on holiday, my dear. I deserve a little fizz and fun, don't you think?' Her smile was answer enough. This was certainly too good to be true... especially if he continued to sit there looking like a one-eyed raccoon, as Davy Crockett, the great American hero, might have said. 'Excuse me, my dear. I think I'll wash.'

He locked himself in the bathroom. The picture in the mirror was not what Nigel would have considered enchanting. Dirk Bogarde he was not. Not even Humphrey Bogart. What a sight, Nigel Haversham. What a bloody awful sight.

He washed his face carefully lest he damage the stitches. The result was remarkable. More than half of the sheer bloody awfulness of his face was erased. What he assumed were cuts or scars turned out to be mere encrusted trickles of blood that slipped off his face and down the drain. He was a little deflated. *I'm not half the monster I used to be,* he thought to himself, subconsciously humming Lennon and

McCartney's 'Yesterday'. At least his eyebrows still looked like misty grey brambles above ponds where something had been slaughtered. His eyes were blue, yellow, and bloodshot, showing all the fatigue and trauma he'd been through over the last twelve hours.

He poured the official Le Grand Extravaganza aftershave, so thoughtfully provided by the management, into his hand from its miniature bottle (very much like the sort one gets when one orders Glenfiddich on a plane). He splashed some on his face as a sort of antiseptic. Then he unbuttoned his shirt and ran a little under his armpits and over his chest. He wanted to be discreet, but a change of clothes, he decided, would have to wait until after Penelope left, and that might be a while, if he was lucky. Good thing his years serving abroad in the tropics had toughened him to these sorts of conditions. Nowadays he sweated no more than a stuck pig. At least with the cavalry twill, one would hardly ever notice.

He brought his tie back to its moorings against his throat, passed his aftershave-dampened hands over his slick, silver hair, stroked his moustache between his index fingers and thumbs, and decided it was the best he could do.

When he unlocked the door and re-emerged, he found Penelope sitting on the bed, watching a soap opera on the telly.

'Well, that's better,' he said. 'Almost feel human again.'

'You look a lot better.'

'Thank you. Shall we step outside?'

Good Lord, he thought to himself, already I'm having to compete for her attention. Allowing a young woman a glimpse of a soap opera on the dreaded box was like giving an alcoholic a drink; there might be no way back.

'I rather like the view,' he added, which was certainly true as he followed Penelope's tight pink jogging shorts onto the balcony and flipped off the television with what subtle, polite, and inoffensive sleight of hand he could muster.

Penelope shaded her eyes with her hand and leaned on the railings.

'There it is, Los Angeles. The City of the Angels, isn't it?' he queried as he breathed in air that seemed to scrub the oxygen out of his lungs. 'I very much admire your palm trees, I must say.'

Penelope smiled at him. He wondered if she considered him an idiot or a master of obscure double entendres. Frankly, of course, he felt like an idiot.

'You know,' he said, the thoughtful man of the world, 'L.A. is a great deal like Israel. In both places, the Jews have made the desert bloom.'

'What do you mean?' she said, squinting against the sun. She'd left her sunglasses inside.

'Well, I mean, they're both deserts, aren't they?'

'Yeah, but, like, what about the Jews?'

'Oh, you know, movie producers, that sort of thing. A lot of them are Jewish, aren't they?'

'Oh, yeah,' she said, squinting back out at the tall, shiny buildings.

'And of course, Israel, when I was unofficial adviser to dear old Moshe Dayan back in the Six Days War...' Where the bloody hell was the room service?

'I've got a Jewish friend. He's in med school.'

'Oh, studying to be a doctor, is he?' No, you fool, he's studying to be an accordionist.

'Yeah, his father's a really well known psychiatrist in Newport Beach. They've got a really nice house. They've got *lots* of money,' she said with heavy emphasis, nodding her head and twisting her mouth as if to say, 'I mean lots of money, know what I mean?'

She sat her elbow on the railing, her chin in her palm, and let her fingers probe between her lips. 'Have you ever been psychoanalysed?' she asked, looking at him lazily.

'No,' he said; and I'd rather not be right now, if you don't mind, he thought to himself. 'Do you think I ought to be?'

'You can learn a lot about yourself. His father psychoanalysed me. You don't know how much pain I've been through.'

'Oh, really? Anything I can do to help?'

She shook her head. 'I've had too many tragic relationships with men.'

'How perfectly dreadful. Well, you mustn't let them take advantage of you. That's what fathers are for... to protect you, I mean. You do have a father, don't you?'

She laughed. 'Yeah.'

Well, that might have been obvious, but Nigel knew there was a great deal of divorce in California, and a great many brave new world things, like sperm banks, artificial insemination machines for lesbians (well, they have them for cows, so why not?), and God knows what else. One couldn't be sure of the most normal things nowadays, so one was obliged to ask inane questions. It was a time of *o tempora, o mores*, as he knew all too well.

There was a knock on the door and not a moment too soon, as far as Nigel was concerned. A bit of bubbly and things would run smoother all the way round.

'Come in, my good man, come in,' said Nigel, opening the door to the waiter who did a double take at the spiffy but badly bruised English gentleman in cavalry twill before him. 'Set the table on the balcony, if you don't mind.' And keep your eyes to yourself, Nigel thought as he glanced up at Penelope, who was sitting in a white plastic chair at the table outside.

Yes, it was hard being a jealous man in love with a beautiful woman in tight pink jogging shorts, which, if Italy were a leg, were riding up near Trieste. But there was a certain chivalry in jealousy; the desire to take a chair and a whip and defend one's beloved from the animal passions of anyone other than oneself, who of course was deserving of gratification and ownership and proved it by one's jealousy.

But of course, he didn't really love her. How could he? He'd barely probed the wonders of her mind. He hadn't the slightest idea of her no doubt deep and worthy religious convictions. And he didn't have time for that sort of thing anyway. But the mere thought of it did add a sort of enjoyable *frisson* to his evolving plan to make good use of her in a worthy cause, or so he told himself.

The waiter laid the table with great care and made brief, smirking remarks to Penelope, who returned them all too eagerly. Nigel waited inside.

The waiter returned with his cart. 'Would you like me to open the bottle, sir?'

'No, I can manage, thank you,' Nigel said, stuffing a wad of bills in the waiter's hand, shoving him out of the room, and slamming the door shut, knocking the cart into the waiter's shins.

'There now,' he said, tearing the foil from the champagne bottle, 'what sort of sandwiches did they give us?'

'One's tuna—that's yours, I don't really like fish. And this one's vegetarian—avocado and sprouts.'

There was still no sign, mercifully, of those green things you have with Christmas dinner.

'Well, so long as you're happy. There we are,' he said, deftly popping the cork and filling their glasses. 'What shall we drink to?'

'How about your staying alive?'

'That's awfully kind of you. I'd already forgotten about that. All right, to my survival and to you and your fair city.'

She didn't seem particularly taken by the compliment. Perhaps it was putting it on a bit too thick to call Los Angeles 'fair'. Perhaps her mind rebelled at such side or imprecision. All right, here's to you and your overcast metropolis, he thought to himself. He slapped a little of the bubbly on his tongue and felt better.

'Were you born in Los Angeles?' he asked, looking for the best approach to consume the rather large sandwich before him.

'Yeah,' she confessed, as though she were embarrassed never to have left her native city.

'Good,' he said encouragingly. Time to turn Plan A into Operation Alexandra. 'Perhaps you could show me around. I could use a native guide.'

'Sure. How long are you here for?' She said it pleasantly, but with a certain understandable suspicion, he thought.

'Oh, I don't know. A week, perhaps. Now that I'm retired, I don't really have to be anywhere.'

'Well, like, what do you want to see?'

'There is one thing I'd like to do. The daughter of a friend of mine is living here in Los Angeles, an English girl about your age. I was wondering whether you could help me find her?'

'It's a big city, Nigel.'

'Yes, of course it is. Now, I don't actually have her address, but I did receive a postcard from her recently. It was postmarked Los Angeles, CA, 90025.'

'That's West L.A. We could call information.'

'I doubt if they'd be any use. You see, she's rather an independent character. She likes springing all sorts of surprises on her mother, but doesn't like leaving any traces. I have a picture of her here. I know it's highly unlikely you've ever met her, but it might give you some insight into what sort of girl she is.' He reached into his wallet and drew out two photographs of a high-spirited, arrogant-looking blonde, perhaps twenty, laughing and dancing barefoot on a well-kept lawn.

'She's beautiful,' said Penelope, admiringly.

'Yes, she is, rather. She comes from a very handsome family.' Penelope returned the photographs to him and he filed them in his wallet. 'Her father and I were very good friends. We served together in the Army. Unfortunately, he died, killed in the line of duty in Northern Ireland. That happened some time ago. The girl never knew him. I'm the child's godfather, and I've always felt something of an extra responsibility for her. I know it's rather a sentimental thing, but I would awfully like to see her. The trouble is, I've got no further clues about where exactly she might be in Los Angeles.'

'I don't think I can help you,' Penelope said. He guessed her suspicions were rising again.

'Well, Los Angeles is Raymond Chandler–land, isn't it?' He saw he'd have to wait a long time for an answer to that one, so he plunged ahead. 'We can do a little detective work of our own. It might be rather fun to try and solve the mystery, don't you think?'

She was starting to look bored. Where's your sense of adventure? he thought of asking her. But that, no doubt, was a line for young men, not for young, female Californians of the X generation.

'We can start,' he said hopefully, 'by putting ourselves in her shoes. Tell me, my dear, if you were a young lady, new to L.A., where would you spend your evenings?'

'I don't know. L.A.'s a happening place.'

'Well, I mean, when you saw me you immediately thought of the

Guards—very flattering of you, I must say. Now where might a girl like Alexandra go? That's her name, by the way, Alexandra.'

'There's so many places.'

I'm losing her, he thought. Never could handle women properly. But there was another tack to take. Nigel had already marked Penelope down as a woman with a powerful thirst. He'd noticed that in the Guards. He refilled her glass and held up the fast-emptying bottle by its neck. 'Oh, this will never do. Will you join me for another?'

'Sure.'

He stepped inside and rang up for a second bottle, putting his faith in *in vino veritas*. It had rarely failed him in the past. And he had another card to play. Americans, he believed, were quite taken by the glory of England's finest families. Perhaps the excitement of riding to hounds after a wayward young aristocrat would stir her lazy, sun-tranquilled blood. The smell of hawthorn in the sun and bracken in the wet...

He sat his charger alongside Jilly Cooper and Dick Francis, who looked on, gape-mouthed, as Penelope of the Pecos, golden blonde hair pouring from beneath her ten-gallon hat, held a smoking six-shooter, circling her Palomino around the poor fox, drilled dead as a Boot Hill desperado. 'Yee-hah, Nigel! This is what I call fun!'

He ferried an envelope, its seal jagged and torn, from an aeroplane carry-on bag he kept near his bed. He tapped the heavy paper against his palm and chuckled to himself. A sort of *pièce de résistance, n'est-ce pas?*

'I say, this tuna is quite smashing,' Nigel said, returning to his own white plastic chair. 'I don't believe I've ever eaten better in my life than here in America.'

Penelope's smile was wan.

Right. Time for the cannonade. 'Here,' he said, handing her the square, peach-coloured envelope. 'I thought you might like to see this. It's from Alexandra's mother. She's rather eager I should find her daughter too.'

Penelope took the envelope hesitantly.

'Go ahead,' said Nigel. 'Read it.'

She reluctantly withdrew the letter, unfolded the heavy, eggshell Churston Deckle paper, and passed her thumb over the embossed escutcheon at the top. It was handwritten in heavy black ink, directed by an old-fashioned, elegant hand.

My dear Nigel,

　　Thank you ever so much for seeing me and agreeing to take on 'your mission'. I'm so very thankful to you. And though I know you share my sorrow and anger at what's happened, I can't help noticing how excited you are by the chase. You are a wonderful sportsman. So, tallyho and accept all my love.

　　　　　　　　　　　　　—Pandora

Penelope said nothing, but returned the letter to its envelope and handed it back to him. If anything, she seemed embarrassed at being shown things that were none of her concern. The Brideshead gambit had had no positive effect at all. Everything, evidently, would rest on a champagne-generated warming of her friendly spirit, if he didn't fritter away all her latent goodwill with his clumsy, off-putting overtures to enlist her support.

'Pandora's a wonderful woman,' he said with desperate charm. 'And the Williamsons, of course, are a fine, old family. Odo de Guillelmo came over with the Conqueror. Ranulf was with the

Lionheart at Acre...' Best to find yourself a graceful way out of this. It seems the Americans are more democratic than you realised, old boy. 'Of course, it was d'Arcy Williamson who had rather a soft spot for Patrick Henry. How's your sandwich?'

'It's fine,' she smiled lightly. 'Would you like me to plan your vacation for you?' she said, waxing more eager. Planning things evidently appealed to her practical American spirit.

He shrugged his shoulders indulgently. 'If you'd like.' Then more craftily, 'I'd like very much to see L.A.'s nightlife.'

'Okay,' she said, suddenly flush with enthusiasm. Quite peculiar, women.

She was telling of the dinosaurs rising out of La Brea's tar pits when the waiter arrived, knocking at the door. Nigel thought it best to meet him there and prevent any further contact between the slick young Lothario with a towel over his arm and his own charming cicerone. Bottle was exchanged for cash, and the slick-haired young man gave Nigel a huge, drippingly salacious wink.

'I say, lad,' Nigel said, smiling and beckoning the young man forward and then driving the butt of his palm hard into the base of the waiter's throat, knocking him, choking, across the corridor. 'If you so much as wish my daughter good morning, you mangy cur, I'll have your guts for garters. You understand?'

The young man's eyes were blazing black, but he couldn't speak, and daren't stand.

'Now off with you, or I'll have the management after your rotten hide, you despicable scum.' He closed and locked the door, unwrapping the foil from his next bottle of seductive *vino*, only for an instant entertaining the idea that he'd been a little harsh on the lad, before reminding himself that all young men needed to be put in their place.

'Here we are, my dear,' he said, popping the cork. 'Looks like you could use some more. A fresh glass is as refreshing as a fresh-cut flower, I always say.'

'WE'LL HAVE TO SPEND A DAY AT MALIBU,' she said, and he nodded. Malibu sounded perfect. As did Disneyland, San Juan Capistrano, Santa Catalina, and all the other Spanish names that were as familiar to her as the Iron Duke's peninsular campaigns were to him: Vimiero, Fuentes d'Onõro, Salamanca—and all the other places where the British had gone around killing people. But then again, those people needed to be put in their place too; they'd been French after all.

The second bottle was nearing exhaustion when Nigel decided it was time to sign the contract. They'd strayed a bit from the reason for their lunch. It was time to bring her back.

'Now, Penelope, old thing, I do want you to promise me that we'll crawl among the nightclubs and look around for my goddaughter. Is that still on your schedule?'

'Oh, sure,' she said.

'Good. This is awfully kind of you, my dear.'

'It'll be fun.'

Perhaps, but now was the time to make it serious and official, he decided, and the best way to do that was with *baksheesh*.

'But I'd like to make it worth your while, too,' he said. 'And I'd like to hire your friend, what's her name?'

'April.'

'Yes, I'd like to hire April as well. I'll cover all expenses and pay you a hundred dollars a day for every day we spend looking for Alexandra and a five hundred dollar bonus on the day we find her.'

Penelope's face showed a little colour. He supposed she was torn between her latent suspicion, her pleasure at being paid, and of course her champagne-warmed feelings of goodwill to all men, though Christmas was still some way off. 'Thank you,' she said.

'Not at all. It'll be simply charming having you as my guide, but it'll be a job for you for all that, and you ought to be paid for it. And if it's any further incentive, I can assure you that when we find Alexandra, you'll have the sincere thanks of one of the greatest families in England. And you know,' he said, chuckling, 'that could come in rather useful if you'd ever like to honeymoon at Elkstone. I'm sure Lady Williamson would insist on your using it. I think you'd find it quite delightful.'

Penelope didn't know what to make of it at all. She'd certainly never heard of Elkstone, she had no immediate plans for going on a honeymoon, and if she did, it certainly wouldn't be to some draughty old castle with hot water bottles and Stilton cheese as its main attractions. Or at least, that's what Nigel read in her eyes. Hawaii, he thought to himself, was rather more on her mind, with long, passionate grapples in the warm tropical evenings, she and her lover thrashing about like grunions in the sand. (He'd read about grunions in one of his travel guides, how they spawned on the beaches of California and Mexico. Funny, but the only beaches Nigel had spent any time on were in the Falklands, watching the Royal Marines and Two Para go ashore. Not at all the same thing.) Nigel thought of the ocean caressing Penelope, its stimulating fingers smashing over and away, over and away in passionate blue and frothy white lather.

Nigel decided he'd rather like to keep staring at Penelope's sleepy blue eyes for some extended period—perhaps a Hawaiian weekend when this was all over. After all, he'd spent some time in the tropics.

Perhaps he deserved some time holidaying there in the service of Bacchus for all the years he'd spent there as a servant of Mars.

He suddenly saw himself wading ashore, like MacArthur in the Philippines, Penelope draped across his arms, an Aryan mermaid, of whose company he was quickly relieved by muscle-bound surfing Adonises, of which this country had far too many.

Oh, bloody hell, he sighed inwardly.

'Well, what do you say, my dear? Shall we have another to solidify our relationship?'

'Yeah,' she smiled exultantly.

Nigel started hoisting himself to his feet, but Penelope jumped up to stay him, her hands outstretched. 'Oh, let me do it,' she said excitedly. 'And I've got to call April. Can I invite her over? She's part of our partnership.'

'That would be splendid,' he replied, none too happily, seeing no reason for a chaperone. It rather offended his sense of honour. His eyes followed her pink jogging shorts inside, then stared gloomily at the buildings in the smog.

When Penelope hurried back, her excitement almost tipped her over, as her tennis shoes became entangled stepping onto the balcony.

Nigel smiled diplomatically. 'Is she coming?'

'Yeah,' said Penelope breathlessly, blushing as she staggered like a filly. 'She's coming right over.'

'Marvellous.'

'Woow,' she said, plopping into her chair and wiping her forehead. Nigel looked at her too full mouth with its too big tongue and wondered how sometimes physical beauty overwhelmed its own imperfections, while at other times it was crippled by them. In Penelope, beauty overwhelmed everything.

She smiled at him in that knee-jerk way he'd noticed American girls are wont to do. But Nigel didn't return her smile. That would have shown an accommodating weakness. Instead, he acknowledged it by a slightly raised eyebrow and a thoughtful expression, which showed complete self-mastery and no contemptuous desire to please. Nigel might never have married, but at his advanced age he had the disinterested capacity to know the vanities and perversities of the female mind without having his vision blurred by youthful male romanticism.

'When do you want to start?' she asked brightly.

'Tonight, after a rest and a bath, I think. Let's get a bit of L.A. nightlife, shall we?'

'Okay.'

'Any ideas?'

'Hmm.' Nigel noticed her legs were rocking back and forth under the table as she cogitated.

'Is there somewhere where young people like you might enjoy going slumming, perhaps? Somewhere that caters a bit to the rough trade?'

Penelope's smile turned reflective and coy. She liked talk like that.

Nigel heard room service's knock on the door. He rose to answer it. Penelope didn't move a muscle, but lay lazily in her chair, gazing thoughtfully at the skyline, smiling and dreaming of sleazy bars for Nigel.

Nigel opened the door and saw a champagne bottle, chilled and perspiring, standing alone on the floor, a note wrapped around its neck with a rubber band. He removed it and read 'Charged to your account.' A grin passed quickly over his face. He closed the door and locked it.

As he turned and ambled back to Penelope, he couldn't help chuckling to himself. The lion has roared, he thought, the lionesses have gathered, and the hunt is on. Not a bad innings, old boy. Not bad at all.

CHAPTER THREE

APRIL'S SHORTS WERE A phosphorescent lime green. Her thick, bouncy hair was tied back in a ponytail, and she wore a matching lime green sun visor. She also wore white ankle socks, bright white tennis shoes, and a thick white T-shirt advertising a Mexican beer. Nigel found it hard to remember why he'd ever begrudged his balcony to such an adorable sun-kissed creature.

Penelope stood with her arms folded on the balcony's railing, watching the traffic pass by, rhythmically twisting her ankle back and forth. They still hadn't settled on a venue for the evening.

But April, bless her, slashed that Gordian knot without the slightest trouble. Bubbling glass in hand, bouncing on her toes, her ponytail prancing merrily, she burst out with teeth agleaming, her body twisting to face her interlocutors (Penelope, who stood behind her, and Nigel, who sat in front of her): 'The Club E.D.! Let's go to the Club E.D.! It'll be really fun, Nigel.'

Nigel's eyes looked to Penelope for her expert approval.

Penelope smiled broadly and nodded. 'Yeah, okay.'

'The Club E.D. it is, then,' said Nigel, toasting April. 'Would you be so kind as to pop over here at nine o'clock? That should give us time to recuperate for this evening's work. You know, a hot bath, a change of clothes.'

'Sure,' said April, putting one tanned leg before the other, flexing it on her toes, and twisting it back and forth as though she were exhibiting herself at a beauty contest.

The unconscious action of a trained model, Nigel surmised; one wonders if all California girls are like this, or is one just lucky?

Penelope tossed back the remainder of the champagne in her glass. 'Okay. Goodbye, Nigel.'

'Bye,' said April, brushing her hand sympathetically over Nigel's shoulders. 'We'll see you at nine.'

Nigel nodded and watched them step inside to collect their stray sunglasses and handbags. His carefully trained lip-reader's eyes— which had recorded many enemy conversations through binoculars— observed the following whispered conversation, begun by April.

'He's looking for his goddaughter?'

'That's what he says.'

'Well, he's kinda cute in an old limey sorta way.'

'*And* he's loaded.'

'No kiddin'.'

'Like, totally.'

Nigel slumped in his chair and saw their shorts slide to the door and disappear.

With effort, Nigel tottered to his feet and stamped inside, slipping off his coat and undoing his tie. A good, warm bath, a good afternoon's nap, and a good, fresh set of clothes should put him in shape, he thought. It had, after all, been an arduous eighteen hours, hadn't it? From car wreck to hospital to champagne luncheon to his pub crawl this evening, he still kept the hard-riding schedule of an officer on active service—and it was special operations executive service at that. Not bad for a man his age. Not bad at all.

He slipped out of his shoes and tossed the rest of his clothes on the bed. He padded into the bathroom.

Ah, American plumbing, another marvel comparable to the American phone system. Quite marvellous. Shiny, modern, always worked. The hot water was always hot, the cold water always clear.

SuperMac, who'd never had it quite so good himself, was surely right when he said our role was to play Greece to America's Rome, thought Nigel. But it didn't seem quite fair that we should settle for the Yanks to have all the good plumbing and all the good phones. The fact that we Greeks had once sacked their Rome—Washington— nearly 190 years ago, seemed small compensation.

He stepped into the steaming tub, full of decorous suds. Now, this is luxury, old boy, relaxing all the senses. Just don't fall asleep and drown on me.

After his bath, Nigel slept the sleep of the just, and it was only thanks to his setting the alarm on the clock radio courteously pro- vided by the hotel that he managed to wake in time to dress in his blue Guards blazer, white shirt with open neck, and loose-fitting grey trousers. Best to be a bit casual this evening, he thought. I don't know that a black eye goes very well with more formal attire. An open neck's a bit jaunty, and a jaunty man is apt to be flippant at the wrong time, hence my eye. The awful rude bore struck me. No sense of humour at all.

Nigel topped himself off with a pair of dark glasses. Movie stars wore these when they went out, didn't they, to avoid being recognised? Well then.

Nigel took the lift to the lobby and stepped outside the hotel into the hopeful, warm Los Angeles evening, the sort of evening weather, Nigel thought, that was made for long walks along a beach, an evening full of promise and joy.

He paced in front of the hotel, but hadn't long to wait before April's red Ford Taurus pulled up. Penelope was in the passenger seat with her window rolled down.

'Oooh, Nigel, I like the shades,' she said.

'The... er?'

She tapped his glasses' frames.

Nigel stepped into the back seat. 'Oh, thank you.'

'Hey, Nigel, very stylin',' said April over her shoulder.

'Thank you, my dear. Do I remind you of Dirk Bogarde at all?'

'Dirk Bogarde? Is he on *The Young and the Ruthless?*' she asked, looking at Penelope. Penelope shrugged.

'Oh, I really like this song,' Penelope said, thrusting her hand to the radio and turning up the volume so that further conversation was impossible.

Nigel looked out the window and watched the scenery pass by.

The flashing neon sign for the Club E.D. came at the end of a slightly seedy strip that boasted a pizza parlour, a couple of ethnic restaurants, a laundromat, and a small art-house movie theatre. One entered through a battered wooden door that led onto a tattered red carpet and a dark-haired, Italian-looking young man in dinner clothes standing behind a cheap wooden podium. Behind him was a diving black metal spiral staircase. The floor beneath their feet vibrated to the raucous rhythms thundering below.

'Do you ladies have i.d.?'

Penelope and April fished for their drivers' licences from out of the small handbags they carried on thin straps over their shoulders. Both wore simple, short dresses that Nigel guessed were designed to allow full freedom of movement for dancing and plenty of ventilation for hot weather—or some such practical thing. Neither one of them wore stockings, and their heels were of a serviceable height. Penelope certainly didn't need to be any taller.

The girls produced their identification, Nigel stumped up the cover charge—$10 apiece—and they passed on to the black metal spiral stairs that brought them down to the ear-numbing noise below.

The interior of the Club E.D. struck Nigel as a sort of underground, miniaturised version of the Colosseum in Rome. There were three horseshoe-shaped levels of booths until one reached the crowded dance floor. At the opening of the horseshoes was a small rectangular stage where a live band jumped up and down and screamed into unnecessary microphones that were unnecessarily amplified through unnecessary speakers.

Where once decaying Roman aristocrats, perhaps at the onset of the Dark Ages, might have tried to relive the decadence of the past with gladiatorial combats in a dark atmosphere like this—more suitable to cockfighting, one should think—now young people gathered for their own entertainment, to have their eardrums pounded and give themselves over to some strange onset of St Vitus's Dance.

'A booth for three? Follow me, please.'

Nigel took off his glasses to get a better look at his surroundings.

It looked, frankly, like Juvenile Delinquents Day at the United Nations. The disgusting, libidinous hormones of the four corners of the globe had gathered here to drug themselves with drink and music that smashed one's cranium like a jackhammer. This was worse than he expected. Surely Alexandra couldn't be in a dive like this.

'What do you think, Nigel?' April screamed to be heard above the din.

'Charming,' he replied. 'Could we please have a round of beers?' he continued to the waitress before she could get away.

'Do you want a pitcher?'

'Three pitchers, I think.' He'd need a great deal of solace to get through this evening's ordeal.

'Bud, Coors, or Coors Light?'

Nigel motioned to the girls, who chorused, 'Coors Light.' Nigel nodded to the waitress in confirmation. 'Coors Light, if you please. Are there any hops in that?'

'Wow, Nigel, were you in a fraternity?' asked April.

'No,' Nigel reminded her. 'The Guards.'

'We should have bought him a keg,' laughed Penelope.

Nigel gazed affectionately upon his companions, whose attentions were quickly turning to the band. Their heads rhythmically bobbed to the cacophonous throbbing from the speakers. They were still beautiful, he thought, if in desperate need of a finishing school with a strong curriculum in music: Elgar, Vaughan Williams, Gilbert and Sullivan—the great masters. But there was a natural grace to the girls, their necks like swans', with shimmering hair that begged for a kind hand to stroke it.

But though his companions were clearly happy, he couldn't help feeling sad, overcome with a sense of waste and futility. *The image came to him of two giant marble Roman goddesses in the Libyan desert, come to life, smiling and rhythmically bobbing to the beat of tribal drums as swirling dervishes swarmed lubriciously around them, swinging from their marble necks, hanging from their marble arms.* Good Lord!

The pitchers arrived, along with three chilled mugs.

'Here, girls,' he said, raising his in toast, 'to the wonders of California,' adding to himself, Aren't I just looking at them now?

The girls weren't much inspired by his toast, but they lifted their mugs perfunctorily and sipped the foam from them.

Coors Light, Nigel decided, whatever its considerable merits, nevertheless lacked a certain weight, a certain *gravitas*, which could only be made up for in sheer volume. He looked around in desperation, but clearly no one had heard of real ale. And so it wasn't long before Nigel had finished his own pitcher, polished off a large portion of Penelope's and April's, and consumed most of a fourth.

By now it may have been mixing with some of the afternoon's champagne, or perhaps it was merely the sorry spectacle on the dance floor before him, but Nigel's face looked sad and wrinkled as a bloodhound's, as he rested his elbows on the table, face in his palms.

'How are you feeling, Nigel?' shouted April.

'Fine,' he yodelled in return. 'Here,' he handed her his wallet. 'Order whatever you'd like. I'll be back in a moment.'

He slid out of the booth and down an aisle. He got a few odd looks, an old man with a swollen black eye, weaving his way through a lightly sweating human traffic coming to or going from the dance floor. They glittered with gold chains, brief black leather skirts, and shirts that seemed to be missing all their upper buttons. Biceps or ankles were tattooed in jagged black shapes that looked hideously liked barbed wire. What was that supposed to prove?

He turned a corner and brushed past a few hirsute young men slouching and talking together next to the gents. They looked at him somewhat surprised, somewhat hostile.

He pushed open the door of the men's room. There were two

athletic-looking black men wearing baseball caps—one forward, one backward—who quickly put their hands behind their backs, like playground bullies caught smoking cigarettes.

'And, like, who the hell are you, man?'

'Haversham. Nigel Haversham,' he said, with John Bull's belligerent pride in his tone.

They walked past him, as though they were going to leave, but did not. 'Well, brother, why don't you knock next time? Sheet, can't even get no privacy in a fucking bathroom.'

'Sheeet! Who the hell is he?'

'Whoa, that muthuh? He's Haffer-shem. Ni-gel Haffer-shem.'

Nigel looked at himself in the dirty mirror, but there was nothing to say.

'Hey! Old man! Whoa! Look at that eye. Get yourself to bed, old man!'

'Thank you kindly for the advice. I think I shall very soon.'

There was an obscene click and Nigel turned to see the glittering edge of a switchblade poised and weaving like a cobra before him. Nigel should have known better than to go unarmed into darkest downtown L.A. He'd faced a flick knife before, along the Falls Road during his second tour of duty in the Province, but then he'd been in a colonel's flak jacket with half a company at his back.

In his current circumstances, he could poke the fellow in the eyes, stamp on his toes, or insult his mother. But any of these things might result in his immediate demise. Discretion, he had learned at Sandhurst, was the better part of valour. He smiled serenely at the knife carrier. 'Call of nature,' he said and disappeared into a cubicle, smartly locking the door behind him.

'We can wait all night, muthuhfuckuh!' Nigel heard the black man shout. Nigel waited the appropriate time, read a few of the more interesting offers and phone numbers on the wall, then flushed. When he emerged, the two men converged on him.

'Oh no,' Nigel groaned, staggering and holding his left arm.

'Hey, man,' the knife wielder said. 'What's your problem, man?'

'It's my heart,' croaked Nigel. 'Triple bypass. Please. Air. Must... have... air.'

'Sheet, man. You are one sick muthuhfuckuh. Give me a hand, nigguh,' said the knife man to his unarmed partner. 'We gotta get Ni-gel some air.'

They each draped one of Nigel's arms over their necks—and carefully plunged their fingers into Nigel's pockets. They found nothing of interest except his dark glasses, which they threw to the floor.

Nigel groaned. 'Air. If... no air... it's... murder.'

'Come on, man, don't die on us now.'

They dragged him out of the stall, out of the men's room, down the passageway, past the slouching, hirsute men. 'Man, this muthuh is sick. I done never seen no muthuh look so pale, man.'

A whispering voice: 'Where we takin' this muthuh?'

A whispered response: 'We gotchta take him outside, man. Dump this muthuh. Here man.'

'But it say "Employees only".'

'Fuck that, man.'

Now it was into the kitchen, through the steam, past the gleaming steel of pots, pans, and cookers, past the staring waitresses and cooks, to the rear exit they knew must be at the back. But a big, fleshy man stepped into their path and blocked it, crossing his arms over his chest to show off his tattoos. He was bald, with a compensatory moustache, and he glared at the would-be muggers with little piggy eyes.

'Hey, what're you doin'?' he said.

'Hey, man. Our friend here needs some air. He's got three bypasses already, man. Don't let him spoil your kitchen. Sheet.'

'Who is he? Is he drunk?'

'He's our friend, man. He's Ni-gel Haffer-shem, muthuh. Now, get out o' the way.'

'Where'd he get that black eye?'

'Hey, man, you think we give him that? You think a black eye happens just like that? Man, you is ignorant. Ni-gel been mugged yesterday. Fuck, man, we're here to protect him. Look, Emile, show the man Ni-gel's pockets.'

He turned out Nigel's trouser pockets and demonstrated that there was nothing in his coat pockets.

'He got no wallet. How much money you got, Emile?'

Emile brought out his wallet. 'Twelve dollar, man.'

The other black man drew out his wallet. 'I got two dollar, man. Now you think we robbed this muthuh for two dollar or twelve dollar? You just think we mugged him cuz we black, don't you? Well, that's racism, man. And I don't like it.'

'Yeah, man, that's racism. Uh huh.'

'Aw right, aw right, aw right. What you gonna do with him?'

'I told you, man. We just gonna give him some air.'

The big man nodded doubtfully. 'Okay. Out that way. But next time, use the regular exit. Customers aren't allowed back here.'

'Customer not allowed back here,' the mugger scoffed. 'It's a medical emergency, man!'

The muggers dragged Nigel outside onto the concrete landing and then up the two dozen concrete steps that led to the street behind the Club E.D. The big man followed them onto the landing and watched.

'Sheet, Ni-gel. You done gained one hell of a lot o' weight. Wutch you been eatin', man? Sheet.'

They paused to rest at the top of the steps, next to an industrial rubbish bin the size of a lorry, and called down to the manager. 'He's feelin' much better now, man.' He put an ear to Nigel's lips. 'Wutch you say, Ni-gel? Oh, uh huh. Ni-gel say thank you, man. Thank you.'

'Okay, come on, nigguh.' They hoisted him up again and dragged him out of sight behind the bin.

'Is he gone, man?'

The other peered round the bin. 'Yeah.'

'He's gotta have somethin', man. What about that ring?'

Nigel blinked his eyes open. 'Given to me by Lady...'

Emile screamed, and the other man defensively slapped his hard fingers against Nigel's mouth.

'Fuck this shit, man,' Nigel heard, and he saw a knife wrapped in a mugger's fist, a fist that hit him like the crack of a cricket bat. He felt blood trickling from his mouth, his body slumped, eyes closed in pain.

'Is he dead?'

'He ain't dead. Give me a hand, nigguh. We gotta dump this muthuh, 'fore he comes to life again.' They strained, lifted him up, toppled him into the bin, and raced away.

CHAPTER FOUR

FOR A BRIEF MOMENT, Nigel saw bright stars on the dark velvet background of a beautiful, if spinning, California sky. Then it went black and his mind drifted to the last time at Elkstone...

It was there that Nigel had first met Sean Stalker, at a garden party on behalf of the Morris Minor Society of Great Britain. He remembered the moment, strolling over the green lawn, gazing at the colourful pavilions with Jaguars and old MGs and the occasional Rolls or Bentley parked nearby between rows and rows of Morris Minors and dogs—setters mostly—frolicking around the gentry, both young and old, who were dressed in tweeds and sweaters, wellies or brogues, a few with flat country caps, all with drinks in hand, mingling with the anoraks who drove Morris Minors.

It was the sort of social setting—now more and more of a rarity, of course—where Nigel actually felt somewhat at home. It helped, naturally, that the party-giver was someone of similar sentiments, taste, and age. Lady Williamson and Nigel had been poured from the same

cask, bearing a traditional aroma, flavoured by common experi-
ences—he as an officer, she as an officer's widow.

He was resting on his shooting stick, watching a particularly handsome blond labrador, when another young blonde with a croquet
mallet over her shoulder came eagerly towards him, followed by a
black-haired chap with a mallet in each hand.

The young blonde was Alexandra, his lithe and leggy goddaughter,
whose small, sloping nose always reminded him somewhat of a rhesus monkey's—not that this detracted in the slightest from her beauty.
Nigel conceded that it more likely reflected the surfeit of time he'd
spent in dripping jungles with baying monkeys scampering amongst
the verdant vines and branches above him, as if intentionally trying to
point him out to the enemy; it was in these circumstances that Nigel
mastered that neglected weapon, the slingshot, and was able to treat
his men to monkey-head soup.

He was far more protective of Alexandra's head, and given that
she was such a sprightly young thing, Nigel gladly served as her sen-
ior adviser on all matters related to her life—from the importance of
not attending university, especially Oxford or Cambridge, so as not
to strain her eyes, to the equally important necessity of not holding
hands with any young man who had not already received his
approval.

And indeed, she generally, he thought, had followed his sage coun-
sel. Certainly, she'd followed his advice about university, which was
an excellent turn of events, as it brought her to London, where she
worked as a secretary to a publisher, making her a convenient, occasional luncheon companion. Nigel didn't know much about publish-
ers; had he done, he might have been less pleased with Alexandra's
decision.

'Hello, General,' she said, smiling brightly. Nigel nodded in order to admire her up and down. A fine figure of a woman. He certainly needed to keep a sharper eye on her in the future. 'I've been simply dying for you to meet Sean. General Haversham, Sean Stalker. Mummy asked us to set a good example for the others by playing croquet. Care to join us?'

'I'd be delighted,' Nigel said. But to himself he thought, he simply won't do. Points scored, of course, for having romantic, handsome features. One could see how a young girl might fall prey to him. But one could just as easily see from the cut of his jib why she shouldn't.

For one thing, he seemed to Nigel a rather sexually confused individual. On the manly side, he had dark eyebrows crawling towards each other like caterpillars and dark, wet Byronic locks curling over his forehead. One might like that sort of thing—a matter of taste—but Nigel didn't. On the feminine side, the young chap was built on a disturbingly thin frame—as though he were a bulimic fashion model. And like a fashion model, he had a beautiful woman's high cheekbones and luxuriant long eyelashes. Beneath his sharp, undersized nose was a thin, stubbly, black moustache. As indecisive as his sexuality, Nigel thought.

It was that horrible thing, a *sensitive* face—and with brown eyes, which Nigel, leaping to his prejudices, tried to place somewhere in the animal kingdom. They were clever eyes, but of the scheming sort. A fox's eyes. And like a fox, Nigel had already decided, he'd have to be hunted down.

'I believe I start,' Alexandra said, lining up by the peg. 'Then it's you, General. And Sean, darling, I'm afraid you're last.'

'Oh well, what is it they say? "Lucky in love, unlucky at games".'

Nigel felt the bile rising up in his throat. Oh, God. What is it they say? Lucky bisexuals frolic and play, unlucky bisexuals Nigel castrates today.

Alexandra played extraordinarily well, dispatching her ball through the first three hoops in only two strokes. She looked back happily.

'Oh, well played, dear girl, well played,' Nigel said distractedly. He was much more intent on intimidating Stalker with his narrow, appraising look.

Alexandra said, 'I don't know if Mummy's told you anything about Sean, but he's really a most amazing screenwriter.'

'Oh, really? Anything with Roger Moore? Sean Connery? They seem rather the sort of chaps one can identify with.'

'No, I'm afraid not.' Stalker smiled ingratiatingly, and Nigel noted with despair that he had dimples—a lady-killing accessory that would be hard to combat.

'Well, I daresay, I'm probably the wrong person to talk to. Don't go in for that sort of thing much. Too passive. Backgammon, that's my amusement. I don't suppose you play?'

'No.'

Nigel watched his goddaughter score hoops as easily as if she were picking apples from a tree—and she looked damned attractive doing it. What did she want with this black-haired, bisexual, non-backgammon-playing pretty boy?

'Give us a chance, will you, Alex?' the pretty boy said.

When, in God's name, did he get the right to call her Alex? Surely that was the prerogative of godfathers and others more intimately connected with Elkstone. In Nigel's grandfather's day, a chap didn't shorten his light o' love's name until he'd marched her to the altar and thrown her into bed.

'So you haven't made any documentaries about great backgammon players?' Nigel said.

'No, sorry.'

'Seems a pity. Do you think there'd be a market for one? Omar Sharif could play the lead.'

'I don't know. But if you'd be willing to put up the money, I'd be willing to consider it.'

'You're up, General,' said Alexandra. 'I took pity on you.'

'That's the trouble with being a screenwriter,' Stalker continued, 'unlike, say, a painter or a novelist. You can write a book or paint a picture, but you can't just make films.'

'No, I don't suppose you can,' Nigel replied, sending his ball through the first two hoops.

'Films cost a great deal of money. So you need backing.'

'Blast.' Nigel's ball had ricocheted off a hoop. 'Backing? You mean from someone like Cesare Borgia or the Earl of Southampton—a patron?'

'Any money will do. The government should do more, of course. But there's not much hope of that while the present lot are in power. Too busy lending each other money for houses. Not to mention the Dome fiasco they inherited from the Tories, who were even worse.'

Nigel snorted: a whining artsy-fartsy pinko in the bargain, though he had a point. Stalker cleared the first two hoops in good position for the third.

'Even so,' Stalker went on, 'there's plenty of room for private investment. There's no reason why people who can afford all this,' he raised his head from sighting his mallet and took in the glory of Elkstone, 'shouldn't contribute to our common culture by investing in Britain's visual arts.'

Now, to Nigel, of course, Elkstone, its lady, and her daughter were the very embodiment and triumph of Britain's visual arts. The great house, with its classic Palladian front, had been in the Williamson family for generations. Old Arbuthnot Williamson had lent the East Wing for convalescent officers in the Great War, but otherwise it was untouched and splendid. Old England at its best.

'I'll grant you, there's the lottery, but it's only a pittance, not nearly enough, and they've certainly never given me any money,' Stalker complained. 'What we really need are higher taxes on the wealthy who can afford it, and an arts minister who's willing to take risks—you know, someone like Sir Peter Hall.'

Sir Peter Hall! That overstuffed, politically correct, preening, subsidy-gourmanding exhibitionist! A choleric redness rose from Nigel's neck to his cheeks, as he watched this bounder, this Irish Stalker who had somehow put himself even farther to the Left than Tony Blair's spin-doctored socialists, drive his ball ahead of Nigel's own. He silently rejoiced, however, when Stalker's next shot was scuffed.

'My turn again, is it?' said Alexandra. She easily reached the opposite peg and was through the next couple of hoops on her return before she unaccountably missed a stroke.

'Are you interested in supporting the arts, General Haversham?'

'Oh, yes, do quite a lot of it, actually.' Nigel lined up his shot, then paused, fixing Stalker in his stare. He could all too easily imagine that slimy bisexual's arms turning rubbery, stretching to reach his lapels, and, with delicate, adept, filching fingers, probing the wallet in his coat pocket and helping himself to a few tenners in the name of 'our common culture'.

'Oh, really? In what way?'

'Oh, you know, one does buy *The Spectator* on a weekly basis. And I went to the ballet once. Must admit I fell asleep.'

Nigel's mallet struck his ball perfectly, sending it through the hoop and smack into Stalker's own. Nigel grinned toothily, and Stalker gave an embarrassed chuckle.

'Oh, yes,' he said.

'Afraid I'll have to send you packing.' Nigel squished his shoe onto the enemy's ball. *Whack!* 'Oh, dear me. I do hope you're still on Williamson property.'

'You're such a brute, General,' said Alexandra.

'Oh, no, that's the nature of the game,' Stalker said evenly. But Nigel thought he saw a darkening of the young man's brow. 'Kill or be killed.'

He watched the wretched young man march out to his ball. With those thin arms of his, it would take him a few strokes to recover his ground, Nigel thought. Stalker swung his mallet fiercely—too fiercely by half, topping his ball so that it merely hobbled forward an inch or two.

'Oh, bad luck,' said Nigel.

'Shall I go ahead and finish then?' Alexandra said. The cheeky minx. Even if she was his goddaughter, she shouldn't be so sure of herself. He had no intention of indulging her with an easy victory. One did that sort of thing for children, but not for grown goddaughters. The Haversham comeback was about to begin. He watched with satisfaction as she bent her splendid, supple form, rocking her mallet back and swinging it forward too lightly, leaving her ball short of the hoop.

Nigel rubbed his mallet between his hands. His shot wasn't an easy one, but rather than playing it safe, lining himself up for his next stroke, he swung straight for the hoop. He met the ball solidly. It bounded fast across the grass, hit the hoop, and bounced through.

'I hear the footsteps of a general on the march,' Alexandra said, gratifyingly.

Luck deserted him on his next stroke, though. He had too much adrenaline pumping, and his ball—hit far too hard—galloped past the hoop it was meant to go through, taking him off the course, on a forward parallel with Stalker.

Nigel had no great desire to converse with his goddaughter's dark amorato, but he decided a little small-talk might break his concentration. 'So, what sort of films do you do, then?' asked Nigel.

'Well, I can't claim to have done any yet. I haven't the money.'

'But Sean is building up the most impressive collection of important contacts,' piped in Alexandra. 'He's always taking me to the most exciting parties...'

Now there were words to warm every guardian's heart—'he's always taking me to the most exciting parties.' What did that mean nowadays? Drugs? Rock stars? Members of the Labour Cabinet? (Thank God so many of them were homosexuals.) Wretched excesses of every sort?

'And all the most important people at these parties always know him.'

'And like him?'

That threw Stalker off his mark. His mallet crashed against his shoe and rebounded into his ball. 'Ouch!' His ball rolled over once, twice, and died.

'Well, of course they do, General,' Alexandra said, wide-eyed. 'Whatever did you mean by that?'

'Oh, nothing, nothing. Just an innocent question. So, you're quite the *bon vivant*, I take it, then, Master Sean.'

Through gritted teeth he said, 'It's important to know people, obviously. You know, I believe I may have broken my toe.' He took a few tentative steps to test it out. 'As you say, I need to find a Borgia.'

'Or a Southampton. But so far you've only found a Williamson.'

Stalker's eyes sprang at him. They were fox's eyes, all right. He'd flushed him out. Looking to raid the roost, eh? It was Reynard, it was Chanticleer all over again.

'Well, yes,' Stalker said, trying to recover his equipoise, 'and thank God for it. A delightful girl.'

'General, are you being a pain in the arse again?'

Nigel stepped close to Stalker, as though to proffer assistance, ignoring the profanity from his goddaughter. After all, she had gone to Roedean.

'I'm her *godfather*, you know,' he whispered. 'You've seen the film, I take it. Bear that in mind, lad. Bear that in mind.' Stalker's limp made a nice touch, Nigel thought, as though he'd already been knee-capped by the Haversham Mob.

'I've given you a reprieve, General,' said Alexandra, who had gone through only a single hoop before misfiring. Nigel chipped himself back into position for his next opportunity.

Stalker made a cautious approach to his ball.

'Do be careful,' offered Nigel.

Stalker stretched his lips in annoyed acknowledgement.

'So once you find your Borgia, what sort of films do you aspire to make?' Nigel asked, just as Stalker was bringing back his mallet. His ball sliced terribly, putting him in a hopeless position for his next approach.

'I don't believe in being creatively restrained—not by categories or anything else,' Stalker said vigorously. 'It would be fair to say, though, that I'm more interested in the dark side of human consciousness, in manias and fetishes rather than say...'

'Backgammon?'

'Backgammon among other things. Though, of course, I could imagine making a film about a cannibalistic serial killer who plays backgammon using the severed digits of his victims as pieces.'

'Oh really now, Sean,' Alexandra laughed, as well she might, being through the next hoop and well placed for her next turn.

'No, seriously, it could be quite interesting. That's what I mean by not limiting oneself as a creative artist. It could be a quite riveting dissection of how all of us are really just pawns in a big game, and only a killer like our protagonist can really see through to that and act on it.'

'Pawns would make it chess rather than backgammon,' Nigel said sourly. He'd missed his shot—on target, but short. 'I don't mean to frighten you, but it's your turn.'

Stalker swung wildly and got off a decent shot, bringing his ball in line with the hoop. But his sagging shoulders and adolescent frown betrayed that he no longer cared.

'Jolly good try,' said Alexandra, who now proceeded to knock her ball through hoop after hoop, with all the skill of a champion snooker player clearing the table. Her ball thudded against the peg with the finality of a clod of earth being tossed on a coffin lid.

'Now you two have to battle it out for second place.'

'I'm not sure my toe is up to it, Alex,' Stalker whinged.

'But surely *you* want to keep playing, General?'

'No,' Nigel said, swinging the mallet jauntily over his shoulder. 'I've had my fun.'

And unfortunately, it looked as though Stalker was preparing to have his. He sidled up to Alexandra, smiling and begging sympathy for his self-inflicted wound, like a coward who's shot off his toe so he can come home to Blighty and live it up with the nurses at Netley, while his brave comrades soldier on in the trenches.

And then—good Lord! Nigel's jaw dropped as he saw the bugger put his unspeakable hand on Alexandra's bottom. She—thank God!—quickly moved it to her waist. Good girl that she was, she gave Nigel an over-the-shoulder embarrassed glance and pleading smile. That did it! She *knew* the bugger was no good.

But how could Alexandra—Alexandra of all girls!—succumb to his sort? Nigel would never have expected it. She was a soldier's daughter after all, with a soul of iron, even if she, quite properly, draped it in silk.

Oh, the vagaries of youth. Perhaps they simply no longer knew what to aspire to. She never knew her father, so he couldn't read her Rider Haggard, still less G. A. Henty or Dornford Yates or the incomparable Kipling, the tales his father had read him. It was authors like these that had shaped his own catholic taste in literature so that he enjoyed everything from the novels of John Buchan on the thoughtful literary-political Left to the somewhat sounder *Bulldog Drummond* books of 'Sapper' on the literary-political Right. They wrote of men who knew what to do—men who would have made short work of Stalker. It was a struggle of captains versus canapés.

Alexandra shouldn't yearn for the grudging affection of some wheezing Irish idler like this bastard Stalker (with a name like Sean, surely there must be some Irish blood in his veins; and Nigel's memories of the Shankill Road were too raw to welcome that).

No. Nigel knew what sort of man she needed. She needed an officer rather like Nigel was in his youth. Full of pluck and daring, and raised on aspirations to adventure. Yes, he could see him now. Bronzed by the sun, and rippling with muscles earned not in a gymnasium but through hard, dutiful work, perhaps trekking through the vast, unexplored jungles of Burma.

Yes, it was steamy and sticky hot. One couldn't see the sun for the thicket of tropical vines, branches, and fronds that formed a canopy above him, but his clothes were soaked with sweat.

His trackers and bearers were rustic hill country men, wearing practically nothing save skimpy loin cloths, scarves tied around their heads, and geometric tattoos roaming over their bodies and across their faces. Together, they had set out on an expedition to confirm a rumour that the young officer had heard from a blind holy man in a market bazaar.

Deep, deep in these jungle-clogged hills, there existed, or so he'd been told, a settlement of Englishmen that few had ever seen. They had come more than two hundred years ago, and because of the arduous terrain, they'd been cut off from and eventually forgotten by the East India Company. But to this day—perhaps once every twenty years—a hunter would come from the hills and tell of seeing them and their remarkable civilisation.

And now, as the young officer freed his boot from the boa-like grip of the slimy, muddy, tangled undergrowth, he brought his machete crashing down against a wall of green that fell like a broken sail.

It was as though he'd suddenly raised the curtain on a stage. Before him, not more than twenty-five yards away, was a pyramidical temple. And sitting atop it was a beautiful young woman. She looked to him like a great white goddess—though her nose was a bit like a rhesus monkey's, perhaps the tragic outcome of some interspecies miscegenation many generations ago in this dangerous, isolated place.

She was sitting at breakfast, plunging her spoon into a grapefruit half, smiling at the juice spraying over her. And when the grapefruit had slid down the sluice of her tongue, she sent her spoon scimitaring through a cantaloupe.

Her table was overflowing with fruit, and she, dressed all in white, her golden tresses arrayed beneficently about her, laughed daintily as juices splashed from the force of her spoon.

She was quite alone. Not even the jungle dared to approach the pyramid. It formed a disciplined square, a respectful distance away. He stood at the jungle's edge and saw a sky of the most perfect cerulean blue. The sun was shining, and she basked under its rays, which seemed, at this spot, neither hot nor glaring.

He crouched on his haunches to shield himself from being spotted, and motioned for his men to do the same. And as they watched, tribesmen appeared from out of the jungle, gathering around a sort of platform or stage that skirted the temple.

The goddess calmly finished her refreshing light breakfast, paying no attention to the natives beneath her. Then, she descended the steps of the temple to the platform set above the masses. She waved a gentle arm over them, and upon their ignorant faces she cast her own generous, benign gaze.

The natives bowed their heads. The young officer was astonished to hear a band—it must have been on the other side of the pyramid— strike up 'God Save the Queen'. A Union Jack rose up a flagpole atop the temple, indicating that the Church of England sanctioned its services.

Then the goddess spoke, with a voice as perfect as any trained at Buckingham Palace. 'I have brought you beauty,' she said. 'I have brought you charm and learning. I have brought you the example of

*the unbought grace of life. And my people shall bring you law and
material progress...'*

'Shall I get you a drink, General?'

Nigel's mind snapped back to the young girl before him. 'Oh, no,
thank you, my dear.'

'Well, if you don't mind, we're going to wander on and perhaps
get something for ourselves.'

'Oh, by all means.'

'I'm sure I'll catch you later,' Alexandra said. 'Are you staying for
dinner with Mummy? Sean, poor thing, has to go back to London.'

'Yes, yes of course.' Though if it were up to me, Nigel thought, we
wouldn't send young Sean to London, we'd send him to blazes. Oh,
Alexandra, you weren't born and bred for... him. You were born to
be... well, by God, to be worshipped—by natives in Burma, if available—or at least romanced by an appropriately hardy, adventurous,
and scholarly Englishman. That's your heritage, by God. It shines
through you like lasers from your fingertips.

Think of your family, you foolish girl. Have you not been bred,
trained, and disciplined by the tradition of centuries to embody all
that's best in England—the necessary hauteur, the imperturbable
centre, the ready superiority capable of mastering every situation?

Of course she had. And it was not to be thrown away on some
worthless, simpering, Hibernian rascal interested only in drinking her
money away and striking his blow for the masses by marrying above
himself. No, by God, it wasn't.

He thought bitterly of how, in his ignorance, he had rejoiced at her
coming to London to work for a publisher, thinking it the suitable
thing for a girl of her looks, her social standing, her intelligence.

But now—now when it was too late—he saw clearly all the horrible temptations that London and publishing must put before her. It exposed her to a whole universe of importunate bastards like Stalker—broke, libidinous, subliterary riffraff… skinny, whining, pseudo-Celtic bards… Dylan Thomas poseurs… all trying to seduce her while cigarettes dripped with saliva from their drunken mouths and they trotted out whatever rubbishy affected pose sold to young girls nowadays.

Nigel suddenly realised that he was shaking his walking stick at no one and nothing in particular, and that Lady Williamson was approaching him with an amused look on her face.

'Is something wrong, Nigel?'

'No, no, nothing at all.'

Lady Williamson was a very handsome woman—tall, with long, thin limbs and hands, and a face of fine proportions: almond-shaped eyes, long eyebrows, a straight, pert nose, and a mouth that was slightly too small. It was a sign, perhaps, that she was no sensuous Frenchwoman. Rather, she was more the Artemis type—the sort of Englishwoman used to leaving the men to their cigars and their port knowing that she was smarter than all of them, and who looked cool and dignified no matter what the situation.

'You know, Nigel, I thought I could read your mind for a moment.'

'Really, my dear? And what was I thinking?'

'Met Alex's new boyfriend? Rather like to strangle him?'

Never could pull anything over on this woman. She's like a damned Red Chinese interrogator. 'Yes, as a matter of fact, I have, and I would. Remarkably unimpressive chap on first acquaintance, I must say. And he gets rather worse after that. Surely she's not serious about him?'

'It would appear so.'

'Well, then, something must be done, Pandora.'

'What would you recommend?'

'Flogging at a minimum.'

'For him or for her?'

'For him, naturally. And surely Italians aren't unknown in these parts. I'm sure there must be plenty for hire. I mean, we might not have Mafiosi on the scale of America, but...'

'Oh, do be quiet, Nigel. If I were to blame anyone, it would be you for neglecting your duties *in loco parentis.*'

'*In loco parentis?* Neglecting my duties?' But before he protested too much, he had to confess to himself that there might very well be something to that. He hadn't exactly kept sentry watch over Alexandra, aside from their occasional lunches. In fact, he'd hardly given her a thought. When her father had been killed so pointlessly at that street corner, blown sky high by a device placed there days before in the name of Sinn Fein, Nigel had sworn always to protect the dead man's lady, the elegant, ageless Pandora. And protect her he had, by his lights. When Alexandra was born, it was Nigel who hired the nanny, though he knew nothing about such things. It was Nigel who put her through Roedean and then, somehow, lost touch. Well, there was his second tour of duty in Derry, and he *was* Lieutenant Colonel commanding, and then there was the endless round of jog-trotting exercises, inspections, and diplomatic hoo-has from Kenya to Hong Kong to Brunei to the Falklands, and a dozen other places, before he retired. And while he saw Alexandra occasionally now that she was in London, what, after all, was a man in his position to do? Involve himself in the intimate affairs of young women? Well, yes, perhaps Pandora was right. He'd have to consider that in the future.

'I don't mean to be hurling accusations, Nigel, but I surely cannot supervise her from here. And in any event, it's not entirely our concern, is it? We know Alexandra, and we should trust her and have faith in her judgement.'

'Should we? Yes. Hmmm,' Nigel replied doubtfully.

'And anyway, Nigel, what could we do even if we wanted to interfere?'

'I've already told you, kill the bloody bastard.'

'Really, Nigel,' she said, dismissively.

'Well, I mean, a whimpering twit like that slobbering after Alexandra. It's intolerable.'

'Nonsense, Nigel. It's hormones. And if you don't talk sense, I'll abandon you for one of my guests who's sane.' She wasn't, of course, including any of the Morris Minor fraternity in that.

'Well, I must say, Pandora, I find it rather unfair to be accused— as a confirmed old bachelor, bear in mind—of having failed in my duties—*in loco parentis* if you please—and then to be denied any effective means of disciplining my charge.'

'Killing her lover?'

'Well, I trust it hasn't gone as far as all that.'

'Oh, Nigel, for a man of the world you are astonishingly innocent.'

Now there was a horrible thought. Lover? That pale, consumptive Irishman, her lover? Alexandra, the vestal virgin violated? And by an asthmatic pseud?

It was beyond belief. It was too horrible to contemplate. And so, of course, it haunted him. It rang in his ears like the old Puritan refrain: 'In Adam's fall, we sinned all.' At Alexandra's misguided call, a slimy Irishman had a ball.

But surely not one petal of that English rose could have willingly opened itself to be despoiled by that Irish vagabond. There was, after all, a limit to the sins that could even be considered by a properly brought-up girl of Alexandra's sort. What had they taught her at Roedean? She could not be—she simply could not be—that bastard's complaisant lover.

NIGEL STAYED ON AT ELKSTONE that night, when the Morris Minor Society had gone. They talked of this and that over the candle-light, easily as old friends do, getting mellower with the port.

'Why do you have these ghastly bashes, Pandora?'

'The Morris Minors? Oh, just a little fund-raiser, my dear. For charity, you know.'

'Which one this time?'

'Unesco. Enormously worthwhile. Another?'

Nigel allowed his hostess to freshen his glass.

It was several such later that he wandered along the corridor and up the swirling staircase to the little visitor's room. He'd rather over-done the tawny, he realised as he collided with the corner. What he hadn't realised was how the croquet game had developed his biceps. He'd demolished half the masonry.

'Oh, that,' Pandora said airily on his return. 'I'm having the land-ing redecorated next week. I've been a little neglectful, I'm afraid.'

Indeed she had. Nigel couldn't help but notice the odd peeling paint on the woodwork, the fading of the wallpaper. For the life of him, he couldn't remember Pandora, Lady Williamson, being quite so *shabbily* genteel.

'Tell me, Pandora,' he mused, relaxing like Fred Burnaby on the Williamson sofa. 'Do you ever miss the stage?'

'Lord, no,' she told him. 'My acting days are well and truly over. But it's sweet of you to remember, Nigel. Why do you ask?'

'For one horrible moment I thought that bastard Stalker might have touched you for some money for one of his infernal film projects, promising you the lead, or something.'

She laughed her tinkling, musical laugh. 'Some of us aren't so gullible. But if you're really worried about Alex, give her a ring sometime.'

IT WAS NOT UNTIL the passage of some weeks, when he could bear the strain no longer, that he rang Alex at her work and arranged for her to join him for luncheon.

Lunching with his goddaughter was always a most enjoyable experience. It was quite satisfying to indulge his very dated taste in sartorial elegance—pinstriped shirt, chalk-striped suit, a red rose in his lapel, a black bowler on his head, a long, black malacca-handled umbrella in his hand—and to bask in the ready appreciation of the girls who worked with Alexandra in her office. They fawned on him and always left him with a warm feeling and rosy cheeks—rather the sort of feeling one gets when savouring a fine brandy beside an open fire.

And they were just as appreciative on this afternoon. In fact, their charm rather softened him up, and he feared he wouldn't be able to perform as a proper Torquemada with Alexandra after all.

He sat across from her at an unsteady table in a grotty little Greek taverna, somewhere off Great Russell Street—her choice of course.

'Do you know what you'd like, General?'

'Well, I was rather taken by the unshorn lamb's head topped with eggplant, but it seems rather heavy on a day like today. What do you recommend?'

'Two falafels in pitta, please, with a small tabouleh salad,' she told the waiter, and then explained to Nigel, 'We'll share the salad.'

'Yes, fine,' he replied, not having any idea what had been ordered on his behalf, but handing the waiter the menus.

'It's awfully nice to see you, General.'

'Yes, well, I've been meaning for us to have this conversation for quite some time.'

He looked at her seriously now and was a bit perturbed. She looked very tired. Her eyes, he noticed, were tinged red. She wiped one of them hurriedly. 'Are you all right, my dear?'

'Yes, of course,' she said.

Nigel looked at her sceptically. 'Here, give me your hands. Now tell me, what's the matter?'

'It's nothing. Really it isn't. I know he still loves me. It was just so sudden.' She looked at him, but he said nothing, waiting for her to explain. 'It's Sean. You remember, General, you met him at Mother's.'

'He didn't harm you, did he?' His hands took an insistent grip on hers.

'No, not physically. Please, General, you're hurting me.'

'The bastard,' Nigel exclaimed, throwing her hands free. 'I'll hunt him down and...'

'No, you don't understand. He went away to America.'

'What?'

'He's gone to Hollywood. Oh, I know I should understand. There are so many more opportunities for him there.'

'You mean the bastard's hopped it?'

'I wouldn't say "hopped it", General.'

'No, no, of course not. But left, departed, gone to seek his fortune.'

She nodded. 'Well, my dear, we shouldn't be too upset about that. We should be celebrating.' He thought of ordering champagne, then realised ouzo was probably all they sold.

Alexandra looked at him pleadingly, eyes and mouth wide with dismay.

'I mean,' Nigel explained consolingly, 'that we should bottle up our own personal feelings, no matter how deeply they may run, and celebrate the sacrifice he's made to pursue his muse. It's all for the best—don't you think, my dear—for the bastard… I mean, for Sean, to be happy.'

'Of course I want him to be happy. It's just—it's just that it happened so suddenly.'

'Yes, I know, but no long, extended, tearful partings—that's a good thing. I hate to see a grown man cry, don't you?'

'But only a telephone call?'

'He probably thought it was cheaper than posting a letter.'

'He could have come to see me.'

'Yes, yes, I grant you that. But perhaps he wasn't feeling well. You know, all the excitement of a big journey across the seas. Apt to make a chap a bit uneasy in the stomach, if he's the nervous sort.'

'Nervous? He was worse than nervous, General, he was positively abrupt. He called me from the airport—the airport, mind you—and said, "Goodbye, I'm off to Hollywood. I can't stay here any longer." And then he rang off. Nothing about "How are you, darling? I have a bit of exciting news." Sometimes I think I should hate him.'

'Mustn't be too hard on the chap. He probably thought it was his duty.'

She smiled ruefully. 'That's generous of you, General. I must confess, he wasn't nearly so kind to you.'

'Oh, yes?' *Contemptible little swine.* 'How did I come into this?'

'Oh, you didn't,' she said, plaintively. 'I mean, I just remember that afternoon after he met you... well... General, the two of you are just very different people.'

'I should say so.' Damned Irish bog-trotter.

'Forgive me. I shouldn't have mentioned it.' She sighed. 'It's just that all my memories of him are tumbling around in my head. I don't know whether to condemn him or forgive him.'

'I think condemning is permissible in this case. You know, Alex, perhaps I should confess myself. I never really thought he was, shall we say, appropriate for you.'

'But I love him, General. He's so...'

'Irresponsible?'

'He's devoted to his work, you said that yourself.'

'Poor?'

'Yes.'

'Weak?'

'He's sensitive.'

'Selfish?'

'He's an artist.'

'A chiseller?'

'An artist,' she insisted.

Nigel grunted. 'The real point here, Alex, is that he's fled your presence, hasn't he? And in a manner less than distinguished. You should write the blackguard off. In fact, I'll write him off for you. If we're lucky, you'll never hear from the little swine again.'

'Oh, he did promise to write. I neglected to mention that, didn't I?'

'Thoughtful of him.'

'I thought so. Just suppose, General, that Sean is a success in Hollywood. I suppose you'd think very differently of him then.'

Nigel grunted his doubts. He hadn't enjoyed a film since *The Sands of Iwo Jima*—not bad for Americans.

'With invitations to attend the Academy Awards in Hollywood?'

'Have you ever read anything this fellow has written?' Nigel asked sceptically. 'I mean to say, for all you know, he's as talentless as he looks.'

'I've never actually read anything, no, but he's told me about some of his ideas, certainly.'

'And in your opinion, do they have any merit?'

'In my opinion, yes, but—and I don't mean this in any way as a criticism, General—I don't expect they're the sort of films you'd enjoy. They're rather dark-sounding things about drug-crazed murderers and people tormented by emotions they can't control. They could be very powerful—as films, I mean.'

Nigel looked as though he'd just lapped up some curdled milk. 'You mean to tell me that's the sort of chap you want to spend your time with? Someone whose diseased imagination is always flying off to dream about grotesque murderers and grotty, kitchen-sink melodrama, with some drunken floozy called Blanche and a bloke in a string vest? I mean, that hardly sounds healthy. You always have to wonder about chaps like that.'

'I told you you wouldn't like them.'

'Yes, but what separates thinking from doing, my dear? That's what I'm driving at. You know I take no pride in the fact that I've seen plenty of killing in my time. But people like that give me the shudders, I tell you. I certainly wouldn't be interested in spending much time with them, lest I end my days chopped up in their basement. I'm sure they'd write it off as being a "Jack the Ripper for art's sake" or some such rot.'

'Really, General, I think you're exaggerating.'

'Am I? Well, those things happen, don't they? And who do you expect does them?'

'Yes, I'm sure they're all aspiring screenwriters.'

'Now, don't get smart with me, young lady. You know very well that that class of people aren't the most responsible lot. They can always chalk it up to their "temperament" or whatever the devil they call it. They're not "inhibited by bourgeois morality" and all that stuff and nonsense. Is that what you want?'

'I think there's no further point in talking about it, General. As I said, you and Sean are very, very different. I don't expect you'll ever understand each other. But you must understand, General, that I love him. Now, where are those sandwiches?'

'WHERE'S ALEXANDRA, Nigel, do you know?' It was Lady Williamson.

Nigel mumbled something unintelligible along the lines of 'Uh huh, uh huh, uh hum'.

He was sitting quietly in a deep, padded armchair in his small, slightly scruffy, but very comfortable Knightsbridge flat. In front of him was a tray on which he had his usual at-home luncheon—crackers, pâté, Stilton cheese, and an invigorating Guinness, which Nigel knew was good for him.

Across the room was his old black and white television, a bitch for watching snooker—'he's going for the grey ball in the middle of all the other grey balls'—but for everything else it was all right. He had been watching the horse racing, one of the only things on the telly that amused him, when the phone rang.

'I have to tell you, Nigel, I'm a trifle concerned. I haven't been able to reach her on the phone all week. I wonder if you'd be willing to pop over and make sure she's all right. I'm sure it's nothing, but I'd be ever so grateful if you paid her a visit.'

'Come on, Heart of Ravioli! Come on, Heart of Ravioli!' he exclaimed as a horse on which he had a substantial bet broke from the pack and started moving from sixth, to fifth, to fourth, to third—and with a furlong to go. Brough Scott was screaming the commentary, threatening to drown out Pandora across the wires at Elkstone.

'What did you say?'

'Come on, old girl, come on!'

'What do you mean, "come on"?'

'There you go, there you go, well done!'

'Really, Nigel, if this is an inconvenient time...'

'Yes, by Jove, she's done it.'

'Perhaps I'll ring you back...'

'She's done it! Oh, no need, my dear. The bally horse did it. I just took the packet.'

'Are you wounded?'

'Oh, quite the contrary. Heart of Ravioli just came in at 5 to 1.'

'Well, congratulations are due, I'm sure.'

'Thank you, my dear. Now, you were saying about Alexandra?'

'She's disappeared. No one knows where she is.'

'She's not off on some book launch or something—weekending in Paris or some such thing? Frankfurt Book Fair, I shouldn't wonder.'

'If she is, no one knows about it. That's what has me worried. I did ring her at work. And they were wondering where she'd gone to as well. She's just disappeared. When did you see her last, Nigel?'

'Well, let me see. What was it? Two weeks ago, perhaps? A week and a half? It was when she gave me the glorious good news about wretched Master Stalker doing the right thing and clearing out for America. Two hundred years ago we'd have sent him in a convict ship to somewhere unpleasant in Georgia, mucking out swamps for a Williamson or Haversham plantation. But those days are gone with the wind, I fear. I know I rang you about it. Did she ever say anything to you?'

'No, she didn't. And it's made me think. Thwarted young love, "Romeo and Juliet"...'

'Surely you're not implying suicide?'

'Of course I'm not. How despairingly literal-minded you military men are sometimes. But I do think Alexandra might have done something rash—perhaps even purchased an airline ticket and gone to America herself. Whatever she's done, wherever she is, I should like you, as my man in London, to find out.'

'Certainly, certainly. I shall make enquiries and a recce immediately. Anything else?'

'Yes, Nigel. Next time you have an insider's tip on a horse, I should like you to ring me.'

'As you wish, my dear. I'll ring you as soon as I have any information. Goodbye.' But no great hurry, of course. Catch the next race first. Finish the rest of my Guinness. Then I'll drop by my charming young goddaughter's flat and hand her tissues while she moans listlessly about her flu. I'm sure that's all it is.

CHAPTER FIVE

ALEXANDRA'S FLAT WAS IN SOHO, where red-coated huntsmen had once chased the fox. It was a poky little thing, just off Dean Street. Not at all what Nigel would have chosen had the choice been his, but she found it 'colourful', 'exciting', 'inexpensive', 'so convenient for everything'. Those were the words she used, as far as he could recall. An estate agent's dream, was Alexandra.

To Nigel, however, it was the sort of place where one expected to find a card announcing Mistress Demona of Discipline. The narrow streets surrounding it stank of fish, rotting vegetables, and God knew what else. It was that part of London where Chinatown met Greek Street, and no one, as far as Nigel could see, was the better off for it. If this was food, it wasn't something that often turned up in the officer's mess, thank God; and in the Army, one never saw its detritus lying about the gutters.

Nigel was well used to operating in muck, mire, and gore—it was a professional hazard—but dressed in his usual civilian black elegance, with woollen coat, bowler, and all the rest, he was a little sniffy about it now. He deftly avoided stepping on fish heads, varieties of squashed salad, or the odd Chinaman rushing about with a crate in his arms. He carefully sidestepped the ear-ringed and tattooed delivery men shouting 'oi' at one another. He navigated between the young thugs who trudged down the street looking like giant thumbs eager for a bit of orgiastic eyeball gouging. Ah, the cosmopolitan life.

He trotted up the rickety metal stairs to Alexandra's flat. Behind her forest green door (painted such in honour of her country upbringing), he'd find sanctuary. They'd share a pot of tea. There would be toast and marmalade, water biscuits and Brie, and as a garnish, pills of vitamin C. He'd hand her tissues, take her temperature with his palm on her forehead, and volunteer to run down to the chemist for Lucozade. She'd tell him funny stories, admonish him not to be silly (she could go to the chemist herself), and make him a gift of one of her firm's new books. They'd recently launched a series of naval adventure stories he was rather keen on. Perhaps there was a new one. He reached the landing on the second floor wondering what might be on offer: *Frogflayer: Part Six of the Captain Fraser Chronicles,* or *Armada Be Damned,* or *Peglegs and Lion Hearts.*

The forest green door was open—not wide, but cracked open, as though she were expecting someone and didn't want to miss his knock. But surely this was not the place to leave one's door unlocked. Who knew what might happen? A whey-faced man wearing a dirty mackintosh and dark-rimmed glasses mended with sticky tape might wander in, bewildered: 'I'm sorry, isn't this the Flagellation First Edition Bookshop?' Or some pimply-faced prole might pop in and say, 'Oi. You Doris de Mona, then?'

But now he saw the door was frayed and splintered at the edges, as though it had been rammed or jemmied open. His extremities tingled—his fingertips, his feet, his brain. It was what Army psychiatrists, he knew, called 'the flight or fight reaction'. For Nigel, by temperament and training, it meant fight. He approached the door cautiously, running his gloved fingers along the frame. He didn't like the look of it.

A rash man would have flung the door open. But Nigel knew that would achieve nothing. If tragedy had occurred, there was no use rushing into it. He eased the door forward, watching it move, hoping it would offer clues.

It could have been simple burglary, surely a common enough occurrence in Soho. But it was easy to imagine the worst: Alexandra spread-eagled in an armchair, her throat slit, her clothes drenched in blood.

He stepped over the threshold. The door, still only partially open, blocked his view. He stepped round it and was hurled across the room, his shoes stumbling against a small, feeble servant's table, his hands hitting a wall, which kept him upright. He kicked the table away and spun around, his hands shooting up, instinctively straightening the lapels of his heavy coat.

In front of him were three brooding black men with steel wool hair knotted in dreadlocks that drooped like cat turds from their rainbow-coloured knitted caps. They were tall, gangly, laughable-looking bastards—Jamaicans probably, and probably drugged into imbecility, he thought. Surely not too much for him to handle. After all he was armed—with a brolly. *And* he'd fenced for Eton once upon a different time.

'What the devil's going on here?' shouted Nigel, raising his umbrella in defiance, in the quarter of sixte.

They charged him—all three at once—but *whoosh*, Nigel kept them at bay, swinging his brolly like a shillelagh. One of them foolishly lunged, head first, and on a fierce backstroke Nigel nailed him a wailing blow on the temple. 'Ha!' he shouted. 'Haven't used the *flêche* in a long time.'

But the jolting impact delayed his recovery swing, and the other two sprang forward. There was nothing for it but to counterattack. He shot the umbrella open like an air bag to repel one of them. Then he pivoted and kicked the other scoundrel in the knee.

But before he could strike his next blow, the shillelaghed Jamaican slipped behind him and seized his arms. Another, hopping on one leg, swore mightily, planted himself, and drove his fist into Nigel's face, sending his bowler flying.

Nigel felt as though he'd run full force into a huge live-wire cable. A shocking volt burst through his chin, up his nose, and into his brain. Something squirted onto his tongue and down his nostrils—blood, no doubt. He remembered the taste. A thin grey curtain slid over his eyes, then another, then another, then another, getting darker, and darker, and darker.

He was in Ireland, sitting at an enormous wooden table—a wake table, he believed they called it—that dominated the sitting room in what appeared to be a humble cottage. 'Woman of de house,' he heard himself bellowing, straight out of The Quiet Man, *'where's me taters? And don't you be washing 'em, now. I want de full dirty flavour for meself.'* His teeth came down on little flecks of gravel and he woke with a start.

He thought for a moment he was on a snooker table. But then he realised it was merely the thin, dark green carpet in Alexandra's flat. The gravel in his mouth was blood or perhaps dirt from the carpet. From his vantage point, he had a perfect mouse-eye view of the flat. As a mouse, he'd like it. Lots of crumbs on the carpet for food, and lots of dust to use as camouflage.

But as a wounded godfather inhaling the wretched stuff, he wasn't so pleased. It was true Alexandra might be lying murdered in the next room, but if she wasn't, if she was merely tied up and gagged or something, he was going to give her a jolly good dressing-down. It's slovenliness like this, he thought, that builds upon itself until disasters like making love to Stalker result. The woman was clearly a stranger to vacuum cleaners.

He pushed himself onto his knees and brushed off his overcoat. This qualified, he thought, as the first time he'd ever been mugged. Not an experience he'd like to repeat, certainly, but he didn't feel too bad. Damned heavy headache, of course. Good thing they were such skinny chaps, clapped out with marijuana and what not.

He took a handkerchief from his pocket and ran it carefully over his nose. It felt cut, but not broken.

He rose to his feet, paused for a moment to make sure he was all right, and then looked around the room again. Frankly, it appeared that Alexandra's flat had come off rather worse than he had. It had been torn apart: lamps lying wounded on their sides, cushions upended and disembowelled. And he could peer into Alexandra's bedroom and see drawers lying empty, her clothes flung about.

He knew what he had to do. He made a quick reconnaissance for Alexandra's body, stepping over various obstacles of overturned furniture, ignoring the shambles of her rooms, looking only for her. She was nowhere to be found, which ruled out murder, he thought. Kidnapping was a possibility, of course. But all this destruction—it wasn't from a struggle. The bastards were looking for something, weren't they?

He gingerly fingered her clothes lying haphazardly in the bedroom; he examined the cutlery spilled onto the kitchen's ancient, faded, chequered tiles; he peered into the bottoms of lamps, stared helplessly at the exposed and broken guts of the telephone, and carefully returned picture frames—cracked glass and all—to their places. He'd spent a professional life making sense of violence, but nothing in her trashed flat spoke to him.

He swung the broken green door closed, trotted down the black iron stairs, and searched the smelly streets of Soho for a red phone box. He was out of luck. They'd all been converted to glass. Even so, it was time to ring his friend the Inspector.

'FRIEND' MIGHT HAVE BEEN a bit presumptuous. He'd met Inspector Byron Tanner after writing a letter to the Home Secretary— during the days when nice Mr Major, a man of what Nigel regarded as 'the tolerable Left', occupied Number Ten—volunteering his services as a recently retired Army officer. 'I'm sure you share my feeling,' he had written, 'that the typical British bobby well represents the finest police force in the world. But is he prepared for the ultimate challenge? On top of his normal duties of protecting innocent women, children, and dogs (in which capacity he appears overwhelmed, as our intolerable crime rate shows), is he really prepared—*does our force have the proper leadership*—to meet the very real threat of massive civil unrest?

'I think not. That is why I humbly offer my services should such difficulties arise. Should you find that animal rights activists or communist/anarchist/homosexual insurgents need to be taught a lesson à la Peterloo, the General Strike, and so on, I would be proud to serve in the nation's interest. It's not just *The Big Issue* and Gay Rights people haranguing the Archbishop of Canterbury in his own pulpit, it's the very foundation of our civilisation that's at stake.

'I've had a mass of experience in these matters and can promise a severe, sharp shock to the malefactors that in the long run will protect property and innocent lives while sending the vermin running—preferably out of the country. Acquiring a new penal colony, however, having lost Georgia *and* Botany Bay, is something I must leave to the government. Still, might I suggest Liverpool?'

So read his letter in part. No doubt because it was such a generous offer to a shaky Tory government well in need of friends, Inspector Tanner had rung him up—at the Home Secretary's suggestion, he said—and offered to meet him over a pint.

'Oh, yes, the Home Secretary's very impressed with you, indeed,' Inspector Tanner had assured him. 'But just a friendly word. He's such a busy man, I shouldn't write to him again if I were you. You've made a very big impression already. Everyone at the highest levels of the Force is well aware of your patriotic desire to serve. It's a great comfort, I can tell you.'

Nigel remembered the words because they had warmed his heart. But now, on the phone, the Inspector sounded harassed and harried.

'Yes, General Haversham, what is it?'

'I thought you might like to know,' Nigel replied, somewhat put out, 'that I've been assaulted. Trio of black chaps. Jamaicans, I think. Thought you might like to do something about it.'

'Are you hurt? Do you need an ambulance?' The voice was cold and bored.

'No, I don't need an ambulance. But what I do need is for some of your chaps to come over and do some detective work. These fellows assaulted me in my goddaughter's flat. It's been ransacked, and *she's* been missing for more than a week.'

'Where are you?' the Inspector asked more urgently.

IN THE THIRTY HOURS since the police had searched Alexandra's flat and questioned Nigel about his assault, he'd had plenty of time to brood and worry. But nothing made sense unless the explanation was the most anodyne one. It was simply impossible to associate Alexandra with the idiots who had attacked him. With no body, no ransom note, and no motive, all the indications were that Alexandra's flat and Nigel himself had been random victims of Soho criminality. Alex had no doubt run off on some secret holiday, perhaps to forget her lost love. In her absence, her flat had been burgled by crazy Jamaicans in a frenzied search for money to support their drug habits. Nigel had merely stumbled upon them at exactly the most inopportune time.

That was Nigel's reading of the case. But he was interested to learn what Inspector Tanner thought, especially since the good Inspector had taken the trouble of ringing him to arrange a meeting.

They sat at a dark corner table in the White Horse and Crow. Nigel sipped his Guinness and saw Inspector Tanner peering at him with insistent, aggressive eyes over his own pint of bitter. He was a large, carbuncular man, with a pockmarked face, wiry zebra-coloured hair in disarray, salt and pepper moustache, small but intense brown eyes (Nigel therefore assigned him to the animal kingdom; 'angry warthog' fitted best), and a girth that indicated high blood pressure. From their first meeting, Nigel imagined him as someone who'd worked his way up the ranks—copping juvenile delinquents by the ears and hurling them in the clink; intervening with wearied annoyance in the imbecilic domestic disputes of East End hovels and riots in Notting Hill; stubbornly pursuing vicious murderers and doggedly filing evidence so overwhelming that even liberal judges would be compelled to sentence them to Broadmoor rather than to Butlins.

Now, as an Inspector, his waist was expanding, his ears ached from being ever-pressed to a phone, and his head was throbbing with a permanent headache. Instead of the officer-on-the-beat's regular sense of accomplishment, he had a schedule of infinite demands and an in-tray full of mind-numbing, bureaucratic annoyances. Desk jobs, Nigel knew, were the worst.

The Inspector pounded his glass on the table with the ashtray rattling force of a judge wielding a gavel. His perfunctory attempt at small talk was obviously over. 'Do you know a Sean Stalker?' he asked bluntly, like a round fired at a target five feet away.

'Stalker? Yes, I know him. Not willingly and not well, but I know him. I regret to say he was my goddaughter's suitor—at least temporarily. That's over, thank goodness. Not my sort of chap at all. He's gone to America, I understand, to make his mark in cinema.'

'How well did Miss Williamson know him?'

'I should hope not terribly well. You know these young girls— minor infatuations cropping up all the time, guardians like ourselves helping to knock them down. But surely Stalker can't be involved in this burglary. I suspected him of being Irish, but certainly not Jamaican.'

'How long did she know him?'

Nigel felt the most awful suspicions. His eyebrows closed ranks over the bridge of his nose. 'Well, I don't know, exactly. I didn't spy on the poor girl, after all. But surely...'

The Inspector interrupted him. 'Stalker didn't go to America to costar with Sharon Stone, he went to save his neck.'

'To be perfectly honest, Inspector, I don't care why the bastard hopped it. Good riddance is what I say—and *très bon voyage*.'

'Don't you understand? He's left your goddaughter in danger. If she's not with him, that is.'

'With him? Certainly she's not with him. The bastard abandoned her. I told you that yesterday.'

Tanner ignored Nigel the way a locomotive ignores a twig. 'Stalker's a petty drug dealer and a thief—you should know that. He stole a quarter of a million pounds from a Jamaican drug gang—that's who you met in Miss Williamson's flat. Do you understand now? If we don't find her before they do, we'll have to collect the pieces in parcels. They think you were just a bumbling old man. They think Miss Williamson can lead them to Stalker. They've linked them.'

'But surely you're not accusing Alexandra...'

'No, no, of course not. Why should I accuse Miss Williamson of anything? I don't care—at least for now—whether she's run off with her boyfriend who's pinched a small fortune—why would she ever do that?—or whether she's in hiding because she caught wind of what was happening. It doesn't matter. What does matter is that these Jamaicans want to get Stalker, and he's put Miss Williamson in danger. If you hear from her, you must let me know. She needs our protection. Do you understand?'

Well of course he understood. He understood from the moment he clapped eyes on Stalker that some calamity like this would arise. The bastard. If only the Jamaicans had told him what they wanted, she would gladly have helped them. Together, they could have combed the flat for a lock of Stalker's hair. Then, tapping the buggers' native skills, the voodoo doll assembled, they could have passed an amusing afternoon, they with their ganja, Nigel with his scotch, each taking turns twisting the pins.

But now he had real worries. Alex, definitely in danger. And Nigel, with no clues, no communication, and no control over events.

There was nothing for it but to brood and go for long, morose walks in the brisk autumnal air that took him past Green Park (which was looking rather brown), St James's Park (he always paused respectfully at Buckingham Palace and checked whether the flag was up), up Regent Street, through the crowds of Piccadilly Circus, and back again; or to the Achilles statue in Hyde Park (it reminded him of how he had looked when he was young—without the fig leaf, of course), up Park Lane, down Bayswater Road, around Kensington Gardens, and back to Brompton, where he would return, rosy-cheeked, perhaps sniffling slightly, up to his flat for a Guinness or a scotch and in the darkness of his sitting room console himself with the thought that all he could do was wait for news—anything else was futile.

But after only a couple of days, Nigel's brisk walks took on a more determined pace, his fists clenching and unclenching beneath the black kid-leather gloves that occasionally startled bystanders by shooting up with right crosses or left hooks, sometimes—most dangerously—with brolly in hand.

It was after one of these more vigorous sessions that he was sitting in his armchair reading a particularly violent novel about the SAS, written by a chap who claimed he was there, when there was a knock on the door.

'Yes, who is it?' Nigel shouted. Brave Sergeant Flaherty, bending the Queen's Regulations a little, was holding a bayonet to the evil Arab terrorist al-Washid's throat and yanking on the wet leather thong he'd tied around the Arab's testicles. Would al-Washid break and tell Sergeant Flaherty where the bomb was hidden? It was a horrible time to be interrupted.

The knocks came again. 'It's me, Nigel. It's tea time. Have you put the kettle on for me?'

But... but... goodness gracious, it's Pandora, he thought, shocked to his very marrow. She never visited his flat in London. It was always a matter of being summoned to Elkstone. And to call unannounced...

But that voice, surely it *was* her. Nigel tossed his book aside, jumped to his feet, and checked himself in the mirror. His old Norfolk jacket was straightened, his hair smoothed back, the knot on his tartan tie given a slight twist, his moustaches twirled.

'Why, my dear, what an incredible surprise. Here, let me help you with that,' he said, taking her plastic carrier bag.

Lady Williamson tossed her mac onto a chair and followed him into the kitchen. 'Oh, don't worry, Nigel. I'll take care of it. I just popped across to Harrods. Mr Fayed couldn't have been more helpful. Don't these sandwiches look delightful? Now, where do you keep your plates? Do you think you can put the kettle on? I thought we might even play some backgammon this afternoon, at say a penny a point? Just put the things on the work surface there. Tea, whisky, crumpets, jam. Where's your toaster?'

Nigel stared in amazement as Lady Williamson busied herself in his kitchen. She was looking quite svelte in a simple tartan skirt and brown turtleneck sweater. 'What are you staring at?' she asked. 'Was your mugging that traumatic? Have you never regained your senses?'

'No, well... to be frank, my dear, I was just wondering what the devil you're doing here.'

'Nigel, darling,' Pandora sat down suddenly, her slim hands knotted together. 'I'm sorry, I'm gabbling, aren't I? The problem is I'm worried sick about Alex. The police came round the other day. An Inspector Tanner. Said he knew you. He said he'd do what he could, but it was difficult. Oh, yes, there's the special relationship, and Tony Blair is very chummy with some of the people in Washington, but there are so many police forces in America, and tracking Alex down could take years. He said it's even possible—that we must face up to the fact—that we might never see her again, that she's mixed up with something terrible and violent. Think of it, Nigel, *never see her again*. Alex. I couldn't bear it.'

'There, there, old girl,' he patted her shoulder. 'What can we do?'

She looked at him, sniffed, and sat bolt upright. 'Ridiculous of me, carrying on like this. Here,' she reached into her handbag and removed a postcard. 'It's from America, from Los Angeles.'

He saw a picture of a crowded beach. The message on the back was brief enough. 'Dear Mummy, having a simply wonderful time. The sun in L.A. is marvellous. Sorry I had to leave so suddenly. I do hope you don't panic and ring the police. That would be such a bore for you. Love, Alex.'

Nigel grunted. 'But you did ring the police.'

'No, they rang me. Looking, it seems, for any detail that might link to Sean Stalker.'

'You showed them the postcard?'

'No, it only came this morning. I thought of you straight away.'

'I can't believe it…'

'You were Reginald's closest friend, Nigel. Alex's godfather.'

'No, I mean, that Alex has gone with that bastard Stalker.'

'Nigel, I want you to fetch her.'

'Fetch her, my dear?'

'Yes. Bring her back. That wretched Inspector spoke of a drugs cartel, whatever that is. I won't have rumours and allegations hanging over our heads.'

'From America, you say? From L.A.?'

'I would consider it such an enormous favour if you would.'

'Well, then, my dear, how can I refuse?'

Lady Williamson smiled. 'Thank you, Nigel. I knew I could count on you. You're such a stalwart old soldier. Shall I have someone make the arrangements?'

YES, THAT WOULD BE EVER SO KIND, Nigel thought, blowing a bit of lettuce from his nose. I'm too old to be travelling rough these days, don't you think? If it's all right with you, I'd like to travel first class, luxury hotel, a room with a view. He plucked a banana peel from his chin, brushed an empty vodka bottle from his cheek, and stirred uncomfortably in the rubbish bin.

CHAPTER SIX

HE BOBBED LIKE A DOWNED PILOT, struggling to stay afloat in a thick sea of rubbish. The night air was brisk and invigorating. So much so that when he coughed there was a slight wheeze in his chest, and he felt chilled.

It was warmer in the rubbish, he thought, as he bobbed down again, but his nostrils railed against the putrid smell, and his skin had a horrid eruption of formication, as though hundreds of honey-dipped ants were swarming over him. He kicked like a swimmer back to the surface, and pulled himself up and out of the bin, onto the ground, slapping the rubbish from his sleeves, shaking the imaginary ants from his legs. He was in L.A., he remembered. And he'd nearly been mugged. And him, a boxing Blue... Well, almost.

He felt in his pockets. A brief jolt of panic shot through his brain. His wallet was gone. Well, that's what happens when one nearly gets mugged. It took him a short while to remember he'd given his wallet to April. And in another pocket he discovered his card to let him into his hotel room.

He paused to look up at the deep, dark blue of the sky. The smog hadn't settled in, and if it weren't for the smell of rotten fruit in his nostrils, the grime coating his skin, and the wheeze in his chest, it would have been a very pleasant evening, the type, as they say in Hollywood, that dreams are made of.

He saw he was in an alley. He turned the corner and came to the main street. He walked until he found the entrance to the Club E.D. It was closed, of course. No sign of April or Penelope.

He looked at his watch. Four o'clock in the morning. He sat on the kerb. There were two things, he thought, he wanted to avoid: hospital and the police. Once morning came, he could find his way out of this. But he couldn't spare the time to be carted away again.

He got up and walked slowly back to the alley. Might as well sleep it off, he thought, in some out-of-the-way space. It would be at least nine o'clock before one could find a shop that would let one use the phone. And it would be unconscionably rude to wake Penelope before then. He walked down the steps to the service entrance of the Club E.D. and sat on the cold concrete. This was as good a place as any. It would be warming up soon. It was California, after all. He flipped up the collar of his coat and bent the lapels over his chest, feeling like Paul Muni in one of those '30s Depression films.

He closed his eyes and woke with remarkable punctuality five hours later. Stretching up on his toes, he made an attempt at a couple of deep knee bends, decided against it, and stomped up to the alley.

Of the shop fronts on the street, everything was closed, except the laundromat, which was bustling with business. It was actually a laundromat cum dry cleaner. There were a few young professionals picking up their dry cleaning at the front desk from a pair of smiling Koreans. Behind them, another four were busily sewing and mending.

Nigel waited his turn in the queue.

'Yes, sir?' said the woman.

'Good morning.' He smiled briefly. 'It seems I had a little too much to drink last night and lost my wallet. I was wondering if anyone here would be kind enough to lend me the fare for a taxi or drive me to my hotel.'

'Oh!' she said. 'Oh!' She turned to the man standing next to her and said something to him in their native tongue.

The man stepped forward. 'No, sorry. I call police.'

'No, I'd rather you didn't, actually. I'm on holiday, and I'd rather not spend all day giving testimony in a police station.'

'Did you say you lost your wallet?' Nigel turned to see a young man, balding and bespectacled.

'Yes, I have, I'm afraid.'

'Where's your hotel?'

'Le Grand Extravaganza.'

'I can drop you off,' he said, matter-of-factly. 'Just let me pick up my shirts.'

Nigel made way for him at the counter. Well, he thought, there's another good thing about America. It's so full of Quakers, Good Samaritans, and other heretics that one always had a decent chance of finding some friendly assistance.

The helpful young fellow—an engineer in the oil business, it turned out, who had worked for two years in London—dropped Nigel at Le Grand Extravaganza, refused any payment, and wished Nigel well, saying, 'I'm sorry you got such an annoying welcome to L.A., but at least you're just visiting. It's worse if you live here.'

What an extraordinary lack of patriotism, Nigel thought, as he stepped into the glorious California sunshine, wishing he could afford a few hours to bask by the pool. Unfortunately, there was no time. There was work to be done. He hurried through the hotel lobby to the lifts, directly to his room, and then to his bath, where he soaked and plotted. When he was refreshed and re-dressed, he called the front desk for his messages. There were none. Then he found Penelope's number.

'Hello?' The voice on the other end was fuzzy and listless.

'Penelope, it's Nigel.'

'Oh. Hello, Nigel. Where did you go last night? We lost you.'

'I know you lost me, Penelope. I was nearly mugged. I awoke this morning in an alley.'

'Oh my God, Nigel. You're kidding me.'

'No, I'm not kidding you, my dear. You might have looked for me.'

'We did look for you, Nigel.'

'Well, next time, my dear, you might look harder. I'm afraid I shouldn't be able to pay you if I were to be kidnapped and assassinated.'

'We have your wallet.'

'Well, thank God for that. But I think we'll need a bit more effective teamwork if we're going to find my goddaughter on our pub crawls.'

'I didn't know it would be dangerous, Nigel.'

'It's not dangerous in the slightest. It's that damnable music you listen to that's dangerous. And those horrible men you associate with.'

'What horrible men?'

'At the Club E.D.'

'What men at the Club E.D.?'

'No men in particular.'

'What men then?'

'Just those sorts of men in general.'

'What are you saying, Nigel?'

'Does it matter? The important thing is this: I've got a wretched headache, and I need a rest. So your day is free. But please think about where we might find her. You can pick me up here at eight. All right, my dear?'

'All right, Nigel.'

'Oh, and one more thing. I've had an idea myself. Send April over to visit me this afternoon. Ask her to call me first. I need her to run an errand. Now, back to bed. I'm sorry I disturbed you.'

IT WAS THE BLACK GENTLEMEN he'd met the night before who inspired him. And of course, he'd had some professional training in the matter: commando raids on moonless Cyprus nights and so on. He'd given April very specific instructions, and, amazingly enough, she'd come through. As the two of them stood before his bathroom mirror, they couldn't help but admire their mutual handiwork.

'Wow, Nigel, you'd never know you had a black eye.'

Yes, he thought, or that I am Brigadier Nigel Haversham, British Army, retired.

The wig was shaggier than he knew was fashionable, but that didn't really matter. And though the application of his makeup had been laborious, it looked sound.

The one thing he couldn't hide was his age. So he decided to forgo flashy clothes and unbuttoned shirts. Instead, he dressed in a conservative blue chalk-striped suit, white shirt with thin blue stripes, and a red tie with blue and green polka dots. It also saved having to apply burnt cork to any more of his body.

'Oh, Nigel, you look just like Don King!'

'And who, pray tell, is Don King?'

'Oh, he's on TV all the time, Nigel. You look just like him.' She burst into giggles.

'I take it Don King is black?'

'Oh, yes.'

'Well, that's good enough then.'

'But Nigel...'

'Yes?'

She looked at him sympathetically. 'Like, what about the way you talk? You can't say tomahto. Black people don't talk like that.'

'Then we shall have to say I was raised in Barbados. Trying to learn a new language at such short notice would only lead to disaster. I'd be unmasked. And anyway, I need not talk much at all. I'll leave that to you.'

There was a knock at the door. It was twenty past eight. That would be Penelope. April skipped over, threw back the locks, and let Penelope in, directing her attention, in good game-show style, with a graceful, balletic movement of the arms, to the bathroom, where a nattily dressed black man stood. Penelope screamed.

AFTER A DISCUSSION IN WHICH April and Penelope each tried to outdo the other in professions of not caring where they went, it was decided their first stop would be Penelope's favourite, the Funky Frog.

The neighbourhood of the Funky Frog appeared to Nigel to be fashionably derelict. Inside, it was crowded and noisy. A bar lined the left side of the entry room, packed with occupied tables and groups of young people standing and drinking. Another crowded room, adjoining on the right, was devoted to dancing. A French or German, black and white, silent film was being shone on the wall directly ahead of him, and other walls were draped with cryptic such sayings as: 'Meat was once alive', 'Does life begin at conception or at digestion?', 'Whales are people too'.

The clientele was young, almost exclusively white, except for a group of Japanese businessmen who busied themselves videotaping the proceedings, and in every state of dress from casual American collegiate to punk. With such a variety of clothing styles mixing amiably amidst the intolerable noise in this perplexing, vaguely Berlinesque atmosphere, he wondered why he appeared to draw so many stares. Perhaps it was because he was black.

He sauntered up to the bar with a new, bouncing sort of walk he'd affected. He waved the bartender over. The man looked at him askance. 'Can I help you?'

'Rum and pineapple juice, please. And two light beers.'

'We've got Busch, Coors, or Stroh's on tap.'

'Stroh's please. Is Alexandra here tonight?'

'Who?'

'Alexandra.'

'No Alexandra works here.'

Nigel grunted. 'Oh, I see.'

The bartender put the drinks on the bar and rang up Nigel's bill. 'Where you from, anyway?' he asked suspiciously.

'Barbados, de islands.'

'Oh.'

The girls came up to help him with the drinks, and then they all huddled in a corner and sipped them, while this circus of bizarre, youthful humanity yelled its various conversations at one another.

Nigel was determined that this evening's search for his goddaughter would be more aggressive. Under normal circumstances he would have been perfectly content to be crushed in a corner, sandwiched between two such agreeable young women as April and Penelope. But not tonight, and not with a Japanese businessman filming under his nose.

'Will you get that thing away from me,' Nigel said, pushing the camera aside. He took a firm grip on his rum and pineapple juice and strutted to the dance floor.

'Are you in line?' a girl yelled in his ear.

'In line for what?'

'To be velcroed,' she said, pointing ahead of him. And there he saw the most extraordinary thing. Young people were donning outfits that allowed them to be hung—velcroed, actually—on the wall, upside down.

A corner of the dance floor was devoted to this activity, and a good half a dozen young people were hanging like so many bats.

'Yes, I suppose I am, actually,' he replied, suddenly doubting the stickability of his wig. 'Are you?'

'I'm right behind you.'

'How grand.'

'I'm Monica.'

'Well, hello, Monica. Are you from Washington? My name is...' what sort of names did they have in Barbados? 'Bongo Topaz.'

'Ooh, Bongo, I love the way you talk. Where are you from?'

'I am from Barbados, de islands. De England of de Caribbean.'

'Wow, that must be nice.'

'Hmm,' he nodded.

'Okay, sir, you want to be velcroed?' said a strapping young man in an official-looking T-shirt.

'Uh, no, I was holding Monica's place. Oh please, do go ahead, my dear.' Nigel smiled and bowed slightly, directing her forward. As she passed him he instinctively adjusted her beret as though she were a private on parade. Then he stepped briskly away from the velcro corner and sent his eyes searching through the writhing bodies on the dance floor. No sign of the young woman he sought.

He rejoined his companions, scanning the bar crowd on the way, and bought another round for Penelope's sake. Then it was off to their next stop.

The Screw Inn was the size of a warehouse, with a sawdust-covered floor, an enormous area for dancing, and a long bar ostentatiously studded with screws. Rotating giant television monitors hooked to the ceiling with gargantuan decorator screws gave an ever shifting view of the dancers. The music was incredibly loud. Nigel never expected that the noise of the battlefield would become dance music.

He paid their cover charge to an enormous black bouncer who sat on a stool just inside the door. His huge muscles made his official red T-shirt—*The Screw Inn, Get Down and Twist It*—look like a Roman breastplate.

'Geez,' the bouncer said, his eyes blown big with shock, like someone who'd just seen a traffic accident. '*Who* are *you?*'

'Bongo Topaz,' Nigel remarked coolly, 'from de island o' Barbados. But my cash is pure American, brother.' He twisted his trunk and bounced his arms in rhythm with the music, thinking this might remove any questions about his *bona fides*.

'Okay,' the bouncer said, still staring wide-eyed at Nigel and his companions.

Nigel chose to ignore him. If he couldn't comprehend a gentleman of colour who preferred to dress with a bit more elegance than a red

T-shirt and jeans, that was surely his own problem and no concern of Nigel's. It was axiomatic, he thought, that a conservative black gentleman from Barbados would have no great sympathy for Garibaldi, red shirt and liberal ideas rolled into one.

Taking possession of a table, he dispatched April to find them drinks, while he and Penelope watched the monitors. They offered a depressing spectacle.

Certainly some of the girls up there on the telly were damned fetching with shimmering long hair swaying back and forth, barely concealed breasts bobbing up and down. In a different age, these girls could have been good English wenches, serving up ale and laughing with the salty sea dogs whose pluck and daring were plundering the Spanish main and setting the stage for a new English empire of dash and freedom. But these girls were different—more wholesome in a way. The Americans, thought Nigel, *are* wholesome, so full of optimism, naïveté, and Puritan religion. But what were Puritans doing in a place like this? Didn't these girls have parents? And didn't their parents care whether their daughters hung around in opium dens where the rape of the Sabine women was repeated every night? However much the Sabine women might have enjoyed it?

But perhaps there was nothing to be done. Perhaps American parents were too awed by youth. Perhaps they felt they had no recourse but to surrender to their children's wanton desire to have purposeless, thoughtless, animal stupidity driven into their skulls with an African beat. After all, one often forgot that this was a democratic country made up of the rootless dregs of the world. Quite remarkable they did so well.

April came back with three beers; beer too weak; music too loud. Nigel leaned over to Penelope.

'Do you come here often?'

'What?'

'Do. You. Come. Here. Often?'

'Oh. No.'

He smiled and nodded and sat back in his seat watching the monitor, admiring, up to a point, the way the women moved. Some of it was quite entrancing in fact. But when he looked back at his companions watching the monitors, he thought: But not for my girls, please.

And as warm paternal concern spread down from his darkened eyebrows to the black-stained top of his white collar, he let his eyes drift slowly back to the monitors to see a particularly graceful, particularly beautiful, particularly tanned, bare-legged, miniskirted young girl, a handbag on a thin strap slung across her body, cavorting with a large black chap straight from one of Leni Riefenstahl's later photographic safaris of the Nuba—though he was dressed a bit differently.

Nigel looked at the girl again and suddenly felt as though someone had stuck a needle in the back of his neck and was furiously pumping helium into his head—panic, anger, fever! *Oh my God. Good Lord. It's Alexandra!*

'Nigel.'

'It's Alexandra!' He started after her, but stopped momentarily to turn back and add, 'Don't abandon me this time.'

He plunged into the writhing bodies, pushing his way through. It was a maze of coiled human cobras. He hacked in one direction, plunged ahead, and then hacked in another.

The cobras changed rhythm. A new, more violent beat had taken over. The main lights dimmed and searchlights swept over them. It was a nightmare of digging in a worm-filled tunnel at Colditz.

He had to check himself from diving for the ground when a voice boomed over the loudspeaker. 'Ladies and gentlemen, and the rest of you cats, stand back while we showcase tonight's special guest.'

The spotlights wove into focus on him. He could hear the whistles screeching, the dogs barking...

'It's Don King!'

Nigel looked up at the spotlights, dazed. He looked around him. He was at the centre of a circle of applauding, laughing people. At least, he thought they were laughing. Their mouths were yawning violently, as though they were laughing. But all he could hear was the pounding artillery coming from the speakers.

'Dance, Don, dance!'

He stared back blankly, helplessly, cold blue eyes blinking in the coal black face.

'Go on, Don! Strut yo' stuff! Give us some rope-a-dope!'

He raised an eyebrow and cocked his eye at his audience. Very well, then, he thought. He bowed, stuck out his left arm, brought his right arm over his chest, and trotted sideways to the left. Then he reversed positions and trotted to the right. He did an about-face and repeated himself, trotting in a curve, so he could get a better view of the crowd. He saw April and Penelope waving at him and laughing hysterically.

Blood surged to his head. There she is. Alexandra, with that muscular Nubian with his arms around her waist. And sitting behind them!—Sean Stalker, disguised with dark glasses and without his moustache, laughing and sipping some nancy-boy drink with an umbrella stuck in it, looking weedy, thin, dark, and dissolute as usual. Of all the luck.

Nigel trotted towards Alexandra, looked her in the eye, and took her hand in his. She hadn't the slightest idea who he was, but smiled and blushed slightly, and looked at the Nubian. He grinned and released her. She looked back at Sean Stalker. There he was, damn him, her thin, pale seducer, with his black hair wet and messy, handsome, but with an anaemic, nervous touch to him. Nigel guessed his age at only twenty-two, but with his vitality rapidly draining away through the use of opium and other unspeakable vices.

Stalker nodded to Alexandra and waved her away—scandalously unconcerned, it seemed to Nigel, about her fate.

Well, there are some who do care, he thought to himself, as he trotted her out to centre stage, some who do recognise your true value, my dear.

Together, they bowed.

'Go, man, go!' roared the loudspeaker.

He grasped her firmly and tangoed one way, then the other, and then ploughed a passionate furrow back again.

'Everybody come on, let's dance!' shouted the loudspeaker vehemently.

The spotlights went off. The room was momentarily dark. Then dim lighting rose on a frenzied dance floor. Nigel broke for the door with Alexandra firmly in hand.

'What are you doing?'

He paused for a moment, then screamed over his shoulder, 'April! Penelope!'

'Let go of me!'

He paused again. Unless he was mistaken, Alexandra had adopted an American accent. He held her at arm's length and stared at her.

'What are you doing? Let go of me!'

Oh dear. Could he have been mistaken? 'Alexandra?'

'If you don't let go of me, I'll scream!'

Oh, dear Lord God, definitely American, and here comes her extremely large Nubian friend. 'I say, old man, er... brother... Jolly good dancer, your girl is, what?'

A hand the size of a football grabbed his tie. 'Are you going to let her go, man, or do I have to kick yo' ass?'

'No, absolutely,' Nigel replied, freeing the girl. 'No ass-kicking required at all, really. Just a case of mistaken identity, that's all. You wouldn't happen to know a girl named Alexandra Williamson, would you?'

The Nubian thrust him aside, grunted an epithet, and wrapped his enormous arm around the girl's slender waist, leading her away.

Nigel stumbled disconsolately back to his table.

'What were you doing?' asked Penelope, with an enormous grin.

'I need a drink, a real drink. April, will you please fetch me a large scotch and soda?' He slumped in his chair, his face in his hands. He rubbed his palms against his pinched eyes and wiped them down his nose. It was an act of exhaustion, but the effect was like bleach. He was no longer a black man. He was a mere octoroon.

Penelope laughed. 'You look ridiculous.'

'Thank you, my dear. Just what I needed to hear.'

'I mean, Nigel, just think about it. Like, this isn't Halloween.'

'No. It's not a dream, is it?'

'And that girl? What were you doing with her? You shouldn't mess with football players' girlfriends. Nigel, listen to me,' she said, touching his sleeve, 'like, you don't do that in L.A. Those are the kind of people who get violent, follow you outside, and shoot you.'

'Perhaps it would be all for the best. Put me out of my misery.'

'Here's your scotch, Nigel.'

He downed it in a gulp.

Penelope laughed again and April joined her. 'Do you ever drink anything but alcohol in England?' Penelope said it affectionately, but it took Nigel a long way from Achilles' statue in Hyde Park.

'All right,' he said soberly. 'Let's go.'

Together, April, Penelope, and Nigel swept up from their table and needled their way past the bar. The girls slipped past the red-shirted black bouncer, but as Nigel approached, he slid forward from his stool and blocked the way, muscles rippling in every direction.

'Excuse me,' Nigel said innocently.

The bouncer ran a big black finger, hard, like a piece of sketching charcoal, down Nigel's face. Nigel saw his eyes flame.

'What the hell?' the bouncer said.

'Kindly keep your hands to yourself and let me pass.'

'Do you think that's funny?'

'Funny? What do you mean?'

The bouncer slapped his palm against Nigel's cheek and pulled his fingers like anchors across Nigel's face. 'I mean this, Al Jolson!' he said, waving his dirtied fingers in front of Nigel's eyes. Nigel knew a punch was coming.

'Come on, Nigel, let's go,' he heard Penelope say pleadingly. But there was no way for Nigel to get around the bouncer. As Nigel braced himself for the inevitable blow, he heard April's perky voice from behind the bouncer's enormous shoulders.

'Hey, let him go!'

'What the...' The bouncer glared over his shoulder at her.

'It's not against the law to dress up as Don King,' she affirmed, acting the part of constitutional lawyer, as Nigel believed all Americans did. 'If you hurt him, we'll sue.'

The bouncer seized Nigel under the arms, like a forklift, and dumped him at the door. 'Get the hell out o' here! And don't come back!'

Penelope dragged Nigel onto the pavement, while he protested. 'Illiterate baboon. Unhand me, girls. I must teach him a lesson.'

'Will you shut up!' Penelope screamed, waving a condemnatory finger at him as though she were his nanny. She yanked a handful of tissues from her handbag, tore off his wig, and attacked his face. 'We're taking this off right now! I'm not going to be seen with a totally idiotic racist like you!'

She daubed his face hard, as if every stroke were meant to be a snap from a cat-o'-nine-tails, though of course from her it felt like the delightful, delicious, if somewhat heavy-fingered proddings of a Swedish masseuse.

'I say, old girl, you're destroying the work of hours.'

'Shut up!'

He acquiesced and enjoyed a peculiar sensation: her nannyish hectoring; the pleasure of her touch, even if it was not meant to please; the odd sense of despair. It took him back to the blackout in the War and Nanny Carey putting Dettol on his cuts and bruises. It felt like childhood. But enough of that. The night was young. His liver was still functioning. There was work to do.

'You're such an idiot,' Penelope said, wadding the tissues into a ball and stuffing them into her handbag. (She's a Green, Nigel thought, not wanting to litter.) She straightened his collar, and, most amazing of all, ran her fingers through his hair, trying to comb it into place. This wasn't childhood, Nigel thought. He felt more like Odysseus with Calypso. 'Now, where are we going?' she asked.

It was a welcome question, for Nigel had worried that Penelope, whose moral fibre he'd already calculated was not of the strongest weave, would be ready to throw in the towel, dump him at his hotel, and go simpering off to the sauna—or wherever it was Californians went simpering off to.

But no, this tall, indescribably beautiful daughter of Thor had scarcely appeased her enormous thirst for mead. He had a sudden vision of Penelope, her golden locks in twin Viking braids, head tilted back, flagon raised high, a honey-coloured brew spilling down the sides of her lips, trickling down her gulping throat, as the Norsemen cheered her on: '*Ja, Penelopehilde! Ja, Penelopehilde! Ja!*'

Their next stop, the Club Exotica, was perhaps the oddest of all. The entrance was through a lashed bamboo door, opening to a green-carpeted tunnel decked out like a cave and ending in a pitch black bar. The waitresses navigated by means of electric torches, like usherettes in an old-fashioned cinema—'Plenty o' room in the one and nines, ducks.' Customers, however, had no such advantage. It was a bump-and-go process until they found an empty table. It was also deafeningly loud—though he'd come to expect that. The dance floor was evidently through an archway one could dimly make out in the distance. Some sort of rhythmic obscenity belched out of it, and on either side of the arch, giant birdcages were hung, the thrusting silhouettes of go-go dancers trapped within them outlined against the faint light of the dance floor.

The girls ordered beers, Nigel a double brandy and soda. It being so dark, there was little to attract the girls' attention, and he saw their spirits drooping. Penelope's full, pouting lips were pouting more than usual, and April's 'all-American' eagerness was slipping into a vacant, zombie gaze. He couldn't blame them much. He didn't care for the place himself.

'I suppose they spread a lot of Aids here,' he said suddenly, by way of conversation.

'It's not a gay bar,' said April.

'You don't have to be gay to catch Aids,' reminded Penelope.

'No, I suppose this music has something to do with it, too,' he replied.

They sat stupidly at their table. Even if Alexandra were here, he thought, they wouldn't be able to see her. But he felt no compulsion to press on. He was overwhelmed by a sense of ennui. He ordered another brandy and soda and drank it down. He wanted to get drunk. Already his mind was telling him, there's always tomorrow. This evening's adventures were doomed, doomed ever since he made a fool of himself at the Screw Inn. What a ridiculous spectacle he must have made. His sad eyes roamed to April. He wanted another drink, but nowhere in the darkness could he spot their waitress. His stomach growled. He hadn't eaten all day.

April caught his glance, and her bright look returned. 'Do you want to dance, Nigel? There's a dance floor in the back.'

'Oh, yes? Through that archway there? Satan's tongue? Well, why not? We're certainly not achieving anything here, are we? If you'll excuse us, Penelope. Oh, and, my dear, would you mind ordering me another drink and a sandwich when our waitress returns? Thanks awfully.'

They staggered into the darkness, knocking over waitresses and accidentally groping strangers, until they approached the pulsating archway. Above him were the go-go dancers in their giant birdcages. He paused to admire them for a moment.

'What long legs they have, don't you think?'

April tugged him forward and his shoes hit a hardwood floor.

Before him opened a dark cavern. It was full of frantic mating insects disguised as human beings. They'd obviously been drawn here by the light. It fell on them like confetti from a rotating, spangled globe hanging from the ceiling.

'Good Lord, April. This is horrifying.'

'What's wrong, Nigel?' She pulled him closer to her and out onto the floor. Her body felt warm and soft in the crook of his arm. Her hair smelled as though it had been washed in a stream of fragrant flowers. Rather nice to be alone with her, he thought. But one hoped she wasn't thinking of marriage again. Granted, he wasn't too old for that sort of thing, and now that he was retired, he had more time for a wife. He was free of his martial vows now. He'd done his bit—forty years' worth—for Queen and Country. Now he could afford to uncinch the belt of restraint. The Havershams were long-livers, after all. And he was fit. He'd surely be able to play cricket with his sons well into his eighties.

April broke away from him and whirled like a dervish, her head swinging wildly, sending cascades of hair in all directions. To Nigel, she looked like a particularly supple and attractive Sufi of the Northwest frontier who had achieved spiritual ecstasy and dance-inducing visions through hashish. It was dazzling to watch, dizzying even. Nigel knew better than to remain aloof. If he attracted suspicion, the insects might overwhelm him in frenzied hatred at his not being 'one of us'. So he slid side to side and did breaststroke motions with his arms.

For Nigel's benefit, April slowed her pace. She looked happy, her long, shimmering, brunette hair waving wonderfully around her. Occasionally she joined him, laughing, in his landlocked aquatics.

Quite a girl, he thought. It was a great pleasure to see her so happy, so beautifully happy. Indeed, he felt himself loving her for her very happiness. But it was her he loved, and the fine curve of her torso (those hips so ready for childbearing), not this awful, buzzing, throbbing, crepuscular cavern that cast a dark, corrupting shadow over everything decent and good...

He looked up at the spangled globe. How ridiculous it looked. How ridiculous all this was. And then... everything went black, and silent, as though one were in a cinema and the film had suddenly broken and the projector light failed... or, perhaps, as if one were dead. He shook his head, fluttered his eyelids, and the deafening sound returned. He was dancing with April, who smiled as though nothing had happened. He stared at the spangled globe. Odd, wasn't it? *Crack!* The globe exploded, as if struck by lightning, and a hundred fearful screams pierced the darkness.

Nigel seized April and bound her tightly to his chest, shoving their way to a wall. He pressed her against it, his back a windshield parrying stampeding insects. 'We'll get Penelope as soon as we can,' he yelled in her ear. April was wide-eyed, but didn't scream. She was frightened, clinging to Nigel like a barnacle—a barnacle with cool, sweet, alcoholic breath. Crazed people—shadows swerving out of the darkness—rebounded off his back, knocking the air out of him, but he wouldn't give way, defending April like a grey, puffing Hercules.

Gunfire exploded on the hardwood floor. They had to move. Now! Nigel pushed April ahead of him, off the dance floor, back through the archway. The bar was almost deserted. Everyone was crammed against the tunnel, screaming and fighting to escape. Penelope, thank God, hadn't joined them. With more presence of mind than he would have expected of her, she had waited for them, crouched under their table. Nigel sent April crouching in after her.

'Stay here! I'm going to take a look round.'

April gasped, 'Nigel, don't! You're crazy!' But Penelope pulled her close, and Nigel crept away—back towards the dance floor.

The gunfire flashed in sudden, erratic bursts. Then came a voice: 'Ni-gel! Ni-gel Haffer-shem! We wants yo' muthuhfuckin' ass and we wants it now!'

'Well, you don't have far to look for it,' Nigel replied, stepping forward, arms akimbo, his chest thrust out. He wasn't taking any more lip from anyone. He hadn't devoted his life to the Army to be nearly mugged, harassed, and terrorised in his retirement. He'd bloody well had enough.

'Nigel! Nigel!'

'Take your hands off me, you bastard. Drop that weapon immediately.'

Something like insecticide sprayed in his face. He spluttered.

'Nigel, are you all right?' It was April.

He looked about him. He was in a car. A parked car. Penelope was in the driver's seat, looking down at him over her shoulder. He was in the back with April holding a bottle of perfume under his nose.

'We're at your hotel,' April said. 'Are you all right? Do you want me to help you inside?' She smiled. 'You don't remember anything, do you? You fell asleep on the dance floor, Nigel. I had to, like, carry you out, just like you were a baby—but a *lot* heavier. Are you all right now?'

'Oh, yes. Fine, my dear, fine. Yes, rather a strenuous day, wasn't it? Care to join me for a nightcap?'

CHAPTER SEVEN

ALL RIGHT, SO HE HAD to confess the Bongo Topaz gambit was an utter failure. But surely there was no reason to abandon all hope, ye who have entered L.A. After all, there were worse places to be doing detective work. Afghanistan, for instance. Afghanistan would be nothing like this.

Nigel sat on a white plastic chair at a white plastic table shaded by an umbrella beside an enormous, sparkling swimming pool. He wore deck shoes, white socks that rolled up his calves, white Bermuda shorts, a Hawaiian shirt, sunglasses, and a Panama hat, with a Paisley scarf wrapped neatly around the base of its crown, much after the manner of the Raj. Penelope and April, dressed in bikinis, were stretched out on long plastic lounge chairs. All three of them were drinking iced tea.

Nigel sat thinking, his index fingers resting on his lips, his hand in a wide-fingered prayer. There was obviously a need for a change of strategy. Trawling aimlessly through American pubs would yield him nothing. His prey was too slippery, the ocean of youthful nightlife too vast.

It had been sheer conceit, he saw it now, to think it would be so simple: setting up an observation post at the lip of the jungle, waiting for Alexandra to come to the salt lick at twilight. No, that simply wouldn't work. Los Angeles was not Africa. Alexandra was not a water buffalo.

Worse luck for him, in a way. He looked up at the sun and luxuriated under its rays. But at least here one didn't have to worry about malarial mosquitoes.

'Nigel, I'm trying to ask you a question,' April said.

'I'm sorry, my dear. What is it?'

'What do you think? Is marriage 75 per cent sex and 25 per cent money or 75 per cent money and 25 per cent sex?'

Penelope clicked her tongue and rolled her eyes. 'How would he know?'

'What? Really, my girl, I can't be bothered with such silly questions. I've got a great deal on my mind.'

'See,' Penelope said in ferocious triumph. 'He didn't answer the question.'

Nigel regarded Penelope narrowly. He was right about her, he thought; definite Viking blood; moody and unpredictable like all the Scandinavians. 'If you don't mind, I'm trying to think. We need to avoid further embarrassments like last night.'

'Huh, that's easy,' Penelope remarked dismissively. 'Like, just grow up. You still haven't answered the question,' she insisted.

'What question?'

'You said we were stupid, but you couldn't answer it.'

'What question?' Nigel repeated, his moustache quivering.

'Is marriage 75 per cent sex and 25 per cent money or 75 per cent money and 25 per cent sex?'

'How the devil am I supposed to know? I can't be bothered with Platonic rubbish about marriage.'

'Marriage is *not* Platonic,' said Penelope vigorously.

'I'd like to hear you, Nigel,' April coaxed.

'Marriage isn't the point.'

'Maybe it's not *your* point,' harrumphed Penelope.

'Oh, good God. Can we be sane for a moment?'

'I'm going for a swim.' Penelope gracefully slipped out of her chair, across the concrete, and into the pool, as though it were one smooth, continuous balletic motion. The grace of it was like a slap in the face. You're an idiot and I'm beautiful, it said.

Nigel's teeth bit savagely on the straw in his iced tea.

'Don't get stressed, Nigel,' said April. 'At your age you could have a stroke.'

'At my age...' but his voice merely spluttered into a growl.

'Have you tried meditation? Just think of something pleasant, Nigel.'

'Look, my dear, I've been through sandstorms, wars, and disasters beyond number. I'm hardly going to be undone by a twenty-year-old Californian with more legs than brains.'

As soon as he said it, he regretted it. April was such a well-meaning creature. Shouldn't bark at the poor dear. He considered buying her a drink to make up for it, but ruled against it. It was too early and their livers could use a rest. They sat in uneasy silence until Penelope rose out of the water like Venus and came dripping to her betowelled chair.

'How's the water?' asked April.

'It's wonderful.'

'I'm going in too,' April said, leaping to her feet. 'Come on, Nigel, let's go.'

'I'm sorry, my dear. I neglected to bring my bathing costume. But you go ahead.'

She dived like a natural athlete in the deep end of the pool and zoomed to the bottom like a submarine until she came up for breath at the opposite end. 'Wooo,' she said, breaking the surface and shaking her wet hair. Wooo, indeed, thought Nigel.

'Nigel, I mean, like, what's the point of your spending all this money in bars?' Penelope was stretched on the lounge chair beside him again. 'It's not a very good investment.'

He felt as though he'd been stuck with a cattle prod. Was Penelope giving *him* advice on tactics and strategy? Were his failings that manifest? 'No, I quite agree with you. It makes me ashamed to call myself a general. I've been drifting with the wind, completely ignoring the need for a proper strategy, the need to mount a regular campaign. Our objective is highly mobile, hard to pin down. So obviously we need to offer bait that will flush our quarry out into the open. We can't go gallumphing along as we have been. Is that your thinking as well?'

Penelope's mouth hung open for a moment before she spoke. 'Like, whatever. I mean, Nigel, with all this money you've got to spend, why don't you invest in a business?'

'A business?'

'Our image consulting business.'

'What the devil are you talking about?'

'That football player last night reminded me—and the bouncer too. There's so many guys with great bodies here, but, like, they're totally ignorant about how to sell themselves. April and I can do that with our image consulting business. I mean, like, Nigel, it would be a gold mine. We'd charge for counselling and, you know, like a whole makeover—with self-esteem building, image improvement seminars, dressing consultation, portfolio arrangement. And we'd charge a commission, acting as their agents. The money would be just, like, totally, awesomely flowing. There's no way you wouldn't make a totally great return. Are you listening to me?'

'Oh, yes, indeed. Image consulting, the wave of the future, I've no doubt. But it's not my primary interest at the moment.'

'Well, it should be,' she said, rebuking him. 'I mean, think about last night. You were such an idiot. You're not going to get anywhere dressed like Don King. Like, that's the ultimate in bad image. I mean, even a moron can see it doesn't suit you. You need image consulting in the worst way.' She shook her head as though she'd never seen such a horrible case.

'All right, then,' Nigel threw out hypothetically, 'what could you do for me?'

'Huh, a lot more than that. I mean, Nigel, this is L.A. Nobody cares about Don King.'

'I didn't mean to be Don King,' Nigel replied testily. 'I don't even know who the blighter is.'

'Well, who were you then? I mean, face it, Nigel, an old white man trying to get on *Soul Train* is just ridiculous. Or like this Army thing. Nobody cares about that. Only morons go into the Army.'

Nigel grunted.

'But your accent. We could work with that. I mean, what about— you know—,' she framed his face between her hands and slid her head from side to side like a Balinese dancer, 'British movie producer or director come to L.A. to check things out.'

'Really? You think so? And what would that do for me?'

Penelope shook her head despairingly, as though she had the job of teaching football to Stephen Hawking. 'Only everything. I mean, you'd be interesting then. Like, people would want to talk to you, Nigel. Who wants to talk to Don King?'

He was just about to explode with another denial that he was Don King, when he thought: just a moment. There could be something in this. A new disguise for a new trap. 'Film producer, you say?'

'Like, why not, Nigel? Everybody wants to know a movie producer. You'd be popular.'

'I see. And what if I indulged this whim of yours—in a small way? What if I let you use me as a trial run?'

'Fer sure!' she said, with all the excitement of a Jehovah's Witness finding a door not slammed in her face.

'I'll need a film, won't I?'

'Sure. We can work that out.'

'It'll need a title.'

'How about *Blaze in the Morning?*' Penelope said, savouring its poetry.

'*Blaze in the Morning*? A film about the bloody fire brigade? *Blazing Blitzkrieg Bombshells* is more like it. Sort of *Saving Private Ryan*, but British.'

'I think *Blaze in the Morning* sounds nice.'

'No, sorry, totally inappropriate. Haversham Productions never made *Blaze in the Morning*—or *Blaze in the Bloody Afternoon*, for that matter. No, we need something more literary, something to attract a bisexual, tubercular, pseudo-aesthete bounder—if you catch my drift. What do you think about Thomas de Quincey?'

'You mean like *Quincy*, the TV show?'

'No, I mean like Thomas de Quincey's *Confessions of an English Opium Eater*,' Nigel chuckled. 'Yes, I think that's rather good. Rather good, indeed.'

'Oh, come on, Nigel,' Penelope whined. 'You're not even trying. Like, what sort of image can you expect with a movie like that?'

'Just the image we want, I should think. Penelope, dear, I want you to establish the image that we're looking for a scriptwriter to adapt Thomas de Quincey's *Confessions of an English Opium Eater* into a film, an important film with an enormous budget. There are drama society newspapers for that sort of thing, aren't there—to advertise for screenwriters and such?'

'Yeah,' she said, shrugging her shoulders sourly. Poor girl must have had her heart set on *Blaze* for quite some time, Nigel thought. Still, one can't be sentimental—not when there are lives at stake.

'Very well, then. We must make up an advertisement and put it in one of those papers, whichever one everybody reads. Don't worry, I'll pay for everything—and I'll help you with the spelling. We can hold the interviews here, I think, in my room. Set the date for as soon as you possibly can.'

'Are you serious?'

'Absolutely serious. Now, get cracking, Watson. The game's afoot.'

Penelope rolled her eyes like an exasperated government clerk interrupted on her forty-third tea break. 'Like, my last name isn't Watson. It's Davison, okay?'

'TELL ROOM SERVICE TO SEND UP three Bloody Marys, please, April. And heavy on the Worcestershire sauce on mine, will you?' Nigel was sitting in a plastic chair on his balcony. He was dressed in jodhpurs and riding boots, a white shirt, tweed coat, sunglasses, and a cloth cap. The sunglasses were Penelope's idea. The rest was his own contribution to overhauling his image. Felt quite natural, really.

He looked with admiration on the advert Penelope had placed in the arts section of *The Los Angeles Times*: 'SCREENWRITER WANTED. Rorke's Drift Productions seeks screenwriter to adapt Thomas de Quincey's *Confessions of an English Opium Eater* into Major Motion Picture. Must have experience of subject. Interviews to be held at 10.00 a.m.' He sent Penelope to see how long the queue was outside his door.

'I'd say at least fifty. I can't believe it's only nine o'clock.'

'Well, we might as well get started. Perhaps we can finish early. Ask April to take up her position at the door and send them in one at a time. I'll sort them out quickly enough. You can sit here and take notes.'

'I WAS THINKING OF, LIKE, *Confessions* meets *Back to the Future*. You know, the opium eater comes to present-day L.A. and sees how much more is, like, available to him. I mean, like meth...'

'Next!'

'I SEE STALLONE AS THE OPIUM EATER, though, let's face it, who eats opium anymore? We'll have to make it steroids.'

'Next!'

'I'M SO EXCITED ABOUT THIS THING, because it's so relevant. I mean, everybody's got addiction problems, whether it's drugs, or sex, or television, or shopping, or abusive relationships, or fat, or smoking, or...'

'Next!'

'I COULDN'T FIND IT ANYWHERE. Do you have a copy? I must have called every bookstore in Venice.'

'Venice? Damned expensive, I'm sure. Not to say wet. We'll let you know.'

HE WAS SURE TO COME. Nigel had to play his part, of course, interview everyone in turn, not skip through the queue. But *Confessions of an English Opium Eater* would surely attract Stalker the way a corpse attracts flies. Nigel knew he'd turn up. He had to.

The previous two days had been hectic beyond imagining, slapping the advert together at furious speed to meet their outrageous deadline, arranging a wire transfer from Coutts and Co. to pay the exorbitant cost of the advert space, receiving free image consulting from Penelope on how to appear as a proper film producer—an exhausting process. And the girls had been working round the clock, bless their souls, with Nigel nodding and advising where appropriate.

'I say, where did you girls learn to do this sort of thing?' he asked as he watched them design the advert on Penelope's laptop computer.

'Oh, in school. We were both Communications majors,' said April. 'That's where we met.'

Penelope turned from the computer to correct April. 'No, we met in an African-American dance class, and then we took a couple of condom safety and awareness classes together.'

'You did what?'

'Oh, that's right,' April agreed with Penelope, patting her on the shoulder. Then she told Nigel, 'It was in college. It was really stupid, but you could take it three times for credit. So we did. We took "The History of Birth Control", "Condoms in Transnational Perspective", and "Contemporary Issues in Contraception". And it was all really hands-on. We got to sample a lot of different kinds of condoms—you know, different textures and tastes. We got to practise putting them on cucumbers. And they always gave us plenty to take home.'

'How very practical,' Nigel replied, his knees buckling.

'It wasn't such a big deal,' said Penelope over her shoulder. 'I mean, like, they do that in junior high school now.'

'Uh huh,' April giggled. 'I shouldn't tell you this, Nigel, but they even showed us a porn film once to show us that all the famous porn stars wore them and could still, you know, enjoy themselves having sex.'

'Huh.' Breathe in, breathe out, stay calm.

'It was really sort of controversial. A few feminists, you know, got upset.'

'Oh, needless to say.'

'But as Communications majors, Pen and I watched it more from a sort of technical perspective—you know, like camera work. It was really pretty basic.'

So much blood had flowed to Nigel's head that it almost burst off his neck.

'Pen and I even made a rock video as our project in one class. Do you remember that, Pen?' Pen did. 'It was really fun. Do you remember that song "It's Orgy Time" by the Screaming Skulls at Ten?'

Nigel pursed his lips, as though in thought, and shook his head.

'Well, it's really good, and we made this really fun video. You know, we lip-synched the song, and danced through a bunch of condoms blown up like balloons to promote safe sex; and we had all these guys from the crew team wearing sunglasses and black bow ties but no shirts—like the Chippendales.'

'Like Chippendales?' he exploded. It was one shock too many. 'You mean, you dressed them like furniture?'

'What?'

'You said Chippendales. You mean they were dressed as tables and chairs and things?'

'Like strippers, okay?' April rolled her eyes and continued. 'Well, anyway, it was really fun. But it was really hard work, filming it, editing it, and getting the sound right. And we got an A, and got to show it to the whole campus. So we worked with some computer geeks to design ads to hand out and post around. And like, we thought it was fun. We do all our party invitations on Pen's computer. And I mean, it's amazing. Here, look at this.' She ruffled a newspaper in his face. 'Pen and I were looking through the paper for ad ideas—and I mean, look at that, Nigel. Wouldn't you think Madickweed could afford to do better?'

'That's her name, is it? Madickweed?'

'Do you think she's pretty?'

'She looks like a cheap Liverpool whore—and 'tis a pity she is one. If she had a proper father, he'd have put her in a nunnery where she could have done something useful—like pray and knit socks. Kindly take it away, will you?'

'*She's in great shape!*' April exclaimed, as though Nigel had missed the point. 'And she makes a lot of money. It says here, she threw a great party in New York, with a chorus line of gay British sailors—

you should like that, Nigel—a woman who can smoke cigarettes with her reproductive organs, and an indoor movie screen showing her having sex with a bottle.'

'Her what? Good Lord! Throw that paper in the fire, April. For goodness sake, don't soil your hands with it.'

'I think the ink is dry,' she said innocently.

'She should be put down as a menace to public health.'

Penelope spun in her seat, like a ship turning parallel to deliver a broadside. 'Madickweed's sold more albums than anyone in the history of music. Did it ever occur to you that Madickweed might dress like that because she's someone who's trying to make you think, to challenge your assumptions, to make a statement, who might be an artist?'

Obviously the poor girl had been working too hard, getting a trifle edgy, looking for a fight. Nigel appealed to the common sense that must be lurking, somewhere, deep within her. 'By having sex with a bottle?'

'What's wrong if people like it? Who are you to say?'

'People like flogging too, but I should hardly think it a good thing if we had a booming flogging industry with million-dollar floggers mincing about in tight leather pants.'

'If people want it, why not?'

'Because we're supposed to be civilised.'

'You're being judgmental,' she said, pointing her large Icelandic finger at him (it reminded Nigel of a fish finger, it was just as brown).

'Judgmental? Judgmental? Is it judgmental to think that women shouldn't have sex with bottles—at least not in front of the public?'

'Yes.'

'All right, then, I'm judgmental.'

'Like, you haven't even seen her perform,' April whined imploringly.

'Well, I assure you, if I ever do have the misfortune of being trapped in the same room with her, I'll jolly well keep my bottle of Glenfiddich under lock and key. Now, let's get back to work, shall we?'

HIS MIND DRIFTED BACK to his interview, and the thin, brushy-moustached man before him.

'Just love the girls. Nice touch. The one out there is Vanna, and this one—Marilyn Monroe? But tell me—Nigel, is it? Oh, I just love the way you talk... and that moustache! But tell me, dear, *where's the casting couch?*'

'Next!'

And then he saw him, stepping onto the balcony, relaxed, dressed in an open-necked shirt, flexing his dimples. The skinny, scheming bastard! Look at him! With his eyes glued on Penelope! So, the preening pantywaist wasn't content with stealing one's goddaughter, eh? Had to make off with one's bloody image consultant, too?

Nigel leapt from his chair, yelling into the room—'All right, April, dismiss the others. We've found our man.'—and slamming the sliding glass door shut, leaving Penelope, Stalker, and himself alone on the balcony.

'What? Already? But we haven't even talked yet.' The bastard was still smiling, though a trifle bewildered, as though he'd just won a lottery he'd never entered.

'Sit down,' Nigel said, putting a hand on Stalker's shoulder and shoving him into a plastic chair. 'Try this.' He thrust what looked like a barrelless pistol into Stalker's ribs.

Stalker bounced uncontrollably, stiff-legged, open-jawed—like a marionette handled by an overcaffeinated lunatic. 'Aaah!'

'Stun guns, they call them. Women use them in this country, apparently, to ward off unwanted advances. Pity Alexandra didn't have one. Might have saved us all a lot of bother.' Nigel removed his dark glasses. 'Let's see how that works again.'

'Aaah!'

'Jolly good.'

Stalker slumped, gasping, clawing at the chair like a shipwreck survivor clinging to a raft.

Penelope shouted, 'Nigel, what are you doing?'

He ignored her. 'Where is she?' he said to Stalker.

'Jesus,' Stalker panted. 'For God's sake, you don't need that thing.'

'Where is she?'

'Half a moment. And a cigarette. Jesus. I'll tell you everything. It doesn't matter. They're in my pocket. Matches too.'

Nigel nodded to Penelope. Like the ministering angel he didn't deserve, she stroked the cigarette between his lips and lit it. Stalker squinted at her. He was trying to mount a flirtatious smile, Nigel reckoned, but couldn't manage it.

'All right, that's enough,' Nigel said to Penelope. He prodded Stalker with his riding boot. 'Talk.'

Stalker puffed for a long while before he spoke. 'You haven't made it easy,' he breathed finally. 'What do you know?'

'I've talked to Scotland Yard.'

Stalker nodded and puffed. 'What do you want, then? To arrest me?'

Nigel held the stun gun like a grenade. 'Where's Alexandra?'

'There's one thing we need to get straight, General.' His breathing grew easier. 'I didn't ask her to come. You can't pin that on me. She came because she wanted to.'

'Bollocks.'

'Not that it wasn't convenient. They wanted some collateral. She happened to be available...'

'Who are "they"?'

Stalker made another attempt at a smile—a jagged line, curled at the edges. 'Los Lobos Colorados.' He tried to say it with a flourish.

Nigel's cool blue eyes waited on him like a stork waiting for a fish.

'Why don't you put that thing away?' Stalker said, pointing weakly at the stun gun. 'I'll explain. You know about the Yardies, I take it?... The Jamaicans?' Nigel remained silent and staring. Stalker sighed heavily. 'I need another fag.' Nigel motioned for Penelope to light him another.

Yes, the bastard's dimples were definitely coming back. The licentious rat was flashing them at Penelope for all he was worth. But if he wanted a real stunner, he just had to keep it up. Nigel's fist tightened around the gun. He'd make his hair stand on end.

'Don't mind that I smoke?' Stalker asked her. 'God knows, most Americans do.'

Penelope smiled briefly. 'No,' she said quietly.

'You're a rare one.'

'Wait for us inside, dear,' Nigel said. He didn't want any further distractions.

Stalker caught her eyes as she left.

'Alexandra?' Nigel reminded him.

Stalker turned to Nigel, puffing hard. 'Right. I'm getting to that. If it weren't for your damned toy, I'd have told you already.' He paused to take a long drag and sighed. 'All right, then,' he said. 'Let me see.

You *do* know I ripped off the Yardies—though, of course, you don't care about them, do you? Deserved it, brutal bastards. Raking in disgusting amounts of money, and not one of them isn't completely imbecilic, wreathed in ganja smoke twenty-four hours a day. And they're vicious buggers, totally without a conscience.'

'Alex didn't know about this, did she?'

'Puh, of course not. She acts like she was raised in a bloody convent.'

'Might have been—except she's C of E. Get on with it.'

'Well, naturally, I had to escape. Vicious, bloody Yardies. It's not as though it's a lot of money to them. But it's the example, you know. If blokes like me can get away with it... So I came to America. I thought I could find protection here, and I did.'

'Who?'

'Los Lobos Colorados,' he said, with the air of a flamenco dancer. 'They're a drug gang. Mexicans, obviously. We cut a deal. I give them new markets with the Hollywood elite, they give me protection and a share in the profits. It's amazing what our accents can achieve in this country. They think I'm a Beverly Hills insider. And with their drugs, I will be. Coke can be a great letter of introduction. Meet and greet, sell and snort.

'I've warned them about the Yardies. But they don't mind. I wouldn't be surprised if they made killing a Yardie an initiation rite. Bloodthirsty buggers. Ugly too, though some of the women aren't half bad. Then there's Alex.' His face creased in a grin. 'She makes the perfect hostage, doesn't she? If anything happens to me, she's dead.'

'Where is she?'

'They have her. You see, there's a catch. They're making me buy my first shipment from them. No need to worry about that. The

Yardies gave me my down payment. But they also wanted another symbol of my good faith—collateral, a hostage—something to guarantee I wouldn't take the drugs and run. So I gave them Alex and pretended to be heartbroken about it.'

'You utter bastard.'

'Oh, I don't know. I think I've been fairly enterprising. If you can't find a Borgia, why not be one, eh?'

'You insolent bastard.'

'Why insolent? I've told you everything. You've had my complete cooperation. And why not? There's nothing you can do about it, is there? Not if you want Alex back.'

'You seem pretty bereft of protection now. Where are they?'

'It wouldn't be convenient if they followed me everywhere. I prefer to keep them separate from this part of my life. Slightly risky, of course, but I can't imagine bringing them to Beverly Hills parties, or to meet film producers. I don't know why, but Mexicans lack the radical chic of blacks. So I suppose I've taken a social step down in that regard. Still, one can't always choose.'

'Why shouldn't I take you hostage? Demand Alexandra's release? A life for a life?'

'They'd never pay my ransom. They'd just kill her and be done with it. They're not very nice fellows, these men. And you don't know how to contact them, anyway. So you see, it's quite hopeless for you. Mind if I light another fag? I think my fingers are working now.'

Stalker lit up another cigarette. 'And I know you won't even think about ringing the police. Far too risky for Alex. If there's any trouble, guess who's their first target? The best thing for you,' he said, pointing to Nigel, the cigarette between his fingers, 'is to stay out of the way and let me handle things. The shipment's due in just a few days. Once I pay for it and once I sell some of it, once I show them I can deliver, I'm sure Los Lobos will be ever so much more reasonable about setting Alex free. And when she is, she's yours. And we can both breathe a sigh of relief that we never have to see each other again. Trust me.' He slowly rose to his feet and carefully paced a few steps. 'Ah, there now, that's better. Looks like your faith has healed me already. I can walk again. So, goodbye, General, and don't worry. I might even call later. Rather fancy that blonde number. Maybe I'll give you a ring. Cheers.'

'Blast!' The word pounded between Nigel's teeth as soon as Stalker was out of earshot. It was unbelievable. There the bastard was, sitting not two yards away from him, the key to finding Alexandra, and there was nothing, absolutely nothing, to be done. He cursed himself for his own ineptitude, his impotence, his own blockheaded dullness. Surely there must have been something to hold over Stalker? But whatever it was, he couldn't think of it, and now it was too late. All this ludicrous work—all of it for nothing! And as Nigel cursed his luck, Penelope and April marched onto the balcony, looking like Page Three girls about to take industrial action.

'We have a right to know what's going on,' demanded Penelope, hands on hips, the scolding shrew.

'Blast it to blazes, woman!' Nigel tore the cap from his head and hurled it to the floor. 'Can't you leave me in peace for a moment? We've just suffered an enormous disaster. Isandhlwana all over again.' He walked to the railing and gazed at the Los Angeles smog.

Penelope tapped her foot. 'Well?'

Nigel ignored her.

'Then we're leaving,' Penelope said, storming inside with April.

Blast! Blast! Blast! He couldn't afford to lose them. They were too deeply involved, and they were the only native guides he had, damn it. Must regain control, old man. 'Penelope!' It was a parade command.

She stormed back, April following in her train. She folded her arms over her chest. 'If you won't be honest with us...'

'I'll be honest, all right. But we've got to be clear about one thing. I give the orders, you obey them.'

'Hey, like, this isn't the Army.'

'No, it's not, worse luck. But now I've got you into this, it's best if I get you out, and that means discipline and taking orders. You can't run out now. I won't appeal to your sense of honour or duty, because I'm sure they're lacking. But the fact is, your lives are in danger now. He's seen you, both of you. You need my protection or *he'll* get you.' The shadow of the bogeyman would put the wind up Penelope, he was sure of it.

'Who is he?'

'Well you heard part of his story. He's a drug dealer who dabbles in white slavery. That's what he's done to my goddaughter, sold her to some Mexican gang to ship across the border. You might have noticed him looking at you. He was thinking about how much you'd be worth. He told me he thought your best market might be Central Africa. Plenty of corrupt dictators looking for a white woman like you evidently. When I told him you weren't for sale, he got pretty angry. He said, "We'll see about that. You can't watch over her twenty-four hours a day." I said, "Oh, yes, I can." So you see, Penelope, I can't let you go. You're my responsibility now. I'm sorry I don't have a better arsenal to protect you than your own stun gun, but I'm sure it'll do. They may out-gun us, but we have the superior brainpower, and we'll have the superior strategy. I can't claim to be the Desert Fox, but I've ridden after a few.'

A nervous smile passed over her face; she swallowed hard and fear crept into her eyes. She dropped into a chair and leaned with yearning friendliness to Nigel. 'You're not kidding, are you?'

'No. We've been playing for high stakes. And I'm afraid they've gone even higher.'

Penelope's head fell into her hands so that all Nigel could see was a thicket of blonde hair. 'Oh my God. I've got to go home to my dad. He'll know what to do.'

'Sorry, old girl. I wouldn't recommend it.'

Her head flipped up. There were tears in her eyes. 'What do you know? He fought in Vietnam. He's got lotsa guns. He'll protect me.'

'Penelope, listen. If you leave here, you'll never make it. They'll snatch you off the street before you can say "Jack Robinson". Now, get a hold of yourself, girl. You'll be safe enough here. We just have to take precautions.'

Her palms folded over her eyes. 'I can't believe it.'

'I hardly believe it myself. April, ring up another round of Bloody Marys—doubles please—for all of us.'

WHILE THE GIRLS STARTED on the drinks, Nigel bit the bullet and rang Pandora on her mobile. It wasn't a number he could memorise so he kept it on a scrap of paper in his left shoe—an old Cypriot custom he'd picked up.

'Pandora? Yes. It's me. Listen, old girl, I've got some news...'

'So have I. Oh, Nigel, isn't it awful? Five million. It's outrageous.'

'What?' Nigel frowned into the phone as though the thing was making him hallucinate.

'Five million. It's what they're demanding for Alex's safe return.'

'Are they?' For an instant, panic hit Nigel. Then the old calm under fire returned, and he was himself again. 'Who are they?'

'Los Lobos Something,' he heard her sob. 'They sound like a

singing group. Four identical chaps in sombreros, boleros, and guitars. But this is reality, Nigel, not some joke. They've...' he heard her
voice break, 'they've sent me a lock of the poor darling's hair.'

'The bastards!' Nigel felt his knuckles whiten on the phone.

'We'll have to pay it, of course.'

'Pay it? Can you?'

'Not personally, no. But there's a trust Reginald left. Unfortunately,
Alex can't touch it until she's thirty-five, but given the situation, surely
the trustees will cough up, won't they?'

'I'm sure they will,' Nigel tried to reassure her. 'Contact them.
Show them the note. And get in touch with Tanner at the Yard. Fill
him in. He's got something tangible to go on now. He's a good man.
He wanted to be a regimental bandsman, you know. Tuba was his
thing. But the poor chap got stuck in it during his audition. After they
extracted him, they had to invalid him out of the service. Herniated
disc or some such disaster. How the Yard accepted him after that, I
don't know, but...'

'Nigel, will... will we ever see her again?'

'Yes, of course we will. She's a Williamson through and through.
Now, you get the banker's draft sorted out and get it to me at Le
Grand Extravaganza Hotel, Los Angeles. And don't you worry, old
girl. You won't lose a penny over this, I promise you...'

CHAPTER EIGHT

'YOU OWE US BIG TIME, NIGEL. You've been completely unfair.'

Yes, Nigel thought, but at least I've managed to get you drunk, which is a marked improvement. It was barely tea time, but their only pause from drinking had been to wolf down some room service sandwiches at noon. From Bloody Marys—which, Nigel pointed out, when taken to excess can upset the stomach—they'd graduated to champagne. April had done what was expected of her and was taking a nap on the bed. But Penelope, the hardy Viking's daughter, was still matching him glass for glass.

The two of them sat on the balcony, Nigel wondering how much more champagne he'd have to pump into her before she fell asleep. Perhaps he should try something stronger. Vodka? Tequila? Surgical spirit? A simple blow to the head?

As long as Miss Viking Cruise Ship kept nattering on like a drunken Norwegian sailor, he'd never be able to think. And thinking was imperative. He *knew* that Stalker was behind all this. He needed a new plan to rescue Alexandra, of course, but he also needed a scheme for billeting Penelope and April.

'Yes, yes, quite unfair,' Nigel remarked absentmindedly. He supposed he could take a sheet off the bed and suspend it from the ceiling to divide the room in half. The girls could perhaps share the bed while he camped on the carpet. Or perhaps he could ring down for a folding bed. Or... there was a knock at the door.

'Oh dear, we didn't ring for another, did we? Maybe they're congratulating us on being such good customers by providing us with complimentary tea cakes. Damned thoughtful. Though, I must say, I'm not quite in the mood for one. Are you?' Penelope shook her head. The knock came again. 'Well, it doesn't matter. Go ahead and see what they want.'

'I think you should go.'

'Oh, they won't snatch you up here.'

The knock came more insistently, but she didn't budge. Silly girl. As though that bastard Stalker would dare cross swords with Nigel here. No, he'd need his whole contingent of Los Locos Constipatos or whatever they were called. Damned Mexican bandits. Never been to Mexico, of course. No call to. But he knew about Pancho Villa and General 'Black Jack' Pershing's sending of young Douglas MacArthur south of the border on a bit of derring-do. He remembered the lecture at Sandhurst vividly. Nigel wondered if they still wore sombreros, with bandoleros crisscrossed over their fat bellies, as Pandora had imagined them, tequila rising from their breath. That was obviously why Mexicans danced on their hats. He might like to see that. He'd always rather fancied the American West, where a man can be a man, and so can a woman.

Knock, knock, sounded the door. Who's there?, thought Nigel, chuckling to himself. 'Shall I do it then, my dear? Very well. Rest easy.' Nigel strolled inside. He should, of course, have looked through the peephole. But he'd had so many people traipsing in and out of his hotel room—from Penelope and April, to the screenwriters, to a continuous round of room service—that he'd grown complacent. It was probably just the manager to make sure everything was satisfactory, or the maid come to drop off a lavatory brush, or... whoever it was, he wouldn't recognise them anyway. He only wanted to get rid of them.

But when he flung the door open, they were far too recognizable. Their appearance hit him like a fist, and he felt flares shooting off in his head. Oh Lord, not again. The four of them sprang through the open door and shut it quickly behind them. For the umpteenth time, it seemed, his face was held by steely black fingers, a switchblade rested lightly on his neck.

Nigel's eyes rolled to see the other three—all sunglasses and dreadlocks—as they hurried through the room. One stopped by the sleeping April and looked to the knife man for instructions. 'Just wahtch over her, mahn,' he said in his rhythmic calypso tongue.

Nigel saw the other two race out to Penelope, muffle her screams, and drag her inside. 'Shut up, bitch. Or fuhst he die, den you die,' the knife man said. Nigel still had the stun gun in his pocket, but it seemed a singularly inopportune time to use it.

'You surprised to see us, mahn?'

'Damned surprised.'

The knife man laughed a deep, rolling laugh. 'Long way from London, huh? But we full of surprises. You too. Fine white ass you got in dis room, mahn. Very fine. Dat's a surprise too, huh? Hah, hah, hah. Here's annutter surprise for you, mahn.' His fingers tightened and the blade tickled Nigel's neck. 'We not aftuh your silly white ass. We wahnt Stalkuh. Where is he?'

'Well, he was here just a few bloody hours ago. I could have used you then. You could have helped me wring his bloody neck.'

'What? You would hurt your friend?'

'He's no friend of mine, God rot him. Like you, he's done me a bad turn. I've come here to track him down and pay him back.'

'Hah, hah, hah. So you be our ally. Is dat it, mahn?'

'Yes, I suppose I am.'

Nigel's head was shoved back, exposing his neck for butchery. The knife rested cold and hard against it. 'Where is he, mahn?'

'I don't know.' Hurriedly he added, 'He was here this morning, I told you. We tried to trap him, but he got away. Believe me, I want him as badly as you do.'

'Uh huh. Dat right, mahn. All right, den. I tell you what. You cahn lead us to him. We'll wahtch over you. Where you go, we go—in de background, so we won't be in de way.'

'What if I lose you—accidentally, I mean. I tell you, you can have Stalker for all I care. I just want to be in on the kill. How can I contact you?'

'Hah, hah,' he laughed his bass laugh, but Nigel knew he was stalling for time to think. 'If we lose you... you ring us. Leroy, write down de numbuh for him. Dat good for you?'

'Yes.'

'Good. And sorry, mahn, but we take de pretty lady wid us.' He lowered Nigel's face to look him in the eyes. 'Dat's good too, isn't it, mahn?'

'Surely it's not necessary.'

'Oh, yes, it's very necessary.'

'But look here... If anything happens to her...'

'What? You lead us to Stalkuh, you get her back. All right?'

'Very well.'

'All right,' the knife man smiled. 'Pleasure doing business with you, mahn. We'll be waiting. You left de numbuh, Leroy? Okay, no noise, pretty lady. Let's go.'

Nigel saw Penelope's face, bitterly frightened and full of accusation, as the four of them hustled her out of his room and closed the door.

Nigel's fists clenched in rage. In the course of just a few hours, he'd singlehandedly thrown away his best, perhaps his only, chance of finding Alexandra, and to top things off, he'd thrown a complete innocent (well, perhaps not the right word) to the wolves. Oh, bloody good show, old man, bloody good show. The Mexicans had Alex and the Jamaicans had Penelope. Perhaps he was right about white slavery after all.

'Ahhhh!' His whole body shook uncontrollably. In his fist-clenching fury, he'd accidentally zapped himself with the stun gun. He took a few spastic steps forward and then fell—not like a trained parachutist, but awkwardly with a knee that slanted crazily inwards. His elbow caught the edge of the bed to cushion his fall, but as his weight came down, it slipped off and his chin hit the bed and bounced. Whiplash. Grand.

With his chin resting on the bed and his body splayed beneath him, he watched as a walnut arm stretched towards the ceiling and rotated from the shoulder, then slid down to a narrow waist and stretched over shapely hips. April rolled over languorously and continued stretching. 'Oh, hi, Nigel.'

He imagined he looked like a begging dog. He opened his mouth to talk, but coughed instead.

'Are you all right?'

His voice was like sandpaper rubbing against sandpaper. His words were completely indecipherable.

'Here, let me get you a glass of water.' April bounded off the bed.

'No, no,' he croaked, rolling to face her. Didn't water and electricity equal death? He motioned her towards him with his head. 'Just slap me, dear girl, will you?'

'Slap you, Nigel?'

'Just get on with it.'

April closed her eyes and gave him a bloody good whacking that stung like a handful of angry wasps doing a Morris dance on his cheek.

Nigel leaned back and exhaled. He felt the muscles throughout his body prodding each other to make sure they were all right. They were, but he was in no hurry to get up. He looked into April's big, wide eyes and thought, well here's some damned depressing business. Oh well, best come straight to the point.

'Are you all right, Nigel?'

'I'm fine, my dear, but, look, I've got some jolly difficult news for you. I'm sure we'll get her back, it's just a matter of how and when, but—damn it all, Penelope's been kidnapped.'

'Oh my God. Like, the white slavers. Already?'

'No, the bloody Jamaicans, damn it!' He rubbed his forehead. 'This whole thing's a bloody shambles. I can hardly believe it. First, to lose Alexandra—well, I couldn't help that, I suppose—but then to lose Penelope. Of all the stupid, rotten luck. How the devil did they find us?'

'The white slavers?'

'No, the Jamaicans. What the devil do they want with us, anyway?' He struggled to his feet, April helping him. He took a few paces and then hurled the chair out from the writing desk and kicked it across the room. 'Well, that's it, by God!'

April stepped back, startled, and Nigel spun round to face her. 'I'm tired of getting kicked around by every bugger from London to Los Angeles—not to mention Stalker and his bloody pistoleros. If it's action they want, then it's action, by God, they're going to get. Listen to me, April, and listen to me well. We're going after her, and we're getting her back—immediately!'

'After Alexandra?'

'No, after Penelope. I haven't the foggiest idea where Alex is, except among a bunch of drunken Mexicans. There's a consoling thought, eh? Probably making her dance round a sombrero while they shoot up the dust to keep tempo. Well, we'll sweep them up eventually. Damned Zapatas! But Penelope... Look at that slip of paper there. It has a phone number on it.'

She picked it up, and he snatched it from her hands. He read it over quickly. 'Wait, hang on.' He paced in front of the bed. 'Right!' he said finally, stalking into the bathroom.

He returned holding a wad of tissue paper aloft. 'Here it is,' he said. He snatched up the phone, furiously punched in the number, and slapped the wad of tissue over the mouthpiece, softly singing out 'Mahn, mahn,' as though he were a choral director seeking the right pitch.

He winked at April, and then a scowl burst over his face. 'Dahmn it, mahn. Dahmn it! Dahmn it! We're lost, mahn. Dahmn it! Dahmn it! What's our address, mahn? Uh huh, mahn. Tanks, mahn.' He rang off. 'Hah!' he said triumphantly to April. 'Not bad for someone who hasn't impersonated a coloured chappie since I played Othello in the Upper Sixth. Not including dear old Bongo Topaz of course. Here, let me write it down before I forget it. Now, there's the map,' he said, pointing to the one he had taped over the mirror. 'See if you can find it on there. And while you do that, I'll get cracking on our plan—Operation Ulysses, what? You know, Penelope, Ulysses... Oh, it doesn't matter—just look, dear girl, look! We've got to find her!'

CHAPTER NINE

'THEY'RE WORSE THAN MI6,' said Bongo Topaz, as he sat in the passenger seat of April's red Ford Taurus. They hadn't seen a single dreadlock since Penelope's capture, and he was sure they weren't being followed. He imagined their surveillance men were collapsed in a smoke-filled stupor with Red Stripe beer bottles in their hands, goats nibbling at their clothes—the Jamaican equivalents of Blunt, Burgess, Philby, Maclean, and all that lot.

April's foot slammed on the brakes, jerking them forward. It was a red light.

'I'm sorry,' April said, her eyes darting nervously left and right. 'Is your door locked? I don't like going through here—especially at night. It's not safe.'

Not safe? The houses that surrounded them looked perfectly middle-class, with gardens, private garages, and cars parked in front. True, standing on the street corners were groups of large, menacing-looking young black men, obviously well-fed and positively polished to a fine shimmering mass of muscles. But they looked rather like those muscle-bound, stripped-to-the-waist Nubians one saw in the background of pictures of ancient Egyptian courts. Nothing to worry about. They were probably all eunuchs.

Otherwise, they were quite friendly, if culturally alien to him. Cars full of similar looking fellows would race up to them and drive alongside, their car stereos booming—*puh dum-dum clang, puh dum-dum clang, puh dum-dum clang*—so that their cars actually vibrated with the noise. Ever the entertainers, Nigel thought, as he watched the drivers and passengers rock rhythmically back and forth. Occasionally, they'd look at Nigel and April and flash hand signals as though they were inviting them to play scissors, rock, paper. April, poor girl, was nervous and gripped the steering wheel even harder, her eyes locked resolutely straight ahead. Nigel, however, leaned forward to smile and wave. It must be the custom here, he thought.

The light turned green, and April's car squealed ahead like a nervous piglet chased by a fox.

As they neared the address of the suspected Jamaican hideout, the houses faded away and April turned down several unattractive industrial streets—barbed wire, chain link, smokestacks, buildings made of corrugated metal. One of these streets emptied onto a row of locked-up warehouses and boarded-up shops.

'That's it,' April said, pointing at a decrepit building of about four storeys surrounded by buildings of similar size and neglect. She turned down a side street and stopped at a corner across from what looked like an old, abandoned department store. The building on its left was the suspected Jamaican hideout.

Nigel removed his Bongo Topaz wig, slipped out of his blue blazer, and pulled on a balaclava helmet—SAS, for the use of. He was now dressed entirely in black. He slipped a coil of rope, which they'd painstakingly painted black, over his shoulder. He looked out of the car window at his objective.

'I think the best approach might be that fire escape over there... then across the roof, and onto the roof of Jamaican HQ. Right. Remember, wait for us here if you can. But if anyone starts after you, take up a new position—keeping that building in sight. When we come running out, honk your horn, flash your lights, and come after us if you have to—but do it fast, so they have less chance of tracking you. All right?'

April nodded. 'I wish we didn't have to do this.'

'Wish me luck.'

He was off, scrambling across the street, reaching the far corner of the abandoned department store. Beside him, reaching down like a black, skeletal hand were the metal steps of the fire escape. He started up their zigzag course, moving steadily but not running, not wasting his strength.

The fire escape emptied onto the roof. He knew it wasn't the proper, safe thing, but he couldn't help but stop to examine the view. It wasn't terribly inspiring. No matter. He'd no time to paint it anyway. He crouched and scuttled across the roof like a crab. His building and the Jamaican hideout were equally tall. If they had guards posted on the roof, he'd need to be careful. He peered at the building across from him.

No sign of anyone, but it was dark and the roof was dotted with chimneys, a square shack in the middle, and other excrescences that provided cover. He uncoiled his rope and fastened one end on a chimney behind him. At the other end he tied a large noose—large enough to hang at least four of the buggers, he thought.

Crouching by the wall that marked the end of the roof, he hurled the noose across the street, aiming for the nearest chimney on the Jamaican side. It fell short. He hurled it harder. It fell short again. He spun the rope above his head like a cowboy and threw it. This time it landed on the roof but missed his target. Bronco Billy Anderson he was not. He gave it another cowboy try, and the noose fell over the chimney. He pulled it tight and wrapped the extra, slack rope around his own chimney.

Now came the need for a bit of gymnastics. He stepped carefully over the side, onto a tiny ledge, and grabbed the rope. This was going to be hard; he hadn't done it since manoeuvres in the Cairngorms all those years ago. He took a deep breath and stepped off the ledge, his entire weight pulling on his hands. Thank goodness he was smart enough to wear gloves. He could only too easily imagine the rough rope cutting into his palms and tearing the skin off his fingers.

He tried to kick his feet up to wrap around the rope, but after two tries, he decided he couldn't afford another effort. He needed to move before his hands exhausted themselves and gave way. He hurriedly put one arm ahead of another, pulling himself across. His shoulders started to shudder from the strain.

His legs kicked their way onto another small ledge. He stood, panting a bit, his hands still overhead on the rope. Carefully, he took one hand off and grabbed the wall above the ledge. Then the other hand followed and he pulled himself up and over.

Well, here you are, old boy, on the roof of Jamaican HQ, he thought. He lay there, breathing hard, casting his eyes over the expanse of the roof, looking for trouble.

Satisfied that he was alone, he made a crouching dash to the shack at the centre of the roof. He tested the door. It was unlocked.

He trod warily down the stairs and heard voices. Heavy footsteps were coming towards him. He quickly crept back up and onto the roof. Easing the door quietly closed, he trotted to the back of the shack and waited.

The door swung open and slammed shut. There were two voices, and they were laughing.

'Sheet, mahn, I be freezin' up here.'

'Cigarette, mahn?'

Nigel heard them lighting up and flapping their arms to keep out the slight chill.

'Come on, mahn.'

They were trudging to his left. He tiptoed right, round the shack, until he came back to the unguarded door. Faint heart never won fair lady, he thought to himself. He pulled the door open and quietly closed it behind him. He listened for sounds of pursuit but heard nothing. Faster this time, he glided down the stairs.

They ended at a landing with a door. He eased it open, stepped round it, and locked it by punching the button on the knob.

He was at the end of a dark hall lined by unlit, glass-walled offices, apparently deserted. At the far end of the hall, another flight of stairs took him down to another landing and another door. He crept through the opening.

He was on a balcony, overlooking a large, empty shop floor, punctuated by long tables. To the rear was a forest of racks and metal hangers, the walls lined with shelves. To Nigel's right, along the balcony, were three offices with glass fronts starting about waist high. These were lit, and Nigel could hear voices chanting to a heavy, thumping beat.

He crouched, careful not to be seen from the floor below, and duck-walked towards the offices. He peered into the first window. No one. Just a bare bulb, shining on a bare desk, a chair, and some filing cabinets. He peeped into the second office. Identical picture. The heavy, thumping beat reverberated from the third office. That's where they'd be.

The music was pounding now. Nigel crept to the corner of the window, raised his head as much as he dared, and looked inside.

He couldn't believe his luck. Penelope was alone—tied to a chair, admittedly, but alone. There were no guards. The voices came from a ghetto blaster on a table, pouring forth a stream of obscene rap lyrics.

He sprang to the door and jumped inside, his index finger flying to his lips.

'Quiet, Penelope, not a sound. It's me, Nigel Haversham.'

'Oh my God. Nigel, get me out of here,' she said in a screaming whisper.

Nigel felt her wrists to see if the rope was cutting into them. 'Have they hurt you?'

'No, just get me out of here.'

'Where's the guard?'

'He's wandered off somewhere. I don't know.'

'How many are there?'

'There's lots, Nigel. Just get me out of here.' She sobbed once, before she gasped. Nigel heard it too. Feet clanking up the metal stairs. No time to escape. *Sergeant, order the men to fix bayonets. All right lads, here we go!*

The door swung open and two dreadlocked men in rainbow-coloured caps confronted Bongo Topaz in his balaclava helmet. Nigel lunged forward like a fencer, with a stun gun for a sabre, and zapped the first Jamaican, who screamed and crumpled to the floor. Much to Nigel's disappointment, his dreadlocks didn't spark and shoot for the sky.

The other Jamaican reached for his pistol. Nigel came at him with a slashing backhand, jamming the stun gun into the fellow's neck, sending him to the ground, the pistol falling free. Nigel snatched it up and pulled the pistol from the belt of the other Jamaican, who was still shivering on the floor. He jammed the pistols in his own belt, like a pirate. He gave his victims another jolt with the stun gun and crept outside to look for more.

'Don't leave me here,' Penelope hissed at him. 'Cut me loose! And turn off that fucking radio! I hate rap music!'

First things first. Nigel jumped to the radio, sent the tuner flying down the dial to the local classical music station—which he'd decided, from his experience in his hotel, was not half bad—and tore the knob off. He felt under the table and found, as he expected—this was America, after all—a large wad of chewing gum, pried it off, and jammed it in the hole left by the knob.

He tilted his head 'Samuel Barber's First Symphony, I think.'

'Will you cut me loose, you idiot?!'

He reached into his back trousers pocket and pulled out a small pair of wire cutters. They gnawed away, and he grappled with his fingers to get the ropes off her.

'Oh my God,' she said, rubbing her wrists.

Nigel grabbed her by the hand and ran for the door. 'All right now,' he said, breathing a little heavily, 'just stay calm.'

At that, the window next to them exploded to a crack of gunfire and a shattering of glass.

'Oh my God!' Penelope screamed.

He flung her back into the room and fell on top of her to shield her from any stray rounds. Well, this was going to make it a damn sight more difficult. He crawled back to the door and squeezed off a meaningless shot into the darkness.

'Hold your fire,' Nigel yelled. 'I'm Bongo Topaz from de islands, and I have come to take dis woman hostage, until you pay your debts.'

Silence. Finally, 'What duh fuck you talkin' 'bout, mahn?'

'In London. You haff stolen from our gahng, mahn.' Nigel was warming to his role now. 'Dey send me to make you pay.'

'We pay—wid bullets, mahn.'

Nigel ducked back, as shots cracked and whistled against the balcony. He crawled to Penelope, who was whimpering with fear. Viking blood has certainly gone watery over the ages, he thought.

'Take my hand. Listen to me. It's going to be hard, but we're going to have to run for it. Beyond this door, run like hell to the left. There's another door there. Dive behind it. You'll be safe back there. I'll give the buggers something to think about. All right?'

They crouched together in the doorway.

'Ready. Go!' Nigel jumped forward and fired into the forest of hangers, alert to trace return fire. Penelope scampered down the balcony. He gave her a good head start so they wouldn't bunch up and offer one big target. Now it was his turn. He ran, firing one of his pistols all the way. He dived for the door and crawled through.

'Unscathed?'

Penelope nodded.

'Good.' He cracked the door open, listening for pursuit. It was quiet. 'All right. We can't wait here. We've got to press on. Let's go.'

Penelope led the way, up the stairs and down the hall of darkened offices, Nigel looking back to make sure they weren't followed. Then they stopped. Nigel took the lead. His heart was pounding now. He eased the door open. No one. They ran up the final length of stairs to the roof.

'All right, Penelope. There are two more outside. I'll have to take care of them. If anyone comes up the stairs, come out screaming. Otherwise, wait for me.'

Nigel pressed the door open. He saw one of them standing at the roof's edge, yelling down to a man on the street. They'd found his rope.

Nigel squeezed himself out of the door and around the corner of the shack. He heard footsteps crunching towards him. He'd have to meet whoever it was head on. He saw the glint of the pistol as it came round the corner. In one quick movement, he seized and twisted the wrist behind it and charged into the Jamaican, kneeing him and ramming the butt of the pistol into the kidnapper's face—slamming it home until the Jamaican slumped to the ground, gurgling. Nigel zapped him with the stun gun to make sure he stayed there. He added his pistol to the collection in his belt.

'Yo, mahn, where you be, eh?'

Nigel moved back just around the corner from the door and waited. He heard the Jamaican coming and timed his assault so that he spun straight into him. There was just enough time for the Jamaican's eyes to go wide with surprise before they jumped even wider as Nigel zapped him with the stun gun.

Nigel's victim dropped his pistol and collapsed, still conscious. Nigel grabbed it and stuck the muzzle in the Jamaican's nose.

'I be a man from de islands—Barbados, mahn. You be interferin' wid our trade. You better watch yo'sef, mahn, or I be goin' to blow yo' brains out.'

'Don't do dat, mahn. We be brudders, right?'

Nigel dragged him to the door, and opened it. 'Come on, dear girl.' Penelope scampered out and Nigel rolled the kidnapper onto the stairs where he might slow up pursuit.

'No time to reason why, old girl!' He took her hand and they ran to Nigel's rope. He peered over the side. No one was keeping watch.

She shook her head. 'I'm not going over that.' Nigel thought her eyes looked hysterical.

'My dear, it's either over that or waiting here to get riddled with bullets. Now, get moving. I'll cover you.' Nigel waved a pistol at her, and she stepped gingerly over the side. 'Get a good hold and move fast,' he whispered.

Penelope took the rope, swung her weight down, and gasped.

'Move! Move! One hand in front of the other! Don't look down, look ahead!'

He thought of her poor, manicured hands, the rope biting into them. But worse things could happen. He peered down, looking for Jamaican sharpshooters. He cast a glance behind, looking for pursuit on the roof. Then he looked at Penelope. She was teetering across, but making whimpering noises.

'There you go, dear girl. There you go,' he whispered.

Her legs kicked up onto the opposite ledge.

'Now swing an arm up. Grab the wall.'

She did. But then she was stuck, clinging to the side of the building, balanced precariously on the ledge.

'Can you lift yourself over?'

'No.'

'All right, hang on, I'm coming.' Nigel secured his belt full of pistols, stepped onto the ledge, grabbed the rope, and started across. If the bloody Jamaicans appeared now, he was a sitting duck.

But they didn't. He reached the opposite side, pulled himself over the wall, and reached down to help Penelope. She pulled, he lifted under her arms, and she was over. They collapsed on the roof, gasping together.

'I know we could both use a rest, my dear, but we've got to keep moving. There's a fire escape at the other end—over there. Run for it.'

They scrambled to their feet and ran across the roof. They took the black metal steps quickly, spinning down to the street, where Nigel pressed her against the building and motioned for her to wait while he looked round the corner.

He saw April in the car, still across the street, waving frantically for him to come, but he had to be sure. He stepped out to draw fire if there was any to be drawn. Nothing. He waved Penelope forward and they ran for the car, April flipping the doors unlocked. Nigel jumped in the passenger seat, while Penelope piled in the back. April jammed on the accelerator and spun the car around, its tyres screeching like wildly whinnying horses.

Penelope lay gasping, 'Oh my God, oh my God.'

Nigel kept looking over his shoulder, but no one was following.

'You did it, Nigel!' shouted April.

'Yes, dear. Not so fast, please. We don't want to attract the police.' He pulled off his balaclava helmet. 'Hurray for Bongo, eh?'

CHAPTER TEN

NIGEL SAT ON THE CARPET, against the wall, sipping a cup of tea, watching the hazy Los Angeles sun stream through the window and onto the bed where lay his two gorgeous companions, sleeping soundly and looking terribly, terribly innocent.

Last night, after washing off Bongo Topaz, Nigel had pitched himself on the floor and turned the bed over to his girls. So confident was he that, even before the rescue, one of April's preparatory missions had been to go home and pack a bag for herself and Penelope.

He thought of that now—how she'd stumbled through the door, a suitcase in one hand, a bag full of supplies (the rope, the black paint, the wire cutters, and what not) in the other; how he'd ungallantly watched her struggle with it all because for some reason it amused him.

'Go ahead and put it on the balcony, dear. We wouldn't want to make a mess in here.'

April struggled to the balcony, shifting her shoulders as she shuffled along in rather Chaplinesque fashion.

'No sign of the Jamaicans, I take it?'

'No,' she huffed over her shoulder.

'Remarkably unobservant chaps, aren't they? I doubt they even know who you are.'

'Wheeehuuuu,' she said, dropping her load.

'Drink?'

'Just some water please.' She sat on one of the plastic chairs on the balcony, fanning herself with her hand. It was nearing noon, or roughly twenty hours since Penelope's kidnapping.

Nigel brought her a glass of water and sat across from her. 'Rest easy, old girl. The rope and my camouflage are all we have to do now. We're almost there.'

She smiled and said, 'You know, I was just thinking in the car. Maybe it's because we're about to rescue Penelope, and you know, like, when you're facing death, your life flashes before your eyes. Well, I was thinking I really want to get married.'

Nigel arched an eyebrow like a boxer raising his guard. Oh, yes, he'd heard this before—that infernal, eternal lament. Why was it that the very sight of Nigel drove women to think of marriage? Surely there must be some way to rid himself of this horrible animal magnetism that sent women dreaming wistfully of wedding bells. It was a damned nuisance—always interfering with one's responsibilities.

'I'm sure you shall, my dear,' he said suspiciously. 'You're not thinking of anything rash, are you?'

'Oh, no, it's just that I've got my wedding all planned and I can't wait for it to happen. All I need is a groom.'

Oh dear. As if Nigel didn't have enough trouble on his hands—two kidnapped women and now another wanting to kidnap him.

'A groom is one of the essentials, isn't it?'

'Of course it is,' she giggled.

'Do you have anyone in mind?' he asked with deepening dread.

'That's my problem. Like, there's so many to choose from. Penelope thinks I need to go for an athlete—a professional athlete even, cuz, you know, I'm kind of athletic too. But I don't know. You know, like, with the image consultant business, we'll be surrounded by athletes. Some of them do have the most awesome bodies, but, like, I'm not into sexual-business relationships the way she is.'

'Oh, is she really?' Nigel said, trying to shut his gaping mouth.

'Well, you know her philosophy: "He gives me what I want, so I give him what he wants." And I mean, like, that's kind of a moral way of looking at things—you know, like, I scratch your back and you scratch mine. But that's not me, you know?'

Nigel nodded sagely. Yes, he could see that definitely.

'I want a big house, and a nice, fast car, and a yard, and kids, and a white picket fence. That's what I want. And I want my wedding. I mean, I've been planning it for so long, Nigel. It's going to be so beautiful. And I'd like you to come. That would be special. Especially after all we've been through. And then we'll honeymoon in Mexico.'

'Surely you don't mean *we* will, my dear.'

'Don't be silly. I mean my husband and me.'

That was a relief. Still, Mexico, dangerous place. The home of Los Locos Constipatos, he was thinking. 'Have you been there?'

'Oh, sure, lots of times. It's not far away. Pen and I usually go there in the winter. But last winter we rented a place in Big Bear and went skiing.'

'So you know the border region well?'

'Well, yeah. It depends what you mean by well. I mean, like, Tijuana? Baja?'

With her deep, dark tan she could easily pass for a Mexican, he thought. *He had a sudden vision of April, dressed in a yellow straw hat and those baggy white pyjamas Mexican peasants wore during the day. They were crossing the desert, the sun pressing its sizzling fingers on any inch of exposed flesh. April was trudging on, walking a bit like Charlie Chaplin, as she hobbled along in warped, dust-covered sandals.*

She was leading a mule—his mule—Nigel rocking gently in the saddle. He was smoking a cheroot under his sombrero, his impressive, manly physique discreetly hidden under a poncho to discourage unwanted feminine advances. He was posing as a modest merchant of trinkets, religious items mostly, rosaries, devotional pictures, and pamphlets. Strung along behind him was another mule, carrying his wares.

Their mission—to find Alexandra, held hostage by Don Ameche de Zorro.

April stopped and rubbed the sweat from her brow. 'Don Nigel de Londres,' she said, 'should we not be panting?'

'Panting? What the devil do you mean, panting?'

'I said painting, Nigel. Shouldn't we be painting the rope? It'll need time to dry.'

'Oh, yes, yes. You have everything you need? For tonight, after the rescue, I mean, pyjamas and what not?'

'Everything,' she said, smiling. 'It's going to be fun—like a sleepover.'

NIGEL LOOKED AT APRIL NOW, dressed in an overlarge T-shirt with some sort of alcohol advertisement on it, and Penelope in a huge

American football jersey. Mind you, he thought, coughing to himself, she has the chest for it.

Yes, the girls had everything they needed—and they could rest safely in his care. He'd proven that in the most dramatic of circumstances. But *he* did not have everything *he* needed. He still needed Alexandra. And the prospects of finding her were dim—especially now that *The Confessions of an English Opium Eater* ploy had failed. Plan A might have to develop into Plan B at any moment.

And there were other complications—chiefly the Jamaicans. They could always come back, thirsting for revenge. God knows he'd traded bullets with them. He hadn't exactly expected that. On the other hand, he *had* bloodied their noses *and* made off with a considerable portion of their arsenal. Not bad for a lone chap the wrong side of fifty-nine. That might give them pause. If the buggers were smart, they might prefer to lie low for a while.

He could afford to be confident within limits. Last night he'd proven—to the girls at least and perhaps even reminded himself— that he was no paper tiger. He knew his business; and knew it well enough to realise that without reinforcements he'd never find, let alone rescue, Alexandra. Granted, the Trust money was on its way to him, and he must contact the bank about that. But it wasn't that simple. He intended to use the money as a ruse; Alexandra would be rescued, not ransomed.

He briefly thought of taking the Jamaicans fully into his confidence and enlisting them as allies. After all, here they'd been, knocking on his door, as eager to track down Stalker as he was. But from what he'd seen, they were hopelessly incompetent, they had no local connection to help him track down Los Lobos Colorados, and he had no confidence that they wouldn't bungle things and put Alex into even more danger. How the idiots had managed to get from London to L.A. mystified him. If they were allies of any sort, they were Nigel's Soviet allies, pushing towards Stalker from the East, while Nigel pressed on from the West. And unlike Roosevelt at Yalta, Nigel had no intention of making Uncle Joemaica-mahn any gifts.

No, what he needed was to make an ally of a local warlord—the leader of one of Los Angeles's more respectable gangs (the old Boys of Brompton Cocaine Cartel, Los Angeles Branch, perhaps?)—someone who would know where to find Los Lobos Colorados and who would be willing and able to back Nigel up with firepower if need be.

He had no doubt he'd been lucky last night. But luck can run out. And he could no longer continue, in good conscience, putting his girls in the frontline of danger. He knew it might be the fashion now, what with women snipers in the SAS, women pilots looping the loop over the Gulf, and a woman formerly in charge of MI5, but it was a modern barbarism he could never accept. The very thought of women in the trenches, charging fortified positions with fixed bayonets, made him red with rage. His cup rattled in its saucer. To hang out the washing on the Siegfried Line and find it full of brassieres and lacy, frilly things. Intolerable. If that's what they wanted, why not conscript the bloody Labour cabinet?

April stretched her arms over her head, blinking her eyes, and smiled. 'Hi, Nigel.'

'Oh, hello, my dear. I'm so glad you're getting married and having children. Much better choice than getting bombed, shot at, raped, and mutilated. Rather like to shield you from those things, you know.'

'Oh, wow, like, thanks.'

'Shall I make you a cup of tea?'

She saw Penelope was still asleep and whispered, 'No, thanks.'

Nigel nodded and whispered back, 'I thought I'd pop out for a newspaper, and then take breakfast in the dining room. Care to join me?'

'I'd love to, but...' She looked at Penelope.

'I quite understand—and it's probably the best thing. But if you'll excuse me.' Nigel got to his feet, put his cup and saucer on the writing table, and tiptoed out of the room.

It was a bright, sunny morning with a faint nip in the breeze. Good walking weather, Nigel thought. It'll be hot by afternoon, though.

He ambled along, admiring the wide, spotlessly clean streets, the rows of palm trees marking his advance, the attractive people strolling by, smiling at him on their way to work, and mused that Los Angeles was quite a nice place in its own way—part desert, part tropics, tamed by glittering glass skyscrapers, marred only by the fact that everywhere he went—at least with his cicerone—someone was sticking a knife at his throat. He tilted his Panama and thought—*down these mean streets Field Marshal Slim must go*... He turned off his quiet boulevard and down an already busy shopping street with cars parked everywhere and people hustling out of them to buy styrofoam cups of coffee before going to the office.

Nigel knew there was an international news agent here. The papers were several days old and grossly overpriced, but he wanted to catch up on things back home. He picked up *The Spectator*, of course; *The Week,* a wonderful find; *The Sunday Telegraph,* with a large photo of Liz Hurley on the front page—a not uncommon event and one of the innumerable reasons for his ardent loyalty to the paper (she was so obviously a woman of good stock)—and even found a *Private Eye*. He refused to buy *The Oldie* on principle. As he left the shop, he saw a tall, handsome black man dressed to the nines—sharp black suit, bow tie, severe black-rimmed glasses, a close-cropped, military-looking haircut. He was hawking papers too. Nigel approached him.

'I say, what do you have there, old boy?'

'Boy?' he snarled.

Nigel was rather taken aback by his hostility. 'Well, I mean to say, what's that paper you're selling?'

'*The Jihad Journal-Picayune*, featuring the prophetic voice of the Esteemed Iced Khalifa. Fifty cents.'

Jihad? Goodness gracious, one hadn't realised that holy war had come to Los Angeles. 'Is it of local interest?'

'Here, you blue-eyed demon!' He jammed a copy into Nigel's hand. 'Read it and find out, infidel!'

'Oh, thanks so much, old... man,' Nigel said. 'I'll read it with interest, I assure you.'

A slight wind had picked up, making it impossible to read the paper as he strolled back to the hotel, so he tucked it under his arm until he could unfold it at the breakfast table.

The hotel offered an excellent buffet breakfast, which was full of generous selections—even if their sausages were skinny, dark little things, their bacon was shrivelled and blackened through nuclear-strength frying, and the smallest kipper was not to be found anywhere. The full Californian definitely paled beside its full English equivalent.

Still, he stacked his plate high with scrambled eggs, *their* bacon, *their* sausage, potatoes, hot cakes and syrup, a bowl of porridge, a glass of orange juice, and toast and marmalade. He arranged it before him, threw his napkin over his lap, ordered a pot of tea, and started tucking in, putting *The Jihad Journal-Picayune* next to his teacup.

THE INEVITABLE DESTRUCTION OF THE WHITE RACE, screamed the headline. Ah, yes, Oswald Spengler. Ho hum. He flipped the page. His eyes focused on an advertisement with a strong, forceful-looking, fiftyish man, dressed like the chap who'd sold him the paper, displaying a plastic bottle in his hands. THE ESTEEMED ICED KHALIFA PROVIDES THE SECRETS OF HOLY AND HEALTHY LIVING WITH AFRO-VITA-PACK. Hmm, thought Nigel. His eyes scanned to another picture. Three more of these formidable-looking chaps stood with their arms crossed over their chests outside a tower block. THE SCOURGE OF DRUGS: BLACK JIHAD FIGHTS BACK.

Not the sort of article that would have interested him in the past, but when one's goddaughter is held captive by Mexican drug lords, one tends to want to keep up with narcotics news. He read on: 'Saying that "the self-destruction of the Black race must be stopped", the Esteemed Iced Khalifa sent three of his most Holy and Powerful Men of Discipline on a weeklong anti-drug jihad at the Crenly-Cooper housing project. Destroyer Mohammed, speaking for himself and for Jamal B. Bad and Holy Terminator, said of their weeklong jihad, "We have lifted the siege of the dealers, but now the community must rise up, throw off the chains and shackles of drug addiction, and wage holy war against all who poison our people. Whenever we find dealers of death, we will break them. As our Esteemed Iced Khalifa has spoken: 'Let the blood of the death dealers fertilise our people so that we can sprout new and healthy branches and grow and flourish as the strong trees of God.' " '

Nigel paused to munch on a heavily buttered, and even more heavily marmaladed, slice of toast. Much more virile lot than the Jamaicans. Sort of a black *Wehrmacht* by the look of them. He scanned the paper, searching for an address. Might have to look in on these fellows. Well-trained men are hard to find. And a little *blitzkrieg* down the gullet of Los Locos Constipatos might be just the thing.

What had he told that charming, Christian screenwriter chap the other day? The one who saw *Confessions of an English Opium Eater* as a natural musical starring Pat Boone and the Osmond family? Oh, yes, now he remembered. 'Splendid idea,' he'd said, 'but you see, we're looking for a script about divine retribution, not divine forgiveness.'

Well, here it is, old boy, the wrath of God—not our God, of course, but evidently some sort of Mussulman god. But he would do. Wasn't Allah the god of the sword? Yes, definitely have to look this chap up. What's his name? Ah, yes, Iced Khalifa. Have a parley with him. If not a full-fledged panzer division, at least his chaps might make damned good *askaris* for chopping up the drug-dealing banditos.

In the meantime, he thought, folding up *The Jihad Journal-Picayune* and pulling out his copy of *Private Eye*, let's see what Lord Gnome has to say, shall we? Ian Hislop had a lot to answer for.

STUFFED TO THE LIMITS of human endurance, Nigel tucked *The Sunday Telegraph*, *The Jihad Journal-Picayune*, *The Week*, *The Spectator*, and *Private Eye* under his arm, took the lift to the fourteenth floor, and fished out his room key-card. The door clicked open and he passed into the room.

'Good morning,' he said.

'Good morning,' Sean Stalker replied.

Nigel's hand leapt for the pistol in his coat pocket. Bugger! He'd forgotten. He'd put the pistols in the drawer of the writing desk. All he had was the wretched stun gun. He didn't want a toy. He wanted a weapon. A glint of gun metal caught his eye. Sean was holding a pistol—one of *his* pistols—butt forward, offering it to Nigel.

'Go ahead, take it. It's yours anyway. April pulled it on me. I had to clear up a misunderstanding you created. Go ahead. I know you won't use it. Murder with two witnesses? Not likely.'

Nigel took it and put it in the pocket of his coat. 'What're you doing here?'

Stalker was sitting on the bed, a huge, dimpled grin on his face. He draped his arms over April's and Penelope's shoulders. Penelope was holding a bouquet of flowers and gazing at him admiringly.

'As it turns out, clearing up all the lies you've told. White slavery?' he said, making a face. 'Surely you could have done better than that—that went out with the nineteenth century. We'll have to cover chair legs next so that no one gets too excited.'

'Get out.'

'Oh, I will. And so will Pen. She doesn't like being a part of your nasty schemes any more than I do. And I've discovered we share a common dislike for certain Jamaicans.'

'That bastard's a drug dealer,' Nigel said to Penelope. 'You don't want to go with him.'

'Not everyone's as narrow as you are, General,' Stalker replied. 'Pen understands I'm waiting for my big break. And she understands I need to make money too. Not all of us can inherit it.'

'What about Alexandra?'

'That's an old story, isn't it? Girl wants to be a star in Hollywood. Mummy doesn't approve. Reactionary old git—who doesn't understand anything—is sent to drag her safely home to mummy. That's all it is: an interfering old man trying to treat a grown woman like a child and keep her from doing what she wants to do. Face it, General, it's a lot more believable than your lurid stories.'

'Do you believe him?'

Penelope looked embarrassed. 'Yeah.'

'And you, April?'

'Well, it certainly *sounds* believable, Nigel.'

Stalker said, 'I'm actually in a hurry. Sorry I can't stay for a cup of tea. But I did bring you this.' He pulled a small plastic bag out of a brown paper one. 'Since I'm taking your honey, I thought I'd leave a little sugar—for your tea.' He tossed him the bag.

'I don't want your blasted sugar,' Nigel said, throwing it to the ground. The bag broke and spilt on the carpet.

'That's not very polite.' Stalker picked up the bag, its powdery contents pouring onto the floor. 'Here, I'll leave it on the desk for you.'

'Get out,' Nigel repeated.

'As you wish. Come on, Pen. Goodbye, General. Remember what I told you—just stay out of the way. You'll get Alex soon enough. In the meantime, why not work on your tan?'

'You'll bring the suitcase?' Penelope called back to April.

'Yeah.'

Nigel watched the eloping lovers with contempt. Penelope gave him a quick glance, but that was all. She knew she was going down the sewer, Nigel thought, but some women are just too weak to help themselves, aren't they? Just like Eve, always listening to bloody snakes. The door slammed shut. He turned to see April still sitting on the bed.

'Why aren't you going with them?'

'I wanted to say goodbye first,' she said, rising to her feet and picking up a note by the phone. She smiled coyly, 'And I had to tell you the hotel management called. A Miss Perkins would like to see you. She says you can find her at reception. I think you're in trouble.'

'Trouble? What sort of trouble?' His whole life seemed to be trouble.

April rested the note on her lips and presented her leg in that fashion model way she had. 'Don't I look like trouble?'

His eyebrows came together and shook hands. 'What do you mean?'

'Keeping young girls in your hotel room, Nigel.' She waved her index finger at him in mock admonishment.

'Oh, that's it, is it?'

'You better hope this doesn't get back to Lady What'shername, the one you play backgammon with.'

'Pandora? I'd forgotten I'd mentioned her.'

'You didn't. Sean did. He told us a lot more about you than you ever did.'

'Yes, I'm sure. Look, April, exactly what *did* Stalker tell you and Penelope? Just for the record.'

'Well, it was pretty much like he just said. Alex ran away with him to Hollywood, where he's, like, going to be the next Quentin Tarantino and she's going to be the next Uma Thurman.' That threw Nigel—he wasn't aware of the last Uma Thurman. 'And, like, Alex's mom doesn't approve, so she sent you out to get her back.'

'Nothing about drugs? Cartels? Insider dealing?'

April looked blank.

'April, you wouldn't mind waiting for me while I talk to Miss Nosey Perkins, would you? I'm certain it'll only take a moment. And here—here are some papers to keep you amused.'

He needed time to think, and he needed to retain April—at least until he could come up with a new plan, a new strategy. Plan A had folded and everything seemed to be going wrong. Losing Penelope was one thing—she seemed to be lacking in courage anyway—but losing Penelope *and* April would leave him without a California guide, alone in a country he didn't understand. And Plan B? Well, he hadn't exactly devised a Plan B yet.

He stood morosely at the huge black reception desk, long enough to serve as the runway of a small aircraft carrier, and, out of habit, waited in the queue for the most attractive of the receptionists.

She escorted him down a wood-panelled hall to the modest, but quiet and comfortable, office of Miss Rosalind Perkins, who looked like her office—modest, quiet, though not quite so comfortable. She was a tall, rather elegant woman with narrow, worried eyes, a gentle voice, and enough makeup that if it were scraped off it could be sculpted into a life-sized double.

After the usual polite preliminaries, she said, 'I'm afraid we've had some complaints, Mr Haversham. Now, I want to assure you that we value you as a customer, and I've seen your bill and I know you are making fine use of our facilities. Being hospitable is our business. But there's a pattern developing of *serious* complaints. I could cite, for instance, the enormous disturbance that was caused to your fellow guests by a long line of men, I've heard reports of up to one hundred or more, standing outside your door.'

'Well, that won't happen again.'

'I'm very pleased to hear that, but there have been others. We've even had the police involved. The days of hotel detectives are a relic of the past,' she chuckled, 'but to protect our guests we do have our own security system. Mr Haversham, we discovered some individuals smoking marijuana who were not guests of the hotel and who were disturbing hotel residents. We finally had to have the police escort them away. They claimed they were your guests. I had to tell the police that that was certainly not true, that they weren't registered at the hotel and were certainly not staying in your room. I hope that is true. Do you know them?'

'Girls?'

'No,' Miss Perkins said carefully, as though it hurt her to say the word, 'men.'

'What sort of men?'

Miss Perkins pressed her lips together and rolled her eyes searching for the right word. 'Young men.'

'They wouldn't be black, would they? Jamaican, funny hair?'

Miss Perkins looked pained, but nodded warily. 'They could have been.'

'Not friends of mine at all. And I certainly wouldn't let them stay with me. The buggers probably have fleas.'

'There's another matter that needs to be cleared up, and that is who *is* staying with you? We're not passing judgement of course,' she chuckled again, 'but you booked a single room and I'm told three of you are staying there.'

'A temporary, unforeseen development.'

'But you've only paid for a single.'

'They're leaving today. I only put them up because they had nowhere to stay.'

'Well, we'll have to charge you. Now, we do have a suite that's designed for three—it even has two bedrooms and two bathrooms— if you want to upgrade your accommodation.'

'I don't think that's necessary, thank you.'

An intercom button buzzed on Miss Perkins's phone. 'Miss Perkins? Is Mr Haversham still there? The police are here and would like to talk to him. Shall I send them back?'

'Oh, yes, thank you.' Miss Perkins looked more worried than ever. 'Oh dear. Do you think it's those young men again? The police told me they might have to talk to you about them.'

Nigel's thoughts were much grimmer. It's Alexandra. They've found a body and want me to identify it. Fear and dread licked up his neck like volts coming from an electric chair. If she is dead, he thought, I still have April. Through her I can find Penelope, and through Penelope I can get to Stalker, and then… God, but how to tell Pandora…

'Mr Haversham, I'm Officer Michael Bannon and this is Officer Leslie Curtis. If you'd rather we talk privately…'

'No, go ahead, officer. What is it?'

'Well, sir, it's a funny thing. We came here to see if you could identify the men in these photographs.' He held out photographs offering front and side views of two Jamaicans. 'Can you?'

'Never seen them before in my life.'

'Okay. We didn't think so. But there's another thing. As we were driving over, we got a dispatch call to check up on an anonymous tip. Somebody phoned in that you have a large stash of cocaine in your room. Now, sir, we don't have a search warrant yet, but we've run a background check and we're sure to get one because you're already technically under arrest for driving under the influence. The point is, sir, we can look in your room now or we can serve you with a warrant. If we do it now and the tip is malicious or bad information, we can get it cleaned up and forget it. If we wait for the warrant, we'll have an official investigation.'

'Do I look like a drug dealer?'

'Sir, I've seen all kinds—from grannies to lawyers. Nothing surprises me.'

'Well, I have nothing to hide.' Nigel stood proudly, and silently counted all the things he did have to hide—the so-called sugar, obviously cocaine, planted on him by Stalker; the pistols he'd taken off the Jamaicans (one of which was in his pocket); April, whom Stalker had carelessly implicated by leaving her in Nigel's cocaine-littered room…

Miss Perkins folded her hands on her desk and moaned, 'Oh dear.'

Better to deal with the law upstairs, Nigel thought, than to take action in front of Miss Perkins. It would be safer in his room—fewer witnesses.

Nigel led the officers to the lifts, assessing them along the way. Officer Bannon was a big chap with a heavy black moustache. Overweight, but powerful for all that. He could be a problem. Officer Curtis, on the other hand, was even less physically imposing than April. Badly-dyed blonde hair, a scrawny upper body, hips ballooning with fat—the only threat she posed was to Nigel's aesthetic sense. Perhaps her physique was a warning to other policewomen: Behold the perils of eating hamburgers and chocolate bars as you cruise the streets of Los Angeles! He noticed the holster forced outward by her hips. They were both armed, of course, this being America. But then again, so was Nigel.

'So are you here for business or pleasure?' Officer Bannon asked as they stood in the lift.

'Funny, they asked me that last time. Evidently, I'm here for the amusement of the police.'

They stepped out of the lift and down the corridor. Nigel popped his key-card in the door and flung it open. 'Come in,' he said. He closed the door behind them, gave a glance at April, who looked shocked, and watched with deadened nerves as both officers immediately bent over the spilled white powder. It was all so obvious. Stalker wasn't clever, but he'd timed it well. It was a coup of sorts. And now Nigel's response was simply inevitable. He pulled the pistol out of his pocket. 'I'm sorry, officers, but if you'd both please raise your hands. Thank you.'

'Now hold on, mister, you're digging a much bigger hole for yourself...'

'Alphonsia,' he called to April, who looked at him baffled. 'Alphonsia, take their guns.'

'No, Nigel.'

'... at your age, if you're cooperative, a jury is sure to...'

'Alphonsia, do it!'

'Nigel, I don't want to be involved in this.'

'... put the gun down, sir...'

'Do it now! And you officers can save your breath; I didn't rise to command by shilly-shallying.'

With tears welling in her eyes, April removed the officers' guns from their holsters, handling the weapons as though they were Aids-tainted gloves.

'Give them to me,' Nigel said. He stuck them under his waistband, one on either side. Nigel was beginning to think that piracy must be in his blood. Some old salty sea dogs in his family tree, no doubt. Perhaps he was distantly related to Drake, Raleigh, or even Nelson.

'Now, take off your belts,' he said. No time for ancestral reveries. After all, what had his sixteenth cousin seventy-two times removed said? England expects that every man shall do his duty.

'Alphonsia, take the belts and the guns in the drawer here and put them in your bag. Hurry!' He scooped up *The Sunday Telegraph, Private Eye, The Spectator, The Week,* and *The Jihad Journal-Picayune* and folded them under his arm. 'And do the best you can throwing my bags together. That's it. Just throw everything in there, and close it up. Now if you two officers will kindly lie facedown on the bed. You, sir, with your head on the pillows and you, madam, with your head at the foot—and keep your arms out, so I can see your hands. Good. Excellent. Now I suppose we'll have to tie you up. Alphonsia, get our rope, will you? I suppose we can use the pillowcases for gags. I'm sorry, my dear, but you'll have to do it. I'll tell you how. Nice knot around the ankles. There you go. You've got it...

'Now, I want you officers to know that I am completely innocent of all charges. I've been horribly framed by the real drug dealer you should be after. His name is Sean Stalker—I don't mind telling you at this point—and he's with a gang called Los Locos Constipatos, I mean, Los Lobos Colorados. I'm sorry I don't have time to explain, but I have a friend at Scotland Yard who can vouch for me, Inspector Byron Tanner. That's Byron Tanner. Give him a ring if you have any doubts on what used to be Whitehall 1212. I am sorry I can't go to the station with you and all that rubbish, but I'm on secret service and must move quickly. I'm terribly sorry. Alphonsia, are you ready? All right, then, let's find your Fiat and get out of here.'

Nigel closed the door, grabbed his bags from April, and said, 'Quick, run to the lifts.'

'The what?'

'Come on!'

'Nigel, we can't run from the police.'

'Shh, quiet! The fact is, April, we must run from the police. But everything I told them just now, about having a friend at Scotland Yard—I'm sure you've heard of Scotland Yard—is true. It's all very complicated, my dear, but... Ah, the lift, come on... but I am a sort of secret agent, and believe me, you can't get off now. It's too dangerous. I know it seems dangerous already. But look at it this way, April, the Queen won't let us down. That's ultimately what's at stake here. She stands behind us, and when this business is finished, there will be diplomatic talks at the highest levels, and—you can stake your life on it—when all is said and done, there will be smiles and pats on the back for us and we'll be sent on our way: free, vindicated, and with polite applause. So steady on, old thing. You're on the winning side.'

He knew he was talking the most appalling rubbish. But when one has to communicate with an impressionable young Californian, one was on similar footing as if one were talking to one of the wildest natives of Borneo—one needed to impress and reassure these people with fables and stories of the great white queen. They weren't a literary lot, these Californians. They believed in films, in images, in image consultants, for goodness sake. And who has the grandest image of them all, he thought, but Elizabeth Regina! God bless her!

The lift settled to the ground floor. They hoisted up their bags, and as the doors opened, Nigel stepped directly into Miss Perkins.

'Oh, excuse me,' Nigel said, blusteringly.

Miss Perkins was all nervousness, stroking the ropes of imitation pearls around her neck. 'I was just going up to see what I could do to smooth things over. You don't really have to leave?'

'I've never been so insulted in my life. Those bloody officers poked and prodded all my personal belongings in the most embarrassing way. I think they enjoyed it, the sadistic swine. I wouldn't be surprised if they were drunk.'

Miss Perkins looked doubtful, even suspicious. 'I don't think they were. Are they still up there?'

Nigel looked across the marble lobby to the glass doors that faced the street. The police car was parked outside. 'No, they moved on. Cleared my baggage,' he said, hefting it up for Miss Perkins's inspection, 'and then went laughing to the lift—they said they had to investigate more rooms.'

'Where? They can't do that. They should have asked me.'

'Are you sure they're police officers, Miss Perkins, and not impostors? They seemed damned unprofessional to me. I'm sure that woman had her badge on upside down.'

'Did they say where they were going?'

'No. And I didn't ask—it could be any of the rooms. If I were you, I'd call a fire alarm—flush the bastards out.'

April was as nervous as Miss Perkins, tottering back and forth on her toes. 'Nigel,' she whined.

'But really, Miss Perkins, I can't run your hotel for you. That's your responsibility. But I think someone needs to be punished most severely. Now, if you'll excuse me, I promised this young lady's parents that I'd drop her at her ballet lesson.'

Miss Perkins hadn't noticed April before, but now she smiled and her eyes rolled like ball bearings up and down her tense and bouncing form. 'Oh... yes. And you are?'

Nigel brushed her aside. 'We've been through all that. Goodbye. I shan't be staying here again, thank you.'

'You'll pay your bill on the way out,' Miss Perkins reminded.

'Yes, yes, of course,' Nigel said irritably. But good God, he hadn't time to pay the bill—not with the Jamaicans and the bloody peelers breathing down his neck, Sean Stalker making off for Mexico with every beautiful woman in sight, and two stolen police officers' pistols stuck in his waistband and another stolen pistol in his pocket. He carried his bags to the queue at reception, turned to see Miss Perkins being swallowed by the lift, smiled and waved, and, as the lift doors closed, bolted to the front door.

'Come on, April!' he said, hurrying across the marble floor.

'Oh, sir!' cried a voice.

'April, did you park downstairs?'

'No, I'm on the street.'

'Oh, good girl.' He hoped that would leave fewer witnesses—and no parking attendant—to trace the car.

'Sir!'

'Which way's your car?'

'On the street to the right.'

'Right. You go ahead. I'll deal with this bugger and meet you there.'

'Sir!'

Nigel turned and saw a tall, well-built man in a maroon blazer, an identity card clipped to his pocket. 'Sir, can I help you? Are you in a rush?'

'Actually, I am. I'm going to miss my plane to Mexico if I don't hurry.'

'I noticed you didn't check out. Do you have your key?'

'Oh, yes, here.'

'And we do have your credit card number, of course.'

'Yes, of course.'

He gave Nigel a casual American salute. 'That takes care of it. We'll bill you for any additional charges. Do you need any help with your bag? Can I call you a cab?'

'I can manage, but a taxi would be the greatest help—for the airport, please, I'm going to Mexico. I'll just wait outside for it, shall I?'

Nigel hurried out of the glass doors and turned quickly up the street. He twice glanced over his shoulder and hoped he wasn't being watched by the man in the maroon blazer, by the hotel security, by the Los Angeles Police Department, or by dope-smoking Jamaicans with machine guns.

He wiped his forehead. It was trickling with sweat. Ahead, he saw April's red Ford Taurus in a long line of parked cars running up the street. That was good. Her car didn't stand out. April was cowering in the front seat, but as he approached, she jumped out and helped him throw his bags in the boot. He got in the passenger seat, tossing his newspapers in ahead of him.

'Where are we going?' she asked.

'Out of here as quick as you can without causing a scene.'

He needed time to think. Miss Perkins was in his room by now. She'd have found the police. April's knots wouldn't have held them for long. They'd start a search immediately. The airport story was a feeble dodge, but it might engage a few officers for a short while, as would the bit about 'Alphonsia' driving a Fiat.

'Should I go on the freeway?'

That was the fastest way of getting anywhere (or given traffic jams, was it?), but he had no idea where to go. The backstreets were probably safer. A crowded, unexpected place would be safer still. He needed a bloody map—and reaching down he found one and unfolded it. But of course, it all meant nothing to him. A map was no substitute for seeing the land yourself.

'Get as far as you can away from here and away from the airport... and away from Mexico while you're at it.'

What clues had they? They could link him to his rent-a-car crash, but that meant nothing. They could, of course, trace his phone call to Pandora, and though he didn't want her implicated, what could he do? They also had the false lead of the Jamaicans. That might be useful. If they called Inspector Tanner, he'd be safe. In the meantime, where to?

Nigel massaged his temples. It was maddening, being continually trumped by Stalker. He said, 'Penelope can't really believe Stalker, can she?'

'Why not? *He's* not running from the police.'

'Oh, come on, dear girl! You know better that that. They're merely misinformed, and we haven't the time to set them straight. We've got rescues to perform—your Penelope among them.'

'Then why don't we ask the police to do it? I've never done anything wrong. I've never been in trouble. And now…' Tears trickled down her cheeks.

'Oh, goodness me, my dear. Don't cry. Stalker's a complete rotter. You made the right choice. When the smoke clears, Penelope's the one who'll have to explain things to the police.'

'I didn't have a choice.'

'Oh, yes, you did. You could have surrendered to those two uninspiring police officers. At this very moment you'd be sitting in some dank cell trying to explain why your friend ran off with a known drug smuggler. And blast it all, why *did* she run off with him?'

April sighed with exasperation. 'Like, he came with flowers, and he explained everything and told us you were just an interfering old man and that he was really trying to make it in Hollywood and had gotten into trouble with drug gangs in London, and he was willing to protect us and get us out of all the trouble you put us in, *and*,' she concluded with a certain anger, 'he's kinda cute!'

'Doesn't the confession of drug dealing mean anything to you?'

'Well, like, yeah. It means he has money. I mean, Nigel, what would you do? He's cute, he's got money. Maybe he can help Pen set up her business. And anyway, she was tired of you, and being bossed around, and that nightmare you put her through.'

'*I* put her through! They were Stalker's friends—the ones *he* stole from!'

'It's not his fault she got kidnapped.'

'Oh, it's mine, is it?'

'You got us into all this.'

'Well, I certainly didn't mean for her to be kidnapped or for you to be put in danger. Far from it. I came here to rescue a girl—*from him.* And now I've lost two girls to the scheming bastard. And from the sound of you, I'm in danger of losing a third. Can't you see through him? Those dimples hide a thief, a drug dealer, and a kidnapper.'

'It takes one to know one.'

'I'm a retired officer of Her Majesty the Queen. We don't deal in drugs, or thievery, or kidnapping. In my retirement, I don't conspire new schemes of criminality.' He decided to play the Brideshead card again. 'I dine with dukes and earls, converse with lords and ladies, and when I'm asked to rescue one of their daughters from seducing slimes like Stalker, I do it for the honour of the family. There's your choice, April. You can either stand with the aristocracy of England or you can slink away with a two-faced burglar who's robbed one drug gang and is cowering in the protection of another. You can stay with me and come up victorious—perhaps even an invitation to Buckingham Palace—or you can join Penelope and Stalker and sleep next to tequila-drunk banditos who would rape you as soon as rob you.'

April looked uncomfortable.

'He didn't tell you that part, did he? He didn't tell you that he's cowering for his miserable life with a violent Mexican drug gang. What do you think *they'll* make of Penelope? Stalker already gave them my goddaughter. I'm sure Penelope will be his next sacrifice to Moloch.'

'Who?'

'Canaanite fire god, my dear. Ate children and so on. Don't let it worry you.'

'Oh, Nigel, she didn't know! This is such a nightmare. I can't take it.'

'Yes, you can, my child. You can take it because we're taking it together. You have Penelope. I have my goddaughter. We both have a reason to smash him—and we will, just like we got those bloody Jamaicans.'

APRIL PEELED OFF THE FREEWAY and into the vast parking lot of a shopping mall. Nigel saw palm trees, red tile roofs, walls of white and flamingo pink stucco. But then she swung away from it and parked in front of a café advertising 'quality coffees from around the world'.

'What's this?'

'I never got any breakfast. Can't I at least have a latte and a muffin?' Her eyes were pleading.

'Oh, very well.' He shifted uncomfortably in his seat. He could use a stop anyway to get these damned pistols out of his waistband and into April's bag.

They sat at a table outside, Nigel's face buried in his *Sunday Telegraph*, his diaphragm breathing easier.

April fiddled with his *Private Eye* and picked up *The Jihad Journal-Picayune*.

'What can I get you?' *Smack*. Nigel looked up to see surly brown eyes in an unshaven face. The waiter wore a ponytail, and his hairy legs looked to Nigel like those of a spider. They were certainly far too exposed by his tight brown corduroy shorts and black hiking boots for this to be a reputable establishment. *And* he was chewing gum.

April said, 'I'd like a nonfat, decaf latte and a blueberry bagel.'

'And you, sir?'

'Tea, if you please. Strong and hot... Earl Grey is fine.' He could use a little caffeine to keep himself sharp. 'And do you have any buns, young man?'

'Yeah, and I've been told they're pretty good, but what d'ya wanna eat?' *Smack.*

Nigel glared at him in annoyance and confusion.

'How about a bran muffin?' the waiter suggested. 'They're really good for you. You know, fibre—good for your cholesterol.'

'Didn't I ask you for buns, young man?'

'I'm sorry. We don't have any.'

'But you just told me you did.'

'Sorry, just a joke.' *Smack.*

'A joke? What kind of joke is that?' he said, rattling his paper. 'Do you always joke with customers about the shortcomings of your restaurant? I mean to say, if I came in here and asked you for roast beef, suet pudding, and a Guinness, would you promise me all those things and then say—"Ha, ha, I'm sorry, we don't have any; care for a muffin, perhaps, very good for your health you know"?'

Smack, smack, smack. 'No.'

'Well, then, don't play smart with me. Bring me some tea—and be sharp about it. And I'll take one of your muffins, if that's all you have.'

'Thanks,' the waiter said, rolling his eyes, smacking his gum again, and snatching the menu from Nigel's hand.

'Impertinent prat.'

April flipped through *The Jihad Journal-Picayune*. She paused near the end. 'Nigel, what sign are you?'

Nigel merely growled and rattled his paper.

'I'm an Aries,' April told him. 'It says here, "You are entering an exciting and constructive period in your life. Turn your attention to helping your brothers and sisters in their struggle for empowerment against Whitey and the Jewish oppressors. This week you will enjoy quiet evenings at home with friends." That's weird.'

The waiter brought April her latte and bagel, and then returned with a teapot steeping Earl Grey and a small plate with a muffin stuck to it. He set it clattering on the table.

'The bastard,' Nigel muttered.

April clicked her tongue. 'The Bastard isn't a sign, Nigel. Do you mean Taurus, the Bull?'

'I mean our bastard waiter. This isn't a muffin. It's a volcanic growth sprinkled with tan ashes.' Nigel took a spoon and tapped the muffin suspiciously. 'I mean, this thing would bend a knife and fork.'

'It looks fine to me.'

He tore it apart with his fingers. It was warm and crumbly. And the taste? Acceptable, certainly. He poured himself a cup of tea. He'd had to make do with much worse in the past. He remembered that native chap who offered him grub worms in Katanga.

'What's that you're reading there?' Nigel said, putting aside his newspaper. She handed him *The Jihad Journal-Picayune*.

'It looks pretty stupid to me.'

He opened the paper and his eyes fell on the headline: 'OBEY THE LAW, BUT PUT YOUR TRUST IN BLACK JIHAD'. He read on, 'The Esteemed Iced Khalifa told an assembly of Black Jihad Initiates today that while they should obey the law, their real allegiance must be to Black Jihad. "For decades our people have suffered under the lash of slavery. Now the white folk and our own traitors to our race beat our people down with the deadly stinging whip of heroin and crack. Have the police protected us? No, they have not. They're fat and too busy protecting the white man's wealth. That is why WE must enforce the law in our communities and in our neighbourhoods. Where the police fear to go, Black Jihad will do their work.'"

Nigel heard the compelling snap of snare drums. He stood on a platform before the massed ranks of the King's African Rifles, standing at attention, presenting arms. He stepped down to inspect the men, walking slowly. This would be no cursory examination, but the real thing. It was good to keep the lads sharp. They might not be Gurkhas, or Sikhs for that matter, but one used the tools one was given. And these lads were certainly good enough to fight the bloody Mau-Mau.

But as he got closer to them, the uniforms changed, and suddenly he was facing lines of determined-looking black men with cropped haircuts, black-rimmed glasses, bow ties, and dark suits. Less colourful than the old chaps, but they also looked a good deal more sophisticated and intelligent. He stopped to adjust the handkerchief in a ranker's breast pocket and then said, 'Very good, Lieutenant, carry on.'

'Oh, so you think it's pretty good after all.'

Nigel noticed his fingers were playing with the crumbs of his muffin. 'Oh, yes, yes, delicious.' He rapidly flicked through the pages of the paper until he found the masthead and address of Black Jihad. 'April, old girl, do you mind fetching that street map in your car? I have our next stop.'

CHAPTER ELEVEN

A CALM CONFIDENCE—even a sense of excitement and anticipation—swept over Nigel. To be in command again! Now all the pieces were falling into place. With an army under his wing, he was unstoppable. Stalker would be strung up by morning—perhaps even hanging by his heels like Mussolini. Serve the bastard right. He could see him swinging in the gentle California breeze, Los Lobos Colorados taking baseball bats to pummel him like a piñata for getting them into so much trouble. Africans routinely desecrated corpses. He wasn't sure about Mexicans.

Now, of course, the only trick was to actually get the army—someone else's army. But that was a quibbling detail. Call an *indaba*, a few hours of negotiation, and it would all be settled. British officers like himself had made a profession of commanding other people's armies for generations, centuries even: Charles George 'Chinese' Gordon—a personal favourite—Billy Hicks, Valentine Baker. It was something they did exceedingly well (except for Billy Hicks). He wouldn't be denied his turn at being a mercenary commander. By hook or by crook, he'd be leading a Black Jihad by morning. And as a sort of swagger stick, he'd have an elegant black attaché case full of Alexandra's Trust money, a perfect bait to wave under the noses of Los Lobos Colorados. But bait was all it was. They'd never get the money. Plan B was formulating in his mind.

Screech! April roared ahead at another green light. Green, he thought—that's the colour of Islam, isn't it? He wondered what April would look like in one of those black tents Muslim women wore.

No, he didn't think he'd fancy that much. The veil might add a hint of mystery to her, but the black tent left too much to mystery. Now a belly dancer—that was more like it. That he could easily imagine. Or what about one of those Arabian Nights serving wenches dressed in a gauzy veil, a bright red vest, pyjama bottoms, and colourful slippers with curled up toes. Yes, he could see her as that too. Marriage was always on April's mind. He wondered how she'd take it if she were one of the four wives he was allowed under Islamic law. Who would the other three be? He wished he had a hookah to stimulate his meditation.

But look at her! Poor girl, he thought. She's nervous again—just as she had been when they'd rescued Penelope from the Jamaicans. At every stop one could see her pulse racing, her eyes fearful, as though she expected a violent rampage, a riot, a ghetto revolt targeting young white women in red Ford Tauruses. Even clumps of children crossing the street (he imagined school was over for the day) put her in a state of barely subdued panic, as though she expected them to come at her car with switchblades, slash her tyres, and set it on fire. Perhaps under normal circumstances they would have—but he was with her now. They wouldn't dare. And under Islamic law—which he'd soon be able to enforce, just as soon as he had his army of Bashi-Bazouks—he could have them all decapitated anyway.

When they'd found *The Jihad Journal-Picayune* address on the map, she'd said, 'Nigel, we can't go there. That's Watts. It's the ghetto.'

'So much the better. What policeman would think to look for us there?'

'But, Nigel, it's dangerous. It's full of Crips and Bloods and crime. I'd rather face the police.'

'Trust me, my dear, when this is over, the police are going to give you a medal. I've handled Africans before. I know the dangers they can pose. But not to worry. I know what I'm doing.'

He could tell she wasn't convinced, but he left her no alternative. He'd even, with a show of supreme confidence, disarmed himself—taking the stun gun from his pocket and adding it to the collection of pistols in her bag. It was also, of course, an act of prudence. He didn't want to be found carrying weapons if they were searched by the Esteemed Iced Khalifa's bodyguards. Might give the wrong impression. *Assassin* was an Arabic word, after all. It was something they thought about. Greeting Iced Khalifa with a gun in one's pocket was rather like entering a mosque with one's shoes on—and would no doubt be punished even more severely.

April turned down a tree-lined residential street. He recognised the name. This was where *The Jihad Journal-Picayune* was published.

She pulled up outside a large redbrick house, with an eight-foot-high crenellated wall running round it, making it look like a suburban castle. But the four identical, crop-haired, black-suited, bow-tied giants charging out of the gate didn't look like Frankish knights—more like twentieth-century Moors.

'Oh my God,' said April.

'Turn off the ignition!' Nigel commanded. He didn't want April fleeing like a frightened rabbit. Just because a bunch of Zulu ruffians in bow ties were yelling threatening obscenities and slamming on the bonnet—that was no reason to turn tail. He stepped out of the car.

'You can't park here!' one of them shouted, coming towards him like a walking freight train.

'I've come to see the Esteemed Iced Khalifa,' Nigel replied, drawing himself up.

They surrounded him like a gang of school prefects trying to intimidate the new boy, standing so close that their hot, snorting breath fluttered his hair.

'I think he'll want to see me. I'm General Nigel Haversham. Or I should say, Sir Nigel Haversham,' he lied. 'Haven't quite got used to the knighthood yet. I think I can offer the jihad a bit of help.'

'We don't need no help from no whitey.'

'Oh yes? Well, I hardly see the people of California quaking in their boots about your holy war. I hardly see the drug dealers frightened of Black Jihad. I hardly think, frankly, that you're making much impact at all. I've come here, respectfully, to have an audience with the Esteemed Iced Khalifa, because I have information that can help him change that. I'm coming as quite a high-level contact, in fact. I'm sure he'd like to know. Would you mind telling him?'

'What about her?'

'She's my California assistant. I'm English, you see, obviously new to L.A.'

'No kidding,' he snarled.

'I'm afraid I can't stand here all day. I have a busy schedule. And I must see the Esteemed Iced Khalifa at once, or the opportunity will pass him by.'

They scrummed in even closer, his head boxed in by their massive chests, his eyes compelled to stare at the starched white shirt in front of him. He was like an orange, he thought, about to be squeezed into jam—'Old Whitey Marmalade, the perfect way to eat white people in the morning.'

'Well?' Nigel demanded of the shirt.

The giants exchanged glances over his head. 'Wait here.'

It was an uncomfortable wait, his breath being smothered by the chests of the three remaining giants who stared down at him with fierce, brown eyes that looked like spear shafts behind their severe black-rimmed glasses. Their nostrils let loose a scorching wind that hit his eyelashes whenever he looked up.

He heard footsteps, and the scrum broke apart. 'Follow me.'

Nigel beckoned April to join him. 'I trust your men will watch our car.' He arched an eyebrow. 'I understand Watts is simply black with criminality.'

No reluctant smiles at a bad pun, no heated condemnations for bad taste, just impassive, matter-of-fact menace. Once you were white, it didn't matter what else you did. It was like a murderer trying to shock by stealing a lollipop, Nigel thought.

They were led through a gated archway onto a brief stone path flanked by lawns as close-cropped as the men's heads. The house was attractive, even English-looking, with neat arrangements of red, purple, and yellow flowers growing in plots beneath the windows. The front door was white, with a large, black knocker in the shape of a fist.

He didn't see much after that. They were swallowed by a phalanx of bodyguards. It was just a matter of following along where they marched. They halted so suddenly that Nigel bumped into the chap in front of him—something he couldn't remember doing in even his greenest days at Sandhurst. Nor at Sandhurst had he ever been goosed by a girl accidentally bumping into him from behind—not, that is, if he ignored 'Nancy' Cartwright, about whom none of his fellow cadets had been *quite* sure.

'Whoo! Sorry, Nigel.'

The bodyguards peeled away, layer by layer, until Nigel stood exposed, April behind him, in a room full of decorative columns, imitation Egyptian relics, tall bending lamps decked out with ostrich feathers, and deeply upholstered maroon leather armchairs with leopard skins thrown over them. Nigel appreciated the leopard skins. They helped him imagine he was standing where only Allan Quatermain had stood before.

From the room's huge French windows he could see a large back-yard as carefully tended as the front. Ivy covered the brick walls, and crop-haired men in black suits and bow ties patrolled constantly, walking with their hands behind their backs. He turned and saw two others standing behind him.

'General *Sir* Nigel Haversham,' said the man from *The Jihad Journal-Picayune*'s advertisement for AFRO-VITA-PACK, rising from a deeply upholstered chair. Behind him was a handsome bookshelf lined with expensive volumes held in place by busts of Beethoven, Shakespeare, Napoleon, Alexander the Great, Lincoln. 'Welcome,' he spread his arms wide and then extended his hand to a leopard-skin-covered armchair. 'Please take a seat.' With his dark-rimmed glasses and voice of deep formality, he could easily have been mistaken for an extremely sober and frightening schoolmaster—the sort that took pleasure in humiliating children.

'As for her,' he said with his eyes never leaving Nigel, but with the back of his hand waving dismissively at April, 'I don't believe she needs to be with us.'

But Nigel, like Lord Macartney at the Chinese Imperial Court, refused to kowtow. 'No, I'm afraid she does actually. She's my California guide and aide-de-camp. Assists me with everything.'

Iced Khalifa smiled sourly and pointed to another leopard-skin-covered armchair. 'Sit here.'

April sat—at first primly, but finding the chair comfortable, she curled up in it.

'To what do I owe this privilege, General *Sir* Nigel Haversham?'

'Well, I've been reading about you, Mr Khalifa,' said Nigel, wanting to cross his legs but unwilling to risk it over the leopard's head, 'and it appears we share a common interest in fighting the drug trade...'

'What regiment are you from?' he interrupted fiercely, lunging forward in his seat.

'Lately of the Guards, but officially I'm retired.'

'Who is the prime minister of Britain?'

'At present, we suffer under the Protectorate of Tony Blair.'

'Where is the city of Edinburgh?' He said it with a hard 'g', like Hamburg.

'Scotland.'

'Your Queen, is she Queen Elizabeth the first, second, or third?'

'Second.' Nigel felt like a batsman going for a century. Go on, try another googly.

Iced Khalifa smiled. 'You will excuse me, General. A brief test to make sure you are who you claim to be. You are indeed an Englishman. There are many who would wish to destroy me. Fortunately, your gracious queen is not among them.'

'No indeed, she has always been very fond of the dark... that is, of the dark people of the Commonwealth.'

'You say we are allies in the jihad against drugs. I don't recall our being allies. I have formed no alliances with any white men that I can remember. And why should I? White men don't concern me—except as the historic oppressors of my race.'

'But the men on your bookshelf...'

'I can learn from my enemies. I can learn how to overthrow them. Just as those supposed white men stole from my ancestors. Where would Beethoven have been if it hadn't been for the music of Ali de Khalil, now regrettably lost because of Beethoven's incendiary jealousy, burning all the manuscripts? You see Alexander—an Egyptian, attempting to spread the wisdom of blackness throughout the world. Sheik Speare, of whom your countrymen are so proud, a native of Libya. Lincoln? He feared us and wanted all black men returned to Africa so we would not rise up and dominate this country as we had previously dominated the world. I don't blame you, General *Sir* Nigel Haversham, for your ignorance. You were poorly taught in school. All white people have been brainwashed, fed lies so that they can sit comfortably, fat, easy with their consciences. But I have written several pamphlets, which I will gladly give you, proving that civilisation was born among the black peoples of Egypt and brutally stolen by marauding whites—just as you have continued to steal our women, our dignity, our rights. So perhaps you will concede, General *Sir* Nigel Haversham, that it is impossible for us to wage the same jihad, because we have different objectives in this war.'

'Oh, I don't know,' Nigel said, shifting to keep the leopard's head from impaling his trousers with its teeth. 'It's true I'm not overly keen on the destruction of the white race. But in this case I think it's irrelevant.'

Iced Khalifa's voice boomed with humourless laughter. 'My dear General, how can the very purpose of a jihad be irrelevant?'

'Because together we can smash a *white* drug dealer—put him out of business, permanently. Together, we can intercept and destroy an enormous drug shipment that's targeted at *your* people.'

Iced Khalifa picked up an African horsetail flyswatter and, like some latter-day Prester John, began swinging it languidly at his shoulders. 'Why is this an interest of yours?'

'I have my instructions. But you should know also, on a personal note, he's kidnapped my goddaughter.'

'Nigel...' reminded April.

'As well as a colleague of my aide-de-camp.'

Iced Khalifa twisted his lips and brushed April's friend aside. His eyes bore into Nigel. 'Whose instructions?'

'I'm afraid that's a secret.'

'Then why should I help you? I have no interest in solving your personal problems.'

'I can give Black Jihad what it lacks—professional military leadership—as I've been ordered to do. And I can provide you with a tangible, real example of what can be achieved with trained men, properly led. I can give you the spoils of war: one major drug shipment derailed, one vicious white drug dealer made an example of.'

'You want to train my men?' Iced Khalifa said, shocked out of his feigned indifference.

'Of course. It's essential. But there isn't much time.'

'To do what—precisely?'

'To obey my orders in a sophisticated covert operation. And I've told you the rest already. Our objective is to destroy a drug gang.'

'And how is your goddaughter involved?'

'We'll rescue her in the process.'

'Is she also a dealer in death?'

'For your information, she works in London as a foster mother for black children whose parents are drug addicts. She was kidnapped for that very reason. She's to be an object lesson so that others will be too frightened to fight the drug trade.'

Nigel thought: that should put the chill back on Iced Khalifa. The Esteemed One flicked his flyswatter a few times. Then he said, 'You haven't contacted the police?'

'We're not giving these terrorists the publicity they crave. My orders are to be discreet and effective. That's why we're working outside traditional channels. That's why I'm here. We're seeking higher justice.'

'Is there a ransom demand?'

'We won't pay it. We don't deal with vermin.'

'And a reward?'

'Not officially.'

'But unofficially?'

'Unofficially… for now, I'll have to leave you guessing.'

'You sound like a liar.'

'On the contrary, if I were lying I'd have all these gaps filled. The truth is, I'm bound by orders to reveal only so much.'

'You're laying an incompetent trap.'

'For whom? For the drug dealers, yes, we're laying a trap, but hardly an incompetent one. They didn't order an amateur here, they ordered a professional soldier—and one of rather distinguished rank, if I do say so myself. My other orders are to shield you from risk. You're not to be involved personally. I'm to ask for the assistance of only a few of your men—a half dozen should be sufficient—because you see, there are *some* white people who value what you're doing and admire you for it.'

That one stung him, Nigel thought, like a good, swift jab on the nose.

Iced Khalifa put his hands together as in prayer and pondered the ceiling for a dramatic minute. It was wall-papered, Nigel noticed, with an image of the Sphinx illuminated by starlight. Iced Khalifa waved his flyswatter. 'It is becoming clear to me,' he said at last, lowering his eyes to Nigel. 'Your goddaughter is an aristocrat?'

'One of the oldest families in England.'

His eyes weighed heavily on Nigel, like the eyes of a schoolmaster preparing his *coup de main* for an overly clever student. His voice was grave. 'Has the Queen sent you personally?'

God bless egotistical madmen, Nigel thought. He couldn't help grinning, but he tried to make his grin conspiratorial. 'I'm not allowed to say, officially. But some might find it an interesting coincidence that I was knighted just before I came to California—in a private ceremony.'

Iced Khalifa nodded and bounced his fingertips off each other, cogitating. 'You're on Her Majesty's secret service then, is that right?'

Nigel paused carefully before he said, 'You could say that.'

'Then this is a matter of state, *and of official government contact with Black Jihad!*' he said, shooting forward in his chair, waving his flyswatter frantically. Nigel did his best to look shocked. A smile came over Iced Khalifa. 'You don't need to confirm that. You already have. Yes, I have tricked you, Sir Haversham, and now it is all very clear.' He stood and paced to look out of the French windows. 'Just another symbol of the white man's decadence that now they must come to their scorned slaves for deliverance. Tell me more.'

'There's nothing more to say,' Nigel said, trying to look dejected, as though all his secrets had been winkled out of him.

'You make a very poor salesman, Sir Haversham. You obviously never sold encyclopedias door to door, as I did. The white man who gave me that job made a great mistake, because I read them too. That gave me the beginning of knowledge, which is power.'

'May I have your answer?'

'You want six men when?'

'Now, if you can manage it.'

'You, Sir Haversham,' said Iced Khalifa, pointing his flyswatter at Nigel, 'are an arrogant white man. Now is impossible. And no decent person would ask it. Surely your Queen would not take offence if I took a day of thought and prayer to consider this... this favour that you ask—this favour that Black Jihad must perform for the nation of Great Britain.'

'I must remind you that time is of the essence. The drug shipment is coming soon. If you had a daughter of your own...'

'I do have a daughter of my own!' he thundered, seizing a framed photograph off a table and thrusting it at Nigel. 'Jihad Golightly, the pride of my existence, the reason for my struggle, my hope for the future.'

Nigel admired the rather homely girl in the photograph.

'Well then, you can understand the urgency...'

'When is the shipment coming?' he interrupted.

'A matter of days.'

'When do I get my men back?'

'Immediately—and that's all I can tell you. You must tell me yes or no. We can't afford delay.'

'Where can you be reached?'

'April, give the man your telephone number... Go on, dear, give it to him.'

Iced Khalifa's eyes peered over the black rims of his spectacles at Nigel. 'You'll be at this number? You'll answer the phone?'

Nigel nodded. 'Yes.'

'Then I will call myself. I'm paying you an honour, General. I shall expect to be honoured in return. In the meantime, may Allah be with you.'

'And also with you,' Nigel recited catechistically, then wondered if it was appropriate.

'Merciless Mustapha will show you out.'

CHAPTER TWELVE

'**WHY'D YOU MAKE ME** give that totally scary guy my home phone number?' April whined in the car. 'I mean, God, Nigel, now I'll have to get it changed. I don't want to be called by a bunch of scary-looking black men.'

'Where do you think we're spending the night, old girl?'

'You're the general, you tell me.'

'I am telling you. We're staying at your flat.'

'But, Nigel, we can't. We're on the run from the police, remember? Duh!'

'Think about it. I certainly have been. It makes perfect sense. The police don't know who you are, so they won't track you there. I even gave them a false name for you, remember? The Jamaicans don't know who you are, so you're safe from them. And if Penelope turns up with Stalker, so much the better—though, to be honest, my dear, I imagine Stalker already has her chained by the ankle and sweating nervously over a huge cauldron of beans for Los Lobos Colorados.'

'Oh, Nigel, don't say that.'

'I don't say it to frighten you, my dear. Alexandra's probably chained right beside her.'

'I wonder if they're sharing Ecstasy?'

'*What*?' Nigel bellowed.

'Sean offered us some. I'm not really into drugs, so I didn't take any, but, you know, Pen's more open-minded, and she kinda likes Ecstasy. He gave her a handful for her purse.'

'What, heaven help me, is Ecstasy?'

'It's, like, only one of the most popular drugs around, Nigel. People take it at parties. It's supposed to make you tingly and, you know, experience new things with your body.'

Good Lord! Nigel saw an endless string of beautiful women, addicts all, skipping gaily behind the dimpled, dark-haired Pied Piper of Ecstasy. 'Jolly decent of him to offer, I'm sure.'

'Oh, yeah, it was. I mean, Pen's gotta be impressed. It's gotta be expensive.'

'Oh, yes, undoubtedly.'

'But, fer sure, it's good for business too. You know, like a trial sample. So they've got that in common too—like they're both business minds. They're kinda logical thinkers. Not like you, Nigel.'

Logical thinkers? Sean Stupid and Penelope Pinbrain? You must be joking. *He had a sudden, terrible vision of himself dressed as a Sudanese, an imam even, sitting on a Persian rug with the Esteemed Iced Khalifa ready to impose the sharia law upon Penelope and April. 'You have committed the crime of Ecstasy. Therefore you shall be banished to the custody of the Reverend Ian Paisley, where you will never find it again.'*

Nigel shook his head, dismissing the thought, unworthy and

unsound. One wasn't a bloody ayatollah, after all. One was an officer of janissaries—or soon would be, at any rate.

He saw himself standing before the tall, shaven-headed men of Haversham's Own Islamic African Pistols. Oh, it was just too marvellous. Glubb Pasha, poor sod, was stuck in dusty old Jordan. But Nigel Haversham, that esteemed Brigadier, ran a bloody private army in the wilds of California—with sunny beaches, beautiful women...

'I say, April, isn't there wine country around here? Isn't California quite good at wine?'

'Oh, yeah, but that's all up north—in Napa, Sonoma.'

Sunny beaches, beautiful women, splendid wine... What if he marched the lads north, to sample a few of the finer vintages? Certainly the troops, being Mussulmen, couldn't imbibe, but he could offer them something else—glory, perhaps? It was not inconceivable, after all, given his leadership (think of Clive in India), that California could be theirs for the taking. It seemed a rather chaotic place, didn't it? Rather like the Far East in that regard—or like India. A few disciplined men, promising the people a firm but limited government, could pluck the entire state—like a grape (he hoped they had good reds here, he always preferred the reds)—annexing it for good Queen Bess the Second, Queen of the United Kingdom of Great Britain, Northern Ireland, and California. It would make up for us giving away Oregon after all, not to mention the Thirteen Colonies. Might have to toss a trinket to the Esteemed Iced Khalifa and make the state officially Islamic, but a small price to pay, certainly. If this didn't give England greater stature in the EU, nothing would.

The strains of 'Rule Britannia' soared in his ears. He saw himself being escorted in his whites and plumed cocked hat by a footman down a long corridor full of gold-framed mirrors and regal portraits.

'Brigadier General Nigel Haversham, Governor-General of California, your Majesty.'

'Come and sit down beside me, Nigel,' says the Queen, all smiles. 'We are very pleased with your fine accomplishments and wish to reward you in a very special way—a way that is made possible only by your unique constellation of qualities, which include steadfast loyalty to the crown and to our realm, which you have so generously expanded. We have come to deeply admire you, Nigel, as a subject and, especially, as a friend. Only you can help us in this matter. Only you have our trust and confidence to such a degree that we may ask this very special favour and grant this very special reward.

'As a Muslim, Nigel—a faith we know you chose only for reasons of state, and as Head of the Church of England, we forgive you—you are entitled to four wives. We know that you have already chosen two native Californian wives in Lady Penelope and Lady April. But we were wondering, Sir Nigel...' He noted the addition of the *'Sir'* and wondered breathlessly what it meant. *'We were wondering whether you would be so kind as to take the former Duchess of York off our hands'*—the Duke of Edinburgh appeared, escorting Fergie, who, to be honest, had always rather frightened him, and now, oh dear, it was so much worse, all freckled flesh and lipstick, so horribly close and under regal command—*'by making her your third and most esteemed wife?'*

'This is it, Nigel.'

'What?'

April said, 'That's my apartment complex, straight ahead.'

'Don't turn in yet. Go round. We need to make sure there's no one there.' He said it quickly, instinctively, but his eyes weren't focused on what was around him. His mind was still racing. Fergie! Fergie! Good

Lord! Rather than the Weight-Watching Duchess—whom he had always known was nothing but trouble, even before she impertinently poked his backside with her brolly at Ascot—why couldn't they have called on him in time to rescue that other, more worthy damsel, the People's Princess, before her horrible tragedy. He would have cured her of that 'People's' nonsense soon enough, and her ridiculous affairs.

He could see her now, though nearly blinded by her diamond tiara, her glittering white teeth, her warm, welcoming smile, as though this were the outcome she'd been struggling for all along.

'Nigel, at last!'

'Yes, old girl, glad you finally came to your senses.'

But no, that was only a dream. The grim reality was not heavenly Diana but the former, and formless, Duchess of York! His responsibility! Good God! It would be a political marriage—he saw that—but somehow, perhaps with a separate tent for her, pitched far away, he thought he could manage to be kind-hearted and merciful to his third wife, as Allah commanded. Perhaps she could attend to his camels, teach them proper dietary habits, write children's books for Arab orphans, find a way to ferment figs. His heart rattled his rib cage, his face felt flushed, his hands shook.

'Nigel, are you all right?'

'I'll be fine in a second, my child. It's the strain, you know. Too much thinking, pondering intricate questions of strategy, planning Penelope's rescue. Just drive round and we'll come in this time. Let me know if you see something suspicious. You can tell better than I.'

Her car came round again and Nigel saw a rather unimpressive, weather-beaten, sea green blockhouse two storeys tall. In large green script on the front wall it said *Beach... something Apartments.*

Whether it was Beachcomber, Beachfront, or some other Beach was impossible to tell, because April cut sharply and raced into the parking lot.

'I'm so glad to be home!' she exulted.

'Why?' was the first word that came to Nigel's mind. If she had a predilection for sea green concrete, he failed to share it. As an architectural type, he guessed, it could be classified as California Socialist Realist. He could see over and through a low-slung wall of Spanish arches, looking like a miniature Roman aqueduct, but painted sea green. Behind it, in a U-shape, was the two-storey blockhouse of flats. Planted in the center was a courtyard, which offered at least some redemption. Getting out of the car, Nigel was surprised by the din of constant traffic on the street.

He saw April gazing sadly at a white Mustang convertible sitting forlornly in a parking space. 'It's Penelope's,' she said. But he knew that.

They grabbed their bags and trudged through the courtyard, which was an atrocious patch of unkempt grass with, at its centre, an abstract, concrete statue of a surfer bent over a wave.

'Isn't it cool?' April said. 'Pen hates it, but I think it's neat how it looks like the wind is blowing all over?'

Nigel noticed that the surfer appeared to have been carved by a giant hair comb. The whole statue was sweeping rows of ridges. Nigel thought the surfer might make a very effective cheese-grater— ugly but utilitarian.

April led him up the stairs to the first-floor flat she shared with Penelope, overlooking the courtyard.

'It must be quite something to watch him when it rains,' Nigel said, envisioning cascading channels shooting off the statue.

'Oh, yeah, I suppose that'd be really cool, but I haven't noticed; and you know, it never rains in Southern California.' She added the last phrase liltingly, as though in imitation of a song.

April disappeared with her bag and Nigel dropped his and looked around the spartan sitting room. There was a flimsy bookshelf holding a television, video machine, stereo, and numerous framed photographs of April and Penelope. A few similar photographs were hung on the wall. There was a beaten-up, but serviceable, cloth-covered couch with a glass table in front of it, a few director's chairs, lamps, a small breakfast table off from the kitchen. They were the belongings of itinerant students.

April reappeared. 'I guess you can use Pen's room.'

At the end of the sitting room was a narrow corridor leading directly onto the loo, with bedrooms on either flank. April waved him to the bedroom on the left. It was the shambolic room of a spiteful child. The bedsheets were twisted in big messy knots, clothes were spilling out of wardrobes onto the floor, drawers were hanging open like insulting tongues sticking out of childish faces.

'Sorry it's such a mess. Pen doesn't clean up very often.'

He noticed an easel with a blank canvas in a corner of the room, and on the wall were a few sketches of young men, with a woman's hands always somewhere in view, either massaging a male head or resting on his broad shoulders.

Nigel waded through an ankle-deep marshland of slacks, skirts, blouses, and sweaters to get a closer look. 'These are quite good,' he said. At the very least, they were more than one would have expected. Up to now, Penelope seemed a woman destined perpetually to disappoint him.

But perhaps he just didn't understand her. Perhaps Penelope was right. Perhaps he was too judgmental. The morose recesses of the Scandinavian mind were an acknowledged mystery, after all. Hidden behind her apparent idiocy were probably deep fjords of unimaginably bleak depression. What gloomy thoughts motivated this outpouring of artistic expression, he wondered—pictures of men, where Penelope appeared only as red-painted fingernails. Perhaps it was a bitter sadness that polyandry wasn't practised in the West. She wanted so many men, but she couldn't have them all... or at least, she couldn't *marry* them all... at least not all at once.

And this led Nigel to some sober thinking of his own. Penelope's well-being was now his responsibility, and it was a heavy one. It had to weigh on every decision he made. He prayed that California's imminent conversion to Islam and polygamy wouldn't drive her to despair. He wondered if there were any Islamic handbooks on how to buck up a moping spouse. Then again, perhaps that's what harems were for. Perhaps they were what the Anglican churches were always offering—'a support group'.

'Oh, they're just her boyfriends,' April said. 'You wanna see my room?'

He thought it could hardly be as interesting, as revealing, as Penelope's. Even Penelope's mess was revealing. It was a painfully embarrassing illustration of how much she *needed* to be part of a harem. She *needed* to have little boy eunuchs to pick up after her, make her bed for her, put the toothpaste on the brush for her. He was sure she squeezed toothpaste tubes from the middle.

April's room did provide a shock in a way. It was comparatively neat and orderly. He was not terribly surprised to see wedding and fashion magazines stacked by her bed. What did surprise him were the framed photographs of sports cars with fashion models in bikinis standing next to them.

'Racing cars, eh? Interest of yours?'

'Oh, it's not the cars, Nigel, it's me! I used to model at car shows.'

Did she really? Well then, these certainly merited a closer look. Goodness gracious! It was amazing how much one saw when one had a polite opportunity to stare. Such exquisite lines. Built for speed. There was not a shadow of a doubt—Penelope's moral fibre simply must be strengthened, because Islam was irresistibly on the way.

But just as he was imagining April's dance of the Lotus Super Seven Veils, a far different sort of music from the squealing pipes of Arabia came to his ears. It was like an insistent whisper through the walls. It even had a nostalgic sound. He knew he'd heard it before— often even—here on the streets of L.A. But what was it? *Puh dum-dum clang, puh dum-dum clang, puh dum-dum clang.* 'Shh,' he said. 'Listen.'

He led April to the window overlooking the courtyard and, beyond that, the parking lot. *Puh dum-dum clang, puh dum-dum clang, puh dum-dum clang.*

'Oh my God!' said April. 'It's them!'

So it was. Montezuma's revenge, Nigel thought—a Marlon-Brando T-shirted, dark-glassed, goateed, mocha-coloured army oozing like larvae from their long, low-slung cars that throbbed like insects laying eggs: Los Lobos Colorados.

They were noisy like insects too, chattering like cicadas, but with no fear of being watched. Extremely careless, egocentric, posing like young toughs for each other's benefit—Nigel was singularly unimpressed. With two guardsmen he could wipe the floor with them. They obviously had no discipline, no organisation, no training at all. And there, emerging like dirt from a straining insect, was their would-be leader, Stalker, pulling Penelope out of a car.

'Oh my God, Nigel, what're we going to do?'

Puh dum-dum clang, puh dum-dum clang, puh dum-dum clang.

He tried to think his way calmly through the possibilities, but the incessant rhythm cut through his mind like a tolling doom—*puh dum-dum clang, puh dum-dum clang, puh dum-dum clang.* They were starting to drift across the courtyard now, and he watched them, as an American farmer watches a dark, buzzing cloud of locusts. To his immense surprise, they sounded like readers of Conan Doyle. He could have sworn he heard them calling to each other, 'Hey, Holmes!'

Puh dum-dum clang, puh dum-dum clang, puh dum-dum clang.

No use being creative. There was only one thing for it. 'We've got to hide.'

'Where?'

'No attic?'

April shook her head.

'All right then, Penelope's wardrobe.'

'You want to dress up?'

'No! To hide! Where she keeps her clothes! Come on!'

They ran into the bedroom, Nigel bending to scoop two loads of dirty clothes to stack at their feet. April tore the hangers apart and they plunged in behind them. She slid the wardrobe doors shut and slammed the hangers together. Darkness. Both their hearts were pounding. But Nigel felt an odd sort of calm. He'd been trained for moments like this. He knew what to do. His job was important. He was protecting the beautiful young girl at his side who was giving out little gasps as her breathing kept tempo with the now very faint *puh dum-dum clang, puh dum-dum clang, puh dum-dum clang.* And there was something else—the swaddling comfort of silk and cotton flush against him; the faint, familiar scent of perfume, alcohol, and tobacco. It didn't feel like danger. It felt like a game, fondly remembered from childhood.

The front door snapped open, and strange, raucous voices—not at all like Nanny Carey's—drove into the flat. They sounded like bulls being driven into a pen, with violent snorting and stamping that got louder and louder, like knives stabbing in the dark, closer and closer.

Penelope called to April. Her voice quavered from the stress of trying to sound normal. 'April? April?'

'Hey, any beers in the fridge, Holmes?'

'You're sure that was her car?' It was the loathsome Stalker. 'Let's look in her room.'

The roaring bulls were driven closer.

'Not many, man. Here.'

'That's her suitcase,' said Penelope. 'Maybe she went out.'

Stalker grunted. Nigel could feel his eyes moving into Penelope's room, focusing on the wardrobe. 'Do you need anything in here?'

'Don't go in there.'

'What's the matter?'

'It's private.'

'All right, then, grab the suitcase and let's go. We don't need her.'

The bulls crashed into the door jamb. 'Bingo, man.'

'Hey, Holmes, check it out!'

'Hey, hey, lingerie for your collection, Holmes!'

'Please leave my things alone.'

'Hey, I like it. Frilly pink, man. How 'bout I wear it on my head?'

'Badge of honour, man.'

'Sean, stop them!'

'We'd better go.'

'But we just got here, man, just opened the brews. She got any videos, Holmes?'

He heard a cupboard swing open in the kitchen. 'We got food, man.'

'It's not safe here,' said Stalker.

'Not safe? Who's going to challenge us, man?'

A bull bumped into the doors of the wardrobe. Nigel covered April's hand in comfort and felt his neck tingling. He made a fist.

'Ah, here we go, man! Look at this. Like this is unbelievable, man. Your woman—she's got the gozangas, man!' The laughter was loud, but it was moving away.

'Time to roll, Holmes.'

'But we just got here, man.'

'Time to roll.'

He could hear men grumbling, but it was punctuated by laughter. The voices faded, like dirty bathwater down a drain, and the door closed.

'Oh my God,' April whispered with relief.

Nigel hesitated for a moment, then jerked the hangers apart, flung the sliding door open, and was out, moving quickly to the window. He saw Stalker pushing Penelope into a car. The others were drifting into their cars, casually, engaging in horseplay. He instinctively reached for the gun in his pocket. It wasn't there. As Stalker lifted April's bag into the boot of the car, a sudden bolt of recognition shot through Nigel's brain like a stroke. Stalker was walking off with his entire armoury.

CHAPTER THIRTEEN

SANS PISTOLS, SANS STUN GUN, *sans* Penelope, *sans* Alexandra, *sans* everything, and that was not even to mention that he was still *sans* Alexandra's Trust money or instructions as to where to deliver it. Nigel sat on the couch rubbing his palms against his eyes in exhaustion and vexation. Twilight drifted through the window. He thought of the carved surfer threading his way through the darkness, alone, buffeted by wind and waves, fish flying out of the water, filleting themselves against his cheese-grater body. Unlike the surfer, Nigel could take comfort in that he was not quite alone. He still had his aide-de-camp. He still had her tested steadiness, her transport and knowledge of the area, her warm and comforting voice.

'I feel like I've been violated,' April said from the kitchen.

'What?'

'Stealing our beers! I can't believe Penelope's done this! She hates Mexicans! And my suitcase! And my clothes! My clothes!' She stopped suddenly and looked at her watch. 'Oh my God!' She stood before Nigel, knees bent, one hand waving at him like a signalman, the other on her cheek. 'Nigel, if we leave now, we can make it to the mall!'

He looked at her gloomily. 'Surely they don't sell guns at the mall. And anyway, it's too late. We can't afford the time or the police background checks—isn't that part of the routine?'

'Not guns, Nigel. We need to replace my clothes. And we need dinner. They stole our chips and salsa.'

APRIL DROVE AND NIGEL BROODED. He thought of his contemporaries. Some were still serving, rising to high command and even higher paper-pushing. Others were retired and tending their gardens in Kent or Somerset, or leading local sporting committees, or working for the church, or forming associations to guard threatened national treasures—like the Army. But none, he was quite sure, was at this moment being driven to a mall to look at women's clothes by a delectable twentysomething who was also serving as one's ADC in a single-handed fight against Jamaican drug gangs, Mexican drug gangs, and a drug-dealing kidnapper. Nor were many of his colleagues likely to be wanted by the police or attempting to secure alliances with black fascist Muslims. But it's a funny old world, isn't it?

Somehow he'd never imagined this—not even when he'd taken his assignment from Pandora. He'd thought it would be just another odd scrap in a career of odd scraps, which had taken him everywhere from Cyprus to Aden to Rhodesia to a dozen other places, taking down the flag as decently as possible. He had to admit, it had been a sad career, in a way. Very sad. What others had built, he was ordered to consign to mothballs. The Union Jack down. The other bugger's pennant hoisted high. And then, of course, one was ordered to stay on, sometimes openly or often in furtive assignments, working behind the scenes to keep tottering native governments from collapsing to even worse buggers. It was almost shameful to confess that he'd found so much of his work so exhilarating. Personally, it had given him a splendid opportunity not only to soldier but also to be an unofficial diplomat and secret agent. Sometimes he went so far undercover as to conduct a foreign policy of his own, without the knowledge of Her Majesty's Government, advising the likes of Mad Mike Hoare in the Congo and Ian Smith in Rhodesia—adventures that could easily have cost him his career. And then there were the official assignments to the end of the world—like the South Atlantic. 'For God's sake, Nigel,' Maggie Thatcher had said to him. 'Get out to the Falklands, will you, or our boys will never get home.' He pitied the poor chaps now. Nothing like it.

And now... now he was watching April try on a bright yellow sweater, a saleswoman fluttering around her like a butterfly. 'That looks so great on you. Yellow is so flattering to brunettes. With blondes there's too much of a clash, but with brunettes it really gives you highlights.'

'You really like it on me?'

'Oh, yes. It's definitely you.'

'What do you think, Nigel?'

He banished thoughts of Aden, of derring-do in the ancient, narrow Arab streets, of invigorating recces in the furnace heat of the endless desert. Do yellow sweaters really flatter brunettes? That was the question to engage his faculties now. 'Oh, yes, I daresay, splendid, child, splendid.' He patted the pink blouse with frills down the front that was resting on a small stack of clothes on his knee. Beneath it was a red sweater ('basic,' she said, 'but Pen's stolen my other one'), a white sweater with big blue and orange stripes across the middle ('it'll be good for sailing, in case we have to do an ocean rescue'), a form-fitting purple dress with a narrow waist ('in case we need to go out at night; I think this is conservative enough to go anywhere, don't you?'), and two pairs of pumps (one had black and white stripes like a zebra, the other looked like the golden slippers of a prized concubine from the court of Kublai Khan).

'Do you think that's enough? Well, I guess it is for now. We can always come back later,' April said happily.

Nigel reached for his wallet, but April's hand stopped him halfway.

'Oh, no, Nigel. I'll put it on my credit card. That way my parents'll pay.'

Well, that was something of a relief. For a low-intensity conflict, this certainly hadn't been a low-cost one. And for all the money he had spent thus far he had terribly little to show for it—except perhaps a warrant for his arrest and a second hostage to be rescued. Hardly an admirable accounting. It shouldn't be this difficult, he thought. He'd been behind enemy lines before, capturing enemy soldiers, bringing them back for interrogation. But perhaps this latest fiasco with the guns was just a bit of bad luck, that's all. Given the circumstances, he'd have been jolly lucky to prevent it. And it wasn't fatal. The black chaps in bow ties might fall in behind him. And even if they didn't, he didn't require superiority in weaponry. He'd never counted on that. He knew he could succeed by superior strategy. It was all a matter of brain power and faultless execution, which he should be able to guarantee. That was his job, wasn't it?

'Are you hungry? I'm starved,' April said. Nigel looked soberly at his ADC, who seemed blissfully untroubled, setting a better example than he was. 'It'll be my treat. I've got a surprise for you.'

APRIL BOUNCED ON HER TOES before the rustic, heavy wooden doors—hinged with massive, decorative black steel—of the Goblet and the Cleaver. Inside was a world of darkness lit by rubicund joy. Stout young waiters who looked as though they spent their weekends wrestling on the village green rushed by, decorative cleavers gripped at their waists by wide leather belts. Buxom wenches with masses of hair framing busts that exploded like blossoms out of narrow waists navigated the darkness bearing drinks and looking like ships' figureheads. All around came a crowding din of laughter deepened by ale. Walking past the bar, one almost expected to be crushed against the wall by G. K. Chesterton, with foam dripping from his moustache, saying, 'It's all a problem of usury—which is nothing but use, as in abuse, and misery,' or a swashbuckler (somehow he imagined him as Stewart Granger) dressed in shining black boots rising over the knee, a ruffled shirt unbuttoned to cool the sweat off his massive chest, hot from talk, laughter, alcohol, and flirting with the wenches. 'Nigel, you vicious old landsman,' he'd say, slapping him on the back, his huge forearms looking tanned from his recent foray sinking Spanish ships in the Caribbean, 'when will you sail with me and take a whack at Cartagena?'

'Like it, Nigel?' April asked.

'Glorious.'

A long, hot loaf of crusty bread with a knife plunged through its heart and a huge, sloppy scoop of warm butter moored alongside came to their table on a wooden cutting board. It was almost enough to make him look away from their waitress, whose bodice supported what he was sure Captain Granger would have regarded as two new worlds to conquer.

'Can I get you anything from the bar?'

Yes, Nigel thought, a few more wenches like you, endless tankards of ale, more men like Captain Granger...

'I'd like a Redtail Ale,' said April.

Ale for April? She was certainly getting into the spirit of things. He'd yearned for a scotch and soda, but now he wondered whether rum wasn't more appropriate. 'I'll have a very large rum.'

'Rum and...?'

'Straight, in a large glass. Oh, maybe a splash or two of soda to protect my stomach.'

'Gee, Nigel. Are you celebrating or something?' asked April.

'No, my dear. Drowning my sorrows more likely.'

'What's the matter? There's no reason to be sad. I got really good deals. And at the cash register I started wondering out loud, you know, "Do I really need this red sweater", and she practically threw it in for free.'

'Oh, well, everything's all right then.'

'Sure it is. You've just got to relax. I've noticed that about you. It's amazing you've lived as long as you have. You know, your colour's not very good. You're always turning red. You've really got to watch your temper.'

'Anything else?'

'You eat too much red meat and you drink too much.'

'I see.'

'But you're not fat. In fact, Nigel, if you didn't drink so much and get stressed all the time, you'd actually be in great shape.'

'Thank you.'

'But you ought to try Tai Chi—Penelope's father teaches a class on that, you know, at the beach, and it's low-impact, which is good if you're old. Or you can try plain old aerobics. It's great for hypertension, and they have plenty of classes for people your age.'

'Do they?'

'Oh, yeah. I think they're pretty popular, too.'

'Fascinating. But you know, April, my mind was really rather focused on something else.'

'What?'

'Well, take Penelope for instance.'

'You're worried about Pen?'

'Among other things.'

'You don't have to worry about her. Pen always gets away with everything.' Nigel was dumbfounded and must have looked it, because April explained. 'She has a way with guys. And with her parents too. I mean, like, she's always broke, and some guy will always come up and buy her things, and then if that doesn't work out, she cries and calls home and her mom, who's a doctor, not practising, you know, but she gives advice and stuff to kids, well, anyway, she counsels her and stuff, and her dad, who's in construction and so he's always tan and he's muscular, a really big guy, really tough, with a beard and everything, and he owns the company, so he's got money, and if she gets in bigger trouble, he always comes in and takes care of things. Pen doesn't really like him as much, because, you know, the macho thing bugs her, but, I mean, like, he's pretty awesome.'

'But April, she's held by a Mexican drug gang—a gang with guns, our guns too, by the way.'

'Oh yeah, I know. It's really bad. But, like, she does have Scan with her.'

Nigel rolled his eyes.

'And you know, the way I look at it, the guns don't matter anyway.' He remembered being counselled on strategy by Penelope at the
poolside. 'I mean, look at what you did last time. You were pretty
awesome yourself, Nigel.'

Well, yes, he had to concede that was true.

'And, like, tomorrow you're meeting with those terrible black
men, right? And who needs guns when you have them?' She smiled
triumphantly.

'Yes, but we don't necessarily have them yet.'

'Oh, sure you do. Anybody could tell by looking at that creep that
he thought you were hot stuff—with the Queen and everything. Is
that true, by the way?' Nigel's head bobbed, avoiding an affirmative
nod or a negative shake. 'And anyway, you haven't seen Penelope's
dad. If he finds out she's in trouble, he'll, like, freak. He has a big gun
collection and he's really tough. He goes hunting in Mexico all the
time.'

'In Mexico?' Nigel said. Mexico, like drug gangs, was a new interest of his.

'Yeah. I don't know much about it, but he goes every year. I went
with them once and ate something he shot—I can't remember what it
was: skinless buffalo or hairy pig or something. They made sausages
out of it, too, for breakfast.'

'Didn't Penelope say he was in Vietnam?'

'Oh, yeah. There's this great picture of him at their house. He's
like, with his shirt unbuttoned, holding his helmet on his hip, and you
can see he's got great arms and pecs. He's really handsome, Nigel.'

*Nigel heard the chopper blades and saw the trees and bushes
whipping round. He was led running across the landing zone by a
sergeant who turned him over to a young lieutenant. 'Colonel*

Haversham, sir? Lieutenant Parkinson, sir,' he shouted and saluted, as they both bent against the wind and the noise from the chopper. 'Follow me.' They trotted through a gate surrounded by floppy barbed wire and across a field of red dirt to a sandbagged briefing room.

'Hello, Colonel Haversham. My name is Captain Penelope's Father. Pleased you could join us, even if it's only as an observer.' He lowered his voice. 'I know it's against regulations, but how'd you like one of these?' he said, handing him an M-16 rifle. 'It can get a little hairy out there.'

Nigel took it and smiled. 'Jolly decent of you.' He held the rifle up to admire it. 'Not that I'll be needing it of course—but perhaps a little hunting?'

The Captain grinned. 'Whatever you want it for, it's yours.'

He led Nigel to a map posted on an easel. He slapped a pointer against it, and Nigel was amazed to see it transformed into a sketch of Stalker, with Alexandra standing behind, massaging his shoulders.

'He's a renegade. One of your boys. How he got here or why, I don't know. Maybe you can tell me. But he defected to the NVA. Now he's with the VC. We call him SSS. That stands for Skinless Stalker Swine.'

'That's one Redtail Ale and one large rum and soda.'

'Oh, yes, thank you very much,' Nigel said, and he wondered— could I have met Penelope's father in Vietnam? It would have been a Dickensian coincidence, but...

'Are you ready to order?'

The girl had a way of continually interrupting one's train of thought. Not that one minded of course. But when Nigel looked up he saw she was different from the one who had taken their drinks order. Not as pretty or American wholesome, but she looked exactly like Diana Dors, the British bombshell of the 1950s, which understandably warmed Nigel's heart because he'd once dreamt he'd had an affair with her. She was wearing too much makeup of course, but it was like meeting up with an old friend. 'Ah, yes, thank you for asking, dear girl. Two fillet steaks, please, medium, with baked potatoes and a carafe of your house cabernet.' Nigel had decided to order for April, as a gentleman, by rights, should—and as a guard against her ordering strange, exotic Californian hors d'oeuvres for him.

'You know,' Diana Dors said in her adopted California accent, a smile rising across her scarlet lips. 'I've just got to ask you—are you an actor?'

He was stunned for a moment. 'An actor?' Was Diana Dors about to offer him a role in her next romantic comedy, *A Serving Wench in America*? Was she merely slumming as a waitress, doing artistic research? Had he just been discovered—like Lana Turner in a soda pop shop? 'Why,' he said, 'I was just wondering if you were an actress.'

'You're kidding.'

'No, not at all. You are one, aren't you? I mean to say, you simply must be Diana Dors's daughter.'

'Who?'

'Diana Dors.'

'Sorry. Never heard of her.'

But you must have heard of her, he thought. Just now, when you shrugged your shoulders, blocking my view of your eyes—you *were* Diana Dors.

'Now it's my turn,' she said gamely.

'Don't tell me,' he said. 'Dirk Bogarde.'

'Is that your name?'

'Everyone tells me that.'

'So I was right. You are that guy. "If you want real fish and chips / Don't go with the grease that drips / Come to British Healthy Sea / and we'll give you fish and chips naturally." ' She sang, attempting to mimic his voice.

'What?'

'That's you in the commercial, isn't it?'

'Grease that drips? Fish and chips?' He looked at her with ill-disguised dismay. Was there something wrong with her eyes? Did she suffer from some affliction that made Richard Todd look like a South American leper, Trevor Howard look like a Chinese fortune-teller, and Dirk Bogarde look like a salesman for fish and chips? 'No, I'm afraid not. Don't have that much talent, I'm sure.'

'We get lots of actors in here. It's kinda fun to pick 'em out. What've you been in?'

'You mean to tell me you've never heard of either Dirk Bogarde or Diana Dors?'

'Sorry.' She shrugged her shoulders, blocking his view once more. Incredible—both the view and her ignorance, he thought.

'Have you been in any movies I might have heard of?' she asked, trying to be helpful.

'No, nothing you've seen, probably. Mostly stage work, you know. "Alas, poor Yorick", that sort of thing.'

'Never heard of it.'

'Pity,' he said. 'My finest work, really.'

'Wow. So you're an English stage actor.'

'Yes, that's it.'

'So you know Shakespeare.'

'Not personally, no. But I am told he wrote *Henry V* with me in mind.' That last might have been a fib too far. She looked at him doubtfully. To redeem himself he said, 'Why don't you get me another one of these?' His finger stirred the unwanted ice in his glass. 'And no ice, if you can manage it. Damn stuff just gets in the way, freezes your nose.'

'But you haven't drunk that one yet.'

'Oh, indeed I haven't. Well then, cheers.' He downed it in one protracted gulp (it was a large glass) and it burned all the way. A nice touch and impressive, but it also, he thought, made him something of a fire hazard. If someone lit a cigarette and he belched, he felt certain he'd set the whole restaurant ablaze. He knew he couldn't talk without gasping, so he merely handed her his glass, smiled, and waved.

'Wow, thanks,' she said.

He hoped she ascribed the tears welling in his eyes to a simple, natural, unimportant factor of age and not a sign that the rum was coming back up and spilling through his eyeballs. Thank goodness she smiled and sailed away. He gasped in relief and said to April in a voice that sounded like an awl grating against wood, 'Ah, refreshing.'

'I didn't know you were an actor,' she said excitedly.

Nigel coughed until his voice returned to some semblance of normality. 'Oh, really? I'll have to tell you about it sometime.'

'I mean, gosh, Nigel, what else have you done?'

'Oh, you know, the usual things—won countless wars, been decorated endless times for gallantry, and been mentioned in despatches so often they practically call the blasted things "Havershams" now.'

'Gee.'

'Yes, don't like to talk about it, of course. Mustn't let it all go to one's head. I remember Richard Burton—the actor, not the explorer—

telling me quite clearly, "Humility, Nigel, that's the key." And you know, my nickname used to be Monty, because I was such a dashing cross between Field Marshal Montgomery and Montgomery Clift.'

'Were they famous in olden times?'

'Yes, quite olden times, I suppose,' Nigel said with a look in his eye one usually reserved for when cannibals in the former Upper Volta described their culinary habits.

'I didn't know any of this.'

'Few people do. Need to keep my lives separate, you know. The theatre and the Army—hard to balance. It was a toss-up whether I'd get my K for services to Queen and Country or to the theatre. But still, I managed.' He tried to adopt a distant look, so he could avoid talking. He still tasted the rum, like a hot fist stuck in his chest. It passed before the waitress returned with his next dose of firewater.

'Here you go, rum and soda, with no ice. And I brought your carafe of wine.'

The rum was already working its magic in his bloodstream, and it led him to make one of those slips that happens when one is tired and drinking, and the mind, as if to compensate for the exhausted flaccidity of the body, takes on the role of the sensual, aesthetic critic. 'How terribly well-balanced you are.'

'I'm sorry?'

'I mean to say, what wonderfully great balance you have,' he said, recovering quickly, 'dashing about with all those drinks, never spilling a drop. Remarkable.'

'Well, thanks.'

'Not at all.'

It was odd, but it seemed his mind was funnelling music from a snake charmer's pipes and the insistent call of a muezzin into his ears. He could have sworn he heard a holy man singing out, *'Ni-gell al-Haff-eshem... Allah, blessings and peace be upon him, commands of you the sacrifice of one most blest. A fourth wife is given, a fourth wife you should with praise and thanks deceive.'*

Deceive? Surely, he thought, shouldn't that be *receive?* Or was deception essential in these matters? He couldn't be sure and felt terribly awkward, having, in his ethnocentric way, never created a harem before.

'You know, a girl with grace like yours really belongs in the theatre,' he said and reached into his pocket, extracting a pen and notebook. 'If you'll put your number there, I'll pass it along to my theatrical agent. I'm sure he could find work for a girl like you.'

'You really think so?' she said, taking up the pad and pen.

'Absolutely sure of it.'

But as she set to write her name, consternation hijacked the happiness from her face. Had she seen through him? Californians were entirely consumed by metaphysical mumbo-jumbo, weren't they? Through advanced powers of mental telepathy had she spied into his brain? Had she seen his dreams of Arabian nights?

'What the devil's the matter?' he asked.

She showed him the notebook. There was one entry on the page. JAMAICAN BASTARDS, it said, with a telephone number beneath.

'Oh, the Jamaican Bastards,' he laughed. 'You haven't heard of them? Wonderful performing troupe—simply hilarious. The whole bunch of them once performed the complete works of Shakespeare on unicycles. Amazing.'

'I can't believe I've never heard of them.'

'They're quite famous in England. Perhaps they never made it across the pond. Not all of us have the same transatlantic appeal, you know. But just go ahead and put your number there, my dear, and I'll make sure it gets into the right hands.'

'Thanks.'

She scribbled something and handed him the notebook. Her name was perfect, like that of a romantic female novelist, like Ouida or Baroness Orczy. 'What a marvellous name,' he said, 'Dixie Dorly.'

'You like it? It's kinda different. It's because mah parents,' she said, suddenly adopting a Southern drawl that had Nigel going weak at the knees, 'are frum thuh South, dahlin', from Loosyanna. They all moved back theah. But I,' she dropped the drawl, 'decided to stay herc, cuz, you know, I like it back there and all that, but, you know, with this job I meet such interesting people like you, and now look— like, you're giving me this great break.'

Nigel had a twinge of guilt. 'How about another one of these?' he said raising his still full glass.

She looked at him playfully, as though he were a cute but naughty child.

'Don't worry,' he said. 'It'll be gone by the time you get back.' As he watched her go, he felt completely seduced by her charms, her figure, her way with words. He unconsciously muttered, 'That's it, wife number four.'

'What did you say, Nigel?'

'Oh, I was saying, "Whatever is rum for?"'

'Coke, of course. I think it's really weird drinking it with soda. And how come you never tried to get me in the theatre? She's just a bimbo.'

'What? Oh, yes... usually only have small swigs... straight, of course. Tradition, you know... used to offer a tot to the men occasionally... and in the Navy...' But his voice faded as his mind fell headlong into the land of Scheherazade. *The strings of Rimsky-Korsakov rubbed an overwhelming melody into his ears and before him sprang a vision of She-Who-Is-Not-Diana-Dors's-Daughter. She ran towards him in petite little steps—lest she fall over—while the other dancing girls from the harem waved long ribbons of chiffon like pink waves. Dors the Lesser prostrated herself before him, then leaped up and began dancing. It was the sort of thing, he expected, that harem women made a habit of doing.*

Gazing to his left, he saw arrayed on three ornate, golden thrones (a fourth stood empty) Penelope, April, and the former Duchess of York (who, he noticed, gave him a stomach-turning smile and covert wink and wave).

So this is what it would be like, he thought, to be the California Khalif. A bit heavy on the blonde side, perhaps, with Penelope and La Dors versus April, but he could live with that, and Fergie's red hair was certainly different. The more serious problem was, would they get on together? His own problems were easily a third-tier consideration after the wishes of the Queen, of course, and the needs—the very important needs, one mustn't forget—of the girls. Wouldn't want any catfights or ugly scenes in public. If he was going to have to escort four notable women—notable, of course, because of their marriage to him—to state dinners, he would have to be able to trust them implicitly to be certain they would behave themselves. He wondered whether, as Governor-General of Islamic California, he would be required to dress as T. E. Lawrence did, wearing in his belt the curved sword of the Ashraf descendants of the Prophet. Wouldn't bother him, of course, childhood idol and all that, and he'd probably look dashed debonair in a burnous.

As he took a sip of the splendid California wine, his mind delved deeper into the problems of a possible Islamic California and its place within the United Kingdom. Chief among them would be to what extent sharia law would hold sway. It would have to be imposed in parts, he thought, not whole. In certain matters, strict accordance with English law would simply have to have superiority. He took a gulp of the immensely smooth California cabernet. For instance, it would be a great pity—inexcusable, in fact—to destroy the prized California wine industry. It would be like tearing down the Vatican—something he would certainly oppose during international Islamic conferences.

As Governor-General it would be his responsibility to strike the proper balance—taking four wives as a gesture of solidarity with his Islamic subjects, while continuing to drink California wine, British West Indian Rum, and single malt scotch whisky as a symbol of Imperial unity and tolerance for other faiths within British Islamic California.

He paused for a moment—but just a moment—to consider whether the Church of England would have any problem welcoming an Islamic British possession into the United Kingdom. But no, he thought, if they can swallow women priests, they can swallow anything. 'We need to be tolerant,' he heard the Archbishop of Canterbury intone as he consecrated Britain's annexation of Islamic California. 'There is room for everyone within the wide doors of our church. Guided by conscience and the Holy Spirit, we are free to choose what is best from every tradition, whether it be Druidic or Dharmic, Monophysitic or Muslim. It is, as Aristotle would have it, a matter of the mean, of balance. For how benefits a man, if he gain four wives, only to lose the fruit of the vine, the work of human hands, that symbolises for us our spiritual drink?' Dashed good point. He should like to hear the rest of that sermon.

'Here you go, another rum and soda. But it looks like you tricked me, you didn't finish your last one.'

'Oh, dreadfully sorry.' Dare he recommit his suicidal feat?

'You know, legally, I can't serve you two drinks at the same time.'

'Oh, can't you really? So much for chasers. Well then.' He gave her a sporting eye, lifted his glass, and prayed it wouldn't lead to an embarrassing, sick-making situation. Down it went. It burned too, but the furnace was already lit. It was merely fuel to the fire.

'Wow. You really are a great performer,' she said, and he modestly shrugged off all praise. 'I'll be right back with your steaks.'

'Did you drink a lot of rum in the Army?' April asked in admiration.

'Oh, did my bit, you know.' He paused to cough. 'Supposedly it insulated one from the cold, but I was almost invariably in the tropics—places like Hong Kong, Brunei, Kenya, Aden, and so forth— and so I tended to stick to scotch. You see, I had this theory, which the other officers shared, that it helped vaccinate one, as it were, against malaria. Great supplement for those awful pills they gave one.'

'So you've been all over the world?'

'Oh many times, many times. Really a sort of man of the place, you know.'

'Been there, done that.'

'Yes, that's one way of putting it.'

'Wow.'

'Yes, I frequently say that myself: Wow.' The 'o' sound compelled Nigel to stroke his moustaches. He was still stroking them, rakishly, when the waitress returned.

'Here you go, fil-lay for you and a fil-lay for you.'

'And a pretty little fil-lay yourself, aren't you?' The rum was making him gregarious, and he smiled in his best imitation of Captain Granger. But to his distress, he wasn't greeted by a wench's whoop of laughter, but by a disturbing glare of… he didn't know what exactly. Irritated ignorance? Feminist ferocity? Was it just his imagination or was she eyeing the restaurant for a lawyer? Americans were great ones for flinging about 'sexual harassment' suits, weren't they? Oh dear. He quickly tried to explain. 'You see, in England, we say fillet. I mean, fil-lay, that's sort of froggy, isn't it?'

Thank goodness April, in her two-fisted Americanness, burst in and saved the day. He could have kissed her. 'Well, in America, we say fil-lay—and you're in America, okay?'

'Oh, yes, quite, quite.'

'Will there be anything else?'

'No, no, I think not. Except perhaps afterwards. A postprandial drink, perhaps?'

'Well,' said Dixie Dorly, 'we have coffee and brandy, but I don't know if we have any postprandial.'

'I'm sure brandy will do fine.'

'Mmm. Isn't it good, Nigel?'

'You mean the wine? Oh, yes, superb. I've decided it will survive the Islamic conversion.'

'What?'

'I mean to say, it will survive without aspersion…'—that clearly wasn't good enough—'… and will live long in my heart.' He could easily have added: Like this infernal, combustible rum.

The carafe of wine was gone in a twinkling, and after he'd feasted on his unsurpassably excellent steak and thoroughly enjoyed his relaxing after-dinner brandy, he said with the renewed vigour of a happy man, 'Right, April, it's back to action. Time to visit the Captain of the Hunt for a little pig-sticking, what? Take me to Penelope's father.'

CHAPTER FOURTEEN

APRIL PULLED INTO THE BROAD concrete driveway of a large house in a suburban paradise of large houses. 'It's getting kinda late. Are you sure you want to do this?'

'Never too late to report a kidnapping, my dear. There are lights still burning. I'm sure he won't mind. There's a certain bond between old soldiers, you know.'

'Here, have one of these.' She handed him a breath mint from her handbag. 'They don't drink.'

'What's that have to do with me? I'm not going to press a brandy flask on them.'

'They don't like other people drinking, either.' She popped a mint into her own mouth. 'They don't know that Penelope drinks.' From what Nigel had seen that was hiding quite a lot. 'Or that she smokes.'

'I've never seen her smoke.'

'She smokes when she drinks. That's when most girls smoke. But she's kinda shy about it. She probably didn't feel comfortable with you yet. She needs to get to know you. She only smokes with people she trusts.'

'Oh, yes, I could see she was quite shy,' Nigel said, chomping on his mint.

'No, really, she is. People get fooled cuz she's with guys so much. But she's really shy.'

'I see. And most girls who take Ecstasy—do they do that only with people they really trust?'

'Like, Nigel, that's a totally different thing.'

'Of course,' Nigel said, stepping out of the car.

They walked up the driveway to the house, and April knocked on the door. A tall, powerfully built man opened it.

'Hi, April. I thought that was your car.'

He had steely blue eyes set a little too close together. Gunfighter eyes, Nigel thought, the sort one would expect on a Jesse James or a Billy the Kid. His beard—which, like his hair, was turning grey—added to his rustic, western look. The sleeves of his tartan flannel shirt were rolled up, revealing powerful hands and forearms streaked with black oil. He held a long screwdriver like a dagger. Could rip a chap from stem to sternum with that thing, Nigel thought. He could see him, thirty years younger, clean shaven, an American Green Beret or Navy Seal, camouflage black streaks on his face, rising out of the darkness of the jungle, those steel grip hands seizing a sentry's mouth and driving a dagger into his back. Even now, he didn't look like a man one should trifle with.

He pulled a handkerchief out of his trouser pocket and wiped off the blade and his hands, as if of blood. 'Pen with you?'

'No,' she said, looking embarrassed.

His eyes took in Nigel. 'You're too old to be April's boyfriend, so I suppose you must be her grandfather.'

Fearsome looks, but no intelligence officer, that's obvious. 'No, actually, I'm General Nigel Haversham.'

'*Sir* General Nigel Haversham,' April said eagerly.

The tall man's eyebrows arched back. 'Sir General Nigel Haversham.' He wiped his hands harder. 'Why don't you come in? It's getting a little cool out here.' He called out, 'Honey, company.' Then he said to Nigel, 'Go ahead and sit down. Oh, and my name's John Davison, by the way.' He extended a still greasy hand, and Nigel shook it gladly. The reek of motor oil was comforting, reminding him he was back in the company of men.

'So, you're an Englishman,' he said, continuing to wipe his hands. 'Just visiting the States?'

Nigel wondered how one tells a rather large and dangerous-looking chap, with a possibly lethal screwdriver in his hand, that his daughter's been kidnapped. He might jump to the conclusion that it was Nigel's fault. 'Yes, just visiting.'

'Hi, April.' Penelope's mother had come into the room, a handsome woman, her blonde hair done up in a bun. She wore half-lensed spectacles on a chain and looked like an intelligent, middle-aged, sensible female judge. Though Nigel had never met a female judge, he supposed that they must exist, and if they did, they would look precisely like this. Nigel couldn't help but wonder how her brains and her husband's brawn had produced such a beautiful featherbrain like Penelope. 'I'm Esther Davison. Can I get you a glass of water, orange juice, herbal tea? I'm afraid we don't drink tea or coffee.'

'Please don't bother. I'm perfectly fine, thank you. And the name is Nigel, Nigel Haversham.'

'April just told me it was *Sir* General Nigel Haversham,' Mr Davison told his wife, giving Nigel an appraising, sidelong glance.

'Oh?' Mrs Davison said. 'And how do you know April?'

Nigel noticed that Mr Davison still gripped the screwdriver like an assassin ready to strike. 'It's a long story. Would you like to sit down?' The parents exchanged glances.

'Well, all right,' said Mr Davison. 'If it'll make you feel more at home. I'm afraid I was just doing a little work.' As proof, he thrust forward the screwdriver—like an *assegai*, Nigel couldn't help but think.

'Ah, yes, we have mechanics in England too, with spanners, screwdrivers, and things.' They sat in embarrassed silence, and then Nigel said, 'There's actually a reason for my being here.'

'I was hoping you'd get to that,' said Mr Davison.

'I'm afraid I have some difficult news.'

'It isn't Pen, is it?' Mr Davison said. In one step, he'd sprung out of his chair, looking as though he were ready to grab his elephant gun. The question was—Nigel thought as he stared at the screwdriver— before or after he'd unscrewed one's kidneys?

'Yes, I'm afraid it is. But let me say immediately that to the best of our knowledge, she's alive and unharmed.'

'To the best of your knowledge?!'

'Calm down, John,' said Mrs Davison, looking worried herself, but stoically refusing hysterics. To Nigel she said, 'Tell us what happened.'

'Won't you please sit down?' Nigel said to Mr Davison, who was stalking about the room like a Red Indian preparing for a scalping party.

'No, I won't sit down! This is my house! Now tell us what the hell happened!'

Nigel had hoped to break it gently to Mrs Davison, but the behaviour of her husband Geronimo convinced him that was impossible. Best say it straight out and dare the consequences. 'To tell you the whole story would be an exercise in the irrelevant. What is important to you is that... well, she's rather a sort of hostage... to a Mexican drug gang.'

'What!' Mr Davison screamed.

'Oh my God,' said Mrs Davison, but as Nigel looked in her eyes (porcelain blue, he noticed) he spied what he thought was a shared understanding with him—a certain resignation that sooner or later foolish young girls like Penelope would inevitably stumble into these things, like frightened horses blundering into a bramble.

Her husband did not share her philosophical view. 'Where the hell is she? We're getting her back—now!' Nigel did have to give him points for manly aggression. He liked chaps like this—straight to the point, no fiddle-faddle, attack, attack, attack.

'Well, that's just it. We're not quite sure.'

'Maybe we should call the police,' Mrs Davison said, in a tone that demanded her husband succumb to rationality.

Though this, of course, was not the sort of rationality Nigel wished to encourage. 'No,' he was forced to reply. 'I wouldn't recommend that. You see, there's been a misunderstanding and I'm wanted by the police.'

Mr Davison's eyes locked in their sockets, like bullets settling in a chamber. He stopped circling the room and stalked straight towards Nigel. 'Just who the hell are you and what the hell are you doing?'

'Well, it's quite simple, really. I came here on holiday. I met April and Penelope. And Penelope went and got herself kidnapped.' He wasn't going to spare anyone's feelings anymore. Presumably, this reincarnation of Wyatt Earp would appreciate straight shooting. 'That wasn't my fault. I'm sorry to say it was her own. She chose the wrong sort of company. She has a penchant for the low life.'

'Is that true, April?' asked Mr Davison.

Such was Nigel's keen trust in April that he quickly answered for her. 'I've left some things out, but that's the gist of it.'

'I didn't ask you!' barked Mr Davison. 'April, is that the truth?'

'Well, sort of.'

'What do you mean, sort of?'

'Well, like Nigel said, he left out a lotta stuff. Like he already rescued her once from a Jamaican drug gang.'

'What?!'

'Yes, I regret to inform you, sir, that, in a way, your daughter's incorrigible. In the short time I've known her she seems to make a regular habit of getting kidnapped by drug gangs.'

'You rescued her?' said Mrs Davison. 'How?'

'Well, I've been trained for that sort of thing, you know, and had a fair bit of experience putting it into practice. It was simply a matter of finding her, infiltrating the position, and spiriting her out.'

'He did it with a stun gun,' April added proudly.

'Yes, that was Penelope's, actually.'

Mr Davison ran a hand over his head and shot Nigel a look that said—or so Nigel thought—Welcome to the Hole in the Wall Gang, pardner. 'Is that why you're wanted by the police?'

'More or less. I don't think they appreciate independent military operations on their territory.'

'Well, they're about to get another one,' John Davison said firmly. 'You just tell me who it is, and I'll get the boys and we'll go in there.'

'John, don't be a fool,' his wife said, like a librarian telling a boy to be quiet for the fourth and final time. 'I'm not going to have any violence. We're calling the police. And if that doesn't suit Mr Haversham, then he can go. And thank you very much for telling us about Penelope.'

'I don't know that that's very wise,' Nigel said. 'You can forget my own trouble with the police. It's a mere trifle, even if it is, personally, extremely inconvenient and annoying. But you have to think of your daughter. And I don't believe ringing the police is in her best interest. You see, Penelope joined this gang voluntarily.'

'I can't believe that,' snapped Mr Davison.

'It's true. If you wish, you may even cross-examine April, your oracle of truth. She'll tell you the same. Penelope ran off with a member of the gang of her own free will. Now I have no doubt she was seduced under false pretences and would rather not stay with the gang—Los Lobos Colorados, in case you were wondering—but still it would be rather embarrassing and complicated, I should think, to extricate her legally from an illegal association she freely joined. Very awkward and troublesome, I'd imagine, with a deuced lot of headaches, maybe even a prison sentence for dear old Penelope. And I really don't think the poor girl belongs in prison. Eighteen months in a grotty little cell with a lot of hairy lesbians eagerly inducting her into their wicked ways. What a tragic waste that would be. If she were my daughter, I'd post her to some nunnery in Ireland where she could do work amongst the poor, meditate on the state of her soul, and work out this dreadful fascination she has with brown-eyed men.'

He paused to let Mrs Davison speak, but she only gasped, so he continued. 'Strange as it may seem, I think your husband is right. We need an independent operation of trusted, private commandos. It's the logical choice, really.'

'Damn right. I'll make the calls now.'

'No, you won't!' Mrs Davison was clenching and unclenching her hands in frustration. 'This is madness.'

'Is it?' asked Nigel, adopting the manner of provocative interviewer on the telly. 'April, where's that photograph you were telling me about?' She looked at him blankly. 'The Vietnam photograph.'

'Oh, it's right there.'

Nigel walked over to examine the picture. Mr Davison was standing tall and sunburned, sweat seeping through his uniform, his sleeves rolled up to reveal the arms of a Trojan, one hand resting on a helmet, like Hector's, the other resting on the butt of his pistol, as though on the hilt of a sword.

'How long were you in Vietnam?'

'Two tours.'

Nigel nodded, suitably impressed. Not many men could claim that. It was one of the most foolish things he'd noticed as an observer in Vietnam, the way the Americans rotated their officers in for a year and then out, so that experience was always in short supply, long-term vision neglected, and morale consequently low. Two tours meant he'd volunteered. Two tours also meant he was considered good enough or valuable enough to be allowed to stay. Two tours was a high recommendation.

'Your rank?'

'I left as a captain.'

'Well, Mrs Davison, there you have it. Would you rather trust your daughter's safety to a blundering, hamfisted police force that will arrest her and charge her with drug-dealing, or do you trust the skill and discretion of an American captain with combat experience and a British brigadier general knighted by Her Majesty?' He hated to lie to her, but April had already muddied the waters anyway.

'But this is insane!'

'You've said that before,' Nigel said, adding helpfully, 'but of course it *is* California.'

'Why don't you just leave us alone? This has nothing to do with you. It's a family matter.'

'Yes, indeed it is. I had hoped to leave my own concerns out of it, but since you insist, I should confess that I'll be attempting a rescue whether your husband joins me or not. You see, your daughter's gang also kidnapped my goddaughter. So I have every reason to proceed with caution and to make perfectly sure that our operation is a success. I intend for my goddaughter to be free. And I'm not going to leave it to a bunch of American amateurs like your police force. We get your television, you know. I've seen how they operate—screaming cars, lots of gunfire. Cagney and Lacey. Starsky and Hutch. Abbott and Costello. That's not what I'm hoping to achieve at all. April told you about our first rescue. Sort of a trial run, I suppose. Did it with hardly firing a shot. And that was alone. With trained men like your husband, it will be even easier.'

Mrs Davison stared at him in disbelief, finally removing the spectacles from her nose, letting them dangle from their chain. She seemed terribly shaken and said, 'I'm going to bed,' and disappeared down a passageway, looking like a dazed United Nations peacekeeper retreating from a hopeless operation.

'Well then, old boy,' Nigel said to Mr Davison, 'I suppose you're on board.'

'Damn right,' he said, still holding the screwdriver like a knife.

'Can you put that thing away?'

'My wife gives me hell if I leave tools lying around. And anyway, I might bring this with me. When do we go?'

'Not now, I can assure you. We're still short of intelligence. If any of your friends—and I hardly need emphasise the need for secrecy here—can give us a site for the headquarters of Los Lobos Colorados, it would be damned useful. If they can tell us where it is, we'll need to make a recce of the place. Suppose we meet, you and I, tomorrow at 0900 hours at April's flat—you know where that is of course. We'll look at a map, discuss what you've learned from your friends, and draw up some plans. All right then. Good man.' Nigel took Mr Davison's greasy hand and shook it.

NIGEL WAS EXHILARATED. He might be driving back to the Beach-combing Cheese-grater Apartments, but by tomorrow morning, he'd be laying out Plan C with an American captain, undoubtedly a member of their elite special forces. He was sure to be good. He thought back on the tough-talking American officers he'd met during his brief stay in Vietnam. Worthy fellows, mostly, but dreadfully mismanaged. Fault of the pencil pushers, of course. The same sort of oily bureaucrats who were at this very moment chopping up the thin red line into micro-dots and dashes. Don't know a thing about strategy or tactics—except interfering. And as for man management, one needed to know they were men first, not numbers in a theorem.

'What's wrong?' asked April.

'Wrong? Nothing, why?'

'You were just, like, breathing really heavy.'

'Oh, nothing, nothing. Just thinking, my dear. Necessity of command, you know.' He thought again of Penelope's father. Two tours in Vietnam. Certainly aggressive enough. An excellent find. And with his posse—an armed posse, Nigel supposed—he would be flush with men. And suppose Iced Khalifa also came through with Nigel's hoped for *askari* auxiliaries. Good God, he'd be leading a multinational legion—something out of the latter part of the Roman Empire. *All hail Nigellus Britannicus, Imperator and Pontifex Maximus, Com-*

mander of the Army of Rednecks and Black Islamic Fascists. There was a certain ring to that. He always liked the sound of Latin. Perhaps, he thought, his thinking taking a radical turn, Islam was not the way. Perhaps California would be better suited for conquest as a Roman Catholic colony under the crown. Its Spanish and Mexican history should prove fruitful soil for that sort of conversion. Of course, as Governor-General of a Catholic colony, he would have to renounce all thoughts of having a harem. But for goodness sake, he'd come this far without a wife. That certainly wasn't an insurmountable stumbling block. It might also give him a way out with Her Majesty and the former Duchess of York. He could then honourably take a Catholic vow of celibacy, perhaps entering an order of soldier-monks dating back to the Middle Ages, where blue blood was as important as religious ardour—perhaps the Knights of Malta? Wouldn't that be a pretty turn! And think of the geopolitical consequences. Mightn't the addition of a Catholic California to the British Empire lead to full reconciliation with Ireland? Was it possible that it could even lead to Nigel's beatification? Now there was a thought. If it were a choice between sainthood and having an armada of stockings hanging in the bathroom... well, now.

He could see Sister Marigold lecturing the scrubbed, attentive faces of her students, lilting in her soft Irish brogue. 'Today, children, is the feast day of St Nigel. Now, what is St Nigel famous for? Yes, Seamus?'

'He drove the drug dealers out of California, Sister.'

'That is correct, Seamus. He is our modern equivalent of St Patrick, who drove the snakes from our beloved Ireland. And what is he the patron saint of? Yes, Siobhan?'

'White slavery, Sister.'

'White slavery is correct.'

'Here we are, Nigel,' said April.

'Oh, yes, quite.' Out of a dream world and back to California Socialist Realism. He'd seen more attractive Nissen huts than this.

But he still carried a faint vision in his mind of something more sublime, of smells and bells, of opulent papist ceremonies in ornate, ancient cathedrals built over pagan temples that had been guarded by vestal virgins.

'I say, April, are you a Roman Catholic?'

'No,' she said, and he thought he detected a blush of embarrassment coming over her cheeks. Religion always was a sensitive subject. 'Why?'

"Well, I was thinking, you know, as I said. Merely a matter of curiosity. So you're a Protestant then?'

'Yes.'

'I don't mean to intrude, but do you mind telling me what denomination?'

'Episcopalian.'

'Oh, Anglican. Quite so. And Penelope?'

'She's a Seventh Day Adventist.'

'Oh dear. Oh dear me. Well, at least you're close enough.'

'To what?'

'Oh, you know… to God I daresay.'

Together they stumbled up the stairs to her door. Both were worn out from lack of sleep and too much alcohol. April clumsily stuck her key in the lock. They stepped inside and she hastily shut the door. There was a bit of a chill in the air.

'Brr,' she said. She flipped on the light. *Kerclick.* Stalker levelled a gun at them.

CHAPTER FIFTEEN

'YOU'VE KEPT ME WAITING a very long time.' Stalker looked dirty and tired, like an effete, half-washed coal miner with a spade—or in this case, a pistol—in his hand. He was stretched on the couch, his back propped up by pillows. 'Sit down.'

'We prefer to stand, thank you,' said Nigel. He'd been trained not to give in to threats—and anyway, he knew the American Seventh Cavalry would be arriving by morning. April sighed and slipped out of her shoes. Poor girl must be uncomfortable. Just another outrage to add to Stalker's long ledger of villainy.

'Suit yourself. You'll forgive me if I stay here. I've had rather a rough night. And what about you? I'm not interrupting a tryst, am I? Something that might interest *The Daily Mail*?'

'What're you doing here? Where's Alexandra?'

He smiled that dimpled smile. 'As a master of the obvious, I thought you'd ask me that. I'm sure you'll be pleased to hear she's escaped.'

'Good girl.'

'Maybe. But now you and I will have to be partners, or you'll never find her.'

'And Penelope?'

'Dead, I imagine.'

'Oh my God,' April cried, covering her mouth with her hand. Nigel gripped her other wrist.

'She's got plenty of company—a whole parcel of Los Lobos Colorados, gunned down. Very inconvenient for me, of course, especially because... Do you mind if I smoke? Oh, of course, you don't. We've been through this drill already, haven't we? You see,' he continued, tapping out a cigarette from the pack, 'this part makes me rather nervous.' He displayed a sleek, glittering lighter. 'Like it? I thought I deserved it. I wasn't going to be caught without one after our last interview.' He pulled a few puffs on the cigarette. 'Ah, that's better. You see, this part's rather hard to face—and it's only the beginning of my bad news. Los Lobos Colorados would rather like to kill me, too, now—thanks to your friend Pen. You should have warned me about her incessant whining. I can't stand that in a woman. I'm rather surprised you put up with it. Of course, at your age you might have to. But I don't. I'll just have to be more careful when I poach off you in the future.'

He sighed heavily and took a couple of drags on his cigarette before continuing. 'It should have been fun. We were having a party, and I had every reason to believe that Pen would be a brilliant party girl. It's one of the reasons I poached her from you. Los Lobos had this wonderful nightly tradition of getting drunk *al fresco*, terrifying their neighbours—which wise gangs do—and then slow-dancing with their *señoritas*, who wear the tightest jeans I've ever seen. I wanted Pen for all that. But Pen... Pen was being a bitch. She refused to join in, went moping off in a corner, and left me looking fairly humiliated.'

He sucked on his cigarette and looked at the ceiling philosophically. 'I'm afraid our relationship was never quite the same after she met Los Lobos.' Then he said, as though confiding an astonishing secret, 'She was absolutely *terrified* of them—and she showed it! And of course, she didn't trust me anymore. But I wasn't going to have that—not in front of Los Lobos—and I wasn't about to have our party ruined by some frightened, squeamish girl. So I went to drag her back—and that's when we got hit.' He seemed to wince at the memory. 'The cars rolled up so slowly, it was one of those things where you knew it was going to happen and were powerless to prevent it—like a nightmare. They pulled up close, and the things just exploded with gunfire. Los Lobos fell like... I suppose *you'd* say, like grouse. It wasn't your usual drive-by killing. It was intended to be a massacre. They actually drove back and jumped out of their cars, which was incredibly stupid.

'By that time, the Lobos house was exploding with flames. Bloody smoke everywhere. The gas tank from the barbecue must have exploded. Whatever it was, the house went up like fireworks. And Los Lobos banged the gangbangers back. It got so hot, they jumped in their cars and took off. And I raced like hell to the blazing house, because that's where my money was—all £250,000 of it.

'I didn't make it at first. A Lobo came running towards me, screaming about what a filthy traitor I was. I couldn't believe it. The bugger thought I'd arranged the bloody hit! That I'd gone after Penelope to get out of the frigging way!' Stalker shook his head at the disgraceful lack of honour among thieves. 'Luckily, he was such a raving, drunken lunatic, he never saw the piece in my hand. I knew what I had to do.' He puffed thoughtfully.

'First bastard I ever killed. But I'm a quick learner. Once I got in the house there were three more. They came running through the smoke and never saw me. Buggers went down like ninepins. Have to say they deserved it, distrustful bastards.'

'And Alexandra?'

Stalker looked under his lashes at Nigel and smiled a most obscenely dimpled smile. He waved his cigarette. 'Escaped, clean away.' He took a final drag, then lit another. 'Your Alex is a cool one—not like Pen at all—and a planner. She planned it, just like a breakout from a prison camp, waiting for her moment. She must have shot out of there like a rocket. No trace of her—except one. She's a mean bitch, your goddaughter.' Stalker stopped, as though he expected a reaction, and thrust his pistol at Nigel, who hadn't moved. 'Don't think of trying anything. I've got the gun this time. You need to understand—your goddaughter's a thief. She's got my satchel with the money—a quarter of a million pounds.'

'Good for her,' said Nigel, admiring his filibustering goddaughter; no need for a ransom now, not even as bait; she was actually turning a profit.

'The point is, Alexandra's got the money—*my* money. It was partly my own bloody fault,' he said, clenching his jaw, his face full of self-recrimination. 'Like an idiot, I'd pulled the cash out from where I'd hidden it and shown it to her. And now she's got it. Just to put me up the bloody spout.'

'What about Pen?' cried April.

'Forget Pen. She's not important.'

'Yes, she is!' April shouted.

'She's dead, all right? Are you happy? She's out of it.'

'How do you know?'

'Because it's bleeding obvious.'

'Not if you didn't see her body!'

'I didn't have time to count corpses. I had to run like hell before my own bloody bodyguards shot me.'

'Then you don't know!'

'Look, if she wasn't killed in the hit, Los Lobos would have killed her as a traitor, like they wanted to kill me.'

'But she could be alive!'

'Believe what you want. It doesn't matter.'

'But we've got to look for her!'

'Going back would be suicide—or murder, because we're not going back.' He pressed the pistol forward for emphasis. 'There's no way she got out alive—not between the hit and Los Lobos. And even if she did, she'd have been carved up on the street by some Mexican bitch keening over her dead Lobo. Pen didn't exactly fit in in that neighbourhood. And unlike me, she didn't have a gun, and she couldn't have stolen a car. So forget it.'

'But surely,' said Nigel, who was frantically trying to assimilate Stalker's fantastic information, 'there is another possibility.' There had to be, for April's sake. And surely there *was,* he thought. 'Surely the police and the fire brigade would have been called. What if they rescued Penelope? She could be in their custody. She could be drinking coffee with a police inspector at this very moment, providing evidence against you.'

'Well, General, you should hope not. You don't want the police involved any more than I do. There's only one way to Alex, and that's through me.'

'Then where the devil is she?'

'All you need to know is this: I know where she's going, and we're going to find her together. All you have to do is convince her to give me back the money. You do that, and I'll put this gun away, and you and she can go back to England and eat clotted cream teas to your hearts' content. I wouldn't mind that. It'll be three fewer murders on my conscience.' He pointed the pistol at them in succession. 'You, you, and Alex. Sound fair enough? Of course it does. I'm sure you're an advocate of fair play, General.'

'What happens now?'

'Now, we'll sleep. You can use the bedrooms. I trust you won't jump out of the window or do something foolish like ring the police. It'll be your loss if you do. I'll stay here on the couch and keep watch for burglars.'

'But what about your car? Surely the police will have tracked it. Is it sitting outside?'

'It's a Los Lobos car they have no reason to trace to me. And it's parked blocks away—I'm not an idiot, General—with the keys in the ignition. I'm sure it's been stolen by now. Now, I'm tired. Switch off the light and go to bed.'

SLEEPING IN A YOUNG, single woman's bed was a new experience for Nigel. At least he was fully clothed, except for his shoes and his jacket, and alone. But the room was haunted by thoughts of responsibility. All around him were images—in Penelope's sketches—to remind him of the innocent (well, sort of) young life that he'd recklessly endangered and who was now... where?

As an officer, he was used to taking risks—with his own life and, harder still, with the lives of others. One learned quickly to blot out bad thoughts of things one couldn't help. And for now, there was nothing he could do for Penelope—the poor girl with the bee-stung lips, the big, messy blonde hair, the Bardotesque figure. Nothing he could do but wait for morning and witness the truly impressive spectacle of her father ripping out Stalker's living guts with a Bowie knife. He imagined Captain Davison was quite skilled with a knife, rather like Buffalo Bill must have been. Though Nigel would, of course, have to intervene before Stalker was beaten to death. He did need Stalker as a guide. But he certainly didn't need him completely unharmed.

Yes, the news was generally quite good. Stalker was in his hands. Penelope's father and his gang of retired U.S. Army Rangers, or whatever they were, would soon be with him and cutting slices off Stalker's ears. Iced Khalifa's men might join them, roasting bits of Stalker over an open fire, enjoying the pleasures of their cannibalistic ancestors. And best of all, he knew Alexandra was alive—and not only alive, but performing with the daring and skill of an RAF pilot escaping from Colditz. Good show, old girl! He tried to picture her in his mind. The long blonde hair, the imperial blue eyes, the rhesus monkey nose. Yes, he remembered. And soon he'd have her back at Elkstone. Soon he'd be sipping tea laced with scotch and playing backgammon with Pandora. Soon all would be well. Soon...

He looked at the phone next to the bed. Time to break the news to Pandora.

'Your call is being diverted,' an electronic voice told him. 'Please wait.' And in a moment, Pandora's voice floated across the wires.

'Pandora?'

'Nigel! Thank God it's you.'

'I have marvellous news.'

'You've found Alex?'

'Er... no, not exactly. But she's escaped from the rats who kidnapped her.'

'When?'

'What... er... I don't know. Today. Yesterday. Day before. I'm not sure.'

There was a silence. 'I've had a phone call,' she told him. 'Two hours ago. They still have her.'

'But the shootout...?'

'Nigel, I spoke to the man myself. A Mexican. I didn't catch his name. You're to bring the money in a suitcase. Unmarked one hundred dollar bills from the First National Bank in Los Angeles. That's where I've sent the banker's draft. You're to deliver it in person at a place called Tequila Wells. Can you find that? They'll be waiting.'

'Of course. Look, Pandora, have you brought Inspector Tanner in on this? He can trace calls, check ransom envelopes for saliva, all manner of things.'

'Nigel, this is Alexandra's life we're talking about. I'd much rather pay the money than risk a police shootout. I'm telling you specifically, no police.'

'Very well, my dear,' he reassured her. 'Trust me. No police it is.' No police, certainly. But rescue by an irregular British-officered force—well, that was something altogether different.

After she'd rung off, he had an enormous temptation to use the phone again. Goodness me, he thought; he certainly deserved it. After all he'd been through. One topping bit of fun to cap the whole thing off. Yes, by George, he'd do it. He'd take the initiative, make the call, revel in the possibilities. He tiptoed out of bed and fetched his notebook from his coat pocket. There it was, the number he was looking for.

HE WOKE SUDDENLY to the sound of the phone ringing. Springing out of bed, he leapt over Penelope's unkempt hedges of clothes and dashed to the kitchen where the main phone was kept (he didn't want Stalker picking up the other line). He grabbed the receiver and, turning, saw that Stalker had him covered from the couch.

'Hello?'

'Is this Sir General Nigel Haversham of Her Majesty's Guards?'

'Yes, indeed it is. Good morning, Mr Iced Khalifa, Esteemed Mr Iced Khalifa, that is.'

'Blessings and peace be upon you.'

'And also on you, old boy. Do we have an answer?'

'After much prayer and thoughtful reflection, yes. It has not escaped my knowledge of history that your country, England, was the first to abolish the slave trade. Thanks to Mr William Wilberforce— peace be upon him. Nor that your army conquered and ruled a quarter of the globe, thanks to African soldiers...'

'I hate to interrupt, your esteemedness, but I actually have the Prime Minister waiting on the other line...'

There was a pause. 'You do?'

'Yes.'

'Please give Sir Prime Minister Tony Blair my very best regards on his rise to power. I hope he will adequately fill the shoes of the esteemed Mrs Thatcher, and that other guy in the grey suit whose name I can never remember.'

For a brief moment Nigel had visions of Tony Blair wobbling forward on ill-fitting spiked heels, swinging a red handbag over his head like a bolo to knock some unspeakably cringe-making, pro-Euro Tory backbencher off his perch at Question Time. But he quickly dismissed the image to ponder a more important question: if Mrs Thatcher was 'esteemed', where did Nigel himself stand in Iced Khalifa's hierarchy?

Was he at least the 'Admirable', the 'Honourable', or the 'Revered' Sir General, as Iced Khalifa had it, Nigel Haversham?

Nigel said, 'I'm sure he'll be very glad to have your best wishes, your esteemedness, but he too is eager to hear your answer.'

Another pause. 'I bring you good news, then. It is my honour to inform you—and I ask that you pass my message on to Sir Prime Minister Blair and Her Majesty the Queen—that I have accepted your proposal. There are, however, conditions for my acceptance.'

'Name them.'

'As you suggested, I am not to be involved in any way. My men are not to be armed. They are not to be asked to do anything contrary to the law. And they are to be returned to me immediately. Do you accept these conditions?'

'Gladly.'

'And you will express to Her Majesty and Her Prime Minister the delicacy of my position that requires them.'

'Oh, yes, certainly.'

'I will give you only five men. Less than you wanted, but more than I, at first, thought I could spare. I give them to you as recruits, to receive, in the short time you have them, advanced military training.'

'Funny you should mention that. I had a conversation just last night with a brilliant military instructor, a captain, who should be joining us.'

'Oh? Are your numbers growing?'

'By leaps and bounds—everyone is rallying to the colours. But your men will have a special place of honour as disciplined volunteers representing your struggle for... whatever it is you're struggling for. I mean to say, I don't wish to put words in your mouth.'

'And you will talk to the Queen?'

'Oh, absolutely. Can you hold the line a moment?' Nigel shouted down the hall. 'Prime Minister. Oh, hello, Tony. How's young Leo? Splendid little chap. Yes. Can you hold the line? I have that delightful black fellow on the other line. Sends his best regards, by the way. Yes, I thought you'd be flattered. Thank you ever so much.' He returned to Iced Khalifa. 'Can you send your men over right away?'

Stalker coughed and brandished his pistol at Nigel, who made a face that implied, not to worry.

'That was Sir Prime Minister Tony Blair?'

'Yes, indeed, frightfully chuffed about your high regard for him. Now, about those men.'

'This morning?' asked Iced Khalifa.

'Yes, immediately.' Nigel put his hand over the receiver and called, 'April!' Returning to Iced Khalifa he said, 'I'm terribly sorry. Trying to fetch my aide-de-camp to take notes.'

'Very well. I shall send them this morning. Where?'

'My aide-de-camp will have to assist you there. I'm afraid we have just acquired new billets and I'm not exactly sure of the address.' April appeared in a nightgown, rubbing her eyes.

'Is it truly necessary that I speak to her?'

'Oh, yes, that's what she's here for—to be spoken to, to provide phone numbers and addresses, all that sort of thing. And I'm sorry, your esteemedness, but I really mustn't keep the Prime Minister waiting any longer.'

'Good luck and may Allah be with you.'

'Thanks awfully,' Nigel said, handing the receiver to April. 'Be a good girl and give Iced Khalifa your address.'

'What the hell's going on?' said Stalker through gritted teeth, politely whispering so as not to disturb April on the phone. It was little things like this, Nigel thought, that revealed Stalker for all his Miltonic Beelzebubness. He knew how to behave. It was instinctive with him. But he had wilfully chosen not to conform to the norms of the class, apparently middle, to which he belonged. He refused to obey the law. He denied the canons of good taste. He catered to the illicit desires of Britain's disgraceful 'yoof' in search of quick windfall profits. It reminded Nigel of when Enoch Powell had lectured him, for some mysterious reason, on the substance of immorality. 'Immorality,' said the Prophet Enoch, 'is frequently the desire to get something too quickly, whether it's money, sex, or power; the means become fraud, fornication, and force.' Not that he put great store in Enoch Powell. Rummy fellow who thought too much. But Stalker brought his observation to mind. And as he waved his pistol, thinking he was menacing like Jimmy Cagney, Nigel could feel only contempt for Stalker's puerile posturing. Enoch's stare was more imposing than Stalker armed.

'I'll have the gun, if you don't mind,' Nigel said, extending his hand.

'As long as I have this, I think I'll be giving orders. Now what the hell was that all about?'

'You're about to be outnumbered.'

'I told you not to cross me!' Stalker leapt off the couch and aimed the pistol at Nigel's face. 'That's it, damn it.'

'Shooting me won't solve your problems,' Nigel said calmly, calculating that Stalker was making a melodramatic show. The General had looked down pistol muzzles before.

'I told you—I warned you—you cross me, Alex is dead, you're dead. You're all dead.'

'The fact is, I haven't double-crossed you. We're calling in reinforcements to protect you.'

'To protect me? Right!' Stalker said cynically. 'Who the hell are they?'

'A sort of praetorian guard that will take orders from me. We could use a few more men, don't you think? Now, give me the gun.'

'No.'

'I'd advise it. These men have nothing against you—as long as they don't know who you are. But if they discover you're a drug dealer, if they see you threatening me with that pistol... you're for it.'

'I warned you.'

'And now I'll warn you, young Master Stalker,' Nigel replied commandingly (as generals should). 'You're quite right, we're in a partnership—a partnership in which you are the junior partner. Don't try to bluff me. Better men have tried: Jomo Kenyatta, Ho Chi Minh, Leonid Brezhnev—I won't bore you with the full list. You think you're a hard man. But killing a few gangsters in a smoky, chaotic fight doesn't make you hard or even put you in particular danger. As far as the police are concerned, those killings would be hard to pin on you. You could plausibly argue they were in self-defence. The law might even wink at them. But killing me would be simple, cold-blooded murder. You'll be a top police priority then. The Los Angeles police will contact Scotland Yard. And then you'll have the police of two continents after you. Possibly Interpol as well, now that we're so chummy with Europe. So for your own sake, be a good lad and give me the gun.'

Stalker's tongue darted nervously between his lips. 'You still haven't told me who they are.'

'It's quite simple, really. They're black Muslims waging holy war against drug dealers and the white race, though I've convinced them to focus on the drug dealers and spare the Anglo-Saxons for now. Just don't mention General Gordon.'

Stalker flung his arms down at his side and looked to the ceiling for deliverance. 'But we're meeting drug dealers, you bloody idiot!'

'That's not your concern. You want your money. They want to crack a few drug dealers' heads. Quite a sensible ambition on their part. And it doesn't conflict at all with yours.'

'I can't believe this. Where do you find these people? Black gangsters, blonde bimbos...'

'They're not gangsters,' said Nigel. 'Unlike you, they're men of principle. But this is all beside the point. The fact is, they're coming. So give me the gun—and be sharp about it.'

Stalker stared at him. It wasn't a stare of defiance; it was a stare of ill-concealed bewilderment. 'Damn it!'

'That's not an acceptable answer.'

'I should just blow your bloody head off.'

'Give me the gun. Now.' Nigel stuck out his hand.

He believed they called this situation 'a Mexican stand-off'. Two men facing each other—one a brown-eyed coward with a gun; the other a rather dashing fellow, really, with pale blue eyes set in a ruddy, handsome face that the discerning might compare to a mature, greying, moustachioed Dirk Bogarde. If it was to be a test of wills, a staring contest, Nigel was completely confident of victory. Already Stalker's vulpine brown eyes were wavering.

Stalker stepped towards him, the pistol pointed at Nigel's heart. Nigel kept his hand outstretched, but he no longer expected the gun. The coward Stalker obviously didn't know what he wanted, whether to surrender or play for time. It was up to Nigel to make the decision for him. He'd have to seize Stalker's arm and wrestle him for the gun. He wasn't in the mood for any more nonsense. He wouldn't care if he broke Stalker's arm in the struggle. But then Stalker stopped, and the pistol was slapped into Nigel's hand.

'All right,' Stalker said, sinking onto the couch and weakly rubbing his hands over his sooty face. 'I give up.'

Nigel stared at the gun rather as if someone had suddenly slapped a fish in his palm. He weighed it, let his eyes glide over its silver barrel, and took a grip on it. It seemed appropriate to point it at Stalker. 'All right, then. Where's Alex?'

'Give me a moment, will you?'

Oh, yes, the sensitive type, a poet. He'd forgotten that. Poor fellow might break down in tears at any moment. Stalker lay back on the couch as though he were ready to seek psychoanalysis—and he succeeded in getting a diagnosis of sorts. While Nigel politely examined the sights on the pistol and waited for Stalker to gather himself together, April brushed past him, leaned over the couch, and whacked Stalker a deafening slap.

'Bloody hell,' he said, holding his face. When he moved his hand, there was an enormous rosy welt, and his eyes were glistening with tears of fright, the fright of an unarmed Vichy collaborator surrounded by the Free French, Nigel thought. He wasn't much moved to sympathy.

Someone pounded on the door. Nigel looked at his watch. It wasn't half eight yet. No one was supposed to come this early. Stalker caught his eye. Nigel knew what he was thinking: coffee-coloured young men with cigarettes, tattoos, Y-front T-shirts, sunglasses, and slick black hair—Los Lobos Colorados seeking revenge.

Nigel rocked the gun in his hand. If it were Los Lobos Colorados, what should he do? They'd undoubtedly overwhelm him by sheer numbers. They'd strip the gun from him and then... gag him? They had no reason to kill him. But do drug murderers like these need a reason? And what about April? He wouldn't let her go without a fight. In fact, he'd die fighting before he'd let them kidnap her. That was his solemn vow—no more kidnapped women. Now Stalker on the other hand… he didn't mind their butchering him, but not yet. Maybe they could strike a deal…

They pounded on the door again.

But it might not be Los Lobos. It could be the police, having traced Stalker's car after all. And if the police—who were already under the misapprehension that he was an elderly drug addict—found Nigel holding a gun over a battered Stalker…

Or it could be Penelope, her clothes dramatically torn to shreds, soot-stained like Stalker, exhausted, having stumbled, with her feet sore and bloodied in high heels, all the way to the Cheese-grater Apartments, through gang-infested streets, still shaking with fear from the terrible gang fight…

Or it could be Alexandra, a white muffler tossed carelessly around her neck in true aviator fashion, a sardonic look in her eye. 'Surprised to see me?'

Or could it be…

They pounded on the door again. There was a low, grumbling sound of male voices.

'April, find out who it is.' At least it would keep her from scratching Stalker's eyeballs out. That was one part of him they still needed.

April looked through the peephole and said 'Oh' happily. She flung the door open and Captain Davison breezed past her with a brief hello and headed directly to Nigel, with two big, bearded men in baseball caps following. 'I've brought two of the boys, who took off work. We're ready to go. I even brought you a gun if you want one.' He pulled up short at the sight of the pistol in Nigel's hand. 'But look at this,' he said, taking the pistol and admiring it. 'A Glock. You've got expensive tastes. But what else should I expect from a

General and a Sir.' He put the gun back in Nigel's hand and slapped him on the shoulder. 'We're ready to go. We'll go cruise the Mex part of town and talk to people. They'll tell us where these Los Lobos Colorados are. And then we'll hit 'em, straight on, between the eyes. Cowards who do drive-bys aren't used to people who fight back. Whattya got?'

'What I have,' said Nigel, with a certain prideful flair, like a well-greaved Achaean tugging away the sack in which he's hidden Paris, 'is the man who kidnapped your daughter.'

Davison's gunfighter eyes widened for just a moment, then narrowed and turned on Stalker like the rotating barrels of a Gatling gun. Stalker's welt flushed again, and his eyes wavered under Davison's glare. 'Him?' Davison said, glancing at Nigel. Nigel nodded. Davison's steely blue eyes turned black and rolled to Stalker. They looked as though they were taking aim, like the cold, deadly aim of a Butch Cassidy... or of oneself, Nigel thought. He was overcome with a nostalgic sensation. *He could feel the butt of a rifle settling into his shoulder as he prepared the final blow for a wounded stag stumbling not one hundred yards away in the Highlands.* The rifle cracked, and instead of the stag dropping, Nigel saw Davison's huge fist seize Stalker's collar. The big man threw himself over the couch, rolling over Stalker onto the floor and flinging the lad after him. Stalker crashed into the glass table, on behalf of which April screamed.

Davison jumped to his feet, a ferocious row of teeth shining through his beard. Stalker lay dazed amid the broken glass and the metal legs and frame of the table. He was bleeding from small cuts on his face and hands. Davison stood with his cowboy boots inches from Stalker's face. It was a warning. 'Where the hell is she?'

'Just a small reminder, Captain Davison,' Nigel said civilly, with no trace of rebuke in his voice. 'We do need him alive.'

Davison nodded, breathing like a snarling animal. He hauled Stalker upright and hurled him against the wall, nailing him there with a hand like a garrotte around his throat. 'All right, you son of a bitch. Where the hell is she?' he repeated.

'I don't know,' Stalker replied in a voice as broken as the glass table.

'Let me have a go at him,' said Nigel. He was anxious to spare Stalker a prolonged beating. He wasn't sure how much he could take. 'I think I know how to make him talk.'

Davison growled and shook Stalker's throat. 'You'll talk, if I have to rip your voice box out and play with it.'

Now there was a charming image, Nigel thought: Captain Davison sitting cross-legged on the floor, pressing different sections of Stalker's voice box, calling the tune, as it were, making him sing various songs. Delightful.

Davison stepped aside, like a well-mannered inquisitor making way for another, each allotted a fair share of punishment time.

Stalker was already looking a bit done in. His back curved limply against the wall and his knees were bent as though he were halfway to sitting down. A friendly tap on the shoulder, Nigel thought, and he'd sink to the floor.

'Where's Alexandra?' Nigel said.

Stalker gulped like a fish and said, 'It's a guess, an educated guess. It's where I was going to take you. Tequila Wells.'

'Tequila Wells?' exclaimed Davison.

'You know it?' asked Nigel. It accorded perfectly with Los Lobos' instructions to Pandora.

'It's a piss-ant border town.'

Nigel asked Stalker, 'Why Tequila Wells?'

'That's where the deal's going down. She knows it. She's going to buy it.'

'What the devil for?'

'She knows I was worried about it. Can't I have a cigarette?'

'After you talk.' Nigel remembered he had the gun in his hand, and though he knew it wasn't necessary, he halfheartedly waved it about as a threat.

'I told her if anything went wrong, I was for it. She'll buy the drugs so I can't—to make me look like a liar, a traitor to Los Lobos. She doesn't know I'm a traitor already, in their eyes. She thinks she's signing my death warrant. Nice girl, your goddaughter.'

Nigel knew that. He also knew what Stalker did not—that if Alexandra was going to Tequila Wells, it was not as a free woman, but as a prisoner of Los Lobos. They'd be waiting for him and the ransom money.

'What's this have to do with Pen?' Davison scowled.

Nigel wished the man would shut up. He needed to think. This one was going to take immaculate timing.

'Where's Pen?' Davison demanded of Stalker.

'Captain Davison,' Nigel said aggrievedly, 'please try to understand. It's the same thing. If we find Alexandra, we find Penelope. Where we find one, we find the other. They've been kidnapped together. Isn't that true, Stalker?' He nudged the pistol into Stalker's ribs to remind him that it was.

'Yes.' Stalker was now prepared to say anything for a quiet life.

'Now you're sure of this—that she's going to Tequila Wells?'

'It's an educated guess. But yes, I'm sure.'

'But why the devil should she bother? Why should she go to Tequila Wells when she could just as easily fly home to England?' Pandora, of course, had given Nigel a bound and gagged reason, but she was a good ten thousand miles away; perhaps Stalker could paint in other details.

Stalker's dimples returned, Phoenix-like, out of the soot and blood that scarred his face. 'Here's one reason why.' He pulled a passport out of his hip pocket. Nigel took it and flipped it open. He saw the cascading blonde hair, the confident blue eyes, the rhesus nose, the ironic smile. He snapped it shut and clung to it.

'Why shouldn't she go to the police, then?'

Stalker continued to smile disarmingly and shook his head. 'No, she won't do that. You need to understand women, General. I've been down this road before. Scorned girlfriends don't just run away. And they're not informers. She's out for revenge.'

The first thought that came to Nigel's mind was: But you're not worth it. And then he realised again, with resounding force, that this limp, dog-eyed, dimple-faced, skinny-bodied drug fiend was the reason for this whole misadventure—yes, and for Pen's misadventure, too; you don't have to remind me, Captain Davison.

Here Nigel was, just inches from the creeping, culpable coward. Captain Davison had got his licks in, what about… But April breezed past him, and levelled another mighty whack at Stalker. He didn't slide to the ground, but it appeared he wanted to; he wanted to do anything to avoid her fury.

'For God's sake, will you stop doing that?!' Stalker screamed.

'That's *my* revenge. You said Pen was dead. But she's alive.'

'Dead?!' roared Penelope's father.

'Look,' Stalker said nervously to April, not daring to engage

Captain Davison, 'I said that last night to frighten you. She's not dead—at least I don't think so. The Lobos... the ones who survived... I mean... obviously they must have taken her with them.'

'He told you she was dead?' Davison shouted accusingly at Nigel.

Nigel was unruffled, but he gave Stalker an odd conspiratorial look. 'I knew he was lying. It was obvious. We found him here last night, after you and I talked. He said he'd escaped from a Los Lobos gang fight. He had to give us some excuse for his cowardice, for not bringing Penelope, so he said she was dead. But I knew it was a complete fabrication.'

'How?'

'Because they wouldn't kill someone they intended to ransom. Last night you hadn't received a ransom note. That's not surprising. They didn't have time. But when they do deliver the note, they'll have to prove she's alive to convince you to pay. So of course she's alive.'

'That's guesswork. I want to hear it from you,' Davison said to Stalker. 'And I'm going to hold you responsible. Is she alive?'

'I think so.'

'Is she alive?' Davison shouted.

'Yes.'

'Then if she isn't,' Davison said, jutting a finger towards Stalker like a knife, 'one skinny boy is going to be a helluva lot skinnier. Do you get me?'

'Yes.'

'So if there's anything you can do to keep Pen alive, you better do it, you son of a bitch. You got me?'

'Yes.'

'I knew you were a liar!' spat April.

'All right,' Davison said, taking a deep breath. 'So we're going to

Tequila Wells. That can't be more than two or three hours from here. We're ready. What do you want to do with this son of a bitch?' he asked Nigel, pointing at Stalker.

'I'm afraid he'll have to come with us. He's our guide, the only one who knows exactly what Los Lobos look like.'

'When do we leave?'

'Quite soon. We have to wait for a few more chaps to join us.'

'Like who?'

'Oh, trustworthy fellows, with useful experience of their own. They'll be here shortly. In the meantime, you might want to relax.'

Nigel looked at his watch and heard April announcing to Captain Davison's friends, 'Do you want any breakfast? We don't have a lot, but we have herbal tea: apple and cinnamon, nettle and cinnamon, and Tree Bark Cinnamon Temptation. And we have a full box of Toasted Oat Fibre Crystals—just add milk!'

He stepped towards the window, hoping to gaze at the green and spot his next arrivals. He didn't reach it. He'd only taken two steps when the front door flew open, screaming on its hinges. Men burst through, shouting in exotic voices, fanning out in the sitting room, pulling pistols from their waistbands, putting everyone in their sights.

'Oh my God!' cried Stalker, half in fear, half in utterly hopeless despair, covering his face in his hands.

'What the hell?' exclaimed Davison, raising his hands to surrender, as did his two friends.

They faced a half dozen gunmen whose smiles, beneath their dread-locked hair and sunglasses, somehow reminded Nigel of piano keys.

CHAPTER SIXTEEN

'HAH, HAH, HAH, I KNEW we could trust you, mahn,' their leader said to Nigel. 'You tell us de trute. Dere's Stalkuh.' He sauntered forward, grabbed Stalker's face, and raised his pistol to the dimpled one's mouth. 'Where be de money, Stalkuh?'

'You really don't have to go through all that,' interrupted Nigel. 'It's already settled. He's taking us there. We'll leave tonight. In the meantime, tell your men to put those guns away. These chaps here are our allies. This is Captain Davison and his men. I don't believe I caught your names.'

'Bill Smith.'

'Tim Jeffries.'

'Well, there you are, Smith and Jeffries. Captain Davison, Smith, Jeffries, may I introduce from Jamaica... I don't believe I ever caught your name either.'

'Colin.'

'Colin. Very good, Colin. Your men will be code-named the

Jamaican Bastards, if you don't mind. It'll save me the trouble of learning a new one.'

'Jamahcahn Bahstuds. I like dat. You all like dat?' He looked at his men. They bobbed their heads yes. 'Okay, we be de Jamahcahn Bahstuds. Who de hell are dey?'

'Dey be... they are... well, let's see. Captain Davison, I think Rebel Yell would be an appropriate code name for your men. You rather remind me of that fearsome Confederate commander Nathan Bedford Forrest. Is that all right with you?'

Davison bravely took the initiative to lower his hands. Smith and Jeffries followed his example. 'That'll be fine,' he said heatedly, 'but just who the hell are those guys and what the hell are they doing here?'

'We be de Jamahcahn Bahstuds, mahn,' said Colin, laughing. 'And you be Webel Yell.' He waved to his men and said, 'Stuff de guns.'

'They're a Jamaican drug gang,' explained Nigel. 'Temporarily enlisted on the side of justice.'

'Yeah, mahn, justus, mahn. Dat's what dis all about. Dat mahn dere, dat Stalkuh mahn, he be a teef and a liar. Now, what about sum breakfast, mahn?'

'Yes, they were just talking about that,' said Nigel. 'Will herbal tea and cereal suffice?'

'Whut kind?'

'April?'

April reiterated the list.

'Do you mind if we smoke ganja, mahn?'

'As a matter of fact, I do. We're about to be joined by another unit, code-named Black Jihad, who rather disapprove of that sort of thing—as do I, needless to say. And if I were you, I wouldn't cross either one of us. I've kept my side of the deal—there's Stalker—now keep yours.'

'**SIR GENERAL NIGEL HAVERSHAM**, I am Destroyer Mohammed.'

'Destroyer, how terribly pleased I am to meet you. I hope I can call you that—Destroyer, that is. Met so many Mohammeds in my time, I'd be confused. Good. And who are all these other chaps?'

As Destroyer introduced them, they nodded sharply in salute. It was like watching a chorus line of black Prussians, Nigel thought. 'Jamal B. Bad... Holy Terminator... Awful Ali... and Merciless Mustapha. Jamal, Holy Terminator, and I have fought gangs before— in the projects.'

'Oh, excellent. And why the white carnation buttonholes?'

'The white carnation symbolises the purity of black children like the Esteemed Iced Khalifa's own daughter, Jihad Golightly, for whose future we fight.'

'Oh, jolly good indeed. Sort of a children's crusade, what? 1212 and all that. Now I'd like you to meet Captain John Davison and his friends Bill Smith and Tim Jeffries. Collectively, their code name is Rebel Yell, as yours is Black Jihad. And that chap over there is Colin. He leads these other men who are code-named the Jamaican Bastards.'

Colin raised a black fist in salute. 'Power to Africa, mahn.'

Destroyer regarded Colin with cool disdain, as a boy from Eton might regard a boy from the Nelson Mandela Comprehensive. '*They* are with us on the jihad?' Destroyer asked Nigel.

'Oh, yes. Jihads make strange bedfellows, don't they?' Nigel replied. 'Oh, and there's one more introduction. That battered-looking chap Colin is so playfully slapping around is Sean Stalker, who will be our guide.'

Destroyer Mohammed looked about him. Here he stood in a young white woman's flat, confronting on one side the Dreadlocked-and-Depraved-Betrayer-of-Their-Race criminal classes and on the other the Late Enemy from the South.

'Does the Esteemed Iced Khalifa know about this?'

'Yes, I informed him this morning. You should know these men share our common purpose. But their participation will in no way diminish your vital role. Your exploits will bring new honour to the name Black Jihad.'

Destroyer regarded him doubtfully. 'What do we do?'

Nigel led him to a map he'd posted on the wall and jabbed his finger on it. 'That's our destination, a little speck called Tequila Wells. We leave for there tonight. The drug shipment, according to our informant, young Master Stalker, is coming across tomorrow, shortly before midnight. So there isn't much time. We have three missions to fulfill. First, intercept and destroy the drug shipment. Second, liberate Captain Davison's daughter, held captive by the Los Lobos Colorados drug gang—the gang for whom the shipment is intended. And third, we're to rescue my own goddaughter. Unfortunately, we have no way to contact her, but she bravely intends to prevent the drugs from reaching Los Lobos Colorados. So she's in a fair bit of danger.'

'And what about de money for de Jamahcahn Bahstuds, mahn?' interjected Colin.

'And of course, our friends the Jamaican Bastards have an additional item on their agenda. Master Stalker misplaced some of their funds in Tequila Wells. We'll recover that money as well.'

'The Esteemed Iced Khalifa told us we would be given training.'

'And training you shall have. Captain Davison?'

'Yes?'

'Kindly lead our men onto the green outside and put them through a round of... what the devil's that hobby of yours again? April told me about it, something you do on the beach?'

'Tai Chi?'

'Quite so. Tai Chi. I'm sure you'll find it most enlightening,' Nigel said to Destroyer. Then, to make it official, Nigel marched into the centre of the room and announced, 'Gentlemen, gentlemen, please, if I may have your attention. We have much to accomplish today. We'll start with a bit of training to sharpen our fitness for tomorrow's adventure. All of us have a great deal at stake. All of us must be primed for a grand assault, for perfect execution of our plan, Plan D, which I am now developing.'

Nigel began to pace. 'Given his extraordinary military background as a United States Army Captain, highly decorated, with plenty of combat experience in the rice paddies of Vietnam, Captain Davison will be my second-in-command. Captain Davison, as I'm sure you will come to appreciate, is a man of many talents—and talented with many weapons, including among them the human body.

'Captain Davison, as you can see, keeps quite fit lifting steel pipes and rolling concrete as the owner of a construction company— which, Destroyer, I would highly recommend should the Esteemed Iced Khalifa ever desire to build a resident mosque.

'But he is also a part-time instructor of Tai Chi, that famous, ancient, mystery exercise of the Far East, which is... well, it's rather a sort of martial art, I should imagine. And I need hardly tell you how valuable a knowledge of the martial arts will be when we engage the enemy tomorrow.

'So, gentlemen, please carry on, join Captain Davison on the green outside, and jolly good Chi-ing to all of you.'

Nigel's announcement was greeted with a great deal of glancing about. Was he serious? The Jamaicans broke the deadlock, leading the way out of the door in a rather shambolic procession. Next came Black Jihad. Behind his severe black-framed glasses, Destroyer Mohammed continued to look stern and earnest, sceptical and distrustful, like a devout Islamic pilgrim who suspects he's been thrown amongst Nigel Baba and his not quite forty thieves. But he was under a khalifa's command to do as he was bidden by Nigel, and he led his men out in good order, as though they'd been drilled quite a lot already.

Captain Davison and his men, however, had not moved at all. They stood their ground, like the stubborn, hayseed Confederates they were. *Nigel could easily imagine them standing by a railroad tie, chewing on a bit of hay, floppy hats on their heads, clothed in fraying, grey homespun and battered old boots. Politely, firmly, but somewhat menacingly, Captain Davison would say, 'Now y'all might rep'sent the law for the Yankees. But we don't abide by that down heah. This heah's the sovereign state of Tennessee. So you'll leave us be, if you know what's good for yuh.'*

The real Captain Davison, however, was not so soft-spoken. 'Just what the hell are you doing?' he said to Nigel. 'I came here to rescue my daughter—not to be some goddamned aerobics instructor.'

Even on a short mission like this, Nigel could not afford insubordination. He shot Davison a piercing glance, as he was well capable of doing with his pale blue eyes, his grey eyebrows capping them like exclamation marks. 'Captain Davison, we have but a single day to develop our plan of attack, to organise our supplies and communication, and to turn that disparate rabble into a single unit capable of executing our commands. Surely,' Nigel demanded, 'you can see the benefit of organised exercise to bring these men together as a team. Surely you can see the need to keep them usefully occupied while I develop our plans. And surely you can respect my desire for quiet and privacy while I beat every last vestige of information out of the bastard Stalker.'

'And why shouldn't I be a part of that?' Davison demanded, eagerly rubbing the palm of one hand over the knuckles of the other.

'Because someone needs to be responsible for those men. Surely that shouldn't be Colin. He'd have the whole lot of them climbing palm trees, hammocking in the branches, and smoking ganja. And just as surely it shouldn't be Destroyer. He appears to be under the misapprehension that he's a cadet at Sandhurst, and we should humour him in that delusion. Now I suggest you give these men some idea of discipline and give yourself—and them—a bit of fresh air. It'll do you good.'

'But...'

'No buts about it,' Nigel interjected forcefully. 'We're leaving tonight. We can't leave earlier and we won't leave later. Your job is to turn that shower into a respectable force. Those are the men on whom your daughter's safety depends. Surely that's responsibility enough. Now, get cracking.'

Davison showed a slight sullenness, which was necessary to show he wasn't cowed. But to Smith and Jeffries, standing behind him, he said harshly, 'Come on,' and they tramped out the door.

April looked at Nigel expectantly, bouncing on her toes, her eyes agleam with hope. But since Nigel said nothing, she forced the issue. 'Please, Nigel, can I go too?'

'Of course, my dear, as you wish,' said Nigel. She gave him, as a reward, an enormous, glittering smile, and went skipping out the door.

'So what now?' asked Stalker, who lay slouched in a director's chair. He lit a cigarette. 'Your turn to ram hot spikes up my bum? You're trained in that sort of thing, aren't you? Torture to make people talk?'

'Torture's hardly necessary. Never is, really. Don't get honest answers that way. You'll cooperate because you want your money...'

'I'm not going to get my money!' Stalker interrupted angrily. 'Not with those bloody Yardies around. That was your mistake, General.'

'... *and* because if you don't cooperate, we'll celebrate Guy Fawkes night a bit early and set you ablaze,' Nigel said. 'It's simply a matter of self-preservation, Master Stalker, and I'm sure you believe in that. Much more pleasant dealing with me than with that rather unpredictable Colin.'

'Oh, he's predictable all right. He's predictably moronic. And you are too, for that matter. Do you know how they treat people they don't like? They toss acid in their faces so they're scarred for life—a walking warning. And what makes you think you'll get on with them? That's a laugh. And what about the rest of that horror show you've organised? You can't fight Los Lobos. They might not even be alive. And even if they are, your own bastards are going to be at each other's throats—and at yours. We could have had a nice little partnership, General, and settled things amicably. But now... why should I cooperate with you or anyone? There's nothing in this deal for me anymore. The Yardies'll get my money, you'll get Alexandra, she'll get Elkstone, and all I'll catch is hell from that maniac when we don't find his daughter. That was another bloody moronic promise you made.'

Nigel looked at him steadily. 'There's no need for speeches, young man. All we need are answers to some questions. You can leave the rest to me. I'm not allowing gangsterism here.'

'Oh, right,' Stalker said, snarling cynically. 'You versus the Yardies.'

'We also have Black Jihad and Captain Davison's men. They're loyal.'

'Oh, yes, I've seen that, haven't I? Those bloody Malcolm X's... I'd trust them all right. They only think every white person is the incarnation of Satan, that's all. They're sure to love you, General. And the maniac, he's a very reasonable man, isn't he? I'm sure he'll be calm when you tell him his daughter's dead.'

'We don't know that. We have every reason to suspect she's alive.'

'Yes, of course. You who weren't there; you who didn't see any-thing. I'd trust your opinion.'

'Now I have a few questions. First, who exactly is delivering the drugs across the border?'

Stalker chuckled. 'Aren't you the dogged one? Never lose the scent. The steady huntsman.'

Nigel said sharply, 'You've deceived yourself if you think you shouldn't cooperate. I'm not appealing to your sense of honour—you have none. But surely you're not so insensate as to fail to recognise the perils of your situation. You've been dashed lucky so far, but skidding on very thin ice. Your luck is about to run out, young man—and out there, you have three sets of executioners: the violent commando father of a daughter you've betrayed; a gaggle of black fascist Muslims with a *fatwa* against people like you; and a wretched Jamaican drug gang that—you told me yourself—would like to boil your face away with acid. And they're just the beginning. What about Scotland Yard?

The remnants of Los Lobos? Me, for God's sake? And who knows how many others? And all you have to do—if you weren't such a blinkered bastard—is to cooperate and turn ninety per cent of your enemies into uneasy allies. Are you so blind as not to see that?'

Stalker chuckled again. With a magnanimous wave of his cigarette, he said whimsically, 'All right, General, all right. I surrender. I don't suppose it makes any difference anyway. I'll cooperate.'

Nigel pressed forward. 'Who...'

'Yes, yes, I know, who's bringing the stuff across the border. I can only tell you what I know, and that's not, frankly, a lot. Los Lobos always called them "The Jackals" or "The Jackals of Jiminez". I don't think they were regular suppliers, because Los Lobos didn't seem to trust them. I think that's another reason they wanted me involved in the deal—my money, my risk. They merely provided the muscle, the contacts, and set the thing up. I don't know anything else about them.'

'How were you to meet them?'

'I'd be taken there. It was a place outside town—Mesa Mendoza or something like that. I was to meet a man named Ramirez at the Blue Parrot Cantina in Tequila Wells. He was going to take me there.'

'He's expecting you?'

'He's expecting an Englishman. I gather we're rather rare in Tequila Wells.'

'Does Alexandra know all these... details?'

'She knows the town, of course. She may have overheard Los Lobos and me talking about the other bits. I don't know. Los Lobos weren't very bright, not very good at planning things or maintaining secrecy, living from grunt to grunt. Their only idea of security was to kill someone, just as their only idea of business collateral was hostage-taking—as you know. Suspicious buggers. But I suppose I asked for that when I told them about the Yardies. They thought I'd do the same to them. Couldn't get them to understand the most basic business principles—like building a client base. It's tragic, isn't it, how our past always haunts us? I suppose I'll always be typecast as a traitor.'

Nigel thought about what an easy target Alexandra would be in a place like Tequila Wells. A blue-eyed, golden-haired girl in a Mexican town with wide, dusty streets on which the only traffic were big balls of spiky tumbleweeds, the occasional mule hauling a peasant's meagre possessions, and the scuffed, weather-beaten boots of ferret-eyed, greasy-bearded banditos. The ruffians would be gathered on the town's old wooden porches, watching her with despicable grins, each fancying his chance.

Stalker said, 'I should think you'd be proud. She's a regular dambuster, isn't she? She's not fazed by little things like details—or mercy. She won't stop until she gets her bombs through and destroys her target—destroys me.'

Nigel grunted.

'It shouldn't be that hard,' Stalker continued. 'She's not flying into ack-ack. The entire population of Tequila Wells could probably fit into this block of flats. In a dusty little town like that, if she can't buy information with a few pennies from her—from *my*—quarter of a million pounds... well then, she's not half the Captain Biggles we think she is. I'm sure she thinks it's a piece of cake. I know I would. All she has to do is buy the coke, burn it, or bury it or whatever, and leave poor old Sean out to dry. Simple, if you're a bitch like Alex— or a bastard like me. You see, we're really more alike than you think, your goddaughter and me.'

Nigel grunted again. He was only half listening to Stalker. His mind was whirling with thoughts of action. 'Right,' Nigel said absently. 'Let's go outside and join the others, shall we? I could use a bit of fresh air myself.'

His veins were throbbing with an impulse, but he had to make sure it could be trusted. He needed to weigh it, test it, think on it. And he didn't have much time.

He led Stalker down the stairs to the lip of the green. There, arrayed in rows, broken by the well-combed surfer, was an astonishing spectacle. Nigel had expected a lot of violent grunting, men grasping each other by their lapels, throwing each other about. He had expected demonstrations of shod feet snapping into unprotected chins, men spinning like tops and driving elbows into bellies. At a minimum, he expected chaps to be slapping each other with basic boxing blows or twisting each other into knots through clever wrestling techniques.

Instead, he was confronted with an odd-looking rabble, pressing against invisible boxes and moving in slow motion as though they were mimes on the street, performing for pennies.

'Not exactly the playing fields of Eton, is it?' said Stalker, his cigarette dangling from his lips.

On the green, the Captain was giving directions. 'Now lift the right leg, slowly, keep your balance, and stretch it ahead of you. Breathe deep and press your arms forward.'

Seeing Butch Cassidy turned into Butch the Tai Chi instructor was amazing enough. But Black Jihad were an even more arresting sight. In their bow ties, dark suits, and severe black-rimmed glasses, they looked, Nigel thought, rather like the black equivalent of Englishmen in morning suits performing calisthenics in Hyde Park. He gave them full credit. They were excellently well drilled, doing their Tai Chi in perfect synchronisation. One could easily imagine them as the ceremonial guards at the tomb of the unknown Tai Chi instructor.

Another star performer, though this was hardly a surprise, was April. She looked as though she'd been raised from the cradle with a regular dose of Tai Chi every morning. It was, Nigel thought, watching her closely, a sort of California dream to see her in action—the beautiful, bronzed young thing, looking so supple, doing the most esoteric exercises with absolute grace, near a ridiculous statue of a surfer, beneath the warming rays of an October sun. He thought he could contemplate her for hours, as a Shintoist might meditate on a flower arrangement. Though April, he believed, was a damned sight more inspiring to look at than an aspidistra.

After April's perfect symmetry and Black Jihad's Nazi precision, the Jamaican Bastards looked even more straggly, unkempt, and chaotic than ever. It appeared as though years of ganja-inhalation had permanently disordered their muscular motor skills. They wobbled and stumbled, as though the guns sticking out of their waistbands were tipping them over.

As for Captain Davison's own men—the big, bearded, stolid Smith and Jeffries—they reminded Nigel of nothing so much as brown bears being trained for the circus—not graceful, certainly, but it was remarkable they were performing in tutus at all.

If it had been, as he assumed it would be, a traditional self-defence drill, Nigel would have gladly practised slitting Stalker's throat—an exercise he was sure to find relaxing and that would help clarify his thinking. But Nigel had no interest at all in a slow-motion ballet. He'd have to find his exercise elsewhere, perhaps carrying a suitcase full of five million dollars.

He took Stalker by the arm and planted him between Smith and Jeffries, who gave Nigel rather indignant looks—the sort, Nigel supposed, that hillbillies gave interlopers who stumbled upon their embarrassing Tai Chi sessions in the Blue Ridge Mountains of Virginia.

'Keep an eye on him,' Nigel said.

As he marched across the green he made a point of giving the chaps a cursory inspection, making such helpful comments as 'Keep that leg up there... You must feel the Chi, Colin, you must really *feel* it... Stretch harder, I want no slacking off. This isn't a debutante ball we're going to, you know...'

He took April by the elbow and said, 'Come with me, child. We're going for a walk.'

'But...'

'Come along.' He led her off the green, and they strode out across the parking lot, cutting down to the street, where the roar of the traffic was like a seashell held to the ear.

'Where are we going?' she said.

'We're going for a walk,' Nigel repeated, and then smiled and added as a sweetener, 'and perhaps a small bit of shopping.'

'Okay,' she said, leading the way down to the pavement. He expected she knew where she was going. 'You remember, General, how last night I was telling you to exercise more?'

'Hmm.'

'Well, I really think this Tai Chi would be great for you. I mean, like, it's so slow and gentle—anyone, no matter how old, could do it.'

'Really?' he said. 'How delightful. But you know, April, I frankly don't see myself on the verge of entering a supervised retirement villa in Torquay. I rather think of myself more as a greying commando. I don't need to limit myself to Tai Chi, I shouldn't think.'

'Oh, whatever,' she said happily.

Oh, foolish youth, he thought, how easily you are deceived. This silver hair is a sign of wisdom, experience, and knowledge of the world. It's not a sign of rust, rot, and redundancy.

And as an example of wisdom in action, here he was, walking down a noisy Los Angeles street, about to bare his soul to his most trusted lieutenant. He needed to test his instinct, free it from the beating passions of his heart, and expose it to the smog-obscured light of morning.

'You know, April, I was rather thinking about our little adventure to Tequila Wells. It seems to me there's no point in developing any sort of paper plottings at all. It's a straightforward proposition, isn't it? Get to Tequila Wells as fast as possible—perhaps leaving as early as this afternoon—pinch Alexandra off its dusty streets, and spirit her home.'

'What about Penelope?'

'We spirit her too, in one fluid movement. I imagine we must outnumber Los Lobos now if you add together Black Jihad, the Jamaican Bastards, and Rebel Yell. We might not have to tangle with the Jackals of Jiminez at all.'

He watched closely. She pursed her lips and puckered her eyebrows in deliberation, then said judiciously, 'Well, I don't know who these Jackals are, but, yeah, I suppose that's okay. But I'll need some time to pack.'

It was said with the insouciance of a Drake, a Raleigh, or a Wellington, Nigel thought, but he knew the consequences were enormous. The operation was a go—and it was a risky one. The most obvious risk could come from within their own ranks. Captain Davison would prove a fine officer, he had no doubt—as long as he could keep him pointed at the enemy. But if Penelope wasn't in Tequila Wells, waiting to be rescued… things could take a nasty turn, couldn't they?

Even if she were there, springing a trap on Los Lobos would be much more dangerous and difficult than he'd let on to April. Captain Davison was not a patient man. If they didn't find Penelope quickly, or if Alexandra were liberated but Penelope was not, he'd immediately suspect a double cross, and in his jealous rage he might lash out at Nigel with a screwdriver, a Bowie knife, or some slow-motion, Tai Chi disembowelling movement.

'Let's stop here,' said Nigel. It was a shopping mall, in the shadow of the First National Bank.

'ALL RIGHT, CHAPS,' Nigel said matily, after he'd marched his men from the green into the parking lot. 'The mission is on. We're going now—ahead of schedule. I'll brief you on the details once we pitch camp in Tequila Wells. For now, the key thing is to stick together. To that end, I have acquired insignia for our vehicles. As you see, April's car now proudly flies this small Union Jack from its aerial. I've also affixed a small GB sticker to her bumper. These insignia will identify us as Her Majesty's forces. Travelling in this car will be April, myself, and Stalker. Now then, for Captain Davison and Black Jihad, I have purchased these small American flags for your aerials. I believe this is the Confederate flag, Captain. For your bumpers, I have these "I Support Our Olympic Athletes" stickers. These insignia will identify you as the American forces—large and multiethnic as usual.

'Now, Colin, for your Jamaican Bastards, I've purchased these odd orange cats. They have suction devices on them so you can stick them on the inside of your rear windscreen. And for your aerials, we have these matching orange balls that say "Union 76" on them. I'm sure you'll find them most meaningful and with them we'll be able to identify you as the Jamaican Bastards.' He looked at them good-humouredly. He'd already decided that Stalker was theirs when this was over. He only wanted Colin's promise that Stalker would be an indentured servant on one of their Jamaican plantations for at least five years, preferably with an iron collar round his neck.

'Good,' Nigel continued. 'As I say, I'll answer all inquiries once we're in Tequila Wells and we can begin to lay out our dispositions. All right, gentlemen. Tallyho.'

But what followed wasn't the inspiring, kazoo-like sound of the hunting horns, the snorting of horses, the baying of hounds, the 'so-ho-ho' of the huntsmen. It was a deadly, urban sound, a wailing that came on fast—like a screaming, hysterical woman running towards one at a funeral. It was pitched to penetrate the ear, but it also paralysed the brain with shock. Nigel looked about him. Everyone stood with ears cocked, mouths open. No one could believe it—police sirens sounding like an air-raid warning. The bombs were about to drop— on them.

Nigel shoved Stalker into the back of April's car and said, 'Come on, my dear, let's go!' before he jumped in himself, lugging the leather and very heavy suitcase he'd bought in the mall.

'But shouldn't we wait?' she asked, putting on her seat belt.

'Go, go, go!' Nigel commanded.

The car shot into reverse, scattering Jamaicans, Black Jihadians, and rednecks like so many squawking chickens. Some of them pounded on the car, frightening her. She threw the car into forward gear and jammed on the accelerator. The car bolted like a nervous horse. She flung a right turn onto the street, just as a train of wailing police cars lunged and bounced past them like black and white panthers springing into the parking lot.

'Oh my God,' said April.

'Don't panic, my dear, just keep driving,' Nigel said. He twisted to look out the rear window, praying he wouldn't see a police car bounding after them, its banshee scream proclaiming their doom. 'Take some turns, old girl. It doesn't matter where you go, just get away from here.'

'Mind if I smoke?' asked Stalker.

'Yes!' affirmed April.

'Put that blasted thing away,' Nigel said of the unlit cigarette dangling from Stalker's lips.

'I only wanted to celebrate,' he said, grinning.

'Celebrate?! Celebrate?! To have our entire force collected like so many used milk bottles? Celebrate what?' Nigel exclaimed.

'Bloody Yardies—they're for it,' Stalker said. 'And that lunatic, I'll never see him again, or those bloody black fanatics of yours, thank God. I can hardly believe it. It's a miracle. One clean sweep and they're all gone. Thank God for your neighbours,' he said to April. 'At least there's someone with some common sense around here. What would you do if you looked out the window and saw a bloody army of golliwog maniacs drilling in your backyard? I suppose if you're an American, praise the Lord and phone the police.' He chuckled. 'Oh, to hell with you, I'm going to smoke.'

'No!' said April.

'And you know the best part,' Stalker said, ignoring her, the unlit cigarette between his fingers, 'is that we're partners again, General. Shake on it?' He offered his hand, but Nigel merely growled and looked away, hugging his suitcase to his knees.

CHAPTER SEVENTEEN

APRIL'S RED FORD TAURUS pulled up in a cloud of dust before a decrepit wooden building that advertised itself as the TEQUILA WELLS HOTEL, COME STAY WHERE YOU'RE WELCOME. This sentiment was repeated in big stencilled letters on its barn-like walls, on its slanted, shingle roof, and on a swinging wooden sign on a post in the front yard. A corral with two mangy ponies was a few steps from the hotel. There, a wooden sign read TEQUILA WELLS PONY RIDES, $5.

A Mexican in a straw sombrero and black moustaches was smiling from his rocking chair on the hotel porch. Chickens were pecking beside him, dodging the kicks from his boots and the rollers on his chair. A bottle of tequila was half hidden by a post. Two windows behind him were broken, as though he was in the habit of tossing his used tequila bottles over his shoulder into hotel bedrooms.

'Welcome, amigos, welcome,' he called out. 'Welcome to Tequila Wells. You would like to stay at the Tequila Wells Hotel? Very good rats... er... rates. Come stay where you're welcome, amigos, come to the Tequila Wells Hotel.'

'Look at the ponies,' April said. 'Oooh, I wonder if I'm too big to ride them.'

'Welcome, amigos,' the Mexican repeated, '*and amigas*,' he added with profound emphasis as he saw April stretch out from the driver's seat.

'Thank you,' Nigel replied. 'I take it you have rooms available.'

'Oh, si, si. We have rooms, we serve meals—home-cooked by Mamasita—we have pony rides. We have everything you need.'

'Jolly good,' said Nigel, ascending the steps to the porch. April and Stalker lagged behind—April smiling at the ponies, Stalker staring at the hotel in disbelief.

'Welcome, welcome,' the Mexican said, encouraging them forward. 'You like Tequila Wells?' he asked Nigel.

'Well, we've never actually been here before, but I'm sure it'll be charming. I take it that's the town over there,' Nigel said, pointing across a dusty expanse of desert and scrub where a few wooden shacks and a couple of bigger buildings rested on a flickering lake— a mirage. He hadn't seen a mirage since—where was it? Three decades ago, in Aden? He peered into the sun. The bigger buildings were made of adobe, he thought, and one of them was undoubtedly a church.

'Yes, that's Tequila Wells, amigo, where your dreams can come true. But you should stay here, I think. Big, home-cooked meals for hombres like us from the Mamasita, si? Very good, very cheap. And pony rides for the señorita. In town? None of these things. You not like it so much, I think.'

'Very well, my good man, book us in.'

'Mamasita!' he called back into the hotel. To Nigel, he said, 'Mamasita will give you rooms. You will like it here, I think. Tequila?' he offered, picking up the bottle and taking a modest swig.

'Jolly decent of you, but no, thank you. Not just now.'

A chubby woman came waddling onto the porch, uttering a stream of what Nigel assumed were Spanish curses at her husband. But seeing Nigel, she stopped and smiled, wiping her hands on her apron. 'Buenos dias,' she said.

'Quite,' Nigel replied, nodding and hoping she spoke English. 'We would like some rooms,' he said slowly.

'Come with me, señor,' she said, leading him into the hotel.

Nigel entered a passageway of wooden floorboards that were given an added rustic flavour by being covered with a thin layer of sand, making it sound as though one were walking on a gravel path. Ceiling corners were festooned with ornate spiderwebs that had probably been passed down as a family concern from generation to generation. There were flies buzzing about—keeping the front door open didn't help—but he'd been in much, much worse conditions than this. This was nothing to Aden's malarial mosquitoes, the Antarctic cold of the Falklands, or pints of Murphy's bitter along the Falls Road.

There were even remnants of gentility at the Tequila Wells Hotel. The scarlet wallpaper, for instance, which was drooping like dogs' ears from the walls, might, in Victorian times, have been quite splendid. Now, admittedly, it was stained, torn, discoloured, and shaded by dust. In an effort to keep it in place, painted wooden icons of Jesus and the Virgin Mary, their sacred hearts incarnadine, had been nailed on top of it. Canvasses on a secular theme had also been put into service. These, unfortunately, were of the tenebrous-portraiture-of-unattractive-people-no-one-cares-about school that frighten children with their inescapable eyes.

Behind the counter, where the woman stood, was another dusty shambles: a calendar, five years out of date, posted on the wall; row upon row of dusty tequila bottles lying in wine racks, a few standing upright as a display; a warped sheet of cardboard on which was written \$35 x 1 = \$35, \$35 x 2 = \$70, \$35 x 3 = \$105, \$35 x 4 = \$140, \$35 x 5 = \$175, \$35 x 6 = \$210 (the room rates, evidently, with no leeway for RAC discount); an old, framed photograph of a middle-aged couple who looked English.

She handed him a sheet of paper that read, 'Welcome to the Tequila Wells Hotel, where your custom is always wanted. Please fill in the information below so that we may better serve you.' He noticed a date typed at the bottom: 22/4/66. He'd been in Cyprus at the time, dodging Aoka bullets.

'Have you always owned the hotel?' Nigel asked as he began filling in the form.

'No, the owners, they left many years ago. They left the hotel to us because Pedro and I, we liked working here, and no one would buy it because the well, it went dry and no one comes to Tequila Wells anymore.'

'Well, we have,' he said reassuringly, as his pen hovered over the question *Do you plan to cross into Mexico during your stay? If 'yes', for how long?* 'What exactly is a tequila well, anyway? A festival or something?'

He heard a deep intake of breath. His eyes rose from the form to see her gaping at him in horror. He might just as well have confessed to having leprosy. She called out to the porch. 'Oh, Pedro, come! Come quick! The gringo has never heard the story of Tequila Wells!'

Boots slammed on the porch and came towards him in a medley of pounding heels, creaking floorboards, and leather soles grating on sand. Pedro stood, holding his tequila bottle by the neck, looking dismayed. 'You've never heard the story of Tequila Wells?'

Feet stamped on the floorboards above, showering Nigel with a blizzard of dust. A brace of children came off the stairs, jiggling past him, into the protective arms of Mamasita, to stare in disbelieving wonder at He-Who-Did-Not-Know-the-Story-of-Tequila-Wells.

'No, I'm afraid not,' Nigel said, brushing the dust from his shoulders. 'Is it well known?'

'Ai, ai, ai,' Pedro rubbed his head. 'You've never heard the story of Tequila Wells? You're sure, amigo? You're not drunk? You have not forgotten?'

'Of course I'm not drunk.'

'Never? Not in all your life? Ai, Mamasita, I cannot believe it. Why, gringo, Tequila Wells is where your dreams can come true.'

'Yes, I gathered as much. But surely there's more to it than that.'

'It is because of the well, señor. For many years—many, many blessed years—we could lower the bucket into the well and find bottles of tequila. It was a miracle! A miracle of the Blessed Virgin. The priest, he came back to the church because of it. Some say the bottles, they came from Pancho Villa, he hid them there. But no, that is not true. The well, it is blessed. But the blessing, it has been abused. And now, gringo, no one comes to Tequila Wells anymore, because one day a gringo tourist come and say, "Why don't you haul up all the tequila and sell it?" And we say, no, it is a miracle of God. But then the bottles, they all disappear, and the well, it went dry, and the tourists, they come no more, and the priest, he goes to many churches now.'

'How extraordinary. At least you seem to have no shortage of tequila,' he said consolingly, motioning to the racks.

'Si, señor, I was always a very holy man and I went to the well often with my troubles to call on the holy Blessed Virgin and the tequila.' He crossed himself. 'You see, señor, your dreams can come true in Tequila Wells.'

'Oh, si, definitely. Enchanting place, really.'

'Si, señor. Bienvenidos.' Pedro raised his bottle in toast and stumbled back onto the porch.

'That is the story, señor, the story of Tequila Wells,' Pedro's wife said. 'Will you stay long, señor? There is still much to do in Tequila Wells. There is the church, it is nice. There is the museum, it is always open. And there is still the well. It gives no more tequila, but it is still a holy place. In the evenings some of us, sometimes we say the rosary there. And when gringo tourists, they pass through to Mexico, they throw in a coin.'

'Well then, that should occupy us for at least a couple of nights, I should think. What do people do here, besides run your museum and hotel?'

'Oh, many, many things señor. To the east, there is a farm. Many work on the farm. Then there is the gas station and a market.' Her face grew a little darker. 'And the Blue Parrot Cantina. I not like that place. A single room for you, señor?'

'No, there are three of us actually. Do you have three singles? With private baths? Why don't you like the Blue Parrot Cantina?'

'Three rooms?' She looked pleasantly surprised. 'Si, we have three rooms.' She pointed to the ceiling, which he noticed was still leaking finely granulated wood. 'Upstairs. All private wash basins, señor. But only one bath. The bath, it is in the hall. But the hot water, it always works. And your meals, señor, they are free. I cook breakfast, lunch, and dinner for you. You are welcome here. We will help your dreams come true, señor.'

She had an innocently offensive smile—ominous black gaps, sticky-looking honey-coloured stains on her uneven teeth, her fat cheeks puffed up like big, suffocating balls of toffee. 'Splendid,' he said, forcing a smile in return. 'Do you take?' He held up his bank card.

'Oh, si, si.'

'Now, about the Blue Parrot Cantina...'

'Oh, I no like it. The tourists, they love it, they stay there, much money in it. But no more. Now the men, they go there to get drunk. Bad men there. Men from Mexico. Men with money.'

Stalker stomped in. 'You don't really mean you're going to stay here? There must be rooms in town. Something better than this antique hovel. I mean, the bloody thing's going to fall down any minute. It's not safe.'

Nigel signed the bill, collected their room keys, and leaned back, sliding an elbow along the counter, cutting a path through the dust. 'Oh, I think it'll suit our purposes,' he replied.

'What about that?' Stalker said, jabbing his finger at the wood dust drizzling from the ceiling. It did seem to be falling at a greater rate than before.

'Termites, I expect. But better termites than drug runners. That's our choice, evidently.'

'And I cook breakfast, lunch, and dinner for you, all included, single price,' Mamasita said to Stalker. 'You are very welcome here.'

'There, you see,' Nigel said, taking Stalker by the arm. 'One can't do better than that. And, I say, have you heard the story of Tequila

Wells? Pedro out there is an absolute scholar on the subject.' He led
Stalker onto the creaking porch. The rocking chair was empty. In the
corral, Pedro was leading a pony with April astride it. 'Hi, Nigel,' she
said gaily, waving at him.

Nigel nodded a finger in salute. 'Shall we stroll into town?' he said
to Stalker.

IT WAS AN UNPLEASANT WALK, especially for Nigel, staggering
with the suitcase, which he refused to leave behind, telling Stalker it
was his barrel of tricks; he even ostentatiously chained it to his wrist.
The heat made one's feet swell so that they chafed painfully against
the shoe leather. Deceptive dust clouds collected on one's moustache,
staining Nigel's fingers brown as he stroked it. And Stalker, the lily-
livered, whinged the entire way about how they should have driven
into town, how they were wasting valuable time, how Alexandra was
just waiting to be picked up at the Blue Parrot Cantina and whisked
away to freedom after returning his cash.

But Nigel wanted to see the land on foot. Especially if they were
going to rescue the girls by springing a trap on Los Lobos, he needed
to know the buildings, the streets, the places to hide, the areas that
afforded cover. And walking, he knew, helped him to think. He
always thought better in motion, whether he was pacing in a study or
tramping alone on a country road.

About halfway to town they passed a caravan park. When he'd
seen it from a distance, Nigel had assumed it was a rubbish tip. And
in a way, it was. The caravans were rusting hulks, resembling the giant
exoskeletons of long-extinct, prehistoric bugs. They were looped in a
circle, like conestogas from pioneer days guarding against Red Indian

attacks—a tactic Nigel had seen employed in countless Western films: 'Circle the wagons!'

In the gaps of the laager, he saw young children chasing each other, little puffs of dust at their heels as they kicked up the dirt. Two grey-haired grandmothers sat nearby, unself-consciously staring at the gringos.

In the far distance, beyond the caravans on their left, Nigel could see figures working in a field. Quite a lot of them. But whatever they grew, it couldn't be much—cactus flowers or something.

After the caravan park, they continued through empty scrubland until they reached the entrance to Tequila Wells. There was even a wooden archway with faded lettering on it. WELCOME TO TEQUILA WELLS, it said. In smaller letters below, it read, 'Where Your Dreams Can Come True.'

Ignorant tourists—those who, unlike Nigel, didn't know the story of Tequila Wells—might well ask what sort of dreams those were, because immediately following the archway was a graveyard of chipped and peeling white crosses that lay in front of an old Spanish mission of faded pink adobe and black wooden beams.

Nigel took Stalker round the graveyard, past the tall cacti that stood like sentries at the front steps of the mission, and into the church through big wooden doors that were lashed open.

It was dark and agreeably cooler inside. Two Mexican women, their hair tied up in kerchiefs, were sweeping the aisle. Nigel led Stalker past the worn wooden pews and the Stations of the Cross set in small alcoves on either side of the church's white stuccoed interior. He nodded before the altar. Behind it was a surprisingly accomplished mural in bright colours of a profusely bleeding Christ looking heavenward with calm, obedient eyes, as He suffered on the cross.

'Let's get out of here,' Stalker said. 'They're obviously not around and I can't believe she hid the money here.'

'There's something you ought to know,' Nigel said, still looking at the altar. 'Los Lobos have Alexandra.'

'How do you know?'

'Superior intelligence,' Nigel told him. 'Both my own and my contacts. This paltry £250,000 you continue to whine about is therefore presumably in the hands of Los Lobos, after all. And if Alexandra is here, it is as their prisoner.'

They emerged from the cool sanctuary of the church, blinking at the sun. Around the corner they found the main street of Tequila Wells. On their right was a petrol station, its windows and signs blackened by smashed insects. No one was working on cars or pumping petrol. But three generations of Mexicans in boots and straw cowboy hats sat in its glass-plated office, playing cards and drinking sodas.

On either side of the street were boarded-up shacks which bowed like drunken toe-rags to the Blue Parrot Cantina, its logo splashed huge and colourful above its eaves. ROOMS AVAILABLE! STAY HERE AND ENJOY! Mexican music—full of guitars and hyena laughter—drifted out of the cantina's swinging saloon doors and down the lonely street.

Nigel led Stalker past more dilapidated shacks, past a jagged wall, no more than knee-high, of pink adobe ruins that like everything else in Tequila Wells (except the Blue Parrot Cantina) were crumbling to dust. They came upon another adobe building. A rustic sign, written in Western frontier-style script, read TEQUILA WELLS MUSEUM. ADULTS $2, CHILDREN $1. The door was open and an old man, two days' grey stubble on his face, sat inside on a stool, reading a newspaper. 'Buenos dias,' he called out. He wore a sun visor and a clean white shirt with a bolo tie.

Nigel offered a royal tilt of the hand. 'Yes, just as you say,' and walked on.

Adjacent to the museum was a well, surrounded by a broad, smooth circle of dirt, set in a stone-walled courtyard. There was nothing beyond it, nothing but the ubiquitous scrubland that rose in bumpy sand dunes and disappeared into a blank, dusty expanse. He turned and looked up the street at the Blue Parrot Cantina.

'That's where they'll be,' Stalker said, rivulets of sweat trickling down one cheek. 'They're in the cantina or they're nowhere. There's nowhere to hide. Christ, General, we're wide open out here.'

Nigel nodded. He was completely calm, at least in part because he couldn't believe the gang was actually here. No ostentatious cars, no lookout at the door or on the roof, the locals apparently having their usual good time. This place—this dusty Mexican town in California, with a mission, a petrol station, a cantina, and dashed little else—had nothing to do with Alexandra, with Elkstone, with Pandora. It had nothing to do with England, green hedges, garden parties, or the thronging crowds of London. It was East of Suez (though admittedly West of Suez). It was Nigel's world of desert, dusky peoples, and possible danger, of untrustworthy allies and foreign tongues. It threw him back on the one person he trusted most—himself. But to find Alexandra here? That didn't seem possible.

He led Stalker behind the cantina. Parked in a row were three weather-beaten lorries, their paint faded into tones of ochre and umber and pink-rust red. At the end of the row, like a mark of punctuation, was a single motorcycle.

'I don't suppose you recognise any of these?' asked Nigel.

Stalker shook his head. 'No.'

They came round to the front of the cantina and stepped inside. As his eyes adjusted to the darkness, Nigel saw two Mexican cowboys sitting on stools at the bar and a bartender fixing him with surprised black eyes. On the walls were bullfighting posters, ornate sombreros, and posters advertising Mexican beer. Not a drug lord in sight. He put the case down carefully at his feet. The long chain kept it attached to his wrist.

'Buenos dias, hello, señor,' said the bartender. 'You would like a drink?'

'Yes, I believe we will.' Nigel stepped up to the bar. His every instinct urged him to blurt out, 'Whisky, barkeep.' So he did.

'And for you, señor?' he asked Stalker.

But Nigel slapped Stalker hard on the chest and said, 'Oh, no, not for him. He doesn't like whisky. So give us two beers as well.'

'Dos Equis? Carta Blanca? Tecate...?'

'Whatever you recommend, barman.'

A sullen-looking man rose from a booth in the corner, patting his lips with a napkin. He came up to Nigel. 'I didn't know you would be here so early,' he said. 'There are many hours still. I was just having a late lunch.'

It was obvious that Stalker didn't know him. Not one of Los Lobos, there was only one other possibility...

'Ramirez?' Nigel asked.

'Si, yes,' he said a little angrily, as if there could be any doubt. Anger suited his face. He had a dark, pinched brow that kept his eyes screwed up and agitated. 'Come. I want to finish my lunch.'

Ramirez slid into one side of the booth, Nigel and Stalker into the other. There was a framed photograph of a Mexican football team on the wall.

'Who's he?' Ramirez asked, pointing his head at Stalker.

'My associate, Herr Schweinhund, a German-trained expert in narcotics. I wanted someone to test the stuff. We won't be cheated, you know.'

Ramirez laughed, tore up a tortilla, and began sticking pieces in his mouth.

'Has anyone else been poking about, asking questions?' Nigel asked.

'Puh! No. No one else,' Ramirez said, dispeptically. 'Why should they? Stinking little town. No one comes to Tequila Wells. Not even the Border Patrol. Who would want to come here?'

'No strangers about?'

'Except for you, no. Why are you worried, señor?' he cracked an awful semblance of a grin. 'It is not a difficult thing to do, to sell drugs here. No one cares about Tequila Wells.'

'Men like us need to be careful.'

'Puh! No need for careful here. The Jackals have the drugs. You have the money, yes?'

'Yes,' said Nigel.

'Then no problem. Where are Los Lobos?'

'Well, I don't know if they're coming, actually. They didn't really think it was necessary.'

'Bueno,' he said, seeming very content as he scooped up a forkful of refried beans.

'Whisky and cerveza,' the bartender said, depositing their drinks.

'This is your round, Herr Schweinhund,' Nigel said, nodding at the suitcase chained to his wrist.

Stalker sighed and paid.

Ramirez resumed shovelling food in his mouth. Then suddenly he stopped, a fork laden with dripping cheese enchilada suspended in midair over his plate. His eyebrows parted company for a moment, his face lit up, inspired. 'But maybe we go now.' He nodded his head as though he were in violent agreement with himself and quickly shoved two final forkfuls into his mouth. 'Yes, I think we go now, señor. I will have dinner at home, instead of this stinking town. Come, I take you now.'

'Take me where?' asked Nigel.

'To the Jackals of Jiminez. There is no reason to wait. You have the money, they have the drugs. Let's do it, señor.'

'But we *don't* have the money—not on us at any rate. We've kept it in a safe place.'

'You don't have it?' Ramirez said querulously, eyeing Nigel's suitcase. He pointed at Stalker. 'I think you bring it, then. You bring it now, to us here. Then we go to the Jackals.'

'But that's impossible,' Nigel said. 'We were told midnight, and we'll stick to the schedule.'

'It is not impossible, señor! It is not impossible at all. It is not impossible *unless you are lying!* If you have the money, you bring it, you bring it now, and we go.' He belched and pounded his fist against his breast.

Nigel and Stalker sat in painful silence.

'I think maybe the Jackals don't like this,' Ramirez continued. 'I think maybe you have no money. I think maybe you are liars. I think maybe *you*,' Ramirez pointed at Nigel, 'come with me. And *you*,' he looked at Stalker, 'you bring the money—or you no see your friend no more.' Ramirez put his hand inside the pocket of his metallic blue jacket and aimed the pocket at Nigel. 'Okay?'

He could be bluffing, Nigel thought. He mightn't have a gun at all. Even if he did, he wouldn't dare commit a murder—or two murders—

in front of all these witnesses. Or perhaps—given *these* witnesses—he would. This was the Wild West, after all. This was Tequila Wells, not Tunbridge Wells. Those Mexican cowboys and the bartender probably saw a murder a week at least.

'Okay?' Ramirez repeated.

'And the drugs?' asked Stalker.

'You come back with the money, we'll trade. But you should hurry, señor. I don't think he likes staying with the Jackals much.'

'All right, sounds fair enough. It's a deal,' Stalker said, sliding quickly out of the booth.

'We meet here. In two hours. You be here, señor.'

'It might take me a little while—so don't rush off. In the meantime, shall I carry your case, Nigel?'

'No, thank you,' Nigel grumbled.

'Well, then, you keep a stiff upper lip, old boy.' A grin slipped through. 'Cheerio.'

CHAPTER EIGHTEEN

RAMIREZ DIRECTED NIGEL TO ONE of the lorries behind the Blue Parrot Cantina and told him to kneel. Nigel knew what was coming— not a bullet in the brain, but a hard blow to the skull so he'd be limp and unconscious for Ramirez to throw in the lorry and forget, with no worries about escape. But as the pistol butt came hammering down, Nigel rolled forward. The blow caught him hard on the muscles of his neck, and he fell face first into the sand, feigning unconsciousness. Ramirez was not a particularly big man and he strained, grunting to haul Nigel into the flatbed of the lorry, unaware of the unconscious assistance that made the job easier. The Mexican struggled with the suitcase, wrenching at the chain that linked it to Nigel's wrist.

Nigel bounced on the hot, ribbed metal as they sped across the scrubland. He saw nothing, of course, except the accumulating dirt. He could have hurled himself over the side, attempted his escape, but to what effect, besides possibly breaking an arm, a leg, his neck? The lorry was racing far too fast, and he was curious to see the dreaded Jackals of Jiminez. The lorry swerved to a stop. What had elapsed? Three quarters of an hour? Ramirez came back and unsnapped the tailgate. His pistol was visible now. He waved Nigel forward. 'Come on.'

Nigel saw a dozen well-armed Mexicans, who, for whatever reason, reminded him of the Montagnard tribesmen he'd seen in Vietnam. A heavily muscled young fellow with a chiselled face and early Beatles-style hair came to the front, his wraparound sunglasses glinting. Jiminez, Nigel thought, and these are his jackals.

Nigel had no Spanish, but even if he had, he doubted whether he would have understood more than a few of the words Jiminez and Ramirez spat at each other, their voices crepitating like bursts from automatic weapons. Jiminez fired off a final volley and shouted some orders to his men, who regarded him with impassive, flat, Amazonian Indian faces, obediently shifting their automatic rifles and submachine guns on their shoulders and slouching off. Not the smartest-looking outfit, Nigel thought. But with the weapons they had, they could certainly cause trouble.

He watched them slope away to his right past a small collection of lorries, which blocked his view of everything save scrubland. 'In there!' Ramirez's voice snapped like a whip. Nigel turned and saw a pistol. 'In there!' Ramirez repeated, pointing at a horrible wooden shack that was either a latrine or a garden shed. 'Come on, gringo! Move it!' He shoved Nigel forward. 'Open the door!' Nigel yanked back the bolt and dragged the door towards him, its uneven base grasping at pebbles and sand. He was still pulling when battering-ram Ramirez hit him in the small of the back and shoved him into the darkness, suitcase and all. The door hurriedly bounced shut, the bolt slammed into place.

Nigel knelt and felt the earthen floor. He ran his fingers along it until he reached what felt like sandbags. That was good enough. He sat, resting his back against them, to think, wait, and swelter with the flies, ants, and whatever other creepy-crawlies were his neighbours in the dark. Tarantulas... scorpions... gila monsters...

It was hot and stifling, but at least it didn't smell like a latrine. He wondered what was in the shack. Surely these sandbags weren't filled with cocaine? It would have been awfully rash to store him in their warehouse. His fingers clawed to pry one open. He couldn't manage it, especially with a heavy suitcase lashed to one wrist. He tried to smell them, but all he could smell was dirt. He lay back again and thought.

Everything wasn't black, he told himself—or actually, it was. But his position wasn't *that* hopeless. Quite a decent position, really, when one thought about it. Once he became accustomed to the light, it would be no great trouble to find a tool, hack his way out of the shed, trek from he-knew-not-where across uncharted desert to find Alexandra, spring an ambush on Los Lobos to rescue her and Penelope, spirit the girls to freedom, shackle Stalker, hand him over to the Jamaicans (though he'd have to break them out of gaol first), and then explain things to the authorities so he could fly home and receive his bottle of Glenfiddich from Pandora. Piece of cake, as Stalker would say.

He knew what he had to do. His hands groped in the sand for a tool. He couldn't find a spade, a shovel, or a pick, but he did find a palm-sized, sharp-edged rock. It would do. He crawled on all fours to the rear wall and began hammering, chipping away the wood, the suitcase lurching against his side with every blow.

But then he heard something. Running footsteps partially muffled, thudding in the sand. Mexican voices. He rolled the rock away and crawled to the door. The bolt was flung back, the door hurled open. There he saw the dark silhouette of a man holding a rifle. There was a brief glimpse of the stock before the butt crashed into his chin, snapping his head back. Something else hit him, like a mad dentist testing his novocained jaw with a hammer. He fell back in the sand and dreamt of England.

HE WAS AWAKE HOURS BEFORE they pulled him out. He sat with his back against the sandbags, calm, meditative, trusting to fate, stroking his sore and slightly swollen jaw, and thought of writing a book—*Enduring Beatings: An Experienced Guide For Old Age Pensioners*. His suitcase was safe, still chained to his wrist.

Whatever was going to happen, he told himself, would happen soon, and he'd play whatever new cards he was dealt.

The Mexicans chattered excitedly as they dragged him out of the dark of the shed into the dark of the night and loaded him on a lorry. He wasn't going to be alone on this ride, though. The lorrybed was already full of gunmen. Hands grabbed his arms, planting him in the centre, his suitcase on his lap. The sharp, pointed toes of cowboy boots crowded against him. Someone wrapped a bandana round his eyes, and the truck jerked ahead.

'What you got in the suitcase, señor?' he heard one ask.

'My regimentals,' Nigel lied. 'In case I'm invited out to dinner. You know—mess dress?'

'Mess dress? You queer or something, señor?'

Nigel forced a smile, shook his head, and trusted to foreigners' belief in British eccentricity.

When they stopped, the bandana came off. Men grasped him on

either side and they jumped off the lorry. There were three other lorries, parked in formation, their headlights the only illumination in the
dark desert night. Nigel stumbled as he was shoved forward, and saw
gunmen gathering in the beams.

Their headlights were answered by three other pairs, perhaps
seventy-five yards in the distance. Jiminez shouted something in
Spanish from nearby and Ramirez answered him from the headlights
ahead. Immediately, they were arguing again, spitting fire at each
other, like machine-gunners duelling in the night. Then a crystal voice
cut through the firefight like a flare. It was an English voice, its dic-
tion clear and precise. 'We're not settling anything until you speak
English. Both of you!' It was Alexandra!

Nigel's pulse jumped. He licked his lips and tried desperately to
think of what extraordinary feat he could perform to effect their
escape. Her voice was a tonic, restoring his sense of purpose, filling
him with energy. This was it. The final showdown. He'd found her.
And now all he had to do was escape from these dozen over-armed
Mexican-Indian mercenaries, steal a lorry, and snatch her away. Piece
of bloody cake! The Mexicans tugged a little harder on each of his
arms.

Ramirez shouted something in Spanish. A confident, handsome
young man tapped Nigel on the chest. Nigel didn't recognise him at
first, without his wraparound sunglasses, but it must be, he thought,
Jiminez.

'Speak to them!'

'Hello. Alexandra, dear. Nigel here,' he called into the illuminated
darkness.

'Oh, General, thank God! Are you all right?'

'Perfectly fine, my dear. A few scrapes, a sore jaw, nothing serious.'

A different voice said, 'Good for you.' Nigel scowled. It was Stalker, the bastard.

'They want the money, General,' said Alexandra.

'*My* money,' corrected Stalker.

'Well, then, I suggest you give it to them, my dear. I think it might be helpful where I'm concerned.'

'Well, that's just it, General. It's a problem. I don't have it.'

'What?!' Stalker screamed. 'You bloody liar! Where the bloody hell is it?'

'Yes, my dear, it would be helpful if you could find it,' Nigel affirmed.

'But surely,' Alexandra said, 'you've got it.'

Jiminez tapped Nigel on the chest again. Nigel looked into his big, sombre eyes. Jiminez rubbed his fingers together. 'Dinero,' he said, then drew a finger across his throat, 'or die.'

Nigel called out, 'I don't mean to trouble you, my dear, but it appears they want to kill me. Perhaps we can try something else for ransom.' He had no intention of parting with the Williamson inheritance; the game wasn't up yet. 'What about that rather ornate cigarette lighter Stalker has?'

Sharp whispers duelled in the distance, sibilants clashed like foils. A blade struck; there was a winner. 'Right,' said Alexandra. 'We're sending Ramirez across with it.'

He heard the sand kicked by footsteps. And then, blindness.

It was as though a dozen flashbulbs had exploded in his face. Voices came through megaphones and in the sky he suddenly, faintly, heard an engine. 'Put down your weapons. Order your men to put down your weapons. You are surrounded.'

Now sirens blared and lorry engines roared. He looked up. A spotlight shone from the sky.

'This is the American Drug Enforcement Agency. Drop your weapons and raise your hands.'

'This is the California Border Patrol. Drop your weapons.'

'This is the San Diego County Sheriff's Department. Drop your weapons.'

'This is the FBI...'

There may have been other announcements as well, but Nigel's ears were saturated with spit as Spanish expletives crashed all about him.

Jiminez's eyes flared like a jaguar's, full of anger and contempt. He spat at Nigel's shoes and roared at his men, as a dying beast might roar. Weapons thudded onto the sand and Nigel's arms were freed. Nigel shrugged his weary shoulders, stretched his arms... and Jiminez snarled and slapped him hard across the mouth with the back of his hand.

It hurt like hell, landing flush on his throbbing welts. 'I think that's bloody well enough!' Nigel exploded, stomping his heel on Jiminez's arch, kneeing him in the groin, slamming the heavy suitcase against his nose, and knocking him into the sand.

'Hey, break it up over there!'

The American authorities were drifting in, the men spread out in good style, less vulnerable to sudden bursts of fire. They wore a variety of uniforms, but all of them had their arms ready. They saddled themselves with the weapons they scooped up from the sand, and started handcuffing the Jackals.

'Hey, you! You! I'm talking to you!' An overweight man in a cheap blazer, his tie undone, was striding purposefully to Nigel. He had a large automatic pistol in his hand. 'You Nigel Haversham?'

Nigel was watching two muscular sheriffs handcuff Jiminez. Now, perhaps, it was his turn. 'Yes, I'm General *Sir* Nigel Haversham,' he said, wondering whether his false knighthood might earn him a temporary reprieve.

'Good. Then you're coming with me, you goddamned, interfering limey bastard,' he said, leading him across the sand. 'I've had one helluva lot of trouble thanks to you. I'd appreciate it if you kept your goddamned nose out of our business. You've caused one hell of a big stink, and all this fucking bullshit bureaucracy. Now everybody's getting in on the act. You can just be thankful, buddy, that we got 'em, or so help me, you'd be rotting away in Chino and I'd say "Fuck you" to the Queen.'

'That's rather strong,' Nigel protested.

'I just hope this is one helluva major bust. And we better get some fucking credit for it this time. And as for you, I want you out of here. Go back to Limeyland where you belong.' He dug into his pocket and pulled out a folded sheet of paper. 'Here. This is for you—your "get out of jail free" card. It's a fax from Scotland Yard.'

Nigel unfolded it, reading it by the headlights. It was from Inspector Byron Tanner. It said, 'General Haversham, thank you ever so much for giving me the opportunity of cooperating with the American authorities. It was, indeed, a pleasure. Come home, now, like a good chap. England has need of you.' Nigel folded it up and put it in his pocket.

'General!' He spun round and saw Alexandra standing by a lorry. Beside her, a handcuffed Stalker was being led away.

'Oh, yeah,' said the fat man. 'She's the other one. Take her with you. Now get the fucking hell out of here,' he said, waving good riddance. 'You're free to go.'

'General,' she repeated, as she rushed into his arms.

Nigel held her and blinked, his nose resting in her soft, golden hair.

He wasn't blinking back tears. He wasn't terribly emotional at all, really. He was simply confused. What the devil was going on?

'Oh my God,' Alexandra said. She pushed herself back to look him in the face. 'I can't believe everything that's happened. At least you're safe.' Her fingers felt his chin. 'But that's an ugly-looking bruise. Are you sure you're all right?'

'Perfectly.' Nigel remembered his duty. 'And Penelope, she's all right?'

'Oh, she's perfectly safe—in San Diego. We escaped together.'

'Hah,' he grunted. 'So Los Lobos were lying; trying to get the ransom when you'd already legged it. And April?'

'I sent her after Penelope.'

'Good show.'

'Get these guys out of here!' said the fat man. But he wasn't talking to Nigel. He saw the Esteemed Iced Khalifa standing in all his black-suited, bow-tied glory near a row of handcuffed, guarded Jackals.

'Do you have enough light, Mustapha? Then give me a count of three and take the picture.' He thrust out his chest, arms akimbo. 'Now what about a picture near that truck, consulting with a DEA man?'

A rough hand shook Nigel by the shoulder and spun him round. He was pierced by the deadly bullet eyes of Captain Davison, one huge, gnarled hand seizing Nigel's collar, the other drawing back as a fist. 'I'll give you one chance. Where's Penelope, or I'm breaking your goddamn jaw right now!'

'Your Penelope's been rescued, Captain. Thanks to my intrepid goddaughter here, she's sunning herself on the beaches of San Diego—though, I grant you, perhaps not now, at midnight. Now kindly unhand me.'

Captain Davison dropped his hands, squinting in bewilderment. 'San Diego? What the hell's she doing in San Diego?'

'We thought it the best place to store her. Picturesque, plenty of things to do, secure by the seaside.'

'But she's okay? Nobody's touched her?'

'Would they dare? You've seen what I've achieved here.'

'What *you* achieved? Listen buddy, we're the ones who brought the cops—after you hung us out to dry.'

'I rather thought that was my work,' said Alexandra with admirable, cool-eyed scepticism.

'You stay outta this, missy. I didn't see you at the police station.'

'I prefer to work by telephone.'

'I told you to stay out.'

Nigel raised his hands to signal that he could set things right. 'All part of Plan E, you see. My job was to infiltrate the enemy, and I relied on you,' he said to Captain Davison, 'as I knew I could, to bring these security services here to mop things up.' He produced the fax the fat man had conveniently given him for his little white lie. 'You see, here's my communication from Scotland Yard. Everything was organised at the highest levels.'

Captain Davison read it in front of the headlights, handed it back to him, and looked at Nigel with the round, open mouth and the dull, speechless eyes of a gunfighter shocked to find he's been hit, and not yet ready to sink to his knees.

'Do you understand now?' Nigel said huffily.

Captain Davison nodded slowly and said, 'Uh huh.'

'Very well, then.'

'But wait,' said Captain Davison, reanimating. 'How's Pen going to get home?'

'A trifling detail. Alex, how's she getting home?'

'She has a car.'

'There. She has a car. Now is that all?'

'Well, yes,' said Captain Davison. 'I guess so. But... I guess I should thank you, Sir General Nigel Haversham.' He held out his huge paw.

Nigel took it. 'Not at all, my good man. Let me know if you're ever in London. As you can see,' he said holding up the folded fax, 'I'm being summoned back at once to deal with some internal security difficulty. Could always use a man like you. In the meantime, keep a close eye on that daughter of yours. You simply must stop her drinking to excess with despicable, dark-haired, brown-eyed men.'

'Drink? But she doesn't drink.'

Nigel gave him an 'Oh, really?' look with his eyebrows and slapped him on the shoulder. 'Goodbye.'

Alexandra took Nigel's free hand as they weaved through the law enforcers. 'Now, my dear,' he said, 'how do we make our escape?'

'Over there,' she said, pointing to a motorcycle. It was the one he'd seen behind the Blue Parrot Cantina. 'I'm sorry I only have one helmet.'

'Don't be silly. I only have one goddaughter. Haven't worn a helmet since the Falklands. You wear it. I'm not in the least concerned about scrambling my brains. Let's be off, shall we?'

He mounted the mechanical horse, clicked free the handcuffs with the key he'd carefully hidden in his lapel, clamped the case behind him, and wrapped his arms around her.

THEY CHECKED INTO A HANDSOME HOTEL in the early hours, adjacent rooms along a starlit veranda overlooking a glittering swimming pool. Nigel had barely had time to shower the Tequila Wells dust out of his turnups when there was a knock at the door.

'Mamasita?' Nigel gasped. Did she run *this* establishment too? Had her English benefactors been so generous?

Alexandra's monkey face appeared over Mamasita's shoulder, creased into an elfin grin.

'Mamasita be buggered, Nigel,' the Mexican woman's accent was now pure Mayfair by way of Belgravia. She crossed to Nigel's mirror, sat down, and proceeded to pull cotton wool wads out of her mouth. 'Oh, that's better.'

'Pandora?' Nigel was using the door frame for support, blinking in disbelief.

She turned to him, dabbing at her face with theatrical cream, 'Alias woman with big poodle when you first met April and Penelope.'

'Good God.' He felt Alexandra steady him.

'Alias,' and she switched to her Southern belle, 'Dixie Dorley, honey. Y'all come back now, y'heah?'

'I can hardly believe it.'

'Alias,' she pursed her lips and popped on, from a deep pocket, a pair of butterfly glasses, 'Miss Perkins, from Head Office, General Haversham.'

'But this is incredible.'

'Alias, as you know,' and she sighed as she hauled off a huge padded corset, 'Mamasita, señor, making all your dreams come true.' Her accent vanished again, 'I'm glad you didn't stay for breakfast, Nigel. My tortillas are not, I fear, what they used to be.'

Nigel slumped onto the bed. Alexandra poured a scotch from the mini bar. 'Am I actually awake?' he asked.

'Nigel,' Pandora sat beside him, her face streaked with five and nine, 'Alex and I owe you an explanation.'

'I rather think you do.'

'Tell me, when you were last at Elkstone, did you notice anything?'

'Stalker,' he remembered.

'No, I mean about the house.'

'No, I don't think so.'

'The place is falling into rack and ruin, Nigel.'

'Well, the odd bit of dry rot,' he conceded.

'No, it's far worse than that. The family silver has long gone, I'm afraid. What with death duties after Reginald died and a few unwise investments. And now this blighter Blair is Prime Minister, he's bound to make things worse. So I hit upon a plan...'

'Alexandra's inheritance,' Nigel realised.

Pandora nodded. 'Not available until she's thirty-five. That's another fifteen years, Nigel. I couldn't wait. Sean Stalker was the key.'

'He was in on it?'

'Of course,' Alexandra said. 'He was, as you discovered when you first met him, a posturing prat. He'd do anything for money and had this Hollywood pipe dream. He also had some shady underworld connections.'

'Los Lobos.'

'Exactly. Stalker arranged for them to 'kidnap' me. And with something as horrendous as that—international incident, aristo kidnapped and so on—the tight-fisted Trust would have to put up the money.'

'They wouldn't do it for anything else,' Pandora chipped in. 'I know, I tried.'

'Unfortunately, the whole thing misfired,' Alexandra said, 'and Los Lobos got greedy. So did Sean. I'd promised him a cut, but he wanted more and was already involved of course with the Jamaicans back in London.'

'The Bastards.'

'Oh, they weren't so bad,' Alexandra cooed. 'But it certainly complicated things. He never knew, of course, the actual sum involved in the ransom or he'd never have settled for the little he did.'

'But where did I fit in?' Nigel asked, still bewildered.

'You were my rock,' Pandora held his hand. 'My husband's oldest friend. My knight errant. I wouldn't risk Alex with a degenerate like Stalker. I needed you there to protect her.'

'I didn't do a very good job,' Nigel had to confess.

'My dear,' she kissed his cheek, 'you did splendidly. I couldn't of course sit at home wringing my hands, so I put my theatrical training to good use and popped up every now and again, just to keep an eye. Borrowing the poodle was no problem, and Pedro was only too delighted to be my husband for a day, given the wad of cash I gave him. Le Grand Extravaganza, swallowing Miss Perkins from Head Office, was a *little* more of a challenge, but breeding will out. Did I *really* look like Diana Dors, by the way?'

'Her double,' Nigel smiled.

'Flatterer!' Pandora cuffed him round the ear.

'Well, all's well, I suppose. You'll be giving the money back?'

Pandora flashed a glance at her daughter. 'Nigel, Nigel,' she said. 'We can't possibly do that. We told you, Elkstone must be saved.'

'But Los Lobos...'

'The plan was, they would take possession of the money Stalker took from the Jamaicans and let Alex go. It would be refreshing in this day and age to say we found scum with a sense of honour, but, unfortunately, as you know, they were wiped out to a man.'

Alexandra added, 'Getting hit like that *was* a little hairy. It also meant that mummy had to pretend to you that they'd still got me, knowing that Stalker would have told you I'd got away.'

'But Stalker will talk.'

'And no one will listen,' Pandora said. 'Did *you* believe a word he said? The beauty of it all, Nigel, is that Los Lobos, who were supposed to have received the ransom, were wiped out, and the money has mysteriously vanished. The five million is of course insured. So the Trust is happy because they'll get the insurance money. Alex and I are happy because we get to keep the five million for the glory of Elkstone, and we'll be happy again in a few years' time when the inheritance rightfully becomes Alex's.'

'But it's not honest,' Nigel insisted.

'It's Alex's money,' Pandora told him. 'It's just that she's got it now rather than later. Well, now *and* later, actually.'

Nigel stood up. He looked at them both, the elegant, brilliant widow of his old friend and his impish, reckless goddaughter. He paced the floor, looking now at the suitcase, now at the fancy dress that had been Mamasita, now back at the ladies.

'All right,' he said. 'For the glory of Elkstone. But that still leaves Stalker's £250,000 unaccounted for.'

'Oh, I know where that is,' Alexandra said. 'I'll show you tomorrow.'

'No, you'll show me now,' Nigel said narrowly. 'I want all my ducks in a row.'

'AND YOU SAY YOU CHANGED the money into something else?' Nigel was rubbing his wind-burned ears and looking up at the brilliant stars in the San Diego sky. It felt good to get his legs unstraddled from their narrow-backed steed and to wipe the bleary tears from his wind-tormented eyes.

'Not changed, General, not like water into wine. I invested it.'

Nigel looked about him. They were in the parking lot of a quite splendid hotel. A tall, high-rise, modern-looking thing, clean with wonderful palm trees in front and a shining swimming pool behind. 'Invested, you say? Jolly clever. What did you invest in?'

'In art. You know, the collectible kind. I actually let Penelope choose it. We found it at an auction.'

'Penelope?' Now don't be too hard on her, he thought. The girl's an artist herself. 'I mean to say, is it any good?'

Alexandra shrugged her shoulders. 'It doesn't honestly matter, really. It was just a way to get the money off our hands.'

They crossed the quiet lobby, the desk clerk smiling at them as they walked to the lifts.

Alexandra had called ahead so that Penelope and April would be expecting them, which was a jolly good thing at three o'clock in the morning.

'Nigel!' screamed April as she opened the door, hugging him, pulling him inside, and pointing at Penelope. 'Look, we've got Pen!'

'Hello, old girl,' Nigel said, unable to hide the exhaustion in his voice. Penelope sat on a couch, her long legs curled up, smiling her big-lipped, big-tongued, big toothy smile.

'Well, hello,' she said, and he remembered that strange, thick whine she had.

'And look what she bought!' April said happily, pointing in her usual game-show style to a faceless styrofoam dummy dressed in knickers. Leaning against the wall behind it were six framed paintings.

'That? What the devil's that? That's worth a quarter of a million pounds?'

'Oh, yeah!' said Penelope springing from the couch and assuming the role of art lecturer. 'They're really valuable. Like, I'm amazed we were even able to buy them.'

'What the devil is it?'

'Well this,' Penelope said, directing everyone's attention to the styrofoam figure, 'is the original outfit Madickweed used for her video "The Slave of the Man with the Big Parts".'

'Madickweed?!' he blubbered.

'Yeah, can you believe it? I can't believe we got it. I mean, this must be worth a ton on the open market. And these,' she said, stepping round the styrofoam figure and pointing at the paintings, each in turn, 'are six originals by Barney Paxporte. He's like, you know, the next Warhol. Aren't they cool? They're, like, little, sly essays about consumerism. You know, like, to me, they really make materialism, like, reflect back on itself in a really scarily beautiful way.'

Nigel didn't need to take a closer look. They were horrible enough from where he stood. They weren't really paintings at all—at least, not paintings as he understood them. They were photographs pasted over painted psychedelic backgrounds. The first two had naked young men, one black, one white, looking at the viewer (and, thank goodness, cut off at the waist), sweatbands around their heads (white for the black man, black for the white man), their wrists held up to show off their watches. The next had a well-dressed man striding through an airport, a suitcase prominently displayed in one hand. The other held a leash, leading a naked black woman on all fours.

Nigel's eyes hurried over the last four pictures, each one more ghastly than the last: a flaming red sports car resting on a pedestal of black workmen, a stunning young woman in red heels standing on the bonnet, her red skirt billowing provocatively in the wind; a man sitting on a naked woman's back, reading the newspaper; a litter of infants dressed in business suits and crawling towards one; an emaciated man on his knees, eating a banana, a muscle-bound, whip-wielding, turbanned black slave-dealer behind him.

'What do you think?' asked Penelope.

'Oh, yes, stunning,' he replied. 'But what will you do with them? I suppose you could actually wear... well, those things. But what about these... these pornographic pictures? Surely you're not going to hang them in your flat?'

'Oh, no,' Penelope said, looking very serious. 'They're, like, worth too much money. You're just asking to be robbed. We're going to put them in a vault in a bank, just as soon as we get back to L.A.'

So this was how it was going to end—at least three drug gangs smashed, a British fugitive from justice caught and arrested, two kidnapped women successfully freed, a noble bit of insurance fraud indulged in to provide for the deserving *nouveau pauvre* aristocracy, and, to top it all, the remaining quarter of a million pounds they were all clawing for had come down to knickers and the worthless pictures of a madman, to be locked in a bank vault in L.A. It could have been funny, Nigel thought, but he felt his tired muscles quivering for one last thrust of action. He wanted to kick the bloody things to pieces.

'The real question,' said Alexandra, 'is how we're going to divide them. I suppose, in a way, we should turn the money over to the police, but, you know, General, it doesn't really belong to anyone. I suppose the Jamaicans have a right to it—but do they really? I mean, they're criminals. And where did they get it from? From a wretched collection of pitiful drug addicts, most likely. We'd never be able to track them down. And even if we could, they'd only use it to buy more drugs and support more Jamaican drug dealers. That can't be right. So, it may be a little sin, but I thought we should keep the money and divide it amongst ourselves, and give anything that's left over to charity. There's four of us, and we've got six paintings and the

Madickweed outfit. You've done so much for us, General, that I really think you deserve first choice.'

Nigel pursed his lips and looked at her under his eyebrows. 'I see.' He paced the room, careful not to get too close to the blasted things, because he knew he wouldn't be able to restrain his eager leg. Seconds ticked by, and then minutes, but Nigel paced and said nothing, while the girls watched.

Finally, he turned about and caught them all in a steely blue gaze beneath his surging white eyebrows. 'We're not dividing anything. And we're not keeping the bloody rubbish. You're getting rid of it.'

Penelope pouted, April looked blank, and Alexandra met his blue stare with her more emollient blue eyes. 'I want them sold,' he said. 'All of it. And I want no part of it, not a single pound, do you hear me? And Alex, I don't think you should be involved either. Sell the damn stuff, Penelope. I want your word you'll sell it immediately.'

'But what am I going to do with it?' she pleaded.

'I want you to take the money and do something worthwhile with it.'

'Like what?' The damned hysterical woman seemed close to a virtual torrent of tears. Must be tired, poor thing. It's late.

'I want you to take the money and buy an office. You and April should be image consultants, not proprietors of pornography.'

The tears did flow now, and Penelope ran to him, grabbed him, hugged him, and kissed him on his cheek. He found this rather frightening. For one thing, she was such a tall, Viking girl it seemed dangerous. But more than that, emotionalism never appealed to him; what were upper lips for if not to be stiff?

'Now hold on a moment,' Nigel said, extricating himself. His eyes shot over to April. He wanted to make sure that she, good girl that she was, was happy with this arrangement. She was smiling brightly. All right, then. He reached into his pocket, removed his notebook, and scribbled something. 'And I want this to be your first client. I can provide the introduction.'

Penelope took the notebook and cried, 'The Jamaican Bastards?'

'No, no, no!' Nigel exclaimed. He seized the notebook from her and tore off the appropriate sheet.

Penelope read it. 'William Hague? Who's he? In London?'

'Yes, poor chap needs it terribly. A Yorkshireman, looks like a Mekong, wears baseball caps backwards, and, well, I'm sure you'll know what to do. My dear Penelope, the fate of Britain lies in your hands.'

'Well, cool,' she said at last, smiling and bobbing to some unheard rhythm.

'Good. Get on with it. Selling those things, I mean. In the morning, if you can. All right. Good show. Come here, my darling April,' Nigel said, and then embraced her briefly. 'Here.' He pulled out his notebook again, scribbled down his address, and tore it off for her. 'Do drop me a line. Let me know how business is going. Don't marry without my permission. And look me up when you come to London. All right, then,' he said with a flourish. 'Alexandra and I are off to L.A. and then, thank goodness, back to Limeyland. Thank you, girls. You've been troupers. Goodbye and good luck.'

IT WAS WITH A SENSE OF RELIEF that Nigel stepped behind Alexandra, mounting the motorcycle again. This was it, his adventure finally over, his beautiful, blue-blooded driver (family connection of course) was returning him to HQ, victorious. It had been a campaign reminiscent, he thought, of so many historical British military campaigns—from Khartoum to Omdurman; from Dunkirk to D-Day; from Argy invasion to triumph at Goose Green. First, the inevitable brush with disaster. Then, the inexorable march to victory. Pandora, he knew, would soon be winging her way home on a Boeing 747, and Elkstone's glory would be restored.

His own adventure—the War of Stalker's Dimples, he felt it might be called—was part of a noble military tradition. Suppose it brought him that capstone of recognition he needed, and he was made a peer of the realm. Should Brigadier General Nigel Haversham, conqueror of the Jamaican Bastards and vanquisher of the Jackals of Jiminez, become Lord Haversham of London and Los Angeles? It was something he'd have to consider most seriously.

'Lord and Lady Haversham, mum,' announced the footman.

The Queen said, 'How awfully nice to see you, Nigel, and how terribly well you look, Lady...'

Who would it be, he wondered. Fergie? Oh, good Lord, no, he thought, please no, not the Duchess of Dumplings. But what did duty demand?

He'd have to think about it later. He was too tired. He yearned for clean, warm sheets. He was windswept and cold. It wasn't English cold, not wet and damp, but the sudden, surprising cold that falls on the desert. His ears were chafed by the wind and his eyes dribbled defensive tears. He tried to hide his face behind Alexandra's helmet.

She seemed awfully skilled at handling her machine. As they cruised northwards, he gazed at the attractive lights of the California towns and cities they passed. There were even dark, attractive open spaces, a startling nuclear plant, a pristine-looking Marine Corps training area, the sudden rising of tall, modern buildings, and then, eventually, they were back where it all began, back in Los Angeles.

Alexandra roared her machine over the quiet freeways, through a jungle of tangled overpasses, on-ramps, off-ramps. Nigel heard a squealing in the distance, like some children's toy that squeaks when squeezed. But as it came closer, he knew what it was. It was a police siren. Yes, Los Angeles was an unfortunately murderous place, wasn't it? A huge, rambling, sun-kissed spot, full of palm trees and beautiful, idiotic women, but also full of surging, fuliginous criminal classes who spilled onto the streets, rampaging with violent chaos. What incredible stupidity, he thought. Here was the answer to every do-gooder in the world. Put your beloved, despicable proles in a choking, smoggy paradise that millions would sacrifice their very souls for, and what did they do? They live as they have always lived—murderous like Cain and foul with the vices of Sodom, Gomorrah, and Liverpool. Lord, what fools these mortals be.

As the police car came level with them, Nigel braved a look and risked a wave. He wanted the policeman to know—even as he rushed to do his duty—that there were still some who respected such courage and who honoured those men who risked their lives to maintain order, protect the innocent, and punish the guilty. Nigel continued waving, waiting for the car to pass them. But it stayed alongside. A megaphoned voice said, 'Please pull over to the side of the road.'

Oh, good God, what now? Nigel thought. It could be anything, all of it bad. Perhaps they still hadn't cleared him of the phoney drug charge. Perhaps the police had believed Stalker and were trying to stop Alexandra. Perhaps he would never be allowed to leave California. Perhaps he would be incarcerated in one of the state's most notorious, razor-wired, top-security prisons, in a cell block populated by failed actors from films like *Beach Baptism Bongo* or *Lady Chatterley's Surfing Safari*, who, spoiled by early success and destroyed by early failure, had turned to drugs, prostitution, petty theft, armed robbery, murder, and pop music.

Alexandra parked on the verge and removed her helmet, shaking free a gorgeous cascade of golden hair, which was wonderful to look at, but which sent tiny, stinging lashes into Nigel's eyes.

Yes, they were still in the Wild West, Nigel thought, as he turned his face away from Alexandra's hair and saw the police officer coming towards them with the rolling gait of a gunfighter.

His torch flashed in Nigel's eyes.

'Well, I'll be damned. If it ain't the old limey.' As he drew closer, Nigel made out the handsome, Aryan face of the Cromwellian constable who had tormented him after his unfortunate crash. How long ago was that? 'Can't you obey *any* laws?'

'What can possibly be the matter this time?' Nigel sighed with exhaustion and frustration. 'I'm perfectly sober, as you can see.' He slipped off the motorcycle, performed a couple of deep knee-bends, flung his arms, and touched his fingertips. 'I'm not even driving, for goodness sake. And my goddaughter here I'm sure was obeying every conceivable law.'

'Oh, so she's your goddaughter, huh?' he said, flashing the torch at her. 'Good morning, ma'am.'

'Good morning, officer.'

He kept the torch on her a bit longer than necessary, Nigel thought, and he saw with horror that he had a roguish, lopsided grin—with dimples. But, thank goodness, the Puritan had a sense of duty too. He flashed the torch on Nigel. 'No, she's all right. It's you. Where's your helmet?'

'Goose Green.'

'It's California state law. You gotta wear a helmet.'

'Oh, come now, my good man. It must be five o'clock in the morning. We're leaving for London tomorrow. Surely at this time of the morning with so few cars about, an exception can be made. For goodness sake, I'm an Englishman. I can't be expected to know every last vestige of California law.'

'You see,' Alexandra chimed in, 'we only had one helmet. And it's rather a long story, but we were ordered, by the police, to leave immediately—helmet or no. I was absolutely commanded to pop off with the General as quickly as possible.'

'That's right,' said Nigel, warming to her story. 'It was a matter of security. In fact, I'd like you to take a look at this, young man.' Nigel drew the fax from his pocket. 'It's a message from Scotland Yard, requesting my immediate return to London to deal with some internal police matter. You'll notice he mentions I was helping your own authorities on a particularly sensitive case.'

The police officer put the fax beneath his torch. He puckered his lips and nodded, looking suitably impressed. 'Scotland Yard. Huh,' he said, returning it to Nigel. 'Like Sherlock Holmes or something, huh? Is that what you are? A kind of private detective?'

'Much more hush-hush, shall we say. But something like that.'

'Huh. Okay. I'll let you off with a warning,' he said, and stepped to the rear of the motorcycle to copy down some data.

Alexandra followed him. 'I'm sorry, officer, but can't we just leave it at a verbal warning?' she asked. 'I mean, this paperwork is always so much of a bother, and it leads to so many little problems at home. I promise he'll stay out of trouble. We're popping off to London first thing tomorrow. I really would so much prefer it if we could just have the verbal warning and leave it at that. You see, otherwise his superiors will put another black mark in his file. And he's such a gifted man. But he has such rotten luck with the jealous bureaucrats. I'm sure you know how it is. My godfather always calls them "the damn pencil pushers". They really don't understand the pressures on men like you, do they? And men like my godfather. It would mean ever so much to me,' she said, smiling quite winningly, Nigel thought, and tossing her hair like Rapunzel, 'if you could spare your brother officer that horrible, bureaucratic trouble. Really, it would.'

The policeman put his tongue in his cheek. It must have been quite difficult for the young Ironside—a crisis of conscience. Could he possibly give a wink to two escaping Cavaliers and allow them to ride away?

'Okay,' he said, putting away his pad and pen. 'I'll let you go. But you better be careful. I don't want to be called out for another accident. Where are you staying?'

'We hadn't really made any arrangements,' Alexandra said. 'It seemed so silly, for just a day. I'm sure we'll find something.'

'The airport's that way. You'll find hotels there. You oughta get some rest. Like I said, you gotta be careful. Have a nice trip,' he said. Then, as an afterthought, 'Where's your luggage?'

'Oh,' she said, 'a friend is bringing it for us.'

Nigel thought of Pandora on a Boeing 747, the precious cargo on her lap.

The police officer shrugged his shoulders and said, 'Okay,' in a way that implied, 'If you want to be weird, that's your prerogative, lady.'

Alexandra waited, standing over the handlebars, fiddling with things until the police officer drove back onto the freeway. 'Thank God,' she said. 'Thank God he knew you. It gave us an excuse.'

'An excuse for what? To receive another lecture in California jurisprudence from that jackbooted jackanapes?'

'I mean, if he'd written that ticket...'

'A warning, my dear? Perfectly meaningless. Would have torn the thing up immediately.'

'But don't you see, General? This motorcycle, if he'd reported it, they would have arrested us. It's stolen.'

And with that, she put on her helmet, looking, Nigel thought, for all the world like Britannia. She revved up the stolen engine beneath her, Nigel wrapped his arms tightly round her waist, and the two buccaneering Britons sallied forth into the Los Angeles dawn.

ABOUT THE AUTHOR

EDUCATED IN CALIFORNIA AND ENGLAND, H. W. Crocker III has worked as a journalist, speechwriter for the governor of California, and book editor. He lives in Northern Virginia, midway between the California and English coasts.

Crocker is also the author of the bestselling and critically acclaimed *Robert E. Lee on Leadership.* Former Secretary of Defense Caspar Weinberger called it 'a splendid and inspiring book', while Major General Josiah Bunting III, superintendent of the Virginia Military Institute, lauded the book as 'a masterpiece—the best work of its kind I have ever read'. Bestselling author Dinesh D'Souza called *Robert E. Lee on Leadership* 'a moving and illuminating look at Lee the man', and *Library Journal* praised Crocker's 'very readable prose' and 'thought-provoking ideas for today's present and future leaders'.

The Old Limey is his first novel.